PEMULWUY

The Battle For Sydney

Eric Willmot

MATILDA BOOKS

www.matildabooks.com

Pemulwuy: The Rainbow Warrior
First edition published Weldons Pty Ltd 1987
Bantam edition published 1988, Reprinted 1991,
Matilda Media Pty Ltd e-book released 2012

Pemulwuy: The Battle For Sydney
First edition published Matilda Media Pty Ltd 2013
Matilda Books e-book released 2013

National Library of Australia Cataloguing-in-Publication data
Willmot, Eric. *Pemulwuy, The Battle For Sydney.*
ISBN 978-0-9874389-0-4
Pemulwuy, ca. 1756.1802—Fiction. (2). Aborigines, Australian—
Fiction. I. Title. A823'3

Cover painting: *War*, by the Author
Reverse cover painting: *The Crow*, by the Author

Matilda Books is an imprint of Matilda Media Pty Ltd

PEMULWUY

The Battle For Sydney

Eric Willmot

DEDICATION

Governor King, the third British Governor to mount military actions against the Australians led by Pemulwuy, is credited with breaking the Australian resistance in 1805.

This novel is dedicated to those first Australians who fought and gave their lives against these invaders. It is especially dedicated to a remarkable Australian, Pemulwuy, the man who led the resistance between 1790 and 1802, and in whose blood and upon whose land the city of Sydney and, indeed, modern Australia were built.

MAP OF THE WORLD OF THE EORA

THE WORLD OF THE EORA
Approximate locations of known Eora subgroups are shown in parentheses. Some locations referred to in the novel are shown in italics.

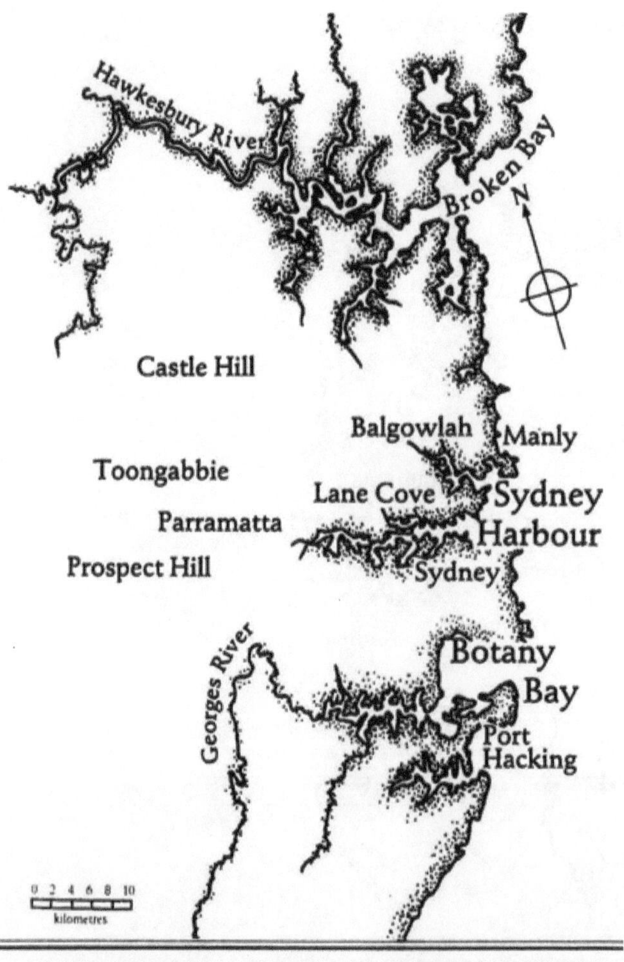

MAP OF THE WORLD OF THE EORA RENAMED BY THE BRITISH

CONTENTS

CAST OF CHARACTERS *(In alphabetical order)*

Australians

Baido—	Eldest of young Awabakal men
Balayoo—	Mixed race child of Nargel and Sean McDonough.
Bennelong—	Bidjigal man
Binkillikin—	Awabakal man
Bintunkin—	Kiraban's father, an Awabakal man
Boorea—	Pemulwuy's fist Bidjigal wife
Boorungoroo—	Young Bidjigal girl who desires to marry James Cawley
Burangaroo—	Knowledgeable old Bidjigal woman
Burrewun—	Eora man
Caesar—	Black American who joins the Eora
Coleleu—	Young Bidjigal woman
Djwordwuy—	Karingai man (from Broken Bay)
Gomil—	Bidjigal man
Gnoorooin—	Gonianna's sister
Gonianna—	Bennelong's promised wife
Kakaya—	Awabakal man
Kiraban, also called *Awabakal*—	An Awabakal man from the Hunter River region of NSW.
Koobee—	Kadigal man, based on historical man Colbee
Maronong—	Awabakal man
Milbab—	Kobee's wife
Nanborree—	Man, promised husband to Nargel
Nargel—	Formal name *Narrewe,* Bidjigal wife of Sean McDonough and mother of Balayoo; later Pemulwuy's second wife
Nungee—	Bidjigal girl, a relative of Koobee, who loves Kiraban-Awabakal (murdered by MacIntyre and Tilmouth)
O'some—	Tharawal woman who becomes the wife of Weong (Bidjigal man)
Pemulwuy —	Also called *Wayan*, Bidjigal man, born about 1760, with a turned eye. (Legend holds that his mother hid him away long enough to avoid any demand for infanticide of an unhealthy child.)
Pinicoolong—	Koobee and Milbab's son
Tedbury—	Pemulwuy's son (Bidjigal man)
Weong—	One of Pemulwuy's lieutenants
Yannerawannie—	Bidjigal man who goes to England with Bennelong (dies in England)
Yella Mundi—	Old Bidjigal man (story teller)
Yenowee—	One of Pemulwuy's lieutenants
Yerinbee—	Bidjigal man who marries Bennelong's promised wife while he is away in England

British and Europeans

Major Abbott—	New South Corps
Mr. Balmain—	Surgeon
George Barrington—	Chief constable of Parramatta (ex convict)
Lieutenant William Carpenter—	Royal Marine
Private James Cawley—	New South Corps
Lt. Colishaw—	New South Corps (killed at Parramatta)
Captain Collins—	Judge advocate
Millicent Copley—	Escaped English convict
Kate (Silky) Donavan—	Escaped Irish convict, married Bain Benu
Captain Matthew Flinders—	Navigator and explorer of eastern coast of Australia
Major Francis Grose—	New South Corps
Captain Hill—	New South Corps
John Hunter—	Second Governor of New South Wales (1795–1800)
Phillip Gidley King—	Third Governor of New South Wales, 1800–1806
William Knight—	Bushranger
Captain John Macarthur—	New South Corps
Sean Macdonough—	Escaped convict, given Bidjigal name *Gurrewe* when he joined Pemulwuy and married Nargel
John Macintyre—	Governer's gamekeeper
Reverent Marsden—	Christian Cleric
Lieutenant Francis Marshall—	New South Corps
Lieutenant Palmer—	New South Corps (saw action at Parramatta)
Major William Patterson—	New South Corps
Arthur Phillip—	First Governor of New South Wales and founder of settlement of Sydney, 1788–1792
Penelope Reid—	British New Zealander, ship owner and writer.
Major Robert Ross—	Commanding Officer, Royal Marines
Sergeant Smart—	New South Corps
Captain Watkin Tench—	Second-in-Charge of Royal Marines
Ben Tilmouth—	Macintryre's convict servant
Petty Officer James Thomas—	Governor's aide
Thomas Thrush—	Bushranger
George Wilson—	Bushranger

PREFACE

Terra Australis—the great dreaming South land—had stayed silent and hidden during the first of the modern world recorded human times. Her human world had come to live in a covenant with this land and the other creatures that lived upon it with them. These humans did not believe that they owned the land, but that they had come from it and were part of it.

Humans are different from any other living things in that they do not accept nature as they find it. They create over it a different landscape in their symbols and imagination. This for them is the real land in which they live. In this relationship, the South Land revealed to the humans the covenant, and the laws that were necessary to govern a near perfect world. This was a first human Earth. Its laws governed the lives of its first human inhabitants and ensured an existence in balance with the world about them. But it was not perfect. Not all humans upon this land obeyed these laws all of the time. Like all other humans, the Eora people in the land of Pemul observed the sun which, except on very rare occasions, seemed to be eternally unchanging and consistent, but *Yanada* the moon, was not. The ancient story tellers told that the moon's capricious nature, and indeed even its existence, was the result of a human who had broken the covenant with the land. The Eora people believed that Yanada, in a changed state, now stood in the sky as a reminder of the consequences of such human action.

As the South Land approached a second human awakening, another human was about to break this covenant again. A slender dark-skinned woman with an infant clasped in her arms, ran from her own people who would take her child from her. She was desperate and clever and hid in the forests of the Eora land until she knew that her child was safe and past the time when he must be returned to the land to be born again.

This woman was almost past her childbearing age and this son was her first live child. The infant bore on his face the mark of a troubled destiny, but she loved him with the ferocity and passion of the *Worragal*. The child was born different and now by her deed she had made him different for all the days of his life. His name was *Pemulwuy* which means 'man of the Earth'.

This novel was originally completed in 1986. It marked this woman's action, and was a statement of witness to the initial Australian response and resistance to the European invasion of this land. Regardless of the different views of early modern history, this land still belongs to its original human inhabitants. It has been so since the first of human times. And, regardless of the sorrow or guilt of the new inhabitants for what their ancestors did here, the land still remains stolen.

This work has been widely read and used in modern Australia for educational purposes. The demand for the book has remained high even though it has long been out of print. This is the first new edition.

This edition presents new characters and the further development of some of the original characters. It presents a wider experience and scope to the general view of that early Australian event while preserving the essential story of the mystery and tragedy of the original novel and the history on which it was based. This work also addresses some other aspects of the very human consequences of the actions of the people involved at the time.

This new edition also explains more closely the mystery of how it was possible for groups of less than six hundred aboriginal Australians, armed with spears and wooden shields, to take on a constantly reinforced British colonial military force armed with firearms and to contain them to a few coastal inlets for twelve long and painful years.

The answer is strange but simple. Spears and muskets were only the minor weapons used by the combatants in skirmishes. The kind of guerrilla tactics adopted by Pemulwuy in the forests and scrublands of New South Wales of that time, made these weapons of little advantage to either side. However, they were very different to the major weapons that determined the outcome of that Battle For Sydney.

The unseen weapons of the British were the diseases of Europe, in particular measles, influenza and smallpox. As well as these, the British were assisted by the very determined settler farmers. They were civilians or emancipated convicts, who had been encouraged to create farms on land stolen by the British from the Eora.

Against these, Pemulwuy employed a singular and immensely powerful weapon of uncontrollable fire upon the land. This was a force of nature that even the modern descendants of the original British settlers are still unable to deal with as witnessed by the disastrous bushfires in Victoria in 2009.

The Eora, like all Aboriginal-Australians, had learned over thousands of years how to use and control these fires. In fact, their fire lighting activities had altered and become part of the nature of the land. This was the method used by Australians to manage agriculture and grazing. These are the same methods used on lands owned by indigenous Australians for the same purpose today. During Pemulwuy's campaign against the British, his people used fire as a weapon of war. They did this firstly to burn crops and prevent farming and grazing. This forced the colony to remain heavily dependent on shipping for food and other supplies. Secondly, they used fires as a terror weapon against the British military, to force them to defend fortified enclaves.

However, it was the British diseases that finally won the war. The rapid spread of disease caused a disastrous reduction of the Eora population, almost to the point of extinction.

That population never really recovered. This, combined with the associated morbidity, broke the resolve of the Eora. The British won by default. Smallpox, called by the Eora *Galgalla*, was the most terrible. Humans with no experience of such a sickness had immune systems that were defenseless. Pemulwuy, along with many Eora believed that the British deliberately infected the local population with this disease. The validity of that contention has neither been proved nor disproved

Eric Willmot AM

THE THREE PARTS OF TRUTH

The bird of night flew into *burnigula,* the setting sun. She rested quietly and the night was heavy in the land of the Eora. The old man, *Yella Mundi,* told his story in the flickering firelight of the camp. The children listened in spellbound silence.

'No rain came and the old people were afraid, but *Yanlarree* and *Gonduwuy* were great hunters. They could run all day in the heat through the mountains. At night they would return, each with a *ganimantj* on his back. The Eora felt secure because they always had food.

There was a berringen whose ordinary name was *Yanada* and she was the promised wife of Gonduwuy. But Yanada had a passion for Yanlarree, and he for her, but Yanlarree and Gonduwuy were *bulumna* to each other, and so she was in a proper relationship in marriage to both men.

The Eora were fearful that if she became the wife of one of the men, they would fight and kill each other and the Eora would starve.

It was clear that Yanada was growing to the age when a child spirit might enter her body and begin to grow there. She would then have to become the wife of one or the other of the hunters and the trouble would start.

One morning the group was awakened to find Yanada beating children and old men with sticks. She was also making strange noises and all agreed that she must be mad.

The old man ceased his story for a while then called the children closer and went on.

'That Yanada was seen to be mad is the first part of truth; that which we can easily see.'

He stopped again and all waited, 'the Eora called a *carrdigan murray* to attend and heal her, but he could not do this. He told them that she had worried so much about the consequences of pregnancy and the fighting between the hunters that her body opened in fear and a mischievous spirit entered her and made her mad. This he said was very sad for her. She must be cast out from the group and she must never have children.

'This,' said the old man, 'is the second part of truth; the truth in the secret minds of other people'.

The old man again stopped and smiled almost to himself—'there is a third and final part to truth. It is the secret truth within each person'.

The old man paused.

'Tell us, *Mundi,*' called one of the children. 'What is the secret?'

'No,' he said, 'I shall tell you what becomes of Yanada. You must think of the last part of truth yourselves'.

The old man reached out in front of him.

'The Eora seized Yanada and carried her to a distant place from which she could not return, and there were no Eora child spirits and so she could not conceive.'

'The great spirit of the rainbow knew her secret truth. He was sad for her but knew that she was *matlong*. But he feared that other young men and women might be tempted by her deception. He picked her up and carried her into the heavens where you see her in the sky.'

'Yanada,' he said, 'Eora will hereafter know you as the new moon. You will be the envy of all women. Each month you will lie on your back and become pregnant. Your stomach will swell and you will bear a child each month and it will be a new star Twiuga, but you must then return to earth for a short time to tell other young women to beware of how they behave and not make trouble between men.'

Yella Mundi then told the children to go to sleep.

Black Caesar, who had joined the group, stood up now and put his hand on the old man's shoulder.

'Yella Mundi,' he said in his deep voice. 'Is it an Eora man's secret or can I know Yanada's third part of truth?'

The old man smiled.

'You can know my friend, but I will not tell you. It is good for men, as well as children, to think of truth.'

The night bird now ascended from the firelight on her silent wings. She looked up at Yanada's luminous body and she knew her secret truth.

THE FIRST PART OF TRUTH

'…that which we can easily see.'

CHAPTER 1

PARADISE LOST

The alien sea thing floated silently upon the water at the entrance to the lake. It was in the time of summer when the strange object had come to this place. Now it lay at ease on the evening tide as the dusk came to the silent land. The hard cobalt sky of a long hot day had softened and come to its end. Now the sky touched the sea, which slowly tumbled and fell upon the sandy shores. Coloured streamers of the day's end formed magic patterns about the little rocky islet of the moon. This marked the place where this lake joined the sea. This is where *Kiraban* stood. His dark body formed a part of the shadowed headlands.

He heard the voice of the sea, the cry of the birds, and now a strange clinking, knocking sound. This new sound came from the strange alien thing upon the twilight waters at the lake's entrance. This, thought Kiraban, was what his people had spoken about in whispers. It had come to this land from the ocean.

The excluded young men of the *Awabakal* people had spent a lot of time lately along the seafront. They worked at fishing as the sea rolled ashore and filled the rock pools. They gathered shell fish and collected the black stones for their fires. Those nights were warmed by fires fueled by the hot tarry smell of the burning stones. For them, this formed the last of their childhood memories. They told stories, jokes, lies—and sometimes even the truth. Some of them still played among the mischievous spirits of childhood, but they had all begun to dream of manhood and of their coming winter status among their families.

Some of the young men talked lately of the alien sea things that had come to the coast of their hidden land. Some of the older people called them 'sea islands'. At first sight they appeared like small clouds on the horizon. Only a short time ago one had come close to the shore. It was obviously a boat of some sort, but extraordinarily large. It had many people on it and seemed to be driven only by the wind. This strange object had disappeared along the coast in the direction of the summer. Now it must have returned and come to rest in the inlet that linked the lake to the sea.

This was a special place for Kiraban, a site belonging to his father, and he always visited it alone. Kiraban was quietly amazed to see so many fires come to life on the sea thing as the darkness settled. It must be very large he thought. Awabakal people sometimes carried fire or burning torches on board their boats to keep away the stinging *binatung* when they were fishing in rivers and creeks; but so many fires must be very difficult to manage. Kiraban felt the urge to run immediately and tell his companions. But he feared that the alien thing might return again to the sea, and make him a liar. He decided to wait until dawn.

During the night he dozed off to sleep and the spirit of the site swept over him and moved his mind to dream of a place where aliens from the sea things lived. He saw himself walk among them and imagined that he could converse with them. He awoke and sang of his dream. During the long night he heard odd, mournful clanging noises.

At first light he was awakened by a new, active sound. He saw a smaller raft-like vessel being propelled by paddles to the shore. Kiraban quickly fitted a spear to his *umana* and flexed the assembly. He moved quietly to a hiding place, close to where the boat would land. He could see now that the small boat was hollow and was really quite large compared to Awabakal watercraft, and it seemed to be very strongly built.

As it touched the shore, a group of aliens who must have come from the larger sea object, alighted and secured it by a long twisted line of some sort. It was strong and flexible, quite different to things made by Awabakal people. Kiraban thought that if they left this device behind when they went away, he would take it back to the old men so that they could examine it. He was most impressed by this simple but very strong and useful thing.

Kiraban could see that these aliens were humans of some sort. However, they appeared to be very different to Awabakal people. They were short, solidly built and heavily clothed in remarkable materials and with covers on their feet. How strange they were, Kiraban thought, to wear such a lot of covering in the summer. The most remarkable thing about them was the extraordinary lack of colour in their skin. Their faces appeared pink or like the colour of the flesh of fish.

This was all too much for Kiraban. They had now marked the earth and his vision was secure. Kiraban fled like a young bird to report this fantastic event and to ensure that it was witnessed.

It was some time before the sun was on high, when Kiraban and three of his companions returned to a vantage point close to the landing site. Tracks in the sand indicated that the aliens had been walking about. They all seemed now to have returned to the landing site and were busy doing something on the shore. The young Awabakal men noticed that they were picking up the black stones; they felt the weight of them in their hands as the Awabakals did. The young men wondered if they were going to try to light them. They were now very curious, because they all knew how difficult that task was. Kiraban's group watched for a time in total silence, and then assembled to discuss the event.

Kiraban told them of his dream and all seemed suitably impressed. But before they could explore the full implications of it, the group was disturbed and bewildered by the sound of a chant. It was singing they knew from their own land and it came from the alien group. They all moved closer and were able to see a man sitting a short distance away from the others, singing and tapping two stones together. They peered carefully at the figure. Like the others he was heavily clothed, but to their great surprise his skin was dark. He was clearly no alien.

The young Awabakal men listened carefully to the chant, but were not able to understand the language. Kiraban announced that the language was Junkal from some distance to the south of where they were. He was not really sure of this, but Kiraban had a growing sense of great fortune regarding the whole event. This thing could offer him the opportunity to establish a rather special position in the group if he could maintain a leading role. Kiraban knew that it was very important for young Awabakal men at this stage of their rise to manhood to exploit opportunities as they presented themselves. He was somewhat disturbed by his possible minor untruth, but after all, there was the dream that could justify it.

Kiraban picked up his spear and to the shock of his companions, stepped from cover and whispered his father's secret name. The aliens and the other man waved and signalled Kiraban closer. Holding his breath, he stepped boldly out of the innocence and perfection of his ancient land.

Almost half an hour had passed by the time the other young Awabakal men joined Kiraban with the aliens. They discovered that the name of the man from this land who was with the aliens and who had been singing was *Burrewun*. He and the aliens came from the place of *Bain Moree*, which the Awabakal people interpreted to mean South Wind. The actual place where they all presently lived was called by Burrewun *Kamay*, although the aliens referred to it as 'Botany Bay'. Burrewun indicated that he was a Kamergal man. The Awabakal had heard of this group from far down the coast and knew that elder Awabakal people traded with them from time to time. However, they could understand very little of the language, although it seemed similar to their own.

The aliens spoke in a strange hissing whistling language which made absolutely no sense at all, so the whole party was reduced largely to sign language.

The Awabakal men were invited aboard the large vessel, but declined the offer. They were presented with a number of small colourful crystalline objects. They examined these carefully, but could see no important use for them. The second gift, however, was quite different. Each of the four Awabakals was given a small weapon or cutting tool. These had a holding part made of wood and a blade made from the most remarkable material. It was thin, silvery grey, and very strong. They found that the edge could be ground on stone and made very sharp. The aliens called this substance iron and the implement a knife. The young men regarded these gifts as something of real value but were puzzled about the reason for so fine a gift.

Apart from their skin colour, the most unusual feature about the aliens was their clothes. They appeared to be made of very finely woven fibres, similar to the material made by Awabakal women, and used for carrying bags. Some of these materials were coloured with remarkable reds, blues and greens; colours that the Awabakal people only ever saw in flowers and in the sky. The aliens covered their feet with pouches made from animal skin, and the overall fashion of these men was very different to the Awabakals.

At noon the aliens returned to the large vessel and left Burrewun to continue discussions with the Awabakals. Burrawun had begun to understand some Awabakal. He indicated that the aliens would return later in the afternoon. Burrewun again pressed the others to go aboard the large vessel which he called a ship. He conveyed the idea that one of the group should go with himself and the aliens to visit *Kamay* and *Tubbowgule*, the other place where the aliens had made camp. This place the aliens called 'Port Jackson'.

Burrewun left the Awabakals for a short time, and a very lively discussion began among the four young men. *Baido*, the eldest by half a year, now began to question Kiraban about his dream. He finally concluded his line of thought by proposing that it was obvious that Kiraban should go as Burrewun had suggested. It was clear to Kiraban what Baido was up to, but he could not find a reasonable way to refute his logic. If Kiraban went off with the aliens, Baido could then end his exclusion with a report of the great event while Kiraban was out of the way.

Kiraban sat apart and thought the thing through. He knew that the danger was that he might be taken to some distant place of the aliens and never return again. This risk did not, however, seem to worry Burrewun and Kiraban had heard that the Kamergal people were trustworthy. Of course he might simply be killed by the aliens or, for that matter, by Burrewun's people. On the other hand, the aliens did not seem to possess much in the way of offensive weapons. They were most probably peaceful people.

The advantages of the adventure were enormous. Baido may make some short-term gains, but if Kiraban did manage to return, his prestige would be very great—and there was the dream.

Kiraban decided that he would go with the aliens. He returned to the others.

'Baido,' he said, 'I shall go with the ship. I will try to understand the mystery of these sea people and return to properly inform our people of all these things.' He paused thoughtfully, 'I shall bring the aliens with me on my return to speak with the old men'.

Baido nodded sagely.

This was a very good situation for Kiraban if he ever managed to return. All in all though, Baido was satisfied. They called Burrewun and informed him of their decision.

The ship left the inlet late that evening on the ebb tide and headed out to sea. It was amazingly powerful and sped effortlessly through the moderate swell. In fact, Kiraban was alarmed at the great speed with which it sailed away from the shore, but then relieved when the vessel began to sail parallel with the coast again.

Kiraban discovered one by one the sources of the strange sounds of the night: blocks and rigging, a bell and other paraphernalia of this substantial sailing vessel. He had a quick look below but then came back on deck and spent a good part of the night lying on a forward hatch cover staring up at the foremast. He imagined that the great whispering cloud of sails above him was lifting the ship clear of the water. Kiraban imagined being carried on forever and that he might never see land again.

By dawn the next day Kiraban realised that the ship had moved much closer to the shore and was approaching a great opening in the coast that Burrewun called *Garrangel*.

During the night one of the aliens had given Kiraban a piece of clothing called *britches*. He donned them eagerly, but felt uncomfortable in them. He also tried on some other items of clothing for the upper part of the body. Unlike Awabakal clothing, he found these tight fitting, awkward, and abrasive. He put most of the clothes aside, but persevered with the britches because the aliens seemed to want this.

He had learned another important fact about the aliens. The language they spoke was called 'English' yet they called themselves 'British'. This word, Kiraban imagined, meant the same as the Awabakal word *Koori*, which referred more generally to local people. Later he found out that this was not quite correct.

Kiraban had also spent a good part of the night worrying about the precipitous action that he was taking. This was really the business of adult men. However, he rationalised that young men in exclusion while undergoing their initiation into manhood are permitted to take prerogatives and undertake dangerous adventures.

By about midmorning, the ship had entered a great harbour that Burrawan called 'Tuhbowgule' and it sailed into a small cove where two similar vessels lay at rest. The cove, he also learned from Burrewun, was called *Warrun* and was the place of the Eora people. This, Kiraban found, was also the place where the aliens now lived. It appeared to be a collection of strange, block-shaped constructions, 'probably shelters,' he thought. Burrawun called the place by the alien name, 'Sydney'.

CHAPTER 2

SYDNEY

Kiraban's first few weeks in this new place were the most puzzling and exciting of his life. The British called this place 'Sydney'. He knew this immediately to be a name given by the strangers because of the hissing sound at the beginning of the word. The place was full of different people from the surrounding districts. It was the country of the *Borogegal.* He found that there were also *Karegal, Kadigal, Gweagal* and even some of the taller *Bidjigal* people. Of all these, the only language that he could understand with any degree of usefulness was Karegal, which had a lot of vocabulary in common with Awabakal, his own tongue. Most of the other languages except for *Daruk* were clearly related to Karegal, but he recognised that it would take some time to master them.

English, which seemed the most common language used by the aliens, was not as difficult grammatically as the Australian languages. Its difficulty was in the use of sounds not distinguished by the locals. For example, Kiraban interpreted 'cot' and 'got' as the same word. He could easily make 'c' and 'g' sounds, but was not used to hearing them as different. The hissing sounds like 's', 'sh' 'ch' and 'th' also gave him considerable difficulty, but he persevered. Kiraban listened carefully to the speech of the British and quietly practised the sounds. He did this often, much to the amusement of other Eora people.

It was a great occupation among the younger men and women to mock the British speech rather than trying to learn it. They tended to make jokes of the strange language by repeating phrases and sentences, exaggerating the English sounds. 'Thisss blassss issss Ssssydney.' The British, unaware of the joke, would correct the consonant in 'place', explaining carefully the difference between the 'p' and the 'b' sound. The sentence then became mirthfully: 'Thisss pulassss issss Sssydney.' The Eora people were equally amused by the British attempts to speak their languages. Most were unable to make some of the vowel sounds, and the subtlety of the grammar seemed well beyond any of them.

So it also became great entertainment among the younger men to make fun of the strangers' attempts to master the local languages. Kiraban found that the problem with all of this was that, with the exception of a few, the aliens were rather dour people. They did not appreciate the local style of humour, and in fact, hardly any of them could tolerate themselves being the object of a joke. This led to quite a bit of bad feeling between the two groups.

Kiraban encountered a further, more complicated problem associated with this language. When an Awabakal is asked the question, which is the equivalent to the English, 'Who are you?' it is interpreted to mean the more common enquiry of a stranger, 'Who are you socially?' or 'Who are you in relation to me and other people?' When Kiraban was asked this question by the aliens he told them his kinship category. This was interpreted by the enquirer as the name of his people. Kiraban realised the error and tried to correct it by using the more general Awabakal term 'Koori', which meant something close to the English term 'people'. He tried to explain what this meant, and that it was different to the term 'Eora'. Unfortunately, the British had already decided their own meaning for this word. They imagined that it referred to all of the east coast people they had met. They also associated this word with an English word 'native', which had no translatable Eora or Awabakal meaning.

Kiraban tried to explain this difference, but without success. In desperation he stood up and said, 'I am Awabakal'. This pleased the British enquirer and, too late, Kiraban realised that his name had become 'Awabakal'. The aliens clearly did not understand the way the local people used names, and it was not worth the effort of trying to explain. So Kiraban became Awabakal to the British—worse still, the other Eora also fell into using this name. The joke among the other Eora young men now was: 'Awabakal, the man who has the same name as his tongue'. Kiraban, now Awabakal, was fast finding the humour of the Borogegal and *Wanegal* almost as painful as the British did.

Initially, Kiraban was fascinated by the industriousness and activity of the aliens, but this fascination only lasted until he witnessed a flogging. Kiraban had observed that the aliens seemed to have a society that was divided into two kinds of people. One group wore clothes of stunning colours; the other wore drab coverings and were often tied together with iron links. This group was made to work for the colourful people. If they refused, they were scolded or beaten. This was certainly strange behaviour, but most of the Eora put it down to some primitive part of the culture of their strange visitors.

The concept of prison or incarceration was incredible to Eora people. Older Eora said that the constant practice of such physical violence must be some sort of cure for a sickness or else a religious rite. The flogging, however, was an event beyond any of the Eoras' imagination. A man was tied to a post and publicly struck with a large instrument until he was bloody, screaming and eventually unconscious. This was apparently done with no intention of killing him. Kiraban was sick for days after the event and decided that these aliens must be a savage people. He decided that he must leave this place and return home with all haste. This was, however, easier said than done.

Among the more interesting older men that he had come to know were *Koobee* and *Bennelong*. The first was Kamergal and the second a Bidjigal man. At first he had got on well with both of them, and very much admired Bennelong.

Bennelong had adopted many of the British customs and frequently visited the friends he had made among the British, including their leader, a man they called Governor Phillip. He ate with them, entertained and was entertained by them. Bennelong had developed a great taste for the substance the British called wine, and even managed to drink the fiery liquid referred to as rum. Bennelong made no secret of the fact that he believed the British arrival to be a great and important happening among the Eora people. Bennelong said that he considered the event an awakening. One day he scolded Kiraban for joining with some other young men in baiting the aliens with language jokes. 'You should help the British to learn our languages, not torment them when they try,' he said.

Yennerawannie, Bennelong's friend, took Kiraban by the arm and said, 'Awabakal! You should listen to what Bennelong says. The British can learn much from us and we have much to learn from them'.

At this point, Yennerawannie seemed to run out of thoughts and looked to Bennelong to confirm his position. Bennelong was impatient with younger men and simply said: 'You should listen more to what the older men are saying.'

Kiraban thought these two men were strange companions. They did not seem to like each other very much, but both were influential men among the Eora. Kiraban found, however, that Bennelong's view was not strongly supported by many of the older men and women of the district. He was, nevertheless, surprised to find that Bennelong's view was quite bitterly opposed by some other younger men. This school of thought seemed to be led mainly by another Bidjigal man who he had never met, but who had a somewhat odd reputation. His name was *Pemulwuy*. Pemulwuy was at once feared and held to be a man of great stature by many of the Eora youth.

Kiraban asked Bennelong about Pemulwuy. Bennelong laughed derisively and said: 'One Eye! He's nothing; he does not understand the British'.

Bennelong's people were Bidjigal, of which Pemulwuy was one. They were hunting people from the hinterland of the great harbour. Koobee's people, like Kiraban's, were mainly fishermen. They lived on the coastal fringes of the region and tended to come into much more direct contact with the British. Koobee's people had gone through some experiences in this contact which did little to support Bennelong's view of the British arrival.

Kiraban became disturbed by the fact that in the Tuhbowgule area of the Eora land, there were so many people from different language groups. He knew that it was not unusual for people from different language groups to visit each other for ceremonial and trade purposes, but the present situation here seemed very different. Kiraban assumed that this had come about because of the presence of the aliens. Koobee confirmed this—and went on to tell him other disturbing things. He told Kiraban that during the time that the British were at Kamay they would catch Eoras and keep them captives like animals.

'One man by the name of *Arabanu* was kept tied up by the neck with a chain,' said Koobee.

'What happened to him?' asked Kiraban.

'He died of a strange sickness. They buried him in the ground over there,' Koobee indicated with his pursed lips the cleared ground between the house of the British Governor and the Bay. Koobee was a smallish man with a sparse beard and a pleasant, open, friendly face. He continued, 'they bring this sickness *Galgalla*. I don't stay too close to them'.

'Are they bad people?' Kiraban asked.

Koobee looked down, 'some of them are all right. That one Phillip, he's all right, I think'.

'What about Pemulwuy. The one Bennelong calls 'One Eye'?'

Koobee smiled, and then looked serious.

'You keep away from him,' he said, 'he's a strange one'. He looked sharply at Kiraban. 'Maybe a clever man, but he mostly stays out in his own land.'

This shocked Kiraban. In Eora society a man described as clever was thought to be involved in certain extreme religious activities and even sorcery.

'He is a close relation of Bennelong,' said Koobee, 'there never was room enough for both,' Koobee added, 'even when they were little boys together'.

Kiraban nodded to show that he understood. He remembered the strained relationship that had existed between himself and Baido. But it would be many years later before he would fully understand this situation.

Kiraban spoke no more about the matter with Koobee, but he did learn more about Pemulwuy from others. Pemulwuy seemed to have reached a compromise in dealing with the British and traded with them extensively in meat. He and his group hunted in the bushlands mainly along what the British called the Georges River, but which Pemulwuy knew as the *Worronnora* River. The British did not much like the meat of the country's marsupial animals, but they were desperate for fresh meat. The Bidjigals gained some metal tools from this trade, but rum was occupying a more and more important place as currency and was used in much the same way that the British used money.

Koobee showed Kiraban a British coin. This also puzzled Kiraban. His own people, and as far as he knew, the Eoras, did not need to use this thing called money in trading. However, he simply put it down to some kind of cultural difference.

Pemulwuy was reputed to disapprove of 'rum' being used by his people. Kiraban observed that it made people silly when they used it. Kiraban found the liquid impossible to drink and marvelled at those who drank it.

Pemulwuy was said to remain a bitter critic of the British presence on this land, and Kiraban was completely puzzled as to why he continued to trade with the aliens, if he so despised them.

The britches that Kiraban had been given on the ship had not weathered well, and after about a fortnight he gave them up and donned the small animal hide pubic covering of the Eora people. He found it very cold in Sydney and had managed to obtain an Eora cloak. He thought that his cloak was not as well made or as well tanned as those worn by his own people, but it was larger and very warm. It protected him from the sharper night time cold of this new place he had come to. It had become a place in which mystery and excitement had now given way to conflict and uncertainty.

Private James Cawley, newly of the New South Wales Corps, had come to Sydney from England on a ship after a very long voyage. This ship first reached land on the far western side of this continent. But the ship then spent a further two and a half months following the coast of the new land to the same destination that Kiraban had reached two months earlier.

James Cawley found the New South Wales Corps regiment to which he had been assigned very different to any British military group that he had so far experienced. A more senior rank had told him that this was colonial service and he had either to embrace it, or perish.

James found Sydney a very rough place. As far as an army base was concerned, this was a pleasant location beside the beautiful harbour, but the people here were either military comrades, wretched convicts or the strange distant and shy natives. They drew away from him when he tried to engage them. James felt that he had come to live in a kind of English capsule here.

On leave in Sydney, he was amazed at how well the natives spoke English. However, he found their languages a complete mystery and managed only to learn how to say yes or no and otherwise the local languages were incomprehensible. He found the male natives rather closed and uncommunicative except when they made fun of his attempts to use their languages. The younger women were more approachable, but they were far more interested in learning English than teaching him their language. The other thing was that he had decided that the women's gummed hair styles looked terrible. James Cawley decided that this was indeed colonial service and the sooner it was over the better.

Over the passing time Kiraban had become aware that Bennelong was antagonistic towards him.

This antagonism, he realised, arose from the fact that Bennelong seemed to believe that the British belonged to the Eora people and especially to Bennelong. Clearly, he did not wish them to become friendly with the Awabakals or any other nearby group. This sense of the British being a 'possession' had become a matter of great personal importance for Bennelong, such that he was even unhappy about the trading relationship that existed between Pemulwuy and a somewhat shady character among the British known as Macintyre.

The summer had almost passed, and one early autumn morning Koobee invited Kiraban to meet with this man called Macintyre at his hut in Sydney. Koobee explained that he had important business to discuss. It was a considerable walk from where they lived to Macintyre's residence, which was among a group of dwellings located on the southern side of the grounds of the Governor's residence. It was a modest building, but well founded. He had several convicts working for him, and although they did not trouble Kiraban, Koobee harboured a distinct fear of one of them—a man called Ben Tilmouth. Koobee told Kiraban that Tilmouth had killed an Eora man the year before, and had been sung.

While most of the Eora lived in some fear of him, Tilmouth himself lived in considerable fear of some of the Eora people; mainly those associated with Pemulwuy's group. When they reached the end of the road, which led on up to the Governor's residence, they opened the gate into Macintyre's house. Before they had taken four paces they were challenged by none other than Ben Tilmouth. The notorious convict had reddish-brown hair and was not very tall, but the savagery of his appearance more than compensated for his lack of stature. A large scar ran down the side of his head, and at some stage half of one ear had been removed. Tilmouth had strange grey eyes and a thin almost lipless mouth.

As they walked down the path, Tilmouth reached out and caught hold of Koobee, who shrunk back. As he did this, Kiraban instinctively lifted his spear. Tilmouth screamed abuse at both of them. The pair fled to the other side of the house, where they met up with a large fat European woman whose white skin had started to become red, blotchy and leathery with the intense sunlight of this land. She yelled something in English at Tilmouth and took the two men to the side of the house, which was shaded from the sun by an awning. There Macintyre was lounging in a chair with another man. He had an amused look on his face.

'Tilmouth's gonna cut your throat one day, Koobee,' he said.

Koobee dropped his eyes to the ground and looked sideways at the other man, a gaunt, hard-looking character in convict garb whom Macintyre introduced as 'Mr Barrington' with a surprising hint of respect.

'Where have you been, you bastard? I asked you to come here and see me two days ago,' Macintyre growled.

Koobee said nothing. He had never liked this man Macintyre. To Koobee's mind, Macintyre was a man who delved in evil things. He had heard from some women that this Englishman drank a lot of rum, and when he did he became strange in the head. If he caught hold of an Eora woman he would abuse her, copulate with her, beat her, and she might even die. Macintyre looked up at Kiraban.

'Ah! Awabakal, the man from Coal River up north. Well I might have a job for you too boy, that is, of course, if I can get you and your lazy bloody companion off your sterns long enough.'

Koobee looked up at Macintyre. 'Bennelong said you have something special for us to do,' he said, and then, looking down, he turned his foot on the ground and made a feeble attempt at negotiation. 'Mr Macintyre, Awabakal and me don't work for you, you know.'

Macintyre spat at them with rage.

'Don't you try those tricks with me, you black bastard. While I'm the Governor's gamekeeper you'll do exactly what I tell you.'

He stood up. Koobee quickly darted out of his reach.

'You had better move, you bastard,' Macintyre snarled. Then he sat down again.

'What is this special job, Mr Macintyre?' Koobee said, somewhat contritely.

Macintyre smirked, enjoying his minor victory. 'How'd you two fellas like a boat ride to Broken Bay?' he asked. He looked towards Kiraban. 'Near this fella's land eh!'

Koobee looked up at Kiraban, then back at Macintyre, and shook his head. 'No, his land long way,' he said.

'Bloody sight nearer than here, boy, I know where Coal River is' Macintyre sneered.

Kiraban had no idea what Coal River meant, but he thought that he would ask Koobee later. The sea voyage Kiraban had made to Sydney had left him confused as to the distance that the river the British called the Hawkesbury, and which he called *Deerabban,* was from Sydney. Because he had travelled by ship, he could not tell how far it was from his own land. Nevertheless, there was some truth in what Macintyre had said. The place called Broken Bay was much closer than Sydney. He looked closely at Macintyre but didn't say anything, even though Awabakal's English had become remarkably fluent during his stay. He had even mastered a considerable amount of the local Eora languages as well.

Macintyre stood up, reached into his pocket and took out a small bent pipe. He proceeded to fill it with the substance the aliens called tobacco.

'There is an expedition after two convicts who are believed to have been seen in the Broken Bay area.' Macintyre lit his pipe and sat down again. 'The New South Wales Corps are looking for a couple of characters who know something about that land. Koobee, you know that district, and this young fellow might be of some use if we have to cross the Hawkesbury.' He looked intensely at Kiraban and then glanced at Koobee. 'How good is his English?'

Koobee pointed his lip towards Kiraban in typically local fashion. 'Awabakal's English is very good. His English is nearly as good as Bennelong's.'

'You know any of those languages across the other side of the Hawkesbury, kid?' said Macintyre.

Kiraban grinned and nodded his head. 'I know many languages of the places north of here, but I don't know how far away this place is.'

Macintyre drew heavily on his pipe and nodded approvingly saying, 'I think you'll do, fellow, I think you'll do'.

Macintyre stood up. 'In three days from now, he held up three fingers, 'you show up at the quay and look for a man called Sergeant Smart'. He knocked his pipe out on a timber railing and flashed another crooked grin at his impassive companion. 'And if neither of you show up I'll send Ben Tilmouth to find ya. You understand that?' He chuckled.

Koobee nodded gravely and looked sideways at Kiraban. It was definitely time to leave.

On their way back to the camp store, Kiraban excitedly asked Koobee what Coal River was and whether he thought that they would journey in a brig or even a ship. Koobee was always annoyed at Kiraban's knowledge of the kinds of sea vehicles the British used. He tried to seem well informed,

'a ship,' he said in English, 'nothing less!'

Koobee said that Coal River was the British name for somewhere a way north of Sydney. Their conversation turned to Tilmouth, the menacing convict who was always at Macintyre's side. Koobee commented that when Pemulwuy was around, Tilmouth kept well out of the way. 'One day Pemulwuy's gonna kill that fella,' said Koobee.

Kiraban was rather startled at this.

'Why?'

'Pemulwuy trades them meat, but he doesn't like that fella Tilmouth. Doesn't like Macintyre either.' Koobee looked solemnly at Kiraban. 'Pemulwuy killed an Englishman one time just 'cos he took a spear from another man,' he shook his head, 'these fellas with women, that's big trouble,' Koobee added, shaking his head.

Kiraban nodded thoughtfully as the image of Pemulwuy grew in his mind. Macintyre watched the two men as they walked down the dusty road towards the small group of buildings at the foot of the gardens surrounding the Governor's residence. He turned to Barrington and offered him a tot of rum.

'A bright boy, that Awabakal,' said Barrington, 'doesn't come from Sydney?'

Macintyre laughed. 'Shows as much promise as you could expect from these bloody heathens.'

Barrington had about him a presence of calculating cunning. He dealt carefully with Macintyre, but found it hard at times to conceal his contempt for his 'master'. Barrington was a transported pickpocket, who was finding that the colony of New South Wales held a promise he had never found in the slums of London. This man Macintyre could be his ticket to freedom and even wealth.

CHAPTER 3

PEMULWUY

The trip to Broken Bay was appalling. They travelled in an open boat the British called a cutter. It was only some thirty-five feet in length. It had a small decked-in area at the bow, and carried a single mast with a gaff-rigged spanker and two fore sails. So much for Koobee's 'ship'. While the seas across the harbour were reasonably calm, they ran into big waves at the heads. All the way down the coast the little boat rolled itself through the troughs of the Pacific Ocean. Both Kiraban and Koobee were seasick, but were rather pleasantly surprised to find several of the soldiers that accompanied the party suffered in the same way from this boat and the sea. Macintyre had come with them, but Tilmouth had not. This was much to Koobee's relief.

They arrived at Broken Bay near the mouth of the river called the Hawkesbury late in the afternoon. They pulled their vessel up to a small timber landing. Sergeant Smart was severe, but seemed a reasonable man; he made them all share in securing the boat. He then proceeded to march the six soldiers towards the military-looking wooden building a short way from the water. Macintyre and the two local men were straggling behind. Macintyre went inside the residence with Sergeant Smart and the other soldiers. Koobee and Kiraban were left to wander off to where a group of Eora was sitting gossiping merrily about the newcomers. Koobee seemed to know them, and addressed them in a dialect that Kiraban could not understand. He introduced Awabakal, and the local group expressed a great deal of curiosity about this strange young man from the North.

These people were small in stature like Koobee, but looked different about the face. One of them could speak a little English, and Kiraban felt rather amused at using a language from somewhere far away to communicate with people who lived no more than five or six days walk from his own home place. This all added to the story that he would be able to tell on his return home. They spent the evening with this group, and although Kiraban tried several dialects of the northern people, it became clear to him that the river the British called the Hawkesbury *(Deerabban)* constituted a very effective language barrier. Awabakal was also impressed by the size of the mountains and the grand beauty of the place in which they spent that night. It was cold, but they warmed themselves by the strong smelling hardwood fire at the edge of this beautiful and strange bay. Kiraban reflected again on the substance of the adventure he had undertaken. Here he was, a young man, not even yet a man in the way of his people. But now he was living and working among strange people who came from some far-off place, some other world. That night he slept deeply and without dreams.

Very early the following morning, the Eora group left their camp and set forth on a hunt that had apparently been arranged previously with the aliens. The leader of the band, a man called *Djordwuy,* strode ahead. Both Koobee and Kiraban were delighted to be able to take part in this hunt. These were people very much like Koobee's own. He was at ease, and so was Kiraban. They could wander freely, so they thought, with very little chance of running into the tall, aggressive Bidjigal people from the inland regions about Sydney.

By late morning they had crossed the ridge that formed the backbone of the bay in which the small settlement nestled. They proceeded down into a valley, and by the time the sun had reached its half-day height they had made two good kills. One was a small *ganimantj* doe and the other a fairly large grey male. Kiraban was aware that for some reason the British referred to these animals as *kangaroos.* He was puzzled by this. He had been told it was not an English word, but it certainly did not come from the Eora or Awabakal languages. Its source remained a mystery to him.

The group did not fare so well in the higher part of the valley, but on the way back to camp they scored a third kill: a large fat *tanti* which the others told Kiraban the British called a possum. They immediately cooked and ate the animal.

Kiraban felt very pleased to see these people use the same flint method of fire lighting as his own. This was a method that Koobee's people did not use, and these people were very impressed when Awabakal volunteered to strike the flames into the fire that cooked the *tanti.* By the time the sun reached its noon peak they had returned to the mouth of the valley. As they crossed the ridge on the way back they saw two more ganimantj, but they were unsuccessful in hunting them down. At this point Djordwuy considered that any further hunting before dusk was a waste of time. They climbed a little way up to the ridge, where there was a large flat rock. They put down the game they had already caught and moved up the ridge a little further to where a sheltered escarpment exposed a huge rock painting. Kiraban stopped and the others nodded. He sat down and went no further.

Koobee went a little way with the others, then he too stopped and Djordwuy and the other man with him climbed to the edge of the escarpment, where there were paintings belonging to their people. They sat quietly and sang a song. Their song echoed faintly across the valley, absorbing its haunting beauty. It assured the beings, and creatures in the painting, that the eternal permanence of this land was maintained.

They reached camp by nightfall, fortunate enough to have killed a third ganimantj. At camp they were greeted with much shouting. The smallest of their catch was prepared for the evening meal. The women took over the task of dealing with this food. The other animals were cut and butchered in a rather strange and unusual way. Kiraban found out that this was the method prescribed by the British. These two carcasses were carried to the residence, and the Eora saw no more of them.

Their second night in Broken Bay was as pleasant as the first. The food was good, and all tension had gone from the group. Djordwuy and the other man spoke with glowing praise about

Awabakal's skill in fire lighting. Koobee also congratulated him on his hunting expertise, for it was Kiraban who had killed the animal that they were eating that night.

The next morning Awabakal had his first experience of life in a British expeditionary force. The force was led by Sergeant Smart, two local corporals and Macintyre. All were splendid in their red coats and armed with what they called muskets. The Eora referred to this weapon as *djurraba.* Kiraban had no idea how it worked and neither did any of the others. There were altogether eight British soldiers and four Eora, Koobee, Kiraban and two men from the hunting party of the day before. The four native men were armed only with local weapons which even the British agreed were better for hunting the *ganimantj* than the musket.

To Kiraban's horror he found that when the British travelled on such an expedition they carried great loads. Each man, including the four local men, was given a heavy pack. Kiraban was sure his was the heaviest. Besides, he thought that carrying such loads through the bush was stupid, but such was the way of the British. The little expedition headed out along the valley in which the settlement lay, and for a day they tracked through the foothills and along the base of a great cliff which formed a barricade at the far end of the valley. By the end of that day Awabakal could hardly walk from the burden of his pack. They stopped only three times during the day, once for a meal and twice to rest. The remainder of the day was spent marching furiously through the bush.

Kiraban was amazed at the endurance of the Europeans. Although sweating inside their robes, they were able to trudge all day long with huge loads on their backs. They made camp that night at the base of a large cliff and were informed the next day that they must reach the plateau at the top. Kiraban slept restlessly, wishing that he had never ever got into this venture. The next day was spent climbing to the plateau, and once on the plateau they marched inland for some three or four miles. That night they camped in a small valley formed at the base of a watercourse; at this stage they must have been some thirty miles from the Hawkesbury *(Deerabban)* river base.

Previously, Djordwuy had walked with Sergeant Smart at the head of the expedition, with the other three Eora men bringing up the rear. That night, however, they were informed that the four local men must scout the surrounding district before they moved on. Kiraban was pleased to find that that was to be done without carrying packs.

The next morning the British part of the expedition set up tents while the Eora men and Awabakal moved out to scout the country. They went in pairs—Awabakal and Koobee to the north and the two local men to the south. By midday Koobee and Awabakal had managed to kill a ganimantj. They did very little scouting during the afternoon, because they were too busy consuming the hindquarters of their catch. They reached the British camp late in the afternoon, armed with the remains of their catch. They were scolded severely by both Smart and Macintyre for taking time off to do some hunting. Koobee seemed untouched by the berating, but Kiraban felt abused and bewildered. He turned to walk away when Macintyre called him: 'Make yourself useful and show Private Cawley here where he can get good water,' he said.

The young, fair-skinned soldier of about his own age stood unhappily holding a variety of containers. Kiraban looked sullenly at him; then moved his head pointing in the direction of where he had seen a waterhole. 'You and me go this way.'

The two left the campsite and wandered off into the fading daylight. Neither spoke, and after about a fifteen-minute walk they came to a small waterhole well hidden in a rocky outcrop. Kiraban squatted down beside the waterhole and said to his companion, 'you can drink this'.

Private James Cawley put down the containers. It was only eighteen months since he, the youngest son of a Lancashire farming family, had joined the New South Wales Corps. He had then endured an extraordinary voyage in a ship to come to this place. This strange land remained very much a mystery to him, and he had heard fearful tales of bad water. Kiraban noticed his hesitation and said, 'it is good water'. He reached down, scooped some up in his hands and drank it.

'How do you know?' asked Cawley, 'you don't come from about here I am told'.

'I listen,' said Kiraban pointing to his ear, 'I learn enough stories from here'.

'What stories?'

'We know by stories.'

'About the land?' asked Cawley, puzzled.

Kiraban nodded; then waved his arm before him. 'Long time ago, when this land was sleeping, a big lizard came here. He walked all about; he wanted to make a place to live.' Kiraban pointed to a nearby hill. 'He dug that up, trying to dig a hole'—he paused—'water filled the holes, like this one'.

'Where did this lizard come from?' asked Cawley curiously.

Kiraban looked uncertain, but went on, 'I think he was sleeping in the ground, where that big river is, before the time of dreams'.

'The Hawkesbury!'

'Yes, that one,' said Kiraban, 'he was a very big lizard, and when he got up the sea came into the hole he dug'.

'Where is this lizard now?' asked Cawley, now very curious.

'I don't know that part of the story,' replied Kiraban, 'this is not my place. Maybe he lives in those mountains,' he said, pointing to the west.

'But, how do you know where the good water is?' asked James Cawley.

'The *gitjis*—kinds of spirits—they followed the lizard…they live in some waterholes.' Kiraban looked seriously at Cawley. 'You can tell if gitjis are in the water,' he pointed to the water-level mark on the rock. 'This one is a good colour, see.'

Cawley began to fill the containers, 'so your people have a story about every part of the land, and that's how you know?'

'Yes, that's how the land was made,' said Kiraban, he looked quizzically at the young soldier.

'How do you know about your land?'

Cawley looked puzzled, 'I don't know...we make maps,' he replied.

'The writing?' said Kiraban.

'No...' replied Cawley, 'more like drawing... You know...pictures'.

Kiraban sat silently.

James Cawley looked at him, 'my land is very small...not like this...people live everywhere'.

They filled the containers, and shared them between them; then they began to walk back to the camp.

As they walked, Kiraban asked, 'are all the men in your family soldiers?'

'No,' replied Cawley, 'I am the only one'.

'Is your brother looking after your land while you are here?' Kiraban asked.

'I have no land. My family works on land that belongs to other people.'

This reply left Kiraban puzzled. 'How can you have no land?' he asked.

'You have to have money to buy land.' Cawley obviously found Kiraban's question disturbing, while his reply completely puzzled Kiraban.

'How can you buy land? Land is what you come from!' Kiraban said.

James Cawley shook his head, 'I don't understand, it must be a heathen thing'.

Darkness was falling when they arrived back at camp. The other two Eora men did not arrive until next morning. Awabakal was awakened by the sound of Djordwuy speaking excitedly with Sergeant Smart and Macintyre. Kiraban quickly learned that Djordwuy had gained information for the British. On the previous night they had met up with a number of people who knew where one of the escapees lay dead.

The expedition broke camp at about five that morning and by three in the afternoon they came across the spot to which Djordwuy had unerringly led them. It was a large rocky ledge overhung by a series of trees, and at its base lay a crumpled human heap in a blood-splattered shirt, accompanied by a brigade of blowflies.

Smart and a couple of the other soldiers examined the corpse and decided that it should be buried where they had found it. By nightfall, a shallow grave had been dug and the corpse laid to rest.

For the first time Kiraban saw a European read from a book. He didn't really understand what he was saying, but he had heard much talk about this reading thing among the Eora in Sydney. They made camp, without pitching tents, near the grave of the convict they had buried. All of the Australians were disturbed about camping so close to the corpse.

Djordwuy spent a good deal of time that night telling what had happened. Apparently the two convicts had been assigned to the settlement at Broken Bay, and about three weeks before Awabakal and Koobee arrived they had made off into the bush. About a week ago it had been reported that one of them had been killed. The examination that day showed that although the man's body was fairly decomposed he had died from a wound in the chest. Djordwuy believed that the wound had been made by an Eora spear. The Sergeant, for his part, was still of the opinion that the man had been killed by his companion. Djordwuy then volunteered a more disturbing piece of information—there were rumours that the man Pemulwuy had been in the district.

The reappearance of this man so far north seemed to make the British nervous. Kiraban was also puzzled and he questioned the two Eora men about the range of Pemulwuy's wanderings. Djordwuy told Kiraban that Pemulwuy had spent his exclusion experience in these hills and valleys about the Hawkesbury. He was very familiar with the area and quite often returned there.

Next morning at breakfast, James Cawley joined the local group. He was shy about this, but Kiraban introduced him as 'Jimmy' and welcomed him among them. Jimmy was the name Kiraban had heard the other soldiers use.

The Eora were eating the remains of the ganimantj that Kiraban and Koobee had caught the previous day. Cawley was delighted to share this as he, like the Eoras, detested the military salt pork rations. Cawley was curious as to why Kiraban accepted Awabakal as his name. Kiraban told him that younger Awabakal people may be given different names as they grow up.

'Nicknames,' laughed Cawley.

Kiraban grinned and agreed, but did not understand what the word meant at all.

'Who is this fellow Pemulwuy?' Cawley asked.

The Eora seemed embarrassed at the question. Finally Kiraban answered, 'Pemulwuy is a Bidjigal man, and a very good hunter...he comes from the bush here'.

There was a short silence.

'People seem frightened of him,' said Cawley.

Djordwuy had told the British that a number of Eora had passed this way some three or four days ago and were now camped about five miles north. Armed with this information, the British expedition about-turned and headed north past their camping spot of the previous day and journeyed on almost two miles further. It was approaching dusk as they came into a small clearing surrounded by trees and dense shrubbery. The clearing was situated on a gentle slope leading down to a valley which, Kiraban imagined, eventually opened out onto the Hawkesbury River again. Djordwuy warned the Sergeant that they were very close to a group of Eora people, and the Sergeant called a halt to the march.

Kiraban and Koobee wandered up towards Djordwuy, who was talking with the Sergeant and Macintyre. He was drawing things on the ground. The two Australians had almost reached them when they became sharply aware of the presence of strangers near them. Kiraban stopped and peered into the surrounding trees. His eyes picked out seven or eight people: they were motionless, almost part of the forest on the edge of the clearing. After a moment Kiraban turned and saw that Djordwuy was also aware of the newcomers. He called out to them and he was answered in a clear Sydney Eora dialect. Four of the strangers then appeared in the clearing. They walked up to the main group, which included Macintyre.

There was a strange tenseness in the air. The group around Macintyre seemed to brace themselves. Suddenly Kiraban knew why. The man at the head of the group of strangers had a powerful sense of danger about him. He moved forward in long, liquid strides. He was tall and well built, with a strange caste in his right eye.

This was Pemulwuy.

No-one had to identify him to Kiraban. He had a large trailing cloak, but he possessed something else that set him apart from his companions. The sunlight fell differently upon him. His face with his turned eye made him look mad and he carried with him an aura of implacable hostility.

Djordwuy stepped forward and made a polite joke; Pemulwuy responded accordingly, but the tension did not abate. Pemulwuy stepped away from Djordwuy and over to Kiraban and Koobee; this was a great breach of Eora etiquette. He stood before Awabakal, 'so you're the stranger from the far lake,' he said in Bidjigal.

Awabakal did not move a muscle. He stared directly at Pemulwuy and did not drop his eyes as he would to an older Awabakal man.

'I am Koori,' he said in English and Awabakal.

Pemulwuy placed the shaft of his spear on the ground and let the tip fall until it struck Awabakal on the chest, piercing his skin. Awabakal did not flinch.

Pemulwuy suddenly extended his right arm and turned his hand down in a snakelike gesture, his face still alight with a strange wildness. He said nothing, then: 'Welcome to my land, Awabakal man'.

He smiled; then giggled. Awabakal joined with him. Pemulwuy lifted the spear and embraced him. The tension relaxed, and both Koobee and Djordwuy joked with Pemulwuy.

Then Macintyre joined the group.

'Pemulwuy, my friend! I hope you are hunting for me,' he said with an affability that rang totally false.

Pemulwuy half smiled and focused on Macintyre. Again the strange wildness swept across his face. 'I hunt for Pemulwuy; to you I give some meat,' Pemulwuy said in the crisp, clipped hissing English of the Bidjigal. Pemulwuy waved his arm across the group, towards the plains beyond. 'Tell me Macintyre, what is it you seek in my land?'

The sergeant now stepped forward and Pemulwuy reached across and lifted his spear. 'And you soldier, what do you want in this place?'

Sergeant Smart drew himself up in a formal manner. 'Sir, you are advised to give us whatever information you can about the killing and the whereabouts of a convict.'

Pemulwuy laughed. 'Sir, I am advised only by the spirits of this land.' He smiled broadly at the Sergeant, 'these spirits, are all Eora,' again the hissing English, 'they know nothing of convicts or anything you do'.

'I insist that you…' the Sergeant began.

'You insist!' Pemulwuy hissed, eyes wide, his voice like sharpened stone chilled in ice.

The Sergeant valiantly tried to regain command of the situation. 'I do,' he blustered.

Pemulwuy stood some six feet tall. This left him only an inch above Sergeant Smart, yet he seemed to tower above him.

'My good soldier of your King,' he said gently, 'would you have me take you to the place where your convict rests, or would you have me take you to another place, and then you shall rest?'

Macintyre quietly intervened. 'Pemulwuy,' he said, 'this is a serious matter. This is not the business of the Eora; it is the business of the British. We do not interfere with the Eora, and you should not interfere with us. If you know where the convict is, you should tell the Sergeant'.

Pemulwuy threw his head to one side, 'I know nothing of your convict. Perhaps he seeks a place among the Eora'. Then, ignoring Macintyre, he walked back over to where Awabakal stood and placed his hand on his shoulder. 'Tell me Kiraban, what do you do with the British?'

Awabakal opened his mouth, but he made no sound.

'Go home to your people Koori. Do not know the British,' said Pemulwuy and then with a fleeting look of fearful menace, he said, 'you soldier! Never come again onto my land, unless you ask and are welcomed. If you do this again, I shall kill you'.

With this Pemulwuy swung around, looked back over his shoulder and called, 'I shall see you in Sydney, Macintyre,' then he stepped into the shadow of the trees.

As silently as they had appeared, Pemulwuy and his people were gone.

Darkness consumed the little group. They stood as though suspended across two worlds.

'That bloody savage,' said Sergeant Smart, obviously still suffering from his humiliation, 'we'll know no rest until we rid ourselves of the bastard'.

'He is a man taken to strange fantasies,' said Macintyre, 'it's as well you showed such restraint, Sergeant. I think it would have gone badly for us had we taken the man to task here and now'.

'He is a thorn in the side of every Englishman in New South Wales,' said the Sergeant.

'But we need him, Sergeant,' said Macintyre, 'he is an excellent woodsman and hunter. You know, if it wasn't for the work he does for us we'd have a hard job feeding ourselves in this hellhole of a place'. The gamekeeper smiled sardonically, 'when the time is ripe, we shall dispense with him and his kind'.

None of the Englishmen's conversation registered with Awabakal. His mind was still taken up with the presence of Pemulwuy. He wondered at his extraordinary use and form of English, beyond even Bennelong's.

Dark as it was, the Sergeant ordered the group to march in single file back towards the edge of the escarpment, away from the place infected by Pemulwuy.

CHAPTER 4

HORSES AND HEROES

A month had passed since Awabakal had met Pemulwuy. This meeting had completed, for Awabakal, his experience in Sydney and the Eora. There seemed nothing more he could learn here, no future for him, and worse still, he felt himself being drawn into the futile existence of so many Eora people in and around the British town. He wanted to go home. Unfortunately, the only person who seemed to have the sort of influence necessary to get him transported back home by the British was Bennelong. Bennelong, however, had become downright hostile towards him since the news of his meeting with Pemulwuy. Awabakal was painfully aware of the difficulty that he was going to have returning to his own place. The thought of tracking across country alone, through the land of others, at his age, was indeed daunting and dangerous. Curiously, he also felt a need to separate himself from Pemulwuy. The man had created a disturbed climate within his own mind, and, indeed, within the Eora community in Sydney. Even Koobee, dear Koobee, with his gentle wife and boisterous children, had been affected by the recent experience with Pemulwuy. Bennelong's differences with Pemulwuy now verged on open hatred.

Bennelong had become very much an intellectual of Eora society, at least in Sydney. His ventures into British society, his apparent understanding of them and acceptance by them, gave him great status among the Eora people. It was a status however, that was always challenged by Pemulwuy. Awabakal feared that they would kill each other before much longer. Awabakal had become sick of this place, sick of the smell of the Eora people and of the British. Only his fear of crossing a great river and the troubling distance to his own place stopped him from running to the source of his spirit.

Awabakal now lived with Koobee some five miles across the harbour at a place called *Kayumy*, which the British called Manly Cove. Koobee had a typical Kamergal dwelling, quite large enough to house his family and Awabakal. *Milbah*, Koobee's hospitable wife, insisted that Kiraban stay with them.

Early in September a whale became stranded on the beach and Awabakal joined Koobee and many others in butchering the creature. Koobee took a large piece of meat and blubber to

Tuhbowgule for Bennelong, who in turn gave some to Phillip. The British Governor was apparently so impressed that he decided to visit the site. When Koobee learned of this, he became worried. Many Kamergal were very suspicious of the British since Arabanu's death, and Koobee tried to dissuade Bennelong from supporting the Governor in his intention. Arabanu had been captured and then befriended by the British in a manner similar to Bennelong, but much before Kiraban's time there and no one seemed to know how he actually died. Bennelong listened to Koobee's warnings, but for his own purposes was determined that the visit should take place. Sydney acted like a magnet to the Eora people living on the foreshores of the harbour. They visited the town frequently. Awabakal and Koobee had been visiting Sydney for a few days, and Koobee decided to return to Kayumy the day before the planned visit by the Governor.

Phillip, accompanied by Bennelong, Captain Collins, the Marine officer, Watkin Tench, and five other soldiers, followed him the next morning. Tench had become friendly with Arabanu before he died, but Koobee worried that his presence might disturb some of the others. Even Bennelong's presence was a concern. Koobee felt that this Bidjigal man bringing strangers onto another's land needed to be done properly, but Bennelong seemed to regard himself above all this. Koobee dreaded the visit.

That evening, Awabakal heard that the Governor's boat had returned without Bennelong, but carrying the Governor with a spearhead in his neck. When he arrived back, he found Koobee in an angry, agitated state. Koobee told Awabakal that the people butchering the whale were very disturbed at the British visit. Phillip had tried to put them at ease, but in doing so had frightened a young man, who threw a spear at him. Koobee was fearful that the British would take a terrible revenge for this deed. The people at Kayumy waited for the expected reprisals, but nothing happened.

Awabakal learned later that Phillip's wound was not as serious as had first been thought and that Bennelong had successfully prevailed on the Governor not to take revenge. Although it was Bennelong who had supported the near-fatal visit, his status rose even more as a result of the Governor's decision. However, Koobee suspected that it was the intercession by the marine Tench that had actually calmed the Governor. Koobee apparently got on well with the marine and had prevailed on him to help.

Awabakal entered his nineteenth year in the Englishmen's October of the year 1790. He had become friendly with a young woman named *Nungee.* She was an Eora woman, a relative of Koobee's, who was living in the town of Sydney. Koobee told him that she was promised as a wife to another Kamergal man. She would be his second wife. This relationship only intensified Awabakal's problem with his own dreaming connections. He well knew that breaching or even becoming involved in such matters could be dangerous even in his own group, but to create an incident in another group could end in a spearing or even death. He had a need to complete his manhood, but he could not do it in this place.

This young girl of perhaps fourteen years old carried with her the charm and bitter sweetness of this strange place called Sydney. He had lain with her one long night on the sands of a beach at Tuhbowgule near what the British called Port Jackson, close to Sydney. That night they walked by the sea together and he had sat with her and examined their kinship relationships. Together under a half-moon, they had rationalised that their relationship was propriety enough within the social order of old Australia, but that was not enough. Koobee knew of their relationship but said nothing to Bennelong, even though the girl was Bidjigal. Koobee had become a good friend to Awabakal and made life bearable in this abyss of humanity that he had come to live in. Nungee, on the other hand, knew Pemulwuy, as she was also related to him.

She told Awabakal the story of Pemulwuy's life. It was a rather tragic tale of a mother who had broken the law and hidden her child from their people because of his strange eye. The world of the Eora would have insisted that she cast such a child spirit back to its source so that it could be reborn without the imperfection that gave Pemulwuy his look of madness.

Pemulwuy's mother was very clever and successfully hid from her people. By the time she returned to her group the child was beyond the age of such infanticide. However, many people of the group expected that he would be an unfortunate child. This shadow fell upon his childhood, but the child overcame it and tended to be better than other children of his age, including Bennelong. As a result he grew up as something of an outsider. Nungee said that he was very clever and excelled at all things that a young man must do, so much so that people began to fear him. This in turn seemed to make Pemulwuy secretive and aggressive, but very much a leader. Awabakal also learnt from Nungee that Pemulwuy had a son called *Tedbury* and that he had recently come to live in Sydney. He was a young man of about Awabakal's age. Awabakal had decided that he would meet with Tedbury. Perhaps then, somehow, the dreams of the long nights would go away. If only he could find a solution to the problem Pemulwuy was causing in his dreams.

Then, early in November, Koobee came to Sydney and sought out Awabakal to tell him of a dreadful thing that had happened two days past. Awabakal met Koobee at Farm Cove. Not unusual for Koobee these days, his face was drawn and concerned.

'Someone has killed Nungee,' he said.

Awabakal fell to his knees, 'who did this?'

Koobee sat down beside him, 'it happened at Kamay,' he murmured. 'It is said that Macintyre took her to his bed. An old white convict woman said that in the night he gave her to Tilmouth. Some Kadigal people found her body floating in the water at Kamay'.

Awabakal flew into a rage, picked up a stone and began to cut his head in the fashion of his own people. Koobee calmed him down. He talked to him for a long while and told him that there was another serious complication. Pemulwuy had been at Kamay for the last two days and had heard of the event.

'Pemulwuy's going to kill both of them,' he said sadly, 'Tilmouth has gone already. Pemulwuy must have killed him'.

Awabakal looked up at him eagerly, 'perhaps Tilmouth has run into the bush'.

'Where would he hide out there from Pemulwuy?'

'He must also hide from me!' Awabakal screamed.

Koobee looked down at the young man, 'if he ran into the bush, Pemulwuy would kill him so quickly'.

'And what of Macintyre?' Awabakal asked coldly.

Koobee reached out and put his hand on Awabakal's shoulder, 'the Kamerigal will sing that man', he said, 'you must come back with me to Kayumy. There will be terrible things happening here,' he added, his eyes widening.

'No,' said Awabakal quietly, 'I do not know how strong the Kamerigal song is; I will now become an Awabakal man. I will make a special spear as I have seen the men in my place do this thing. I will drive it into this beast's heart and Nungee's spirit will be revenged and return to her dreaming'.

Koobee hung his head in sadness and thought to himself, 'Nungee was such a pleasant happy child, now her death ignites such anger in this young man; but even worse—it has awakened a murderous wrath and set alight a fire of revenge in a more dangerous place, in the ferocious heart of Pemulwuy. All will know the pain of this day'.

Awabakal, bitter and feverish in his own anger, made his way towards Sydney, determined that his manhood would be tested by taking the life of Macintyre. With this sense of impending doom, Awabakal walked along the long and dusty road that led to Macintyre's house.

On his way, he came across one of the strange animals that the British called a horse. It was late in the day and the animal was grazing along the roadside. Awabakal walked over to the animal. He knew that these were tame creatures that would allow a man to be carried on their backs. This thought distracted him from his immediate purpose, and for a little time his mind was taken with the idea of riding such an animal. The horse lifted its head and stared at him for a few minutes. While Awabakal observed the creature, it turned and began to walk away from him. Awabakal reached out and patted the animal on its rump and in the next instant he learned something rather special about horses. Perhaps he was the first man born of this land to learn this lesson. He got two solid hooves planted in the middle of his chest. The impact hurled him backwards some fifteen feet into the grass beside the road.

Stunned, and with a great pain in his chest, he watched the animal as it trotted off holding its head and tail high. He was completely bewildered and hurting terribly. He staggered to his feet. He could hardly breathe, and each step caused him great agony.

The trek to Macintyre's house and the great test of his manhood ended quietly, without revenge, in a painful, dreamless sleep.

Awabakal awoke early in the morning with an intense pain through the whole middle of his body. He again staggered to his feet. He had no idea what to do. Two Eora people saw his distress and assisted him on his journey to Sydney.

By the time they reached the main street of the town, Awabakal was almost blind from the pain in his chest, and they took him to a place near the fish market where he could lie down and then they found a *cardigan* to attend him. Here a group of Eora people, including Koobee, came and laid him in the soft sand and made him as comfortable as possible. An old woman sang quietly to him, while he lay silently in great pain. By noon he realised that the physical pain of his chest was greater than any other agony that he had ever known. His need for revenge had completely dissipated. He realised that the only way that he could survive his physical situation was to lie quite still for many days.

It was some seven days before he was able to walk upright with a reduced level of pain. When he did this he felt quite a wise old man, for he knew something about these things called horses. As well as this, he had come to realise that physical pain overshadowed most other feelings. In an unexpected way, he now understood an important principle in attaining manhood of the Awabakal: the pain of the body can be used to relieve pain of the mind.

By the time he could walk without a lot of difficulty, some fifteen days had passed, and his intense desire for revenge had mostly subsided.

In late November he heard that Pemulwuy had refused to trade with Macintyre. Pemulwuy had nevertheless agreed to meet the gamekeeper at Botany Bay.

Awabakal sensed that blood would be spilled at this meeting and the old cardigan at Kayumy had predicted it. He decided that he wanted to be present. With this in mind he set out for Kamay. As he turned the corner at the new British store, he was grasped by the arm and pulled to one side. This sent a sharp pain across his chest. His eyes turned to the person holding him, ready to knock his head off his shoulders, and saw the pink, smiling face of Jimmy Cawley. Awabakal felt excited, despite his pain. The two young men sat down on the side of the new road in this new world, as old friends.

Awabakal said with a pained smile, 'Jimmy, I can tell you so much about horses'.

'I could have saved you all this pain Awabakal. There is only one end of a horse you can do business with.'

The two young men fell to laughing although this caused Awabakal much pain.

'Have you seen a surgeon since this happened?' asked Jimmy.

'No,' said Awabakal, 'but I'm nearly cured. Some old women and a cardigan looked after me. I'm really very well now'.

Jimmy's eyes became very serious. Awabakal realised that they were intensely blue, like the sky on a summer's day.

'Awabakal, I heard about your girl. I'm sorry.'

Awabakal looked down at the ground. 'It's done now,' Awabakal shrugged.

'Were you sweet on her?'

Awabakal looked at Jimmy quizzically, 'what does that mean?'

'You know—love.'

'I don't know what that means either,' said Awabakal.

Jimmy blushed, 'at home, boys have sweethearts, kiss 'em, play around,'. . . he paused uncertainly, 'that's all I know'.

Awabakal looked thoughtfully at Jimmy. He didn't want to offend him, 'I think I understand,' he said, 'I think it's the same'.

There was a short pause.

'Is love important in your place, Jimmy?'

'They say it can make you mad,' Jimmy looked away for a moment. 'In the barracks they say that that man Pemulwuy is looking for trouble. He's got it in for Macintyre, but old Macintyre's not scared. Pemulwuy'd better watch out!'

Awabakal stood up but said nothing. In the Eora way, he held his own counsel on this point, and their moment of closeness passed.

'What are you going to do, Awabakal?'

'I don't know, Jimmy, but I know one thing—I'm going to see that man Pemulwuy again.'

'Don't Awabakal, don't,' Jimmy said. 'Go back to your place, go back to that lake. I've never seen your place, but I've heard of it, a beautiful place. They call it Coal River now. Go back there. It's even harder for me to go home, but I would if I could. This is a bad place.' Jimmy took Awabakal by the shoulders. 'Can I help you get back to where you want to go?'

Awabakal stared into Jimmy's strange blue eyes. 'Can you get me a ship so that I can go home?'

Jimmy looked at Awabakal sadly. 'No, I can't do that. But I will try to get you passage on a ship to Coal River.' He looked sadly at Awabakal. 'That won't be easy either, but I will try and I will find you if I have any luck.'

Awabakal reached out and touched Jimmy on the hand. 'Jimmy, why don't you come back with me to my place? Your place is so far away. You could find a wife and you could live on her land and maybe make your farm. You and your wife and your children would have more land than many English farms together,' he paused thoughtfully, 'Awabakal girls would think that you look a bit funny at first, but they would like your blue eyes'.

Jimmy Cawley smiled wistfully, 'Awabakal, I wish that I could do that, but we are very different, and there is the army. I can't just leave'.

Awabakal nodded, turned away from Jimmy and looked back towards the sea. 'I suppose you're right, Jimmy. I'm going to go back to my camp now to think about this. I think what I should do is go home some other way.' He turned back and looked at Jimmy. 'Maybe you should go home too. You're right, I reckon.'

Awabakal embraced Jimmy, and the two young men parted, one walking towards the sea and the other towards the west wind.

CHAPTER 5

OF MICE AND MEN

Pemulwuy's hunters used to bring their killed and butchered ganimantj to an agreed place near Kamay. Macintyre would pick up the carcasses in a wagon and make his exchange of goods and credit with Pemulwuy. There were never any problems with the direct exchanges, but there were constant disagreements about the credit transactions which Macintyre never understood. Pemulwuy was not interested in British money or goods except for iron and Macintyre was generally not prepared to barter in much of this material. Various members of the Marine Corps had from time to time mediated in these disputes, and they found more often than not in favour of Pemulwuy. The British Judge Advocate, David Collins, and a marine subaltern, William Carpenter, had once been forced to separate an all-in brawl between some Bidjigal men, Macintyre and Tilmouth.

With the arrival of the first contingent of the New South Wales Corps, things had deteriorated quickly. The Marines had willingly avoided any further involvement, and Macintyre had taken the fateful step of trading rum with the locals for their ganimantj catch. This infuriated Pemulwuy. Some of both the British and Eora were concerned that if Macintyre persisted, or was allowed to persist with the trade it would lead to a serious incident.

Macintyre himself was concerned at his increasing difficulties in dealing with Pemulwuy. Nevertheless, the failure of the first crops and the very slow rate at which the colony was acquiring domestic stock made the trade essential and very profitable. The British never really liked the flesh of the ganimantj but as the pressure and demand for fresh meat grew, Macintyre grew in both wealth and influence. Further, he had the ear of the Governor and had been appointed his Gamekeeper. Macintyre was quite competent in dealing with most Eora by bullying and intimidating them, but this approach did not work with Pemulwuy or with other Bidjigals. Macintyre was in real fear of the man now that Tilmouth had disappeared. On 20 November 1790 he set out for Botany Bay, determined to settle the matter with arms if necessary. Pemulwuy had already refused to make any further meat exchanges with Macintyre. Macintyre had sent a message that he wished to discuss the matter with Pemulwuy and would meet him at the place of the exchange. He took with him six men from the New South Wales Corps and was himself well armed.

They reached the exchange place late in the afternoon. There was no sickly sweet smell of marsupial carcasses, and the clearing was bare except for a small group of scantily-clad or naked Eoras sitting beneath the meat-hanging tree. Macintyre thought that he knew exactly why he and Pemulwuy had come to loggerheads. 'Poor dumb Collins,' he said half aloud. Collins had been fascinated by Pemulwuy's contrivance of using the Eora geometric mathematical system to cope with the numeracy of trade, but he could never fathom their weird economics, which involved a strange idea of credit which they called *wea jowinid,* which even Collins did not understand.

'Well, I bloody well can,' Macintyre thought. 'I outwitted that black bastard, and he couldn't take it.'

Macintyre thought that he could handle that problem, but not the business over the woman and Tilmouth.

'It gave that Pemulwuy an excuse,' he told himself, 'now I've got mine, and Pemulwuy'll pay—with interest'.

Macintyre walked boldly up to the Eora group. He knew from the way they averted their gazes that Pemulwuy was close by.

'Pemulwuy, I have not got all day!' he called out.

The men of the New South Wales Corps looked about, anxiously holding their loaded and primed muskets high. Then Pemulwuy stepped from a small patch of scrub about twenty yards away. He was not wearing his cloak, and he looked slim and somehow frail.

Macintyre strode towards him, holding a pistol in his hand.

'No closer,' Pemulwuy called.

Macintyre hesitated. He looked at Pemulwuy's spear, its shaft held taut against its *umana.* The spear head prickled with barbs. This was no *dooul,* this was a spear prepared for revenge and homicide.

Macintyre glanced at the British soldiers and signalled them to lower their arms. He had been told that at this distance Pemulwuy could cast a spear with deadly accuracy faster than the priming powder in a musket could burn. Macintyre decided on a different strategy.

'We should lay down our arms and talk,' he said. 'Look, I will put the pistol on the ground if you put down that spear.'

No reaction from Pemulwuy.

Macintyre glanced backwards again. He checked the priming and then carefully cocked the pistol, bent down and slowly placed it carefully on the ground, watching for the movement that would send the spear hurtling towards him. Pemulwuy did not move.

Macintyre stood up, hands and palms forward, and shrugged his shoulders.

'Come on!' he said, 'I have quit my weapon'.

Pemulwuy released the spear and umana and let them fall to the ground.

'That's better,' said Macintyre. 'We can do each other no harm now. Let's talk.' He smiled at the expressionless Pemulwuy, his gaze hardened, and for a moment, the eyes of the two men were locked together in ultimate metaphor of like and unlike.

Suddenly Macintyre reached down and grabbed the cocked pistol. Pemulwuy hardly seemed to move. He picked up his spear in his toes and seemed to flick it into his hand; then a slight forward movement, and the shaft shot forward from waist high. As Macintyre stood up and fired his pistol he was almost knocked off his feet by the spear that buried itself in his chest under his left arm.

Macintyre screamed in agony and fell to the ground. The soldiers fired almost in unison, but Pemulwuy was gone. The other Eora followed Pemulwuy's lead and also vanished into the scrub, leaving the terrified soldiers standing back-to-back, frantically reloading their muskets.

With his hands clasped behind his back so tight that the knuckles showed white, Arthur Phillip paced the room like a caged tiger. The normally even-tempered Governor's face was gripped with anger. He turned quickly as Balmain emerged from Macintyre's sick room.

'Well?' he asked gruffly. 'What hope, Mister Balmain?'

The surgeon shook his head. 'He is alive, sir, but barely…I have cleaned the wound and administered laudanum for his pain.'

Phillip sat down abruptly. 'So! We may have a murder on our hands. God knows, I've done my best with these people.'

Balmain nodded. 'Sir, this savage meant to kill,' he said. Reaching into his pocket, he produced a wicked-looking spearhead some six inches long, festooned with shell barbs fixed in hard resin. 'I would wish you to examine this barbaric implement, which I have just removed from Mr. Macintyre's wound. It penetrated his flesh to the depth of some seven and a half inches.' Phillip stared dumbly at the weapon. 'When a thing like this is used, it is indeed certain to inflict a terrible injury.'

'And his wound?' he asked almost plaintively.

'Mr Macintyre has lost a great deal of blood. The wound is not clean—quite different from the damage done to your own person by that boy at Manly Cove.' The young surgeon looked hard at the Governor. Balmain was possessed of a fiery temper, and would go down in the history of the colony for his duelling as well as his medical skills, but he obviously failed to see the fight between Macintyre and Pemulwuy as a 'matter of honour'. 'I would not take wagers on his seeing the year out. If complications set in, Macintyre will die a lingering death. I would not wish such a fate on my worst enemy, sir.'

A light seemed to go out in Phillip's eyes. Then his face flushed with fury. 'Pemulwuy is no more than a cutthroat,' he snapped. 'Bennelong has warned us against the man on numerous occasions. We shall have to take action. I have been patient with these natives, and in return they show nothing but contempt for the laws of God and man.' Phillip's jaw set in a hard line. He turned to Balmain. 'That will be all, Mister. Keep me informed of the man's condition.'

The Governor strode out of the room and surprised his waiting aides by issuing terse orders for his senior officers to attend him immediately at the residence.

The sun was high in the sky when the officers, sweating in their heavy uniforms, filed into Phillip's reception room for the conference. Major Robert Ross and Captain Watkin Tench were there for the Marines, while the newly-arrived New South Wales Corps was represented by Major

Francis Grose and Captain John Macarthur; Captain Collins, the Judge Advocate, also attended. The two groups of officers were not at ease with each other—the Marines, with a fighting tradition going back hundreds of years, tended to regard the newly-arrived units as no more than hired jailers, and they made little attempt to hide their feelings.

'Good afternoon, gentlemen,' said Phillip, calling them to order. 'As you will all know by now, a servant of the crown has been assaulted with murderous intent by a native brigand. I have called this conference to decide on appropriate action. Is everyone aware of the events to which I refer?'

The officers nodded uncomfortably.

'Well, what is your considered opinion?' Phillip demanded.

There was a short silence.

Then Ross spoke up. 'I would first beg leave, sir, to make the observation that disputes between Mr Macintyre and the group of natives in question were held within tolerable bounds while Mr Collins and Mr Carpenter were overseeing the business. It is only since responsibility has been passed over to the New South Wales Corps that the situation has deteriorated....'

'You molly coddled the natives,' Captain Macarthur interrupted him, 'these... ah…'

'Bidjigals is the word,' Collins helped with a crooked smile. It was the Judge Advocate's only contribution to the discussion.

'Quite… Previously, these bandits were allowed to cheat us, to make threats—all under the protection of officers of the crown. We, by contrast, gave Mr Macintyre the free hand he needed to buy supplies of meat at acceptable prices, and provided the military protection for him to do so. What could be more reasonable?'

Collins looked up towards the ceiling and said nothing. Macarthur, a stocky, broad-shouldered bull of a man with an aggressively protruding lower lip, was undoubtedly an energetic officer, but he had gained something of a reputation for pushiness since his arrival in the colony. Many, including Collins and the Marines, had serious doubts about whether he could really be considered a gentleman.

'These meat provisions are certainly essential to us,' Phillip conceded.

'But in exchange for rum?' Ross countered.

Grose, the senior New South Wales Corps officer moved in quickly to head off the Marine attack. 'The fact of the matter,' he said, 'is this..., Pemulwuy... and his cohorts have been allowed to believe that they can behave as they wish. I don't think that anyone here would deny that this is a very dangerous state of affairs and that, whatever the incidental facts of the case, we have to take firm action.' He looked around challengingly. 'Mr Macintyre lies gravely wounded, impaled by a spear thrown by a black ruffian. We must act, gentlemen!'

Captain Tench and Major Ross exchanged glances. Both knew of Macintyre's unsavoury reputation, and neither trusted the New South Wales Corps' opinions on most things, but Grose was right this time.

Tench nodded. 'We must take some action. It is true. And it must be decisive.'

'Before the other natives follow this example!'Macarthur said, 'before no Englishman is safe in a British colony!'

'Er... on that matter, Mr Macarthur,' Ross said with a frown, 'I must remind you that the local population is under the protection of British law and that any untoward acts committed against natives will be regarded rather unfavourably by the Colonial Office'.

'It is a matter of apprehending a criminal, sir!' Macarthur growled, 'quite simple! One does not have to explain to London every time one catches a thief or a murderer!'.

The balance moved towards support of a police action against Pemulwuy. Phillip dismissed his advisers for the moment. It was a question, not of whether action would be taken, but of how. He thought Bennelong's advice could be valuable there.

Bennelong was obviously pleased to be granted the ear of the Governor in a private meeting and even more delighted when he heard that it concerned his rival, Pemulwuy. He talked at great length about his views on the political situation and the implications for cooperation between the British and the Eora. In view of his previously conciliatory attitude, Phillip was surprised to hear that Bennelong supported a major punitive action against Macintyre's assailant.

'You believe, then, that we should retaliate strongly against Pemulwuy?' asked Phillip.

Bennelong nodded solemnly. 'Yes, sir, and you will need many men to catch him. He is treacherous and clever.'

'That is self-evident, but what about the feelings of your fellow natives?'

Bennelong paused thoughtfully, pulled a handkerchief from the pocket of his britches and dabbed his forehead as he had seen so many British do.

'Sir, you must not bring too many more British here. Mr Macintyre was not a good man, and Pemulwuy is bad. They both wanted trouble and all because there are too many British here now. This is why Mr Macintyre is greedy for meat, and why Pemulwuy attacks him. If not too many British, there will be no trouble.'

'Of course, of course,' Phillip replied patronisingly. What Bennelong said had some truth to it; but there was little doubt that London would send more and more convicts, and very few of the useful, skilled settlers that Phillip had dreamed of. At the moment he commanded only the sweepings of the English prison hulks, and he was duty-bound to feed them, which meant there had to be trade with the natives through men such as Macintyre. Sometimes Phillip despaired of bringing anything of English civilisation—the real, decent England, rather than a warped, brutal society of soldiers and jailbirds—to this damned place.

'Well, do you really think that it is Pemulwuy's role in meat provision that assures his status among the Eora?' he asked, trying to get down to specifics.

'I... am not certain,' Bennelong muttered.

'Then you cannot help me on this point?'

Bennelong shifted uncomfortably, 'Pemulwuy... he was conceived of a wrong spirit,' he answered. 'This is why he has a strange eye.'

Phillip sighed. Yet again, he had come up against a wall of superstition. It was really impossible. Bennelong was an amiable, well-meaning fellow, not unintelligent, but he and his fellow natives were, after all, little more than primitive heathens.

'I must establish a school for your children,' he said with a grimace, and ended the interview.

Consultations with individual officers followed. Ross refused to support more than a straightforward police action. Grose harboured no such reservations.

'Sir,' he said eagerly, 'I have been giving this some thought. The important thing is to ensure that our authority is not compromised. Should we fail to apprehend this black murderer, morale in the colony—not to mention our position with the friendly natives—will undoubtedly be undermined. We should, I believe, strike ruthlessly.'

'And what would you advise in that case?'

'Capture six men from the fellow's tribe and put 'em behind bars, as an example. Better still; take six of the blighters dead or alive. Then no-one will be able to accuse you of weakness!'

Phillip nodded. 'Certainly there is no room for weakness. However, my previous policy… '

'These Bidjigals are now our enemies, sir! Six Bidjigal heads will show the other natives what befalls them when they dare attack an Englishman!'

On 13 December 1790, an expedition was launched against Pemulwuy. Phillip's orders, following Grose's advice, were for them to capture Pemulwuy and five other Bidjigal males, dead or alive. Six heads For Sydney. The reluctant Captain Tench found himself landed with a New South Wales Corps officer, Lieutenant Hill, as joint commander of a force composed of four officers, two sergeants, two corporals, a drummer, two surgeons and forty privates. Given the limited resources of the colony, it amounted to a major military expedition. The party carried provisions for three days.

The expedition returned seven days later, worn out and half starved. Their horses had all been speared at night, but they had sighted Bidjigal people only once long enough to fire a couple of ineffective rounds at them before they faded into the bush.

Two weeks later, Tench was sent out again with a smaller group of Marines. They stumbled through the bush for ten days and saw not a single Bidjigal.

Contrary to Balmain's expectations and to the benefits of the opium derivative laudanum, Macintyre lingered on into the New Year, dying in January 1791. There were rumours of a dramatic death bed confession, in which he had admitted to all manner of crimes and atrocities in the colony. But by then it was too late: the might of the British had been committed against Pemulwuy. Now he and his people were considered outlaws in all but name. Phillip's policy of peace with the natives was in tatters.

Soon after the gamekeeper's funeral, it became known in Sydney that Tedbury, Pemulwuy's son, had secretly attended the ceremony. Major Grose, in his cups with Macarthur and his brother officers, was heard to remark that, if it was up to him, he would see to it that every black in the town was put under lock and key. And, by God, he would have those Bidjigal heads.

Tench was appalled at the idea of taking heads and did his best to prevent any order to do so. He had commented to Lieutenant Carpenter that these Indians were nothing like the American version. Tench said that, except for the one man he was sent out to pursue, these were in general peaceful people and could possibly be dealt with differently. There was no doubt that Pemulwuy's contacts in Sydney reported all these things to him. And so gradually, almost helplessly, the colony drifted towards a strange, undeclared Battle For Sydney.

CHAPTER 6

ESCAPE FROM SYDNEY

In the first light of dawn five Eora and their European companion left Tuhbowgule and headed south towards the river that flowed into *Kamay*. By noon they had reached the river the British called the Georges River. The existence of the Ross Hill and other settlements now provided a problem. To skirt the settlements it meant that the group had to follow the river for many miles to place a safe distance between themselves and the alien town of Sydney.

The fleeing group was led by Koobee along with a boy called *Bungaree*, whose people came from the area through which they must pass. Tedbury, Awabakal and a young woman called *Nargel* made up the rest of the Eora complement. The European was an escaping Irish convict named Sean McDonough.

Irish convicts seemed to be singled out by the British for particularly harsh treatment. McDonough had clearly been a strapping youth in the past, but the treatment that he had received and poor food had left him physically weak compared to his lithe companions. Their serpentine movements in the rough scrubland allowed them to maintain a withering pace. Even the young woman and much older Koobee were becoming difficult to match. By nightfall they had not covered as much distance as Koobee would have liked, but it was clear that McDonough's poor condition was making him unable to keep pace with the others. They camped at night without a fire and without eating. The soft sounds of the Australian night made up their entire world. The night was somewhat chilly, and they talked for a while about the advisability of lighting a fire. They decided against it and each began to seek out a sleeping place. Nargel lay wide awake. It was she who had brought the convict McDonough with them. Nargel was a young Bidjigal woman, some sixteen or seventeen years old, and although she was not very tall, she had long limbs and the characteristic awkward appearance of Bidjigal youths.

The others were curious about the nature of the relationship between Nargel and McDonough. Nargel was almost as curious herself. She had fallen into a strange state of infatuation with this being. She was not even sure that he was human. At first it had been a caring friendship of unlike creatures but now, whatever he might be, this strange, wretched creature had assumed the status and character of a man among other men. There was about him an intense human maleness. Nargel had thought vaguely that this night would be the time they might become lovers. McDonough, was, however, clearly exhausted, and she felt strangely embarrassed sleeping so close to her friend with her own people nearby.

They were all awakened soon after dawn when Tedbury and Bungaree, who had risen early, returned to the campsite with a magically produced fish of quite startling proportions. Koobee commented to the company that Tedbury had been born to the wrong part of his group and that he had the makings of an excellent fisherman. They all huddled together, eating the animal raw.

Awabakal drew the lad Bungaree aside and asked him about McDonough. Bungaree knew very little, except that he was a convict, whom Nargel had befriended. He was of the British ethnic variety called Irish, and he spoke a different dialect of English. Awabakal then asked Bungaree why he had come with the group. Bungaree explained that he had come far up this river on a British expedition.

'I am looking for relatives I met up here when I came with Captain Flinders,' he said. 'My people at Kamay all died of the new sickness *galgalla*.'

These new sicknesses worried Awabakal. He wondered if he would bring them to his own people on his return.

As the morning wore on, Sean McDonough became acutely aware of the strangeness of his situation. He felt a complete outsider in this group. The months in which he had come to know the girl, Nargel, had created in his mind an alternative to the wretched conditions of a convict life in Sydney. More than this, she had become for him the charming native female companion that he had heard some men speak of. He had come to love her in a European way, and it was this intense emotion that had given him the courage to get this far out of Sydney. His young companion now seemed as alien as the other three people from this land. Nargel chatted to the Eora men in a local dialect which had become common in and around Sydney. Sean McDonough could hear the dialect quite well, but had considerable difficulty engaging these five fluent speakers in useful conversation. After eating his portion of the fish he went down to the river and washed himself as best he could on the muddy bank. This made him feel a little better. Unfortunately, the feeling of freedom he expected was still shrouded by a sense of entrapment. He mused on how he could feel as closed-in as he did, in a continent many many times the size of the island from which his life had sprung. He decided that the place had a sinister feel to it and its people almost the same.

Tedbury took the lead as they proceeded further. McDonough and Nargel at times walked in single file and when they could, hand-in-hand. This magic woman of his dreams, however, somehow transformed into a small native she thing, as strange and different as everything else in this hard hostile land. As the day wore on, this sense of alienation became more and more pronounced. Twice during the morning Nargel had walked on ahead and spoken to Tedbury. McDonough noticed that he replied rather sharply, and he had the feeling that some rift was developing between the two. Each time Nargel returned from this contact she was silent. She made no attempt to hold his hand.

McDonough had the compelling feeling that he should run back along the track following the Georges River and return to whatever Britain had to offer. Then he reflected on the recent years that he had spent there, and a great desperation came over him. Just at this point, Nargel walked up, took his hand, and said something quickly in Eora which he didn't quite catch. She giggled and hung behind him for a minute. Try as he might, he could not seem to rekindle the dream that he had about this young woman. McDonough was a big man and she was much smaller and younger, even childlike. As the sun reached its maximum height, the group stopped in a small shady spot and lay down to rest. McDonough felt hungry now, but these people didn't seem bothered at all with their stomachs. He was further bewildered by Nargel's behavior—she was moody and disturbed and did not seem to want to communicate with him.

McDonough lay down and tried to sleep, but the flies bothered him. He broke off a small twig, which still had a few leaves left on it, and waved it about his head. This helped a little, but these flies were really persistent. He had never seen them this bad in Sydney. Somehow everything was worse now. He must have dozed off for a few minutes because he was suddenly awakened by loud, angry voices. He sat up. Tedbury was there, with Nargel looking up at him arguing furiously. Koobee, Bungaree and Awabakal were sitting on the ground. Koobee seemed quite concerned and in a mind to mediate in the affair. Awabakal seemed rather bored by the whole thing. Bungaree got up and walked down to the river.

The arguing was ended by Nargel quickly turning her back on Tedbury and sitting down. For a minute McDonough thought that Tedbury would kick her, but he didn't. Instead he turned and walked morosely down to the river bank where Bungaree was sitting. McDonough stood up and walked over to Nargel and tried to take her hand. She pulled away, put her face down between her knees and refused to look at him. This was a terrible situation, he thought. He seemed to have completely lost contact with what was going on in the group. He moved towards Koobee, but Koobee stood up and started walking down towards the river, following Tedbury. Sean McDonough turned around and walked back towards Awabakal. By this time Awabakal was lying on his back, his hands behind his head. McDonough sat down beside him and tried to engage him in a conversation in English. Awabakal didn't seem particularly interested, and when McDonough asked him what the fight was about, Awabakal raised himself on one elbow and pointed a piece of grass towards Nargel.

'She trouble,' he said.

McDonough looked at Nargel, then back to Awabakal.

'What has she done?' he asked seriously.

Awabakal placed his head between his hands. 'She belongs, you know. Her family arranged a marriage.'

He looked at McDonough. McDonough stared questioningly at him.

'I don't understand,' he said.

Awabakal picked up another piece of grass and began to chew it. He stopped and thought for a moment. 'I don't fully understand how Eora people do this,' he said. 'In my place, a woman like her is promised to be wife to somebody when they are just little girls, sometimes before they are born.'

He paused, and then went on, 'some girls like her,' he pointed with his lip, 'don't want the arrangement, so they run away and shame their family'.

McDonough was puzzled and said to Awabakal, 'you mean she's betrothed, she's promised to somebody in marriage?'

Awabakal nodded, 'yes, something like that, and she ran away'.

Awabakal didn't seem to be interested in pursuing the conversation anymore.

McDonough stood up and walked over to Nargel. He stood there awkwardly for a moment and then sat down beside her.

'Nargel is it true? Are you promised in marriage to somebody else, some other Eora man?'

Nargel looked at him, with her large brown eyes close to tears. 'I told you long time before, McDonough,' she said.

McDonough tried to take her hand, but she pulled it away again.

'I didn't understand,' he said, 'I thought it was a sweetheart. Are you going to be in some kind of trouble with your people?'

She made no answer.

McDonough stood up, walked over to the tree where he had been lying, and tried to think. He wondered what he had got himself into. McDonough wasn't highly educated, although he could read and write. He recalled vaguely something that he had heard, something relating to interference with native women who are promised in marriage. For that matter, he knew all sorts of trouble that a man could get into in his own society by interfering in betrothal arrangements. This situation seemed much more serious, given the circumstances.

He felt as though he had jumped right into a fire. Life as a convict in Sydney may have been totally wretched, but he could well be walking to his death along this strange river.

About mid-afternoon the group started walking further along the river. By late afternoon there was a welcome cool change, and Koobee said to McDonough that they must go and hunt.

McDonough told Koobee that he did not know how to hunt, and the only weapon he had was a knife. He showed it to Koobee. Koobee looked at the knife carefully and nodded his approval. He smiled and said, 'it is a very good knife. It is long and the iron is heavy'. He looked sympathetically at McDonough, 'it is not good for hunting; only after the hunt is it good. Where did you get such a good knife?' he asked.

'I made it.'

Koobee was very impressed. 'So you know how to make things from the iron.'

McDonough nodded, 'yes that is what I did in Ireland before the British brought me here'.

'Do you make the iron things for the British now?'

'No, I'd be making nothing for those bastards.'

Koobee nodded and handed the knife back. 'Some day you will learn to hunt, but today it will be too hard—you must wait here. Bungaree will look after you. Some day you can show him and the others how to make the things with iron.'

This comment did not impress Bungaree, and when McDonough saw the boy's disappointment, he said, 'I will be all right. Take him with you'.

Koobee nodded and closed the conversation with the comment, 'we must hunt now. It will not be so good on the ridges after we leave the river'.

McDonough said no more. He simply waved goodbye as the group moved off into the bush. When he realised that Nargel was also going hunting, he became concerned, for she carried no weapon. He wondered what her part in this hunt might be. But she said nothing to him as she left, and only looked back at him for a moment and then followed the others into the scrub.

McDonough sat down under a tree, somewhat closer to the river than where they had stopped earlier. He felt totally inadequate, a burden to this group. If only he could do something useful. He thought that he would be happy to teach any of them the art of the blacksmith. Perhaps someday he would, he thought. He looked around, got up, and wandered about in the scrub, not going too far because he had heard many tales of people being lost in this terrible place. He was appalled at the apparent lack of resources. Even near the water it seemed a barren place. McDonough broke a bough off a small tree and began to whittle vaguely with his knife, to pass the time.

If only there was something he could do. Perhaps he could make a line, catch some fish. He wandered back to where he had been sitting earlier, sat down again and looked at the river. At this point the river was quite narrow but flowing very slowly. The water looked clean and sweet, and he decided he would climb down the bank and have a drink.

The water tasted very good; cool and refreshing. His thoughts turned again to Nargel, and to wondering what fate might befall him. If this girl was, as the others were saying, a promised bride, he might well be about to meet the angry jilted bridegroom, who would demand to kill him, or something worse. Perhaps he could negotiate with his metal working skills, he thought; or perhaps when they met Pemulwuy the native leader would be so furious that he would be killed out of hand.

He sat down and considered Pemulwuy. An extraordinary man, but very dangerous, he believed. It was said that he had murdered something like twenty people since the colony had been established. A wild savage, he had been told. He was stunned at the thought that he was running to this man for protection. Then again, perhaps Pemulwuy was just the man he needed for protection—providing the complication with Nargel wasn't going to lead to his own early death. He determined to find out exactly what the situation was when the others returned—if they returned.

Soon after they left the waiting place, Nargel parted from the others and began to follow a small tributary away from the river. She stopped for a time, converted a small sapling into a digging stick by sharpening it on a piece of sandstone, and then continued on her way. She had draped about her shoulders a ganimantj skin which, as she walked, she dropped around her waist, wearing it rather in the fashion of a skirt that left the upper part of her body bare. She now took the skirt off and hung it across her shoulders. She came to a small group of bushes covered in green berries. Nargel pressed several of them in her hands and extracted black seeds. She tasted them and moved on until she located a bush that carried ripe berries. She stooped down and gathered them into a small pile on the ground, then stood up and took the cloak away from her shoulders, laid it on the ground, placed the berries in it and then drew it up as a bag. Now completely naked, she began to go to work on several other bushes. She worked fairly quickly from the beginning of a small valley, almost to the top of a ridge gathering fruits that she recognised, and occasionally stopping to dig up root vegetables. She also engaged in some hunting, first a greenish snake about a yard long which she dispatched quickly with her digging stick, and then a brown and yellow lizard, which gave her more difficulty, but in the end also finished up in her dilly bag.

After about an hour of this gathering and minor hunting she had a considerable burden of this bush food. She now examined the lizard. She smiled to herself and thought that even if the hunt did not go well even though these young Bidjigal men were known as the best hunters, she had gathered enough food to feed them for a day or so. She carried the lizard locked within her hands across her shoulders in the same way as the bag. She stopped, opened the bag and looked at what she had so far gathered. She considered the *goanna* carefully and laid her hand along it. Then she sat down and looked back towards the valley that contained the Georges River. This set her to worrying. She thought through the events of the last two days and suddenly became angry again with Tedbury. Young unmarried men, she thought, or rather boys, who were not yet allowed near women... Why did she have anything to do with them? They were always like that, always moralising and aggressive.

'*Babera gadia*,' she thought.

She smiled at this and idly translated the term into English. At first attempt it came out as 'head like penis'. She took this a little further into Sydney slang and smiled to herself at the outcome.

She dug a stick in the ground angrily. She had had sexual intercourse once with an unmarried young man from her own place. It had been a very clandestine, hurried affair. Such relationships were much frowned upon between unmarried couples in Eora law, and Nargel felt an idiot for having been involved. But then she detested the man to whom she was betrothed. Things were different in Sydney. Many of the Eora young people there paid little heed to traditional laws.

She thought over her decision to run away to Sydney and escape from her betrothal. She cast her mind back bitterly to her family, the people who could have negotiated and found a better end to all this. The whole Eora world, she thought, was upside down. She had decided last autumn that she would leave and go to this magic place called Sydney, where there were strange people from across the ocean.

Sydney had indeed been a magic place at first. She had never seen people like those who lived there. The British and even the Eora people were different in Sydney. There were strange animals and vehicles. The people built huge shelters in which they lived, and they sailed across Tuhbowgule in incredibly large boats. However, after some months this magic passed. She had been staying with some relations who were living near where the fish are marketed. Many Eora people lived there. At first she kept to herself and with relations she had found in the neighbourhood, but in the past few months she had become quite adventurous and had taken to wandering about the town with several of the younger locals who lived around the settlement.

This sort of living was certainly unusual. Women of her age would never be allowed to even associate with unmarried men. Besides, she was very much aware that she had been associating with men inappropriately related to her in regard to marriage. Such association was seen as being worse than sexual activity outside marriage. A few years ago this would have brought serious penalties. But now, in Sydney, although the old people grumbled about it, nothing was done.

Nargel found British society even stranger and to be governed by very different rules. Those relating to mating and sexual association seemed variable. The predominant order of the society seemed to depend on dividing people into one of two groups. These two groups acted like completely different peoples. They spoke the same language, but the actual nature of the relationship between the groups was well beyond Nargel's understanding.

McDonough was one of the categories of aliens called convicts, who had to work for the others. Nargel also learned that he was Irish, although he did speak English. The ethnic mix and languages among the aliens was puzzling to the Eora people. Many Eoras regarded the newcomers as spirit beings and did not expect to find so many of the trappings of normal humans associated with them.

Nargel had first met McDonough when he had allowed her and another Eora woman to sleep in a warm stable on a bitterly cold winter's night. The other woman had been suffering from one of the new sicknesses of Sydney, which had affected her breathing. She died that night, but at least she had died in warmth and comfort.

The next morning, McDonough's master had discovered the dead Eora woman. McDonough's kindness had allowed the old woman to die in comfort, but had got him severely beaten the following day. Nargel felt very sorry for him and after that time brought him bush food and meat to supplement his meagre diet. They had become friends and soon the strangeness between them had disappeared.

McDonough was a man of thirty-two years, and at first he saw Nargel as a bright, sparkling, friendly child. This situation slowly changed; they drifted into each other's dreams and planned McDonough's escape from Sydney.

Late that afternoon by the upper reaches of the Georges River, McDonough was becoming disillusioned with all aspects of these dreams. He spent some time sharpening his knife so that he could help with the butchering of the game. There was no sign of the others returning, so he decided to wash his clothes. He stripped naked and waded into the river waist deep, and set about industriously washing his clothes.

Some ten minutes after McDonough had started his laundry, Nargel arrived back at the camp. She put down her bundle of food and stared with some surprise at McDonough. McDonough was equally surprised, or rather enchanted, by Nargel's lovely nakedness. She realised this, smiled shyly and dived into the river. Nargel swam to a rock ledge near the opposite side of the stream, climbed out and drew back her hair. She stood upright with her hair in her hands; the afternoon sunlight glistened on her dark wet skin, picking out water droplets caught like sparkling gems in her pubic hair.

McDonough's dream was again rekindled, and he swam out with much splashing to the rock shelf. Nargel was sitting on the warm rock surface, and McDonough pulled his large, angular white frame on to the ledge beside her. Nargel had never seen a naked European before. His skin was so white it almost made her eyes smart: it was as though he had been turned inside out. The greatest shock was his body hair. She found this almost unbelievable. In fact it was too much for Nargel, and she slipped eel-like into the quiet river and swam back to the camp as the hunting party returned well laden.

McDonough swam back to the camp site and as he began to get out he heard the others giggling at something and realised that he was naked. He stood waist deep uncertain how he could retrieve his breeches and retain some sort of decorum. Then Bungaree made some comment that made Awabakal laugh. McDonough called out to Awabakal and asked in English what the joke was. Awabakal laughed and said that there was a bad fish in this part of the river.

McDonough, alarmed, asked, 'does it bite you?'

'No! It only eats *mareemy*,' Awabakal replied and everybody laughed.

McDonough squinted and asked in English. 'What is mareemy?'

Nargel had now joined in the mirth. She pointed to McDonough's genital area and said:

'Those things Sean.'

'Ah bejesus!'

Amid great laughter, McDonough vigorously slipped and scrambled his way out of the water. Koobee met him at the bank, pulled him out and handed him his breeches. Grinning from ear to ear, Koobee said, 'Awabakal lies'.

After this diversion the whole mood of the group changed. McDonough recovered his composure and since everyone was using English, he responded jovially that he was not afraid and said, 'that fish does not eat white mareemy. You smart buggers are the ones that must be careful in there, to be sure'.

This brought another peel of laughter.

Awabakal responded quickly to the wit. 'There Nargel, only you can go in the river.'

As sharp as a sewing needle Nargel replied, 'then you be safe for true Awabakal, that fish not know the difference between little girls and small boys'.

Koobee stood up laughing; 'now you all lie'.

Koobee decided that they would have a fire, and all ate very well that night.

The small party came around to the west of the new British settlement of Toongabbie and then headed towards *Waun*. They were now deep in Bidjiga1 country and proceeded slowly and cautiously. After eight days walking they met with a man named *Yenowee*, who was related to Tedbury. Yenowee, it turned out, had been with Pemulwuy when he speared Macintyre. More importantly, though, Yenowee claimed that he had killed Tilmouth near Sydney and had carried his corpse into the bush to be eaten by the *worragul* and the *woyan*. Awabakal silently relished this news.

After two more days, Yenowee led the group to Pemulwuy's camp, where all McDonough's fears were confounded. They were received with a generous welcome.

McDonough and Koobee had become close companions. After they had arrived at their journey's end, he said quietly to Pemulwuy while shaking his head, 'Pemulwuy I bring you a man who can make things with the iron, but no more travelling with boys and girls for me'.

CHAPTER 7

THE ACT OF WAR

The eastern sky was pale with first light and smoke. The sweet smell of morning began to rise from the land, and death visited silently by the bank of a quiet river. Pemulwuy killed the first man as he drew water from the river. *Nanborree* and *Weuong* together speared the second and Tedbury speared the last as he ran from the burning hut. There was no quarter given and none asked. The attack was swift and left only death and ashes by the Georges River in the days of late January 1791.

Yennerawannie and Awabakal were present, but did not take part in the attack. Awabakal was both sickened and excited by the ferocity and ease of execution of the action. Pemulwuy's spear had hardly killed the man by the river before Weuong had set fire to the hut. It was all too easy. The Europeans had fired a few musket shots in defence, but were completely at the mercy of these ferocious Bidjigal men.

Pemulwuy walked over to where one man was lying in pain and with one blow broke his skull with a club. He stretched his arms out up above his head and shouted, 'Phillip! *yatnadiou benang menora'*.

He then began a stick-like dance by the body.

This was very puzzling to Awabakal. Pemulwuy's exclamation meant that he had made the first wound. The dance was different from any Awabakal form or for that matter any Eora form that he had seen. It was frightening. Awabakal decided that he would leave and ran off towards the camp, which was at least a day and a half's walk away.

Bennelong was afraid and confused. The Governor was even angrier than before, and now he, Pemulwuy's antagonist, found himself in the odd position of being forced to defend the attack on the three Europeans. For now he sat silent, his eyes wide with fear, and let Phillip's anger wash over them all, the Marines, Ross and Tench, and Grose and Macarthur of the New South Wales Corps, who were accompanied by another officer, Captain Abbott.

'This is a massacre, pure savagery!' Phillip intoned, staring round the room. 'They are all heathen savages!'

Bennelong winced.

'Well, what d'you say, eh?' jibed Macarthur, turning on Bennelong, 'What price cooperation now? Who's in charge of the Eora?'

'I said Pemulwuy was bad,' Bennelong protested. 'I said he must be punished. I said nothing of six Bidjigal heads, or putting men in prison.'

'Well, what did you expect?' growled Captain Abbott. 'Have your people no notion of justice?'

Bennelong said nothing, and simply stared ahead impassively. Phillip frowned, and glanced at the clock on the mantlepiece.

'I have other duties to perform,' he announced, getting to his feet, 'I will return to this matter as soon as I can, and by the time I do, I want some sensible suggestions from you gentlemen. The benefit of your wide experience,' he added with a sharp edge of sarcasm, 'good day'.

They stood and watched Phillip leave. He closed the door hard behind him. Tench sat down again and stared reproachfully at the New South Wales Corps contingent.

'Bennelong's right, in his way,' he said. 'This is nothing more than a direct consequence of your hotheaded advice to the Governor.' He smiled grimly, 'you wanted six Bidjigal heads. Well, Pemulwuy sent the Governor three English corpses'.

Macarthur glowered back at the marine captain, his prominent jaw jutting forward with fury.

'If you and that idiot Carpenter hadn't tied Hill's hands, we would have taken them!' he bellowed.

It was time for Ross to intervene. 'Come, gentlemen, that's enough!' he barked. 'Major Grose,' he said, turning to his counterpart, 'I believe we should be better served by dismissing our quick tempered colleagues here and discussing the matter between the two of us, with Mr Bennelong'.

Bennelong's face fell. The three junior officers filed out resentfully. Bennelong knew he was going to be the centre of attention now, and he was not looking forward to it.

Grose took the lead. He wagged a finger at Bennelong, like a schoolmaster scolding a misbehaving pupil.

'The consequences for your people are now very serious,' he said.

Bennelong nodded. Then defiance flared up in him.

'You are British soldiers,' he said deliberately, 'you should have killed Pemulwuy'.

Grose threw up his hands in despair.

'Tench is certain that even a major military action would be unlikely to bring the fellow in, alive or dead,' said Ross. He focused on Bennelong. 'Do you know of any other way to apprehend him?'

Bennelong shook his head gloomily. 'Even when he was a young man, none of us could follow him,' he paused, 'he is *gromeda'*.

Grose looked impatiently at Ross, 'what the devil does that mean?'

Ross shrugged, 'something to do with evil spirits again, I think,' he said. 'We'll ask Collins. He fancies himself as a student of such matters.'

'Not that it will help us much,' muttered Grose, 'and as for the rest of this black liar's fairytales—'.

'The three men Pemulwuy killed were hunting for meat,' said Bennelong, without looking at either of them. 'Pemulwuy says that no-one shall hunt on his land.'

'Oh, for God's sake,' Grose snarled, 'now it's the bugger's land, as if he were an English squire! Well, we'll show him whose land it is!'

Ross clucked disapprovingly and told Bennelong to leave. It would be better if there were no native witnesses to this particular conversation, and obviously Bennelong had exhausted his usefulness.

'This is a difficult business,' he told Grose when they were alone, 'demanding heads—even mentioning it as a possibility was not, in my opinion, a well-judged decision, and I say that with no disrespect to the Governor. He will have an awkward report to prepare after this latest incident'.

Grose merely waved a dismissive hand, as if to say 'the Governor's convenience is not my affair'.

Ross rested his chin in his hand. 'Tench believes, however, that if we have the patience to harry him with small forces, we may eventually be able to draw Pemulwuy into the field of battle where he will be lost.'

'Field of battle?' mocked Grose, 'you flatter this savage, sir'.

'Nevertheless, Tench may be right,' Ross said, choosing not to rise to the insult.

Grose looked out of the window and across Sydney Cove. He could see the small cottage that Phillip had had built for Bennelong on the point. A kennel for the Governor's tame nigger, he thought sourly, except that the tame nigger was no longer doing his job by keeping the natives quiet. But the important thing at the moment was to ensure that the New South Wales Corps avoided becoming entangled in this very thorny business. Let these arrogant Marines bear the brunt. When he turned back to Ross, it was with an expression of carefully calculated man-to-man respect.

'So be it,' he said. 'Then we shall advise His Excellency that you will deal with this matter. You and your man Tench.'

Pemulwuy was exuberant when he heard of Phillip's anger. He had the group carve a small mask-like head from wood.

He blackened it with charcoal and then dispatched Awabakal and Tedbury to Sydney to give it to Phillip.

'If Phillip seeks Bidjigal heads,' he said, 'we'll let him have one'.

McDonough was appalled by the news of the massacre conveyed by Awabakal, and sending a mock head was even more frightening. He told Pemulwuy that this action would surely bring the entire power of the British into the bush.

Pemulwuy only laughed, '*Gurrewe*, if they do that, they fight only the wind, and soon they will have to live in the sea'.

McDonough winced at the name Pemulwuy had given him. It meant white cockatoo. He had some difficulty seeing himself as that raucous, silly white bird, but then it was a small price to pay for Pemulwuy's goodwill.

'Pemulwuy, the British will take hostages, and persecute and frighten other Eora to betray you,' he said.

McDonough waited for a response, but Pemulwuy sat listening and did not speak.

'That's how they defeated my people,' continued McDonough.

'Are your people now defeated, Gurrewe?' asked Pemulwuy.

'No! never!' replied McDonough, 'but it is very bad'.

'You Irish are very strange,' said Pemulwuy. 'The Frenchmen also spoke of you when they were here.'

He paused and shifted position, 'the English seem to easily defeat your body, but in your head you are not defeated,' he laughed, 'perhaps that is why they are so anxious to cut off my head'.

'What do you mean?' asked McDonough, puzzled by Pemulwuy's remark.

'Phillip told Captain Tench to bring him my head,' Pemulwuy smiled mischievously.

'Perhaps he thinks that the Bidjigal are like the Irish,' he said as he separated his hands. 'He thinks that he can deal with my body in one place and my head in another.'

McDonough was now completely nonplussed, 'I don't understand. What does that have to do with the Irish?'

Pemulwuy peered intensely at McDonough. 'The British have brought your body here, but I think that they kept your head in Ireland.'

McDonough looked thoughtful for a minute. 'Perhaps I have the edge of what you're saying,' he said, 'but I can assure you...you have little understanding of the Irish.'

Pemulwuy laughed.

'Do the Irish have a great understanding of the Irish?'

Jesus, it was worse than at home. McDonough stood up and turned away. He had more to do, he thought, than chat with a one-eyed black philosopher.

Awabakal and Tedbury happily trod their hidden highway to Sydney. The horror of the massacre had faded from Awabakal's mind. He and his companion were young Eora men with a special mission.

As they approached the town they became concerned as to how they might deliver the carved head. They were keen to ensure that the gift did not include their own heads. Because of this, they had decided to do some visiting while they were in the district.

Koobee had returned to his family and the two young men agreed that they would visit him first. They arrived at the seaside camp a little before midnight. Koobee was delighted to see them but, like Gurrewe, was shocked at the gift they had brought for the Governor.

Koobee's wife, Milbab, was awakened to show the visitors the new child, *Pinicoolong*. Koobee took the tiny infant in his arms and presented him to Awabakal.

'Pinicoolong go to your *ceuelyen*.'

Awabakal held the child close and felt the warmth of the infant and of Koobee's simple few words. Those words made Kiraban's father and Koobee, brothers.

It was a fine, but rare custom in the society of this land that people from different ethnic groups would bestow a relationship through a third person. Although the Awabakal and Kamergal people were involved with each other economically in one of old Australia's most extensive trade routes, they were very much distant nations.

They all talked late into the night about the problem of the carved head. Koobee believed that the project was ill-conceived. He was however, not prepared to be heard to oppose Pemulwuy before these two young men. He gave them instead his best counsel. 'Place the head in the Governor's garden,' he said.

Following Koobee's advice, Awabakal and Tedbury crept into the residence garden and left their gift mounted on a pole in a patch of potatoes.

CHAPTER 8

AFFAIRS OF THE HEART AND THE STATE

Nargel talked excitedly with Tedbury and Awabakal after their return to the *Goman* camp north of Parramatta. Life had become much better for her now that Pemulwuy had accepted Gurrewe, and Gurrewe seemed to have accepted life under the eye of the crow. Woyan, the crow, was Pemulwuy's *rae*, the bird spirit of his birth. McDonough enjoyed his life, industriously adapting to the ways of the Eora and making spear heads and other things from iron.

Nargel was in an awkward position. She did not live with Gurrewe, but her relationship with him was again improving. More importantly to Nargel, though, was the fact that since Gurrewe had adopted the clothing of the Eora his skin had become quite dark. Perhaps, thought Nargel, if he lives long enough with the Eora he will become black.

Awabakal and Tedbury, newly returned to the camp, were talking with Pemulwuy when Nargel walked by.

'*Narewe!*'

It was Pemulwuy who called her by her formal name.

'Tonight you will leave the camp for two days.'

Tedbury and Awabakal stood respectfully as Pemulwuy spoke. Nargel did not speak and Pemulwuy continued—'and do not return before that time has passed'.

Nargel knew that this was important but felt somewhat petulant before the two young men.

'What am I to do?' she said, showing very little respect for the crow.

'Watch your *gomerry*,' he replied sharply.

The young men laughed and Nargel stalked off with her nose in the air, but even though Pemulwuy had said it jokingly she had not missed his important point. Pemulwuy turned back to the two young men.

'Tell me, *garagalong*,' said Pemulwuy: 'Was Phillip pleased with my gift?'

The two young men tumbled over each other in their reports.

After leaving the carved head in Phillip's garden, they waited outside Sydney to hear of his reaction. It was, as they expected, outrage! Against Collins's advice he had the head publicly burnt. On Grose's advice he ordered Tench out immediately.

'Captain Tench,' laughed the two young men, 'is already on his way to Kamay'. 'Who is with him?' asked Pemulwuy.

'Carpenter and many others,' replied Tedbury.

Pemulwuy held up both hands, fingers spread. Tedbury used fingers to make up eighteen.

Awabakal was no help in this. He had not yet learned the precision of Pemulwuy's acquired numeracy. He would have used the Bidjigal term *murri sooco,* which in English would translate as many or much. Pemulwuy was very concerned about this news of Tench. He regarded him as a worthy adversary and was puzzled as to why such a small detachment had been dispatched. He must ask Gurrewe, but tomorrow.

The voice of the Australian night was smothered by human sounds. The sweet burnt smell of wattle and eucalypts filled the air. The fires of Goman drove away the darkness. The old men ringed close to the glowing embers which formed the centre of a large meeting, *alodim gaeray.*

The speeches were singular and long. The form of Bidjigal used was often abstruse and difficult to understand and also made use of secret Eora words. Awabakal was pleasantly surprised to find that Tedbury, a native speaker, had almost as much difficulty in comprehending the directions of some of the arguments as he did.

There were two main strands of concern. The major issue related to Pemulwuy's relations with, and actions against, the British. The second concerned a claim of rights by Yennerawannie for a marriage with Narewe.

Narewe was in a proper relationship of father's father's sister's daughter's daughter to Yennerawannie. Gurrewe, on the other hand, had been accepted as a *bulumna* to Pemulwuy which was also proper in this marriage of concern. The question was one of more elevated rights, and various speakers argued the two cases.

This all seemed rather old men's political and philosophical nonsense to Awabakal. It appeared that the man *Nanborree,* whom Narewe had originally run away from, had more significant rights than either of the other two. Pemulwuy had somehow persuaded Nanborree to withdraw from his claim and constructed the Yennerawannie situation to cloud the main issue. This sort of politicking bored Awabakal but certainly did not bore Tedbury who followed the arguments intently from a respectful distance. Awabakal was also put off by a knowledgeable old woman, *Burungaroo,* who sat close to them and constantly advised them and berated Awabakal whenever he drifted off to sleep.

Awabakal thought that all this was the most dishonest form of Australian politics. Gurrewe was valuable to the crow for advice on the aliens. Pemulwuy wanted to rid himself of the Nanborree problem and take on Yennerawannie, a supporter of Bennelong. Yennerawannie also represented a challenge (but an easily defeated one) to Pemulwuy's actions against the aliens. Nargel herself was to these older men little more than a minor character in a social scenario that they were trying to construct. To a young man she represented sex, children and companionship. The old men seemed to Awabakal to miss that point of being human, or at least that was Awabakal's view of the thing.

After a time Pemulwuy began to speak, and Awabakal became quite entranced by the elegance of his oratory. He did not understand all the nuances of his arguments, or the special form of Bidjigal that he used, but it seemed very compelling. Only once during this part of the session did Pemulwuy remind Awabakal of the stick dance man. This was when he stood up wildly to explain a point. Awabakal shuddered at the memory of the massacre and dozed off to sleep for an hour or so.

When Awabakal awoke, an old man called Yella Mundi was extolling the virtues of Pemulwuy. Awabakal assumed that the crow had won most issues, Burungaroo proceeded to give Awabakal a bad time for his inattention, and so Awabakal crawled out of the firelight. He slid into a deep sleep that carried him back to the Northern Lake. His spirit lifted itself high above the spotted trees of the place and rode the warm south wind to Awaba in the land of Koori. In his sleep he smelled all the sweetness of his own birth place.

McDonough arrived early at Pemulwuy's camp. Pemulwuy's wife, *Boorea*, was up and about and she sat down to talk with Gurrewe. Pemulwuy joined them eventually, but was distinctly seedy. Boorea left the group and returned with some food. Pemulwuy was dishevelled, cold and naked. Gurrewe, bronzed, bearded and looking like a Viking gone wrong, stood expectantly before Pemulwuy.

'I give you your *berringen*,' announced Pemulwuy with a wave of his arm.

'What in hell does that word mean?' said Gurrewe.

It means like pretty girl in English...she is yours, Gurrewe,' you have a wife who is happy to be at your side,' he said.

'Pemulwuy,' said Gurrewe, delighted, 'you are an Englishman's nightmare and Irishman's delight'.

'What does nightmare mean?' Pemulwuy questioned.

'Like dreams, *weeree*.'

Pemulwuy laughed, and then went on: 'The Frenchmen in Kamay told me, ouvrons nous coeurs aux Irlandais.' He paused and added: 'Mon amie' as he held out his hand.

'I don't understand French, but the feeling is good, Woyan.' They embraced each other.

'You know, Pemulwuy, if you weren't so black you would make a good Irishman.'

'Well Irlandais, you must learn something of the Eora way.' McDonough dropped to his knee and listened carefully.

'That old woman...,' Pemulwuy sighted along his first finger at a woman who was sitting nearby. 'Now, you must not talk to her or even look at her. When you are near her you must stand like this.'

Pemulwuy took a particular stance to demonstrate.

'*Minyin*?' asked Gurrewe.

'Because' said Pemulwuy, 'she is Nargel's mother'. 'Begorra!' said Gurrewe, 'you mean I must avoid my mother-in-law. What an enlightened idea'. Pemulwuy laughed.

'But you must give her presents, and you know, support her. Nargel will tell of this and you will be seen as a good man.'

Gurrewe grinned ruefully. 'There is always a catch.'

Pemulwuy laughed again and touched Gurrewe on the hand.

Then this meeting of friendly minds ended, Pemulwuy turned his back to Gurrewe and prodded his wife's fire back to life. He now spoke seriously. 'Why does Phillip send such a small force to oppose me?' he asked.

'I am not sure,' responded Gurrewe. 'I think that he is trying to draw you into open combat.'

'With Tench?'

'Very likely,' Gurrewe frowned, 'there is a trick to it'.

'What is the trick, my friend?'

'I believe he knows that you refuse to use muskets. He wants you to attack an armed force and commit suicide.'

'What does suicide mean?'

'To kill yourself, *twiuga*, you know—a falling star.'

Pemulwuy was thoughtful for a moment.

'They cannot kill me with the djurraba.'

'Codswallop!'

'It is true,' said Pemulwuy.

'Your soldiers are not prepared to learn how to load a musket and so you construct excuses,' said Gurrewe.

'That's not the point.'

'Then why?'

'A spear you can make from the tree, stuck in your foot, anywhere, and you cannot fight. A spear is quiet and made from the land. If you break it or lose it you can easily make another. You don't need the black powder or the shot. This is the weapon to defeat the British.'

'Nonsense!'

'There will be no argument about this. I will not use muskets,' said Pemulwuy firmly.

Nevertheless, the argument continued, but Pemulwuy would not budge from his position. He went to some trouble to explain the advantage of the spear and shield in small group combat.

Finally Gurrewe stood up and ended his opposition.

'Pemulwuy I could not argue your point in the sight of God, but you're probably right. Go and kill Tench if you can, but mind, he has the reputation of being a good soldier,' he paused and looked serious, 'he is a marine. It'll not be like fighting the bloody Rum Corps'.

Pemulwuy smiled indulgently and returned to the issue of firearms.

'Gurrewe, you can't make muskets from trees, you must have iron.'

'There must be iron in some rocks in this place. I believe that I have seen some. I have seen some rocks here that look like iron minerals. Yes, and the black fire stones for very hot fires.'

'But we don't make hot fires, all our containers and tools are made from the trees and stone, we do not make the burned clay that you call pottery, it breaks too easily, and we move around too much. As well as this you must have powder. Do you know how to make it?'

'Yes, but I have not seen the substance sulphur in this land. Pemulwuy, tell me how you know about coal, the black stones?'

'From the Russians who came here—they told me—and Awabakal's people have always known about the fire stones.'

'I did not know that there had been Russians as well as French here. Can you speak Russian?'

'No, but they could speak French and some English.'

Gurrewe wondered at all this and then he asked: 'Why do the Eora move about. Why not build permanent shelters like the English?'

'Because if we stay too long, the sweetness of the land is lost, *Sooco Murri whani guna.* Soon the place stinks like Sydney and Parramatta.' He pointed to the coast, 'when it is time we move and burn the land, it breathes again and the *Ganimantj*, the *Tanti*, the *Bundicut*, the *Gurrewe* and the *Windji* return'.

Gerrewe shook his head and said, 'that makes sense. But the English will never understand it. It's like your trade. You get credit for something you give someone, but you don't have to pay it back'.

'No Gurrewe, it is not like that. If I do something for you, or give you something like an umana, and you accept, like the berringen, then you and I are wea jowinid. There is an English word…yes, you become 'beholden' to me. You cannot pay it back, if you give me something and I accept, then I am beholden to you. Both you and I are like this now as long as we live.'

'The English will certainly never understand such a thing,' said Gurrewe, 'I am not sure that I do and I am your bulumna'.

CHAPTER 9

MISFORTUNES OF WAR

Lieutenant Carpenter drew up his bedroll and sat down opposite Tench. The fire flickered quietly. The bush was silent, except for the nervous laughter of a small group of Marines camped some ten yards away.

'Sir, I must say this is a damned insecure situation,' Carpenter said to Tench, 'out here in the woods and so poorly equipped'.

Tench shrugged. 'Sentries are posted and I don't intend to go through the disaster of horses again,' he said, 'they're scarce, and on the last expedition the Indians picked off most of them. More of a hindrance than a help in country like this, in any case'.

'No,' Carpenter persisted. 'It's the small size of our force that worries me. And we've been changing our line of march more often than the terrain warrants. Tell me, sir, do you think we're being watched?'

Tench made no direct answer, and then said 'we're a tempting target. More so than a larger force. That's the whole idea, old chap. The important thing is that he doesn't catch us off our guard'.

The younger officer peered into the darkness for a moment.

'I see,' he said.

Tench smiled, 'we could never find Pemulwuy. We've tried and failed. But he may be forced to find and attack us'.

'How sir?'

Tench took his time lighting a clay churchwarden pipe.

'Very shortly,' he said, 'we shall return Pemulwuy's act of war. I am sure that he watches us now. From tomorrow, I intend for us to shoot the first native we see. Our man is proud. He'll be forced to retaliate, and when he does, we'll cut him to pieces even the few of us all armed with firearms'.

Tench chuckled with all the casual superiority of the trained soldier, the product of a thousand years of military evolution. The pungent scent of his tobacco filled the air, and the warm night closed silently around the British camp.

Two days passed without sight or sound of their quarry. Tench's party tramped on through the oven-like heat of the bush in late summer cooking even more thoroughly inside their uniforms.

Then, suddenly late one afternoon, they spotted an Eora man gathering food in a clearing. One of Tench's detachments managed to get a shot at the man from some fifty yards away, and he stumbled. As the rest of the expedition moved forward to seize him, however, he regained his feet and crashed off into the undergrowth limping slightly but still moving too quickly for pursuit.

They made camp shortly after this. It was the end of the expedition's fourth day.

'Well, we've made our mark, I suppose,' said Carpenter to his commander, 'what if they bring up a big war party, sir?'

Tench shook his head, 'they're not American Indians,' he told him. 'If they do strike, there'll be just a small band of them, and it will probably have all the subtlety of a tavern brawl. No match for a musket group. Tomorrow we march in three file, ten men to a row. One row standing firing with bayonets fixed, two down loading. That is why we have been changing direction. We must always present a clear area for them to attack.' Tench smiled, 'if he attacks, we will give the blighter a lesson in how to use muskets, eh'.

On the sixth day there was another sighting, this time of a small group of Eora near the place called Toongabbie. They too disappeared before the Marines could get to them. Weary now, and running low on rations, Tench gave the order to stop for a meal. After about half an hour he made the decision to head back towards Sydney. He warned Carpenter to be very alert, 'the blighter might have been waiting for us to turn back'.

The afternoon's march had them following a small watercourse, which in time led them into a heavily wooded valley. It was stunningly beautiful country. At one point there was a huge mass of colourful sceptre flowers, called *waratahs* by the locals. Tench cut one of the blooms to take home with him. With thoughts of the food and soft beds awaiting them on their return, the party continued cheerfully enough along the valley floor. Tench consoled himself with the thought that there would be another time, another chance at this troublesome, fascinating man called Pemulwuy. At that point a peel of laughter rang out from a gang of birds called *kookaburras*.

'Even the damned birds laugh at us in this place,' Carpenter commented in disillusionment.

Then, without warning, spears began to fall from the sky, steeply, like long, deadly hailstones. Four of the party were wounded immediately including Tench, who fell to the ground, dropping his precious bloom. There was a long spear buried deep in the upper part of his right arm.

Lieutenant Carpenter, in his first experience of action, reacted quickly. He realised immediately that the angle at which the spears had fallen meant that they had been thrown from a fair distance, almost certainly out of range and, as his eyes told him, totally out of sight, and they had come from all directions. The Marines were surrounded.

Carpenter yelled at the men to form a small, open square. Two of the wounded had managed to remove the spears from their bodies, suffering only minor injuries. Tench had to be carried into the centre of the square, as did one private who had caught the missile in his stomach. The man's screams of agony echoed through the valley. As the surgeon attended to the two more serious casualties, Carpenter expanded the square a little, to avoid becoming sitting targets for another such attack. None followed and the valley remained eerily silent.

Within half an hour, the spear had been removed from the captain's arm and, though weakened by heavy bleeding, Tench was able to resume his command. The private was a different matter: the surgeon was forced to administer laudanum to ease the man's suffering. It was clear that unless they got him back to Sydney quickly, he would die.

Tench's shock at being wounded was obviously nothing to his humiliation at being outwitted by a band of primitives. The arrogance of the previous days had evaporated. He knew that they were fighting for their lives.

Their tactic with the spears in this sort of terrain reminded him of a North African adversary who had used such tactics in times long past. He told Carpenter that this left them at a very severe disadvantage in this sort of scrub country.

'They can see us, but we can't see them, and the way they throw those spears, they don't even have to come within musket range. This is extraordinary, a novel ambush tactic.'

There was only one thing for it, under the circumstances. If they stayed in the traditional square or in rows, so effective in Europe against cavalry and infantry alike, they risked another lethal shower of spears and they had no shields. Neither could they risk moving through the bush in single marching order. Tench ordered them to undertake a safer, but tortuously slow, process of leapfrogging out of the situation.

He divided the Marines into two groups of equal size, with two of his men carrying their wounded comrade on a makeshift stretcher. One group moved forward about fifty yards and halted. The second group then spread out and formed an open circle around them, forming a protective wall of muskets. The first group then moved out, now moving within a new protective ring for the gain of thirty yards.

As the party began the procedure, tension was high among the men. Carpenter could see that they were still on the brink of panic and were reluctant to leave the security, however illusory, of the familiar square.

'The men fear that we may be picked off if we spread out as you order sir,' he confided to his commander.

The captain shrugged, 'certainly, but we have no choice. By this manoeuvre, we at least ensure that the natives are forced to attack us singularly, if they dare. To do so, the spear thrower will have to expose himself to us, however briefly, and thus risk a musket ball from his intended victim or one of the other men in the vicinity'.

'Yes, sir.'

Tench told Carpenter to take charge of the first group; he would command the second.

'You may explain this to your men,' he said. 'At all costs there must be an orderly withdrawal until we clear this timbered area. Our safety depends on discipline.'

And so they moved off, rather clumsily and anxiously at first, with each man scanning the bush for the death that might lie in wait for him there. Then their confidence grew. It became clear that

Tench had judged correctly, vulnerable though the individual Marines were during parts of the manoeuvre, no Eora was prepared to hazard his own life for the sake of taking a British one. Something Tench observed with interest.

Forward progress was painfully slow. Even when clear of the entrapment, the trip back to Sydney took four days and cost the life of the marine with the stomach wound.

They saw the Eora warriors only once during their retreat, fleetingly and at a distance.

When Tench's expedition limped back into barracks, their arrival signalled a new, ominous phase in the colony's existence. From now on, it was clear. The British were going to have to fight for their foothold in New South Wales. Not only were some of the natives hostile, but they could actually win at least minor actions. The New South Wales Corps despised Watkin Tench, but none would have dared stand in battle against this careful and dangerous British warrior as Pemulwuy had.

A change had come over Governor Phillip since the failure of Tench's expedition. He was no longer an angry man. True, he was prepared to take stern measures. Against Tench's and Collins's advice, he bowed to Major Grose's call for punitive measures against Eoras living in Sydney. A number were rounded up and imprisoned as an example.

Only Bennelong was excluded from the general order. Nevertheless, the Governor seemed more saddened than anything else. Those close to him thought him preoccupied, even fatalistic. This was not the New South Wales he had imagined when the fleet had set sail from Portsmouth almost four years before. His information had been that the natives were hopelessly backward without ideas of nationhood property, military organisation or warfare. Phillip was a naval officer, and he had been prepared to organise a jail for his masters in London. What he had not reckoned with, was such a strange war to gain control of the colony.

For his part, Bennelong had protested strongly against the arrests of Eora people, but to no avail. Some had already been released, but others, including his old friend Koobee, were still in British hands and were being subjected to the same kind of pointless beatings and humiliations that the aliens handed out to their own convicts.

As Bennelong left the Governor's residence, having made a special plea for Koobee's release, he was worried as well as frustrated. The Governor had seemed very distracted during the earlier interview. Bennelong was beginning to suspect that soon his friend Phillip would give up the struggle and sail back to England. The Eora man trudged gloomily towards Judge Advocate Collins's nearby house to seek the advice of his other powerful British ally. He felt the weight of personal responsibility heavy on his shoulders— it was all going wrong. He knew it, and so did the Governor, which was why Phillip would want to go home. How could Bennelong help save the situation? He felt slightly more hopeful by the time he arrived at Collins' house.

This was a substantial stone building, simple enough by the standards of faraway England, but downright palatial for the young colony. Bennelong knocked on the door and was shown in by a female convict servant. Collins was, however, not alone in his simple but tastefully furnished drawing room. Tench and Carpenter, the leaders of the failed action against Pemulwuy, were present, and they broke off from intense discussion as Bennelong entered the room. The convict maid curtsied and withdrew, leaving Bennelong, irritated and embarrassed by this unexpected encounter, fumbling for the opportunity to excuse himself again.

'Mr Collins, I see you are busy. I can come back later.'

The Judge Advocate got to his feet with a welcoming smile, and drew Bennelong into the room.

'Please come in,' he said, 'you're just the fellow we wanted! Captain Tench and Lieutenant Carpenter were seeking my advice on native tactics of war. Now that you're here, we can have it all from the...ah...horse's mouth—so to speak....'

'I shall help if I can,' Bennelong said cautiously, taking the seat offered.

Collins continued his little lecture to the two Marines. He had been explaining that the Eora did not engage in warfare in the sense that Europeans understood it—certainly not wars of territorial aggrandisement—and that this seemed to have something to do with their religious beliefs.

'Their weaponry is designed either for man-to-man combat or for hunting,' he explained. 'I can't understand where Pemulwuy got the idea to use those particular tactics against you—remarkable!' He said, shaking his head in bemusement.

'Nevertheless, he did,' said Tench, 'and in the kind of terrain we were in, such a simple stratagem renders the musket and square absolutely useless'.

Collins raised an eyebrow. 'So, if I might ask, how did you escape?'

Tench explained the leapfrogging technique. 'It was still a dangerous manoeuvre,' he added, 'they could have attacked any part of the group fairly easily, but the rest of my force would have inflicted heavy casualties on them. They chose not to attack apparently, and thank the Lord for it'.

'You obviously did the right thing, Mr Tench,' Collins agreed. 'I congratulate you on extricating yourself from such an awkward situation with so few casualties. Nevertheless, I remain puzzled by the natives' use of such tactics.' He turned to where their Eora guest was sitting, 'perhaps Bennelong can help us'.

'It is not our way, this fighting,' said Bennelong, shaking his head. Then he extended his second finger in the Eora way, 'the convict, McDonough, would he know of such things?'

'Perhaps,' Collins said doubtfully, 'but I find that difficult to believe. I don't think that he was ever a soldier'.

Bennelong pondered the question further for a few moments.

'Sometimes,' he said eventually, 'when there is a hostile group at a distance in open ground, like when there is an argument, Bidjigal people throw spears into the air. This prevents them from having to move in too close. They do not throw their spears to kill, only to frighten. This way the argument is usually finished.'

'That could well be from where the technique evolved,' said Tench, obviously satisfied. Bennelong nodded sagely, glad to have the question out of the way. He went on to express his doubts about the Governor's state of mind and his concerns at his own situation if Phillip were to leave. The British officers were somewhat taken *aback* at his words, and obviously puzzled that he should be taking such an interest in the political situation.

'Well, my dear fellow,' Tench answered, 'you do seem quite well informed, nevertheless,' he added with a superior smile, 'you may have got hold of the wrong end of the stick. His Excellency has troubles, you are right. His problems are, however, more to do with the New South Wales Corps than with our elusive foe, Pemulwuy'.

Bennelong nodded as though he understood. But Tench's reply had done nothing to allay his fears.

Just then, the maid servant put her head around the door.

'If it pleases you, sirs, there are some Marines outside wanting Captain Tench,' she looked at Bennelong, and blushed, 'they got a black man with 'em, and he's hollerin' fit to bust!'

Tench led the way to the front door. Sure enough, there were two Marines holding firmly onto none other than Yennerawannie. He was dressed in the clothing of the bush and looking very agitated.

'Found him sneakin' about round Bennelong's cottage, so we brought him here, sir' said one marine.

Tench stared at the panting, travelworn man. 'Yes, he is a friend,' Bennelong said, even though he knew Yennerawannie had been supporting Pemulwuy lately. This was a difficult situation; he must get the man away from here and talk to him. 'I shall take him to my house, Captain Tench,' he added.

Tench nodded. 'Very well, just keep the chap out of trouble, eh?'

Bennelong made as dignified a departure as he could, with the terrified moaning Yennerawannie at his side. The three white men watched them go.

'I feel a great sympathy for that poor fellow Bennelong,' Collins commented.

Tench shook his head. 'I have little time for him,' he said, 'Pemulwuy is at least honest, in his savage fashion'.

Collins was surprised by the captain's vehemence, but he simply smiled and said nothing

'And now, if you will excuse me, Mr Collins I must return to my quarters. My arm pains me somewhat and I must take medication,' said Tench.

'Of course.'

They said polite farewells, and Tench and Carpenter set off along the dusty road towards the Marines' barracks.

A brooding, thoughtful Tench broke the silence of their walk only once. After a few minutes, he turned to Carpenter and murmured 'Bennelong and his kind are of little account, you know. If we are to have New South Wales, we must beat Pemulwuy. He is the soul of the native resistance. Break him and we break them all'.

'But how, sir?' asked Carpenter.

'If I knew that Mister,' Tench answered, 'I would tell you'.

CHAPTER 10

WOYAN

Pemulwuy sat stooped, staring vacantly at the earth he was marking with a stick. He listened to Gurrewe, who stood before him with his hands on his hips.

'But you could steal muskets, Djurraba as you call them, and powder,' said Gurrewe, irritated by Pemulwuy's distant mood, 'then I would be of some use to you'.

'I have said before, I see no advantage in those things,' said Pemulwuy, 'they are too slow to load and a shield can protect you from the bayonet. You have strong arms Gurrewe; you must learn to use the spear'.

'You are still missing the point,' said Gurrewe. 'You must form ranks to use muskets properly. Each successive rank then kneels to load, while the one behind fires.' Gurrewe used his hand to describe the firing ranks.

Pemulwuy watched Gurrewe's hand, then said, 'if you formed a group of people like that, I would throw spears like this'. He pressed stiffened fingers into Gurrewe's hands.

'Like I did to Captain Tench, and he ran away.'

'Yes that was quite clever,' said Gurrewe, 'but I am glad that you took my advice and did not attack his retreat. You would have lost a lot of Eora'.

Pemulwuy looked up, quite interested. 'Tell me Gurrewe, how do I attack Tench when he does that?'

'You must use a massed attack, but not without djurraba.' Gurrewe shook his head, obviously unsure of this advice and added—'I will think further on this'.

Pemulwuy then pointed his lower lip towards the other Eora people sitting nearby.

'What will you do with the berringen?'

Gurrewe looked slightly embarrassed. 'Nargel and I would like to go away for a while, find somewhere else to live for a time.'

'You must use her formal name, Narewe, when you talk to me like this Gurrewe. This is all her land, you can go anywhere,' said Pemulwuy, then looked slightly amused. His strange eye confused his gaze. He said nothing for a time, and then grinned broadly.

'Irishmen like *yanga callyne*, eh, McDonough?'

McDonough felt offended by Pemulwuy's remark and walked away.

Yennerawannie talked very little on his first night with Bennelong. The next day, however, Bennelong was to learn of his bitterness towards Pemulwuy. Yennerawannie was quite sure that Pemulwuy had simply exploited him in the Nargel affair, using him to get rid of Nargel's problems with Nanborree. Yennerawannie said that he was reluctant but had gone along with this, only to discover that Pemulwuy had betrayed him to support the Irishman McDonough.

They both talked through their grievances against the crow. Bennelong explained in some detail how he imagined the British and the Eora would live peacefully together, sharing the important features of both societies. Yennerawannie failed to comprehend Bennelong's vision of a divided mixed society. He was nevertheless in thorough agreement that Pemulwuy was their problem. They decided on a plan to get rid of him.

The two conspirators confided their plan to Koobee. Koobee, still smarting from a British beating, was hardly the man to take sides with the aliens against Pemulwuy, but Bennelong argued that it was Pemulwuy's actions that had brought the wrath of the British upon them. Still, Koobee would accept no excuse for the British brutality, 'besides, Pemulwuy beat them,' he said.

Bennelong and Yennerawannie were left to put their plan into action. Koobee set out about an hour later, determined to warn the Woyan of the conspiracy.

Bennelong carefully explained his plan to Captain Hill of the New South Wales Corps. Hill took the proposal to Macarthur, and eventually Major Grose received Bennelong and Yennerawannie.

The plan was very simple. Yennerawannie would guide a force of British soldiers to Pemulwuy's main camp. Pemulwuy would be forced to make a stand and defend the women and children and the old people. So that Pemulwuy would not be prepared, Bennelong would lead another force to another camp in order to mislead him. Grose, now desperate, agreed with Hill and Macarthur that the idea had some merit and was worth trying.

Carpenter heard about the plan through a convict servant, who had heard it through his mistress, an Eora woman, who in turn had heard it from Koobee's wife.

Tench was quite amused when Carpenter reported the plan to him.

'Even that sycophant Bennelong wants to play with toy soldiers,' he said, 'Grose is using a mock Hannibal to plan a mock battle in a land that neither he nor anyone else understands.'

'Who the hell is Hanibal?' Carpenter asked.

Tench laughed and caught Carpenter by the shoulders. 'An ancient Phonetian warrior; they don't realise that's a real bloody Hannibal out there!'

Tench explained his reference to the legendary Phonetian warrior Hanibal.

When Grose heard of Tench's remarks, he was only amused and made a joke of it, and said that the black warrior that had troubled the Romans in the ancient past was something that Tench must have picked up in military history. He said that there was a vast difference between a Roman legion of a thousand years ago, and the British Army.

'The next thing he will be threatening us with will be the ancient Briton Bodecea. After all, she came from the West country like him and she also took on Rome and lost.'

The two New South Wales Corps detachments left Sydney very early the next morning.

The force guided by Yennerawannie was led by Captain Hill, with two sergeants, thirty privates and a surgeon. The other group, led by Lieutenant Hamilton, contained two sergeants, twenty-two privates, one drummer and a surgeon.

Bennelong led the second group to a small pleasant lake on the Georges River about twenty miles from Botany Bay. It was a good day's march from Sydney, and the detachment slept well in these pleasant surroundings. Yennerawannie led Hill's group for two days towards Goman camp, which was located higher up on a tributary of the Parramatta River. It was towards evening on the second day when, for no apparent reason, Yennerawannie stopped in midstride, looked at the sky, screamed out, and ran off into the bush. Hill did not know what to make of this behaviour. He headed for the settlement at Parramatta.

It was in the afternoon of the second day that Bennelong saw the crow. The bird appeared to Hamilton to be an ordinary crow, perched on a stringybark tree quite close to them.

Bennelong looked at it and was absolutely shocked. 'Everything has gone wrong!' he shouted, 'Pemulwuy is here!'

Hamilton felt a cold deathlike feeling sweep over him. He called his men together and prepared them for a possible attack. Nothing happened. Bennelong insisted that they turn around and hasten toward Sydney. The sense of impending disaster had passed, and Hamilton regarded his demented Eora companion with some suspicion.

The plan was to wait there for one day and then join the other group at Goman. Bennelong, however, flatly refused to guide them towards Goman. Finally Hamilton led his troops and the distressed Bennelong back towards Sydney.

The trip back was, to everyone's relief, uneventful. Bennelong received a very poor reception from the New South Wales Corps. Yennerawannie received an equally bad reception a day later when he appeared at Bennelong's cottage. Bennelong had walked through the darkened doorway to be frightened half to death by a crying and terrified Yennerawannie crouched beside his bed.

The following day, news arrived that Hill's detachment had reached safety in Parramatta. A couple of days later a conflicting report said that Hill's detachment had been annihilated somewhere between Sydney and Parramatta.

About four miles out of Parramatta, the road passed a small knoll called Gowwon near Rof's farm. The group had stopped to farewell four of the New South Wales Corps from Parramatta who were delivering two convicts to the farm. They were hit with two successive vollies of spears, apparently thrown from behind the knoll. Six men fell to the initial fusillade.

Hill took ten men and charged up the knoll and down the other side, but the Eora had left.

The Eora group then made a running attack on the remaining group, clubbing some of the wounded to death. Four Eoras were shot dead and two others wounded. At this point the attackers quickly withdrew. Immediately Hill returned and was hit with another volley of spears. This time Hill himself was struck. No further contact was made between the British and the Eora.

The group that bore the brunt of the main attack had fired muskets and then tried to defend with bayonets. Their attackers had deliberately impaled their wooden shields onto the bayonets, rendering the weapons quite useless. As Tench put it, it was not so much a battle as a debacle. The one interesting feature of the whole exercise was the rumour among the local Eora that Pemulwuy had been shot with a musket, but had survived.

CHAPTER 11

A LETTER TO ENGLAND

Sydney
26 November 1791

My dear Gideon,

We are at the end of the New South Wales winter. The season was wet and remarkably cold. I find it more and more difficult to recall the soft and sweet meadows of our homeland. I fear that we shall never be able to make this heartless, harsh place in its image.

Almost four months have passed since my arrival. The voyage was miserable; many convicts died and others arrived close to death. Should you travel here, I advise you never to undertake the journey during the antipodean winter. It may be a fast passage, but conditions aboard the navy's supply ships leave much to be desired. I should warn you, moreover, that the conditions of life in the colony are hardly more luxurious.

I trust that Anne and Elizabeth are in good health, and that Jonathan has overcome his difficulties. You are all so far away. I think of you without ceasing.

The news in the colony, which you will no doubt hear of before this letter reaches you, is that the Governor has resigned. It is a rather extraordinary event. Of all things, the strangest is that Captain Phillip remains in New South Wales. No-one seems to have any certain explanation for his reluctance to leave, tho' rumour has it that he is hoping by his presence to restrain the acting authorities in the colony from ill-considered measures.

Mr Collins is Judge Advocate, therefore the second most important man in New South Wales. He has been very helpful to me, as you supposed he would be. Mr Collins is inclined to place the blame for the Governor's resignation squarely with the New South Wales Corps, and in particular with Major Grose, who is the acting Governor of the colony now. I fail to understand his reservations. I have met Major Grose, and he seems to be a fine fellow. Major Ross, commander of the Marines, is a man of somewhat splenetic humour and also no friend of Grose. Confound their politics!

I am personally inclined to believe that our chief difficulty lies in the manner of our intercourse with the Indians, or natives, or call them what you will. At present the few free settlers, and the convicts, must fear for their lives. No-one dares travel outside Sydney without military escort. The military here, especially the New South Wales Corps, can do little to deal with the situation. I must tell you, to my shame, that strong drink is the curse of the colony, and immorality and fornication are common. There is a great despair about this place. Mr Pitt says that he 'knows of no cheaper way' of ridding England of wrongdoers, but I wager neither he nor parliament are aware of the frightful conditions that prevail here, among convicts and free alike.

The great force among the natives is a blackguard known as Pemulwuy. He has stirred up a hatred for us among these hitherto kindly, tho' simple beings. In the letter I sent to you by the last ship, I entertained you with accounts of a comical, good humoured fellow named Koobee, a native well known in Sydney town. He has disappeared and I am told that he has joined Pemulwuy's band in the desolate hinterland. Bennelong, the other native I described to you, still lives in Sydney and remains a friend of our cause in New South Wales, but the wretched creature fears for his life.

I cannot deny that there is much to criticise in the colony. Mr Collins maintains that the only military man who might deal with Pemulwuy and make the colony safe is a marine officer named Tench. The gentleman concerned seems, however, to possess an exaggerated view of Pemulwuy's abilities and importance. Captain Tench saw fit to criticise the Governor in this matter. Lately he has even attacked Mr Collins and accused him of applying British law unjustly where the natives are concerned. Like the knights of old, Tench talks much of 'honour' and such. He holds the view, so I am told, that our only virtuous course is to declare war on the natives and engage them in combat, then defeat them and occupy their land as victors. Like William the Conqueror or Genghis Khan!

Mr Collins, who has studied the ways of the natives thoroughly, insists that Tench misunderstands them utterly. These people, so he insists, have no notion of such matters as war or conquest. They have no civilised idea of property or the ownership of land. They are the lost children of God, a simple, primitive race of wanderers. They must be protected and educated slowly and carefully until they reach whatever level of culture lies within their as yet untried capacities.

They are able to learn. Captain Phillip demonstrated the fact in founding a school for them. They are, however, very slow. The schoolmaster who teaches them has informed me that they learn half as quickly as English children. Nevertheless, there are indications that make me believe that the natives may yet be capable of being civilised. Those who have studied their languages assure me that in form they are not unlike the Latin we studied as boys. They appear to learn English without great difficulty.

Nevertheless, this man Pemulwuy is a pure savage, and we must suppose that at heart many natives are like him. Pemulwuy murdered the Governor's game keeper—a rogue who, Lieutenant Carpenter insists, most probably deserved his fate. The Governor was persuaded to send a military expedition to punish Pemulwuy's tribe without success. Since then, Pemulwuy has caused havoc in the colony. The forces of order appear helpless. A year ago, this was a tranquil place, and now the Governor has resigned and Major Grose and the New South Wales Corps are at the helm, attempting to steer the good ship New South Wales through very stormy waters.

Pemulwuy's attempts to resist civilisation are, of course, doomed to failure. In his odd, primitive mind he harbours the belief that he can hold back the tide, like King Canute. Soon he will be swept aside. Meanwhile, I believe he has killed some thirty persons. Officers of the New South Wales Corps, with whom I have discussed the matter, insist, however, that these are only trivial skirmishes. They say that Pemulwuy and his confederates are little more than glorified footpads, who should be dealt with like common criminals.

I confess that I do not know what to believe. Perhaps we must trust in our military men, for all their shortcomings. Certainly this Pemulwuy is a stubborn, vicious fellow. They say he made friends with the French when they were here. May we trust that we shall not find ourselves murdered in our beds by the cohorts of King Louis, guided and urged on by the savages of New South Wales!

I am having a little house built near the harbour. I eagerly await your news—a year hence?—and wish you all health and good fortune. Spare a thought for your venturesome brother in the antipodes, and say a prayer for us all.

I remain your affectionate
James

CHAPTER 12

THE FIRST LOSER

By the time the winter of 1792 had passed, Bennelong's misery had turned into despair. Yennerawannie, who now lived with him, was hard at work drowning his sorrows in the new-found solace of rum. Bennelong spent the first few weeks of spring desperately trying to talk Phillip out of leaving New South Wales. He failed to understand that the Governor's resignation was final—an official act that could not simply be reversed at will.

The *Atlantic* was expected in Sydney in early November to take Phillip home for good, but the ship's arrival was delayed until the twenty-fourth. When Phillip finally saw its sails entering the Sydney Heads, he knew that he was the first loser in the destructive conflict that was gathering force on the edge of the continent of *Terra Australis*.

After the Atlantic had docked, Bennelong was inconsolable. Phillip feared that he might drift into the state of psychic death that he had observed to occur with captives in the early days of the colony. The thought occupied his mind during his preparations for departure.

Phillip had spent the past few months pondering some of Bennelong's ideas, especially his proposals for the foundation of a new, mixed population. Certainly some kind of reconciliation with the native people had come to seem essential to him, though he had not yet committed his thoughts to paper in the form of an official report. It was pointless to stay in the colony any longer. The business of resignation had affected him deeply, and it was hard to think clearly while he was still so close to the situation. Relations between himself and Grose had, if anything, deteriorated further since he had left office. Nor had he received much help from Ross and the Marines: Tench, in particular, seemed to have become quite demented, and saw Pemulwuy as some kind of noble enemy, a Hannibal of the antipodes. Fortunately he had the wisdom not to put any of this in writing—or so he said. Phillip was convinced that the best work he could do for New South Wales would be back in London, in the corridors of the Colonial Office. And for that Bennelong might be very useful...

The former Governor invited Bennelong to his house the night after the *Atlantic* docked. After Bennelong had drunk almost half a bottle of red wine, enough to ease the atmosphere between them, Phillip looked at him solemnly.

'Bennelong,' he said, 'I have decided that you are to come with me to England'.

Bennelong shuddered. His eyes filled with tears. He looked up at Phillip.

'Your Excellency...I don't understand. What do you mean?'

Phillip smiled at Bennelong's reaction, which he found childlike, 'simple, my dear fellow,' he said softly. 'You will travel aboard the ship *Atlantic* to England. When we reach England, you will be my guest.' He paused and measured his words carefully, 'and you will have the opportunity of discussing the situation in New South Wales with the British government. You and I together!'

'But is it possible for a man like me to travel so far on a ship?' Bennelong asked after a moment.

'Of course! Anyone can travel on a ship!' said Phillip with a booming laugh, 'especially on a British ship. They are the finest and safest made by man! Besides a trip around the Horn in summer can be quite pleasant.'

Phillip started to tell Bennelong stories about London and the other great cities of Britain— of cobbled streets filled with carriages, of green landscapes and hills, of farms and oak trees. And there were courts, palaces, and a king, whom Bennelong would assuredly have the privilege of meeting.

By the time Bennelong set off back to his cottage on the point, he was euphoric. In one single stroke, Phillip had solved all his problems. He would not have to worry about Pemulwuy, and his visit to England would give him enormous wisdom and prestige. His situation was transformed, even though the prospect of a six-month sea voyage was unnerving. Bennelong's bubble burst when he arrived at his cottage and found Yennerawannie, sobbing and drunk on the floor. He took one look at his pathetic friend and fled back to the former Governor's house. He announced himself at the back porch, and a bemused Phillip appeared, curious as to why Bennelong should return so soon after their last audience

'Are you all right, man?' Phillip asked.

Bennelong nodded, 'your Excellency,' he panted, 'can Yennerawaimie come as well?'

Phillip let out another hearty laugh, 'don't want to leave him in the lurch, eh? Yes, he can come. He is welcome aboard the *Atlantic* and will assuredly be welcome in England. He'll be company for you, eh?'

And so it was set.

On 10 December 1792, Captain Arthur Phillip boarded the *Atlantic* with his two dark-skinned companions. As he stood on the deck of the ship, talking rather sadly with some of the men who had come to pay their respects, a soldier arrived, carting a small, scruffy-looking message penned with charcoal on flattened ti-tree bark. Phillip took possession of it to the general surprise of those present—and the consternation of Bennelong, who took one look at the message and disappeared to another part of the ship. Phillip undid the native twine and unrolled the white parchment-like material.

There were strange Eora symbols decorating the note and a short, poorly penned message in English:

FAREWELL. PHILLIP.
NEVER RETURN.

Another draughtsman, probably Pemulwuy himself, had tried to sign the note but had failed and had drawn the Eora symbol for a crow.

There was a short silence.

'The arrogant swine!' said the newly-promoted Major Paterson, 'I assure you, Captain Phillip, that I shall not rest until he hangs from a gallows'.

Phillip shook his head gloomily and made a dismissive wave of the hand. 'That may be your task, Major Paterson. Nevertheless, Pemulwuy is right. He has defeated me. Perhaps he was better advised than I.'

He paused and gazed for the last time across the landscape that had witnessed his humiliation.

'He will, however, never defeat England,' Phillip said. 'His is a troubled soul, may it rest in peace some day.'

Then, gathering what remnants of status he could of his former office, he turned from the group and walked, hands clasped behind his back and head erect, to his quarters in the stern of the ship.

Tench and Carpenter stood on a promontory overlooking the harbour with a light nor'easterly blowing in their faces. They watched the *Atlantic* clear the heads and set sail for her long ocean voyage that would take her across the Pacific Ocean and around South America.

Tench turned away with a sigh. 'That is a hell of a way to go home. Naval men will never understand what war is about,' he said to Carpenter.'They know how to win battles, but they know nothing of conquest.'

Carpenter said nothing. He was still staring at the tall ship, keeping his eye on it until it was out of sight towards New Zealand and Cook's Strait.

The two marine officers walked slowly back towards the settlement farm. Carpenter asked Tench if he had heard about Pemulwuy's farewell correspondence to Phillip. His superior smiled grimly.

'Yes. It is what I would expect from a man of that calibre,' he said.

'But he has not attacked so far this summer sir,' Carpenter said. 'Why in your opinion is this so?'

'Perhaps he thinks he has frightened us off. If so, he underestimates the land-hungry hordes of the New South Wales Corps,' Tench answered. 'The African has also restrained himself these past months. I believe that he and Pemulwuy may be in league.'

Carpenter nodded, 'where in hell did he come from?'

Tench smiled ironically. 'I understand that he jumped ship from an American whaler. Even this God forsaken place is not spared the consequences of the many actions of the English. He was an American slave.'

To add to the colony's troubles, the New South Wales bush had lately been plagued by attacks from an African who, it was believed, had absconded from an American ship and then got himself into trouble with the Sydney authorities. Perhaps Tench was right, and the American negro had sought allies among dissident blacks like himself—which could naturally enough lead him to Pemulwuy.

'Major Grose now has a free hand, it is true,' Carpenter said, 'and if he decides on a policy of expansion to the west and on the Hawkesbury River, then Pemulwuy will use the opportunity to go on the warpath yet again'. Tench made as if to answer, then seemed to think better of it. There was to be a conference at the residence of the Acting Governor the next morning. Better to lay his cards on the table then.

They walked in silence back to the settlement. They did not yet know it, but they were entering the first proper day of the interregnum in New South Wales. This would be a time during which the New South Wales Corps would establish its supremacy in the colony, a stranglehold that Phillip's successors would take twenty years to break. It would be almost three years before the colony had another Governor from London.

The next day's meeting seemed to Tench more like a royal reception than a gathering of officers and equals. Major Grose was clearly relieved that Phillip had left at last, and he showed an aggressive, almost dictatorial attitude to the meeting. Restraint had been thrown to the winds. Tench could see that he, Macarthur, Abbott and the others now considered themselves able to do as they wished.

There was first a hypocritical valedictory for Phillip, during which Tench sat in disdainful silence. Then they got on to the meat of the conference.

'Gentlemen,' said Grose in his new grand manner, 'it will be our policy to continue to establish new settlements along the Parramatta and Georges Rivers. The settlement of Parramatta will be encouraged to grow and prosper. We shall also make further efforts to encourage settlement along the Hawkesbury River in a systematic fashion of course. We must move from the arid lands around the port of Sydney to the lush plains beyond, where there is fertile soil!'

And nice little estates for the jolly gents of the New South Wales Corps, thought Tench, but held his counsel.

At last he spoke. He waited until Grose had put the new policy open to discussion. His fawning acolytes naturally backed him to the hilt. It was with some sour satisfaction that Tench took his turn.

'Your Excellency,' he said, drawing the word out with just a little too much emphasis and not quite enough reverence, 'we should bear in mind that our problem is not the natives in general, but more particularly the man Pemulwuy and his immediate henchmen.'

Macarthur groaned audibly and looked up at the ceiling, as if to say, 'Oh God, Tench's got a bee in his bonnet again'.

Tench pressed on regardless. 'I agree,' he continued, 'that you should order the establishment of substantial settlements and discourage isolated ventures—the latter plays into the hands of the Bidjigal hostiles. Now, I believe that Pemulwuy is attempting to gain allies among the native population as a whole, but from what Captain Collins has told me, with little prospect of success. With time, I think it will be quite possible to encourage divisions among the various native groups. If we assume this, I can only say that your plan is wise and should succeed. It will, of course, benefit the colony enormously, particularly in the area of food production'.

Grose nodded, pleased. The other New South Wales Corps officers nodded too. Macarthur even smiled at Tench.

The marine officer had not, however, as yet finished. 'Having said this, your Excellency, I must add a cautionary note. It is my considered opinion that from a military point of view, we shall not get off lightly. Your policy can only succeed if we are prepared to mount a massive, ruthless military campaign against Pemulwuy and his forces. This would indeed allow us to clear large areas of land for agriculture and to hunt meat in freedom. We must be prepared to maintain such an effort to the limit of our resources until Pemulwuy is cornered and defeated.' Tench paused, playing his audience, 'at which time, Britain can truly claim sovereignty in New South Wales by right of conquest'.

There was a shocked silence round the room. Grose had turned pale and was searching for words.

'Thank you, Mr Tench,' he said after a while, 'your advice will undoubtedly be invaluable, should I ever decide to invade the dominions of the King of France or the King of Spain. At this juncture, however, I am considering an orderly expansion of this British colony into territory where our only hindrance is a small band of primitive assassins'. He stared hard at Tench. 'That will be all, I think, gentlemen,' he said to Tench and to the meeting in general.

Tench left quickly. Grose's close associates stayed behind. Collins and Carpenter walked through the vestibule in a kind of gloomy companionship.

'Tench will achieve nothing by such outbursts. He's a bloody fool,' Collins said with unusual vehemence.

Carpenter turned to him in surprise. There had been differences, but in general, Collins had been considered a friend of Tench.

'Do you believe that the actions of the New South Wales Corps are defensible?' Carpenter asked.

Collins shook his head. 'Their greed is exceeded only by their indifference to local conditions,' he said, 'but what Tench suggests is absurd. We're not at war with the natives. I firmly believe that, even now, Pemulwuy himself could be approached and reasoned with. He has been quiet so far this summer. Negotiations at this time would be both honourable and potentially fruitful. Providing there is moderation on both sides'.

Carpenter respected Collins, however fervent his admiration for Watkin Tench's courage and integrity. But now, even he wondered whether Tench's obsession with Pemulwuy was affecting the marine captain's better judgement.

Phillip remained in his cabin for most of the first part of the voyage and confined his conversation with Bennelong to pleasantries. The *Atlantic* made her way easily down the coast of

New South Wales, taking advantage of the favourable wind. Some 150 miles north of Bass Strait, she picked up a westerly, and the ship swept off across the Tasman Sea towards New Zealand.

Both Phillip and Bennelong were on deck when the shores of Australia disappeared from sight. They watched wordlessly as the sea became their entire vision. The ship heeled in the boisterous wind, and the sounds of the rigging and the ocean were all that they shared for some time.

Eventually Phillip turned to Bennelong and said with some of his old warmth, 'well, my friend, for me I believe the game is over. I shall assist you in England, and I hope you can do something to create the world of which you dream, but for me this is truly over. From now, I can only intervene from a distance'.

Bennelong had nothing to say for a long moment. He was too busy staring with almost dread concentration at the void of sea and sky that had replaced the coastline of his native land. It had disappeared over the edge of the world and so had he. He turned anxiously to Phillip.

'I am ready,' he said. Then, without changing his expression in the slightest, he added, 'but there is Yennerawannie, your Excellency... if you don't order him to shift from my cabin, I swear I'll throw him into the sea. He is impossible!'

Phillip smiled, placed his arm around Bennelong's shoulder and propelled him toward the waist of the ship.

'Bennelong, my dear friend,' he chuckled, 'now you know why we choose our shipmates carefully if we can. I'm afraid that fellow is your problem'.

Their laughter was a release. They disappeared below as the ship spread her white wings across the world, the sea world that Britain had made her own.

CHAPTER 13

DREAMS OF LOVE

'Were you a soldier in Ireland, Sean?' Nargel asked.

'No, me darling,' replied McDonough, who was busily working on a slim timber pole, 'I was, what is called, a blacksmith'.

'What is that?'

McDonough placed the pole on the ground. 'A blacksmith is a man who works metals, mainly iron.'

Nargel was preparing a stranded cord and was rolling it on her hip and in her hands.

'Then why did the English make a convict of you?'

'I fell to making weapons for my countrymen.'

Nargel looked up quickly.

'Could you make such weapons of iron for Pemulwuy?'

'I could! But there are no metals to be easily had in this place, particularly iron, but we might find some eventually.'

Nargel looked again to her work. It was McDonough's turn to ask a question.

'Have your people never had the use of metals?'

Nargel shook her head and looked up again. 'Pemulwuy could take iron from the British if you need it. Will this new weapon that you are making of wood be better than a djurraba?' she asked.

'No! But it ought to be better than a spear for some things.'

Nargel stood up and handed McDonough the cord.

'If it is not strong enough this time, we will have to take sinew from the tail of a ganimantj.'

McDonough tested the strand on a timber bow that he had made. 'This might work and be good for hunting small animals,' he said, 'but t'is still a long way from a long bow'.

Nargel walked away a little then looked back. 'Gurrewe,' she said curiously, 'why must we live here at this place? It is summer and we should move down the river'.

'Nargel, me name is Sean,' McDonough said with some impatience.

'Gurrewe is your Eora name,' Nargel replied petulantly.

'It is a bloody nickname,' said McDonough. 'It is not a true Bidjigal name...besides, if you are to be an Irishman's wife my dark colleen, you must get used to living in one place,' he added, changing the subject.

Nargel walked sulkily over towards a small hut built of fire flattened bark of a eucalypt tree, with an oddly thatched roof. The hut was nestled into the timbered bank on the upper reaches of the Hawkesbury River. It was an interesting combination of technology. It combined Irish thatching with the Eora fire technique for flattening the coarse hard bark of the stringy bark hardwood trees.

Nargel and McDonough had moved to this place after Pemulwuy had decided to abandon Goman camp. The rest of Pemulwuy's group spent the winter in the broad rock shelters further west.

McDonough had never completely mastered the Eora system of spear-throwing, and so the only large game that graced their table was caught by Nargel. McDonough, on the other hand, had proved very proficient at snaring small animals and had become an expert with the multi-pronged fish spear. He had attempted to cultivate a number of native fruit and vegetable plants, but to no avail. This land was impossibly hostile to such interference and made no allowances for dreamers, and strange dreamers they were, these two. They hunted together, made love, and lived in splendid isolation in this remote wilderness. In this place Sean McDonough at last found his freedom. Freedom held secure by the land and its silent, unseen shadow, Pemulwuy.

McDonough stopped working and stared at Nargel with a faint smile. A bit flighty he thought, but bright as a button, a fine young woman and the makings of a good wife. His smile broadened. He wondered what his mother would have to say if he ever took her home. Just then he noticed that Nargel was carefully watching something.

'What are you looking at?' McDonough asked.

'*O'moon*,' she replied and held her finger up to her lips. Then she moved off into the bush and signalled McDonough to follow her.

McDonough followed her some distance away from the river until they came to a large ageing eucalypt tree. He was still puzzled, but Nargel signalled him again to be quiet and patient. Nargel searched the tree carefully with her eyes, and then she flashed a brilliant smile. She pointed to a small opening in the tree which was surrounded by a cloud of small black insects.

Nargel took an iron knife which McDonough had made for her, from her string belt, climbed the tree and proceeded to enlarge the hole.

McDonough caught one of the insects and examined it. It was not much larger than a fly, though longer, with a black and yellow striped abdomen.

'Huh!' he said. 'It is some kind of a tiny bee.'

Nargel descended with her hands covered in a sticky white liquid. McDonough tasted it. 'It is honey,' he said amazed, 'native honey...and the bees don't sting.'

'Are there such things in Ireland?' Nargel asked.

'There certainly are,' McDonough responded. 'But the bees are much bigger—and they sting.'

'Ireland sounds a nasty place,' laughed Nargel as she walked along, sucking her fingers.

Sean McDonough sucked the sweet substance from his wife's fingers, but his thoughts were far away.

'Bees that don't sting,' he said, half to himself. He became aware of the wild blossoms about them that fed these harmless bees.

'Tis a strange and gentle place this land of yours, my love. I wonder if I shall ever know her.'

Nargel looked up at McDonough as he spoke. Her dark eyes searched his face, silently and knowingly. These deep liquid eyes contained all of the mystery and softness of her race and their scented land. But somewhere, thought Sean McDonough, hidden in all this, below the blossoms, must be the complement, the brutal ferocity that spawned Pemulwuy their protector.

Early in August two of Pemulwuy's people brought an escaped convict called William Knight and a young English woman to Gurrewe's hut. Knight was a tall gaunt man and the woman was a shy diminutive red-haired English girl by the name of Millicent Copley. Knight said that the girl had been awarded to a freed settler who had abused her. Knight had stolen her from the farm and taken her off to the bush. The poor thing was obviously distressed to find herself facing life among the Eora. Nargel found the strange red-haired young woman fascinating and tried to engage her in conversation in English. Millicent found the tall angular fierce-looking Bidjigal woman terrifying, and at first she would not let Knight out of her sight. But as time went by Nargel took Milli under her wing and started to teach her how to find food and live life in this strange wilderness.

Nargel made her a kind of very wide hat to prevent her sunburning, something that she had learnt from living with her Irish husband. After about two weeks Millicent had discarded much of her useless clothing and wore a skirt made from hide.

Both McDonough and Knight came to enjoy the sound of women's musical laughter and chatter around the camp. Millicent began to learn Bidjigal under Nargel's tutelage as she became more and more confident in this new world in which she found herself.

One day she approached Nargel and asked shyly, 'Nargel, does your husband beat you sometimes?'

Nargel laughed, 'no, and if he did I would crack his head with a stick'.

'So, Bidjigal men don't punish their women.'

Nargel thought for a moment, 'I am sure that some would like to, but they are not so brave. They shout instead,' she smiled secretly, then asked curiously, 'do white men beat their women?'

'Some do. I don't think gentlemen do, but I don't really know.'

Nargel returned to spinning twine for some purpose and Millicent's attention was focused on the two men at the hut, who were sitting comfortably and chatting.

'After the sun passes on top I will take you and show you how to find and catch the Bandicut,' Nargel said. 'We will need good digging sticks...mostly got to dig them out.'

Millicent looked admiringly at Nargel. 'You know Nargel most people in Sydney are terrified about getting lost and starving out here. You and I can feed four of us without even working very hard,' she looked back at the hut, 'those two bleeding men just sit back like English squires while we do all the work'.

Nargel looked at the men. 'English squires eh!' Nargel replied, 'I'll fix that. Time that we had some big meat. The squires can go and hunt'.

'But Nargel, neither of them can use a spear,' Millicent said in alarm. 'You will have to go with them.'

'No, then I have to carry the kill back. They got a *djurraba* that is supposed to be as good as a spear.' Nargel stood up and walked towards the hut. The men argued for a while, but were soon on their way to the hunt.

'A big Gunimantj, fat…skin it and leave its guts out there,' Nargel called after them. Then, as an afterthought, she added, 'and bring back some salt'.

'Where the hell would they get that?' Millicent asked.

'Gurrewe knows, a long walk will do them good.'

Millicent smiled and asked, 'Nargel, do you think that men are stupid?'

'No, not stupid, just lazy.'

'Why do they have to butcher the kill in the bush?'

'We got no *tungo* here. You know tame dog, big camps have them; they keep the *warrigul* away.

'Are the wild dogs dangerous?' Millicent asked wide-eyed.

Nargel smiled. 'Sometimes, but not to us, but they will take a baby or a little one. For us they are just a nuisance if you leave meat stuff about.'

Nargel put down her work and said to her companion. 'Milli you got to spend some time at a big camp, much more to learn there. Kids, everyone has to learn things in a big camp. A bit like the school thing in Sydney.'

'But what would I do at a big camp?'

'Same as here, but you would spend a lot of time teaching English, particularly with men.'

'Why men?'

'Most of them would think that their *guna* not stink, if they learned English from a white berringen.'

'What does that mean?' Millicent asked puzzled.

Nargel smiled. 'A pretty white girl.'

They both laughed and went back to their work with Nargel singing.

'Nargel, that is a nice song, it sounds like a lullaby.'

Nargel looked up and smiled. 'Sleep song…yes.'

'Will you sing it to your children?'

'No, this one for men.'

'For men?'

'Yes, after yanga callyne.'

Nargel made a sleep sign and a sexual movement.

Millicent blushed and asked, 'why?'

Nargel laughed. 'When you married, your husband keep you awake all night.'

Millicent laughed, 'so you sing them to sleep'.

The two escaped convicts stayed with them for a month before Knight went off to join Pemulwuy who had moved back to the Georges River area. Millicent was sad to leave, but they all thought that she would learn more in a larger Bidjigal camp. Nargel told her that if things did not turn out well, she should come back or send a message and she would come and get her.

Knight agreed with McDonough that Pemulwuy should try to make use of the bow and arrow. McDonough had made several bows of different timbers. He could not, however, reach a balance between the strength of the bow and the weight of the arrow. The weapons that he produced were no real match for the spear and umana, at least not to Pemulwuy's satisfaction.

Pemulwuy visited Gurrewe and his bride from time to time bringing iron. He was recovering from a minor musket wound in the upper part of his left arm. The crow and his band of about thirty men spent the winter stealing almost anything British that they could lay their hands on. They attacked two farms along the Georges River. Pemulwuy had more or less cut off British access to local food in the immediate vicinity of Sydney and the settlement at Parramatta. Pemulwuy told both Knight and McDonough that he intended to attack the Hawkesbury settlements in the summer. For their part, McDonough and Knight failed to see how a man who commanded no more than a hundred men could make any serious inroads into British power.

The night was reasonably warm and windless. McDonough and Nargel lay side-by-side in the glow of their fire.

'Gurrewe!' said Nargel, 'will you go away when the British go home?'

McDonough laughed. 'I doubt that they will ever go away, or that Pemulwuy will get rid of them'.

'Do they also live on your island, Gurrewe?'

'They do that, me darling,' said McDonough. 'It might take us a hundred years to get rid of them, but we will.'

He drew Nargel closer to him. 'Listen, my colleen, there is hope.'

He looked up at the night sky. For McDonough it was an alien sky, different from the roof of his own world. 'There are in Europe other nations who hate the British. One may be able to defeat them.' He paused again. 'I have had enough of all this, enough of it all. If the British leave, you and I shall find a place like the Bounty mutineers.'

'Who are they?' asked Nargel.

'English sailors who rebelled and took over the ship *Bounty*. It is told that they took women from Otahaiti and sailed off to some new land.'

Nargel found all this very puzzling.

'But where could we go, Gurrewe?'

McDonough waved his arm towards the west.

'We shall go into those blue mountains.'

This thought rather horrified Nargel, but she bore with her new husband.

The next morning McDonough announced that they would leave the cabin for a while and travel downstream. He had in mind some change of diet and perhaps the acquisition by trade of some special twine for his bow experiments.

Nargel was delighted. She had heard of a women's ceremonial event downstream. It was not her group, but she had been invited to attend. This worried McDonough a little. He had rather fancied that Nargel would one day embrace the faith of Saint Patrick. He was concerned about the heathen ways of the Eora, although they seemed to be becoming less pagan to him as time went by.

As a child and a youth, McDonough had been very close to the local parish priest. He and the boy's family had planned for Sean to join the priesthood. McDonough had explained this to Pemulwuy at their first meeting, using the Bidjigal term *gogaruk* to translate 'priest'. Pemulwuy was both impressed and amused, since gogaruk referred more to a sorcerer than to a religious man.

The affairs of Irish politics had interfered with McDonough's vocation, but he had acquired a reasonably good working knowledge of Catholic theology as well as some general idea of European history. He was able to reconcile some Eora religious ideas, but others were very much at odds with the tradition he knew. The Eora people, for example, associated the symbol of the serpent with the transcendental creator, whereas Christians associated this creature with evil spirits and devils. And there was a fundamental problem about which McDonough would have liked to consult a learned Catholic priest. He thought that at a pinch he may even settle for an intelligent protestant pastor, if such a thing existed.

The problem was that Christians believed that the spiritual component of the human being contained the entire personality. It was the soul. After death, this spiritual entity persisted and was rewarded or punished. McDonough found that the Eora believed that the human personality was contained in the synthesis of spiritual and mortal parts. The spirit did persist beyond death, but it did not contain the personality of the deceased person. Such a spirit could be quite dangerous and Eora death rites were designed to send this spirit back to its source. Just what the source was remained well beyond McDonough's comprehension. It was neither heaven nor hell. It seemed to be the land. This, thought McDonough, was extraordinary—no heaven and no hell—just some sort of continuum between nature and the supernatural—a most extraordinary form of paganism. God help the children he and Nargel might have, he thought.

Notwithstanding all these weighty concerns, McDonough agreed that Nargel should attend the ceremony. He helped her with some of her body decorations, though not, of course, the secret ones. McDonough hated the thick, matted and gummed hairstyles, but then he thought that women of all races were rather odd about such things as hairstyles.

'Are you sure that I should not come with you?' asked McDonough. Nargel laughed.

'No!' she said. 'This is women's business and besides it is a *Duru* ceremony and you are *Warrangi*.'

'Pemulwuy told me about that,' said McDonough. 'He said that he was Warrangi and Nargel was Duru.'

'Of course,' said Nargel. 'You are bulumna to him and must be from the same part of the world as him, and must marry the other half.'

'Yes, Koobee is Duru, like me, but Milbab is Warrangi, like you.'

'So there are just the two parts?'

'Yes, of course,' laughed Nargel, she looked up at the sky.

'See the white cloud, it is Duru, but the black one is Warrangi.'

'So the whole world is divided up like that?' asked McDonough.

'Yes,' said Nargel smiling. 'Do you divide the things of Ireland like that?'

McDonough smiled. 'Yes, in a way,' he said, 'to all things there is a season—a time to be happy and a time to be sad, a time to be born, a time to die'.

'I don't understand,' said Nargel quizzically.

McDonough laughed at his Eora wife, caught her by the arm and embraced her.

They parted company near the confluence of two tributaries, and McDonough made his way further downstream, anxious to test a new line and iron hook in the estuarine part of the river. The Eora used fish hooks but they were made from shells or bone.

The day was warm and sunny. A light breeze from across the river carried the sharp smell of the sea and sea things. What a splendid day, McDonough thought. A man really could live here forever without any great difficulty.

McDonough cast the line into the sparkling waters. He became so engrossed with his task that he did not notice the shadows that moved differently from the other things of his new-found world; and then it was over. He looked up with stark disbelief at the cold, grey barrels of muskets, and the military uniforms behind them.

McDonough's hands were tied behind his back, his legs bound and hobbled about two feet apart, and a rope was placed around his neck. He was then pushed and led for about three hours until they reached a small, fortified camp about a mile back from the Hawkesbury escarpment. There he was tossed into a corner and left. He spent the night in a state of stunned disbelief. Even a raging thirst could not make sense of this terrible new reality.

McDonough was not fed that night, or the next morning. By the time the sun rose, his hands and feet were badly swollen, his thirst was unbearable. The day was already well advanced when a private of the New South Wales Corps arrived and released the ropes. He was given some water and a tot of rough rum, and then his hands were retied behind his back. There would be new shackles waiting for him when they arrived at Kissing Point, the soldier informed him with a leer. This day, 23 December 1791, McDonough was marched for eight hours through rough country to a second fortified camp near the Parramatta River.

The camp was perched on a sandstone ridge among thick woodland, but its prominence gave the military a good view of the surrounding valleys through which the Irishman had stumbled, bleeding and in pain, that day. McDonough was tied in a sitting position to the base of a tall spotted eucalypt tree and left alone until sunset.

At first this had seemed like a bad dream, a nightmare from which he would awake to find himself at the place he had called home. With Nargel smiling up at him, and jobs to do, fish in the river, and the sun on his strong free body. Now, as he sat trying not to cry out from the rope burns and the angry swellings on his limbs, McDonough knew that this was his reality—the world of the convict—and the dream had been elsewhere, a place already a dimming image in the mind. Freedom and love, the convict's dream, and the convict's cruel awakening. Just on dusk, two privates dragged him to his feet and hauled him over to the large tent in the middle of the fortified compound.

CHAPTER 14

WORRAGUL WOMAN

'All right, my good man,' said an officer who was already the worse for rum, 'I want to know where you've been and how you've been surviving out there: but make it snappy!'

McDonough haltingly described his escape from Sydney, careful not to mention any names. He said that some natives had helped him—Bidjigals who didn't like the British.

The officer asked him a few more questions, and then seemed to lose interest. After a few minutes, he turned to the waiting soldiers.

'Flog this villain!' the officer rasped.

McDonough was pulled out of the tent and suspended by his bound hands from the bough of a small ironbark tree. He knew what was about to happen; as he waited he forced his mind back into the dream of freedom. Dreams were powerful; all Eora people knew that for a fact, and by the blood of Saint Patrick, McDonough would make his dream work for him.

They flogged his bare skin again and again. Each time the lash descended, there were shouted insults. Slowly, McDonough drifted into a state of semi-consciousness beyond thirst, the bleeding place of shame and pain. Images coursed through his mind: the gentle emerald countryside of Ireland; Nargel's smiling dark eyes; and, just before he passed into darkness he felt the bleeding muscles of his back and shoulders expand as, in his mind's eye, he plunged an Eora spear into the red and white chest of a British soldier.

It was Christmas Day 1791 before McDonough regained some awareness of his surroundings. Through his stupor, he sensed revelries in the camp: drinking and shouting, raucous English voices making the best of their crude version of Christmas. By the end of that day, he was still feverish and confused. He felt himself drifting into the psychic death of the Bidjigal. A black well of despair closed in upon him.

As dusk entered the camp, he was dragged to his feet and faced with another British officer, this time a lieutenant in the uniform of a marine whom the soldiers referred to as Carpenter. The officer wore riding kit and had obviously ridden hard that day to get here. He was hardly a kindly soul, but McDonough could see that he was of a different type to the soldiers he had seen since his capture.

'McDonough' the officer said, and it was a statement rather than a question.

The Irishman nodded without focusing his eyes. Carpenter seemed excited, 'you have been in the bush with Pemulwuy, I believe. Yes or no, fellow!'

The name of Pemulwuy came at first dreamlike to McDonough, then it struck through the dark sickness of his mind. He became alert. This man might learn something that could be used against the Bidjigal. He must try to resist all he could. He did his best. No, he didn't know about Pemulwuy then he asked for water. He had lived with various different groups. They were kindly, peaceful people—not like the English at all.

Carpenter ignored the Irishman's bitter joke and his request for water. He was exhausted from his ride, and he could see that McDonough was far from fit.

'Since it's Christmas, you won't suffer another flogging for that, McDonough,' he said, 'but I'll get what I need from you, be sure of it. Give the fellow some water'.

Carpenter turned to the soldiers, 'I'll interrogate him in the morning. For God's sake don't kill the man. Captain Tench and I want him in Sydney in one piece!'

The marine officer stalked off, and McDonough was led back towards his tree. Then suddenly a cockney voice bellowed at him from his right.

'Here, Mick! You speak the bugger's lingo, don't you?'

McDonough turned painfully, and it was like walking back into his dream. He saw Nargel sitting on the ground along with another young Bidjigal woman. Two soldiers were guarding them with levelled muskets.

McDonough stared at Nargel. It was indeed like going back into a dream. Nargel showed no recognition of him. At that moment his mind flashed into a primordial, savage hymn to Pemulwuy. Inside his head he saw the crow smashing open the heads of his tormentors. He must not use his name.

'*Woyan camya*,' he stammered. Nargel replied quickly in Bidjigal that Pemulwuy was not near, but that some Eora were going to burn the country near the camp at night.

'I have come to take you from the British, my husband,' she said solemnly. It was strange, but when he saw her now, after just a few days, she was once again the alien creature he remembered from the flight from Sydney. She was almost ugly. But she was Nargel, his wife. He now saw her for what she was, a determined Bidjigal woman come to take him from his tormentors. In her fiery dark eyes he could see the fearsome image of Pemulwuy. His heart racing, McDonough did his best to look as though the newcomers were of no interest to him.

'They're just locals gathering food,' he mumbled weakly, as if it were taking every last ounce of his strength, 'nothing more'.

'This one fought like a wild thing, we had to drag her here,' the soldier said, pointing to Nargel.

Then McDonough pretended to collapse in a faint. They dragged him back to the spotted gum tree, tied him up and left him alone.

Darkness came and McDonough waited, still stupified from pain and hunger. Perhaps it had all really been a dream, and the cruelest one of all. He slept for a short while. Then, as the moon rose, he awoke to the smell of fire. It took the British a little longer to realise that they were surrounded, on all sides, by blazing wattle and underbrush. There was panic all about. McDonough too felt terror. He wriggled uselessly in his bonds, knowing that if Nargel could not penetrate the camp he faced death by fire. He called out as loudly as he could. As if in response, a soldier, his uniform unbuttoned and without his cap, stumbled over, untied the rope from the tree and jerked him to his feet.

'Over by the tent, Mick!' he snarled.

Before they could move, a small, serpent-like creature leapt from the smoke like a furious she worragul defending her brood. She drove an Eora hunting spear into the Englishman's throat. He staggered backwards, clutching at the shaft. Within seconds, his musket was wrenched from his hands and a club had smashed out his brains.

A small cutting-knife sawed quickly through McDonough's bonds. Wild-eyed, he stumbled into the blazing bush, following Nargel through a corridor of fire. They fled into the bosom of their silent, mindless burning land. The flames leaped into the air and closed any gate behind him with a terrifying dance of fire.

It was in that moment that McDonough knew an extraordinary new certainty: dreams were real, and love had a sweet violent power. So great that it had broken forever the chains that bound him to Europe.

'I understand the secret of your power, Pemulwuy. I have it now, I do not fear death.'

Pemulwuy listened silently while McDonough made his own special commitment to war.

'It's a fact of life that I must die at the hands of the British. I shall fight here and now beside you and with my wife. It saddens my heart that my blood will not fall on the ground of Ireland, but so be it.'

Pemulwuy still said nothing. He pressed his second finger into the white clay in his left hand and marked McDonough's face. He did this carefully and began to sing as he worked. The crow's song called up the voice of the land, and for these two men the blue sky became deep purple. The fingers of the great southern constellation touched the earth. Their death wish flew like a spear on the aboriginal wind that blew from the west into the face of the British.

Major Grose did not move to talk with Pemulwuy, as Collins had hoped. Fortified camps were established in the west and on the Hawkesbury, but no approaches were made to the Bidjigal.

Pemulwuy responded quickly and with a new strategy. The fire that had destroyed the camp where McDonough had been held was the first of many. All that summer and autumn, Pemulwuy used fire. He set alight the whole southern bank of the great River Hawkesbury, and he killed and maimed the soldiers who tried to prevent him from doing so.

Even though Grose would not let Tench have his big campaign against Pemulwuy, Tench and his comrade Carpenter did what they could to aid the fortified staging-camp strategy. Tench reasoned that it was at least better than wandering expeditions of the kind that had earlier come to grief, though he doubted that there were sufficient military resources in the colony for it to be really effective. Pemulwuy remained at large, growing in ruthlessness and cunning.

By midwinter of 1792, Pemulwuy had destroyed the Hawkesbury camps. In July, the New South Wales Corps was forced to abandon its positions along the river. Settlers and convicts from the area were withdrawn to Broken Bay and the upper reaches of the Parramatta River. Many convicts took advantage of the situation and escaped to join the Eora. McDonough removed their iron shackles when he could and forged them into spear points and knife blades.

The British had suffered, but so had Pemulwuy. The Hawkesbury attacks had cost the Eoras heavily, and his group was in no condition to continue any sort of real offensive.

It was a winter of stalemate. Both sides drew back to lick their wounds and wait for summer. The hot weather would return to Pemulwuy this new weapon of fire that he had used so effectively. There were even those among the British, including Tench, who believed that it might yet win the day for the Eora. Nevertheless, it was a two-edged sword, destroying game and vegetation as well as the British camps, and Pemulwuy knew the great danger of it. He sat morosely in the damp, cold shelter in the deep overhanging cliff face. McDonough and Yenowee watched him for about half an hour. He seemed not to have moved a muscle. Finally McDonough walked up to him.

'Pemulwuy,' he said in his now-fluent Bidjigal, 'you have lost only thirty-one men in the whole campaign. New men will grow from their blood'.

Pemulwuy stared at him. His strange, crooked gaze seemed to search his face closely, then suddenly fade and flick away from him. 'You killed four British with your musket,' Pemulwuy said. Then, with a grimace that was almost a sneer. 'Why do you also carry a spear? You move too slowly. Throw one or the other away!'

He sat and glared at the Irishman.

McDonough turned away with a sad gesture of futility. It was quite pointless trying to talk with Pemulwuy when he was in this sort of mood. He rejoined Yenowee, and greeted Koobee, who had just arrived and seemed excited.

'What is it?' asked McDonough testily, still smarting from his argument with Pemulwuy.

Yenowee drew his cloak around him. 'We have an ally,' he said. 'I have just heard that a strange black man from some other place has been attacking the British near Sydney.'

Watkin Tench looked intently at the map Carpenter had spread before them.

'It could not have been Pemulwuy,' he said firmly. 'Unless, of course, he can fly and has come to wear britches,' said Carpenter.

Tench half smiled, 'quite so, and even though it was on exactly the same day as his last attack. You say it was definitely not another native?'

'Ah,' frowned Carpenter, 'I can't be absolutely sure of that. But the Corps thinks it is the negro from the American whaler. The man called Caesar, though his history until now has been of highway robbery and thieving'.

'Well, I suppose we're about to find out whether he has finally allied himself with Pemulwuy, as we suspected he might,' Tench said. 'A nigger and an Irishman, and Pemulwuy. Ye gads!'

'McDonough,' Carpenter remembered ruefully, 'by the time I got to the Berowra camp, those idiots had flogged him half to death'.

'What can you expect from a gang of bone-headed jailers?' Tench growled, 'and losing him to a pack of women at that. No, the Rum Corps are certainly no match for Pemulwuy'.

Since Phillip's departure, the Corps' hold on the rum trade had tightened; in fact, it had become a scandal. Now everyone called them by their new title, especially the Marines.

'Oh, Bidjigal women can be pretty fiery,' Carpenter said, 'I hear the woman the convict lives with is a real she devil'.

Tench was in no mood for salacious details. He looked away.

Carpenter looked down at the map again.

'What do you expect the end of it to be, sir?'

Tench shrugged. 'Poor devils. The natives, I mean. They will be buried by history, I suppose. Particularly if the Rum Corps writes it.'

'And Pemulwuy?'

'He,' said Tench with a long, hard sigh, 'is a different matter. The colony is a fragile thing, and far from home. However, unless he can talk other groups besides the Bidjigal into joining him, he will be buried too'.

'There seems to be a lot of escaped convicts have joined him now.'

Tench smiled coldly, 'none with military training I'll wager. They will be more a hindrance than a help'.

CHAPTER 15

GRO MOK

The large Bidjigal gathering presently camped near an inland cliff face had begun to move towards the coast to a place south of Kamay. It was still cold, there was little food about, but the promised spring hung in the air.

McDonough had been told that there was a great supply of seafood at the place to which they were going. He had been told that they were to attend an important ceremony. This was a *Wanegal* ceremony, but it was one where Bidjigal people also had a part to play. They reached the upper reaches of the Georges River and a group of about two hundred was camped there. Nargel was delighted to find that the Bidjigal group had brought Millicent with them. The two women met in joyous embrace. They were both very different from when they first met. Nargel now had a fearsome reputation to match her wild appearance. Millicent was now tanned and covered in freckles and very much an accomplished, if not an odd part, of her adopted group. Her confidence in her new life was clear. She spoke fluent Bidjigal and had come here as part of her new group.

The two women talked for at least an hour and Milli introduced Nargel to other women in her group. However, as it turned out there was another side to this meeting of friends from the opposite ends of the Earth. Both Nargel and Milli were close to *Coleleu*. This seemed to cause some friction which became more apparent over the following days. McDonough was sitting on the sandy ground beside Coleleu who was, after all, one of the members of Nargel's rescue party that removed him from the British. They were playing string games with a group of children, and there was much giggling and laughter. Yenowee walked up and squatted down opposite McDonough.

'I hope that you are still not trying to turn these infants of ours into cannibals,' he said jokingly.

'No, I have found another god,' said McDonough.

The joke related to a long-term argument that he and Yenowee had had about the Catholic Christian ceremony of the mass. Yenowee had argued that the idea of sacrifice and eating the flesh and the symbolic drinking of the blood was primitive and represented a kind of cannibalism. Knight, a confirmed Protestant, agreed with Yenowee. McDonough had valiantly defended his old faith, but somehow all of these past concerns had faded in his own consuming desire to join with the Eora to defeat the British.

'You know, these Eora kids are clever,' said McDonough. 'They're undisciplined little devils, but once you understand the way they learn, they are very fast.'

Yenowee laughed and took hold of McDonough by the shoulder.

'Gurrewe, they are too young even to have a mind yet. How can you talk about them learning?'

'No, really. They're very good. They seem to learn at almost twice the rate of the Irish children that I have known.'

A great peal of laughter came first from Yenowee and then from Koobee, who was standing close to the group. Koobee knelt down beside McDonough.

'Gurrewe,' he said, 'the teacher in the Governor's school says that Irish children learn at only half the speed of English children'.

There was more laughter, and even McDonough found a place in his heart to join in this Irish joke.

Tedbury and Awabakal walked up to the group in the midst of their mirth. Tedbury grasped Yenowee by the hand and drew his hand back quickly. Koobee's humour faded as he stared at the blood-red mark on Yenowee's hand. McDonough stood up in surprise and stared at the mark, and the children fled. Tedbury laughed and turned his hand over. On his palm there was a small patch of blood-red dye. This relieved the situation a little.

Yenowee looked down at Coleleu and said, 'she should not be here now'.

Coleleu hung her head down and watched the ground, but refused to move.

It was a strange, awkward situation. What was this curious colouring that Tedbury had in his hand? At this point Nargel joined the group. She glared at Coleleu; then bowed slightly before her husband.

'Gurrewe, my Irish squire,' she said with great exaggeration, 'would you and your friends like to eat with those who work to feed you?'

McDonough smiled, and Koobee made a deep mock bow.

'My dear missus, I would be glad to join you,' he said.

They all laughed and walked off with Nargel towards the campfire.

As the evening wore on, McDonough joined Koobee and his family at their fire in a small sheltered portion of what now amounted to an extensive campsite. Awabakal was with them, and he was playing with Koobee's newest son. Koobee was sleeping near the fire when McDonough arrived and he sat down and talked for some time with Milbab, Koobee's wife. As time went by, he asked her about the significance of the strange colouring that Tedbury had on his hand during the day. Awabakal stood up quickly and told McDonough that these things were not to be discussed in the presence of women.

McDonough had had about as much of young men as he could cope with that day, and quickly told Awabakal in English to 'bugger off'. Awabakal put his nose in the air, made a comment to

Milbab about the friends she kept, and strode off into the darkness. Both Milbab and McDonough laughed.

After a little time, Milbab spoke to McDonough. 'Gurrewe, there is some truth in what Awabakal is saying. There are today a lot of men marked with the red spot. I think you should discuss it with Koobee alone. This is men's business,' she smiled. 'I always find Bidjigals painful about such things.'

At this point Koobee sat up and shivered a little, then joined his wife and McDonough. Milbab discreetly absented herself to gather wood or some such thing while the two men spoke of these serious matters.

Curiously, Koobee was very closed about the subject and would not say very much except that it all had to do with some sort of a special Bidjigal secret society. He pointed out that it did not concern him and nor should it concern McDonough. He was quick, however, to explain McDonough's rights. Under the terms of which he had been accepted into the Bidjigal group he was, as a man, entitled to know of these things and be part of them if he so desired.

McDonough was fascinated by the idea of secret societies existing within the Eora groups. Koobee told him that quite often these special groups were formed to carry out certain types of functions. Usually they were pre-ceremony organisations: two such groups existed now and were making preparations for the *dulaia yang* ceremony that was to be held at the coast. Koobee pointed out, however, that this blood-red dye, which men passed among one another, signified a different kind of secret society, often concerned with revenge after a suspected murder.

They went on to discuss the dulaia yang ceremony, which Koobee said he found to be something of a bore. 'It is very popular with young men and women,' he said with a grin, 'but I am too old now'.

Both men laughed; while Koobee went on to explain that it was an excellent social gathering with much food. Koobee was sure that all would enjoy it. McDonough was concerned to know if he would be allowed to attend the ceremony. Koobee assured him that he would certainly be able to attend most of it, since after all he was now a married man within the Bidjigal group.

Their conversation was disturbed by loud voices from across the camp. One of these voices McDonough recognised immediately as Nargel's, and he jumped to his feet.

He and Koobee made their way across the camp to where a large campfire shed a ghost-like light on a broad perimeter. Nargel stood to one side of the fire with a heavy Eora battle club in her hand which McDonough recognised as his own. On the opposite side of the fire he recognised Coleleu, sitting down with two other women. She had her back turned towards Nargel.

Nargel was calling out, abusing Coleleu, and challenging her to fight. She was accusing Coleleu of making advances to her man, Gurrewe. McDonough was astonished at this and was about to step forward and take hold of Nargel when Koobee caught him by the arm and pulled him back.

'Keep out of it, Gurrewe. It is women's business. You can't interfere.'

McDonough threw Koobee's hand off his arm and said, 'Nonsense, it's thoroughly embarrassing before all these people. She is out of her mind. She needs a clout across the ear.'

Koobee grabbed him by the arm again and literally pulled him to the ground. He was joined in this endeavour by Tedbury.

Koobee said, 'Gurrewe, keep out of it. This is the way of Eora women. They are not like the women of the British. They do not hold their feelings. They're outspoken and it is for them to settle. In the end they won't hurt each other'.

McDonough sat up between the two men.

'You two don't know what she's like,' he said, 'she's just as likely to split Coleleu's head with that club'.

'She won't. There will be plenty of people to stop her, but not us; even the new English woman Milli is involved.' Koobee laughed. 'I hope she knows to keep her head down.'

Coleleu now stood up and faced her adversary. The conflict of bad language at twenty yards now escalated to even worse language at ten yards. At this point Boorea, Pemulwuy's wife, rushed up and caught hold of Nargel's club-bearing arm. Boorea was joined by two or three other women, while at the same time a number of women gathered about Coleleu and in a short time the conflict had reduced again to the occasional bad word from about twenty yards.

McDonough went back alone to his camp and lay there thinking of the event that he had witnessed. This young wife of his has risen greatly in stature over the past year or so. Instead of becoming more European-like, as McDonough had hoped, she seemed to have become even more Bidjigal. Oddly enough, McDonough had got used to this.

Nargel joined him about an hour later and sat for some time in a sulk. McDonough thought he might get up, try and reason with her and bring her to bed with him, but then he thought that with the mood she was in, she might whack him with some weapon. He decided to go to sleep and discuss the situation with his bride in the morning.

The next morning, as the group broke camp, William Knight and two Daruk men arrived and joined McDonough's camp. Nargel flirted with them outrageously, particularly with Knight. William, however, had apparently learnt a few hard lessons about the etiquette of relating to Eora women. He was very careful not to respond in any way to Nargel's advances and Milli was careful to note all this.

McDonough observed this and made a point during the day of introducing Knight to Coleleu. This infuriated Nargel and Milli both. McDonough thought better of all this and secretly vowed to keep well out of women's business in the future.

Meanwhile, by the time they had reached the coast, Awabakal had decided that he must make peace. He walked up and joined McDonough and Nargel. He was quite surprised and pleased to find that McDonough did not even seem to remember the occasion of the night before.

Awabakal had never really taken to William Knight, although he was quite fond of Milli. He was also rather ambivalent in his affection for Nargel. He thought it most unfair that she should gain in status so quickly, considering that she was only newly married. He mentally concluded nevertheless, that she was a shrewd, clever young woman, and one to be watched in the future. Meanwhile the connection between Nargel and Milli and the problems McDonough had had the previous night, led him wisely to decide to also keep well out of women's affairs.

As they walked, Awabakal drifted into his own thoughts. What did it matter what Narewe's destiny was. He was a man of the Awabakal people. He was Koori. Some day he must return and take this great adventure with him. He had reasoned in his own mind that he should not return until after Pemulwuy had defeated the British. These would be great tidings to take home. He would be able to tell his people that he, Kiraban, had fought beside the Eora when they defeated the aliens, and that he was a close friend of the Irish metal worker who now made their iron-tipped spear points.

McDonough was chewing *arakui* nuts and handed some to Awabakal. As Awabakal raised his hand to take the nuts, he exposed the red mark on the palm and drew his hand shyly away from the nuts. McDonough looked at him carefully and then pushed the nuts into his hand. They walked on in silence.

Awabakal was pondering these problems when Yenowee ran up to the group.

'Come quickly!' he called, 'we have a strange visitor!'

The three men ran with Yenowee towards a small gathering to the right of the path. They had pushed their way quickly into the centre and were stunned at what they beheld.

Sitting on the ground were three men armed to the teeth with Eora weapons and two muskets. Two of them were tall Daruk people, while the third was the strangest human being that Awabakal had ever seen. This was a large sinewy man, with highly pronounced muscles in his legs and odd shaped buttocks. His face was far more like the Europeans as regards features, but his skin blacker than his own. His hair was tight and curly and he had a look about him of power and ferocity.

The incredible new black man stood up. He was far taller than any man they had ever seen. Awabakal estimated that he stood a half forearm's length above Pemulwuy himself. His body was physically different from the Eoras, and the Europeans. McDonough had thought that Eora had about them a bird-like or serpentine character of movement, this man moved in a smooth sinewy way. He was like some alien animal that had never walked this continent, perhaps like a lion.

The others stood somewhat in awe of the stranger, so McDonough decided to take the initiative. He held out his hand. 'I am Sean McDonough. I am now a Bidjigal man and I am called Gurrewe here,' he stated.

'Caesar; Black Caesar,' said the newcomer in a deep, sonorous voice as he held out his hand. 'I am an American.'

'He is really an African,' McDonough said later to Awabakal and Yenowee.

McDonough explained that the British had captured African people and taken them across the sea to a place like New South Wales, called America. There they were made slaves. He explained that slaves were something like convicts and that these people were made to work for them and were beaten as the convicts were. He also explained that Africa was a large continent like Australia, inhabited entirely by people like this man, Black Caesar.

McDonough enjoyed thrilling the two Eoras with stories of how African warriors were the fiercest people in the world and would attack in thousands. For good measure he threw in that they were cannibals. McDonough found it rather curious that the idea of cannibalism tended to revolt the Eora, but he never tried to find out why.

The following night, they reached the sea at the site of a sandy entrance to a small lake. There were many people there ahead of them, and during that first day McDonough and his group consumed great quantities of the easily available shellfish. McDonough succeeded in offending everybody by failing to throw his used shells on to the large heaps, as was the custom of the Eora. Having had his attention brought to this behaviour, McDonough found the heaps remarkable objects. It appeared that they had had shells thrown upon them for many many years, perhaps hundreds of years. Some of the heaps were quite enormous and people actually built camps on top and on the sides of them. Others were quite new and small. He found one heap buried under a sand dune, obviously very old. These things, he thought, were the most remarkable and well-organised rubbish dumps that he had ever seen.

During the day's march down towards the beach, Caesar had spent quite a time talking to McDonough. He was very curious about Pemulwuy, whom, up to that point, he had not met. He told McDonough of a dream that he had had. In this dream he had met the man, and from all descriptions the image of the man in the dream was that of Pemulwuy, even to the turned eye.

'Mind you keep that to yourself,' said McDonough. 'Eora people place great store by dreams.'

Caesar tilted his head to one side and squinted his eyes. 'You have really become part of these people, Irish,' he drawled. 'This Pemulwuy must be some bucko mate.'

McDonough did not answer, but thought secretly that Caesar might well be a little disappointed when he did come to meet Pemulwuy. Pemulwuy was a big man for an Eora, but his stature was nothing like that of the African. McDonough was pleasantly surprised to have the opportunity of spending so much time conversing in English. Of late he had fallen entirely into the habit of using Bidjigal, even with Nargel and the others. And even Millicent now used Bidjigal most of the time.

They had been at the beach almost a day, and still no sign of Pemulwuy. McDonough knew that he was painting up somewhere. Yenowee had disappeared for the same purpose. Caesar became anxious and kept asking after Pemulwuy.

That evening there was a small pre-ceremony activity, and he assured Caesar that he would then have the opportunity of meeting with Pemulwuy. McDonough was rather curious as to why Pemulwuy had put off meeting this new ally for so long.

Nargel had spent hours trying to decorate Gurrewe. Caesar looked at all this in amusement and eventually demanded that she put some marks upon his deep black hide. After some time, Nargel consented to do this and marked him a few times across the chest. She knew now why it was that European men did not paint themselves. The best you could do with paint was making them look funny. It was impossible to get the dramatic appearance that was obtained on a black skin. And skin as black as Caesar's was a truly marvellous canvas.

Caesar had also heard of the *Gro Mok* society. He had detected that even the mention of the word sent people shying away from him. He asked McDonough if it was a sacred religious word.

'I am unsure about that business,' said McDonough evasively.

He realised immediately that he was really falling into the ways of the Eora. He reacted to his own thoughts and set himself to be a European again.

'The word refers simply to the dye,' he said.

He then went on to tell Caesar that the society was held in some awe and that it was something akin to secret societies in other countries. It had something to do with vendettas.

Music began in a small sandy clearing about a hundred yards away from their camp. Very soon some male dancers appeared, moving their legs in the characteristic stylised step-like motion of the Eoras. Nargel had already gone ahead. She had some part to play in one of these ceremonies, and she was very enthusiastic about it. McDonough, Caesar and Koobee sauntered over to the site. The three felt just a little outside of this particular event.

As they reached the clearing, a group of Eora men, whose bodies were painted in white clay and a brilliant orange-yellow colour, stepped towards them. The leader of the group addressed them.

'Gurrewe, Koobee, it is time.'

It was Pemulwuy, although McDonough hardly recognised him. He was painted with white markings all over his face. His hair was decorated with gum, much in the fashion of the women. The upper parts of his arms had closely bound small coloured grass fringes and feathers attached, and likewise about his lower legs. His body was extensively decorated with colours and patches of downy feathers. He looked ethereal, like a giant seahawk. McDonough stepped forward.

'Pemulwuy. This is Caesar.'

Pemulwuy stared at Caesar.

'*Wedalyi minyin djalarinjî?*'

Gurrewe was puzzled by this question and simply replied, '*Ranma'*. Caesar realised that Pemulwuy's question must have been odd. He quickly asserted himself and stepped forward and held his hand out in the European fashion. Pemulwuy smiled and touched his hand with the spear he held. Caesar grasped the spear and held it firmly. The atmosphere was instantaneously electrified. No-one moved. A smile outlined Pemulwuy's lips, but it was too dark to see the depth of this expression. Caesar's face was expressionless. He stared steadfastly at the apparition before him. Sensing the delicacy of the situation, Caesar released the spear and stepped back. Pemulwuy raised the spear, held it by his side and said: 'Gurrewe will mark your face, friend. Then you should dance with me. After, we will talk.'

THE SECOND PART OF TRUTH

'…the secret minds of other people."

CHAPTER 16

A FUGUE IN THREE PARTS

Major Grose felt relaxed for the first time since taking up his post as acting Governor. With Phillip safely back in England, he was now truly master of New South Wales, and had a free hand to deal with the colony's problems as he saw fit.

The first of these problems—though he would never admit it to London—was the damned natives and their leader, Pemulwuy. On the desk before him this fine morning was a carefully written report from the Marine commander, Major Ross.

Grose leant back in his chair and began to read the document. The early part was typical navy rubbish, he thought—these Marines had spent far too long shooting at ships from the tops of rigging and conducting shore raids—but eventually it became more interesting: leaving us within an awkward comparison of arms. He read:

> 'The natives are using weapons from much earlier times than our own. Their spears, however, find us at a disadvantage, since we have no shields or armour to protect ourselves, and, being cast with great accuracy, they render even the most disciplined musket formations vulnerable. Our musket fire is devastating to them, but lacks their accuracy. They have learned not to present themselves as massed targets. They possess large wooden shields. In hand-to-hand combat, the natives impale these objects on our bayonets and attack with war clubs. These also prove devastating weapons at close quarters.
>
> The natives are very mobile and skilled, much aided by their knowledge of the wooded lands surrounding the settlements. We are severely hampered by a shortage of horses with which to equip mounted patrols. I must add that the natives have also become adept at killing our horses at night, no matter how many sentries we post to protect them. All of the advantages held by the natives are dependent on the wooded nature of the local terrain. The land must be cleared both for agriculture and in order to make possible effective deployment of our military power. The natives use fire extensively against us, yet the trees here seem remarkably resistant to burning. Nevertheless, the population of New South Wales is now 3,500 souls. If we are to survive, we must rapidly engage in closely settled, intense farming.

Our chief strength, I would humbly submit, is our command of the sea approaches and also of the main waterways. With this in mind, I therefore advise that you should base any strategy of expansion on this command and deploy our population according to the following plan:

1. Establish fortified positions in the form of a small garrisoned town on the far side of Port Hacking. One other in Botany Bay, and on the north shore of Port Jackson. Such garrisons must also be established on the north and south shores of Broken Bay.
2. All of these locations can be supplied by sea.
3. Establish fortified positions at the head of the harbour (near Parramatta) and at the head of the Botany Bay estuary. Both can also be supplied safely by water. The land thereby enclosed should be cleared by convict labour, and captured native labour, and intensely farmed to supply the food requirements of the colony. This area is small and of such a nature that it can be secured against serious native incursions.
4. Establish fortified towns linking the north of Port Jackson to the southern reaches of the Hawkesbury estuary. This land can then also be cleared to permit further farming as the population expands. This mode of operation will conserve our military resources and enable them to be exploited effectively without posing a serious threat to the positions of the Bidjigal group, which is led by the miscreant Pemulwuy. At some future time, of course, we may consider...'

Grose put the briefing down and carefully examined the small map.

'Macarthur will not like this I'll wager,' he whispered to himself. 'He's all in favour of hell-for-leather expansion into the inland plains and damn the natives. But there is a good deal of military sense to Ross's proposition. I shall put it to the officers of the Corps tomorrow.

'Absolute nonsense,' said Macarthur indignantly. 'Major Ross knows nothing of farming, and I fear even less about military strategy. With all due respect, I believe that his judgement has been affected by Tench and his henchman, Carpenter.'

Captain Abbott nodded in solemn agreement with Macarthur.

Outside it was a clear, sparkling morning. The sea had started to move, and the sounds of the harbour formed a counterpoint to the sounds of the morning activities in the Governor's residence.

'He writes as though the Bidjigal own this land—as if, whatever nefarious acts they may commit, we dare not offend them,' Macarthur glowered at Grose. 'These natives wander over it, that is all, occasionally killing and eating the primitive creatures that dwell upon it. They are joined by an African and even English and Irish criminals. One of my men even reported seeing some sort of red-headed English slut running through the bush with a hunting party bare breasted, though that may have been a delusion.'

The sounds of wheeled vehicles and horses on Sydney's rough roads now joined the murmur of the sea.

'The very smell of kangaroo flesh makes me ill, sir! I am sure that it is the source of much sickness in the colony. We need grazing land, not peasant farms. We must grow cattle, horses and sheep!'

The morning sun cast gentle shafts of light through the curtains. The light fell in bright pools on the polished surface of the alien timbers.

'Captain Abbott and I both approve of the use of fortified towns—as a first stage—but to connect them all by navigable waterways is totally unnecessary. We also agree that some limited coastal positions should be established. And to a great extent, this has already been done.' A small black fly swept busily into the room, landed on the acting Governor's nose, was struck at and left hastily. Major Grose finally put up a hand for silence.

'I take your point, gentlemen,' he said to Macarthur and Abbott, 'then we shall have to see how we can satisfy everybody, shan't we?'

The acting Governor shifted his chair slightly and dropped his gaze to the map before him. Macarthur smiled in triumph and glanced out of the window into the new Australian day.

'It is more or less a forked development across the fertile inland region,' said Grose. He pointed to the areas marked on his wall map. In the evening of that same new day, his redrawn version of Ross's plan was illuminated by a cluster of candles. The officers looked on in silence.

'The advantage, gentlemen, is that we maintain Major Ross's coastal positions,' he continued, 'while at the same time gaining immediate access to important grazing lands'. Grose referred to the inland areas indicated on the new map as 'secured,' 'the major thrust, as you will see, now follows the valley formed by the Parramatta river, while the second...ah...fork reaches out to intersect the upper reaches of the Hawkesbury river, thus securing the most fertile regions, as I said'.

Tench and Carpenter stood listening in silence. The Marine Captain was tight lipped. After the Governor had explained the new plan, he dismissed all the officers except his immediate circle.

'Macarthur obviously wants to be the grand landowner he could not be in England, and he has got his way,' said Tench to Carpenter as they paused on the porch, savouring the warm night. There was more despair in his voice than anger.

'Major Ross tried to keep them away from Bidjigal land until we had the power to cope with Pemulwuy. Now those idiots will be blundering straight across it. Pemulwuy will cut those western settlements to pieces,' he murmured.

A falling star crossed the sky.

'Twiuga,' said Carpenter.

The new year passed into 1793 and Captain John Macarthur was appointed Commanding Officer of the fortified town of Parramatta. Toongabbie became its first satellite and then Prospect Hill.

SYDNEY FORKED DEVELOPMENT STRATEGY

CHAPTER 17

PRISONERS OF WAR

There was a hollow thud as the spear hit the officer's horse. Half of the spear's length passed through the animal's neck and two musket shots were heard to the right as the horse reared up and fell backwards onto its rider. The sergeant fell to the ground dead. The horse regained its feet with spurts of blood coming from its neck. The animal plunged about and stumbled again over the top of a young private, then galloped off into the scrub. It could be heard crashing to the ground as its blood drained into the earth.

The rest of the detachment scrambled for what cover there was.

'Take cover!' one soldier shouted anxiously.

'Blimey, it's Pemulwuy!' called another. 'He doesn't use muskets!'

'It's Caesar.'

'Where's Cawley?'

'He can't move. He's got a broken leg—the bloody horse fell on him.' The small band fell silent, each watching, waiting for some command.

This was a small detachment of twenty men, led on horseback by the newly arrived Lieutenant Frances Marshall. They had left Sydney early on a spring morning in September 1793, bound for Prospect Hill via Parramatta. They were to reinforce a small garrison there.

Half an hour had passed and still there was nothing. Corporal Moore took command and called the group together. They assembled very cautiously. Two more musket shots rang out and one soldier fell to his knees. This time they could see the gunsmoke clearly. They fired a rally towards it, reloaded, and again waited. Another two musket shots rang out.

Corporal Moore now led the group, and he felt the burden of this desperate command. The commanding officer, Lieutenant Marshall, lay unconscious after his fall from the horse. The sergeant was dead and two other men lay dead or wounded.

The enemy appeared to be few but well hidden. Corporal Moore made the first real military decision of his life.

'Fix bayonets and prepare to charge!' he shouted. He felt a rush of blood to his temples, and his heart pounded as he stood up and led the charge.

The road was on their right and there was a small ridge to the left. The musket shots had come from the western end of the ridge. Moore led his charge clear of the ridge, along the road, then cut across and charged into the scrub at the ridge terminus.

The scrub was extraordinarily thick and the soldiers found themselves struggling through it. The only thing that saved them from a total disaster was the fact that they were strung out during the initial charge. Thus the hail of spears that met them in the thicket only took three men, and then, only one fatally. The cries of the wounded men caused a complete rout, and each man set about securing a position of safety.

It was half an hour before Moore, who had himself been wounded in the shoulder, managed to assemble the remnants of the detachment at the site of the initial attack. He was appalled to find that both Marshall and Cawley had disappeared, along with the muskets and powder.

They searched the area cautiously but could find no trace of either the enemy or their comrades.

Moore squatted down on the dusty track and held his head in his hands. 'Christ, it's a bloody disaster,' he said fighting back the tears. 'But what else could I have done?'

Tench was unsure whether Pemulwuy was the culprit: the spears were certainly Bidjigal. Everyone had been puzzled by the Eoras' lack of response to the fork plan. Tench and Carpenter were sure that the other minor attacks were not the work of Pemulwuy. For a time Tench was genuinely disappointed that his old enemy might have given up the fight. This new attack clearly indicated to Tench that the Eora were still determined to resist. The taking of prisoners was a new and sinister twist to the situation.

Even Macarthur was concerned about this new turn of events, and Carpenter and Tench led two different search parties without any success whatsoever.

Lieutenant Marshall and Private Cawley had vanished into the bush.

Lieutenant Marshall had suffered a concussion and knew little of his abduction. James Cawley, however, had suffered greatly, being taken with both a broken tibia and fibula. The two were carried swiftly down to a small sheltered bay where they were hidden in silence until evening. Cawley's leg was wrapped in bark and tightly bound.

In darkness the two captives were placed in canoes and taken to the far side of the harbour.

Marshall was barely conscious during the harbour crossing, but James Cawley watched the dark waters fearfully.

'Where are you taking us?' he asked his silent Bidjigal captor. He got no answer. They camped until morning on the other side of the harbour.

Marshall seemed somewhat recovered, but Cawley was in great pain. Two Bidjigal men removed the makeshift splint. They stretched his leg in an unusual way until he lost consciousness. He awoke shortly to find a different splint had been applied and bound very tightly. They carried him for most of that day. Marshall did his best to comfort him, but the pain of his leg was all-consuming.

Some three days later, with Cawley still in pain, they reached a large Bidjigal camp near a tributary of the Hawkesbury River.

The attack had been led by Caesar, the American, with Knight and about fifteen Eora supporting him. Not only did they take the muskets and abduct the Englishmen, but they also butchered the unfortunate horse. The people at the camp seemed more interested in the dried horsemeat than the two prisoners of war.

Marshall had recovered fairly well. He made several attempts to talk to the war party without success. As the days passed, he felt more confident that they were not to be killed. He had been troubled by visions of cannibal feasts, but Cawley assured him that the Eora were not known to practice such a custom.

It was a most puzzling arrival. Nobody seemed to be the least bit interested in the prisoners. Marshall and Cawley stood in the sun for about ten minutes and then moved under a shady tree.

'If you were not so badly hurt we could practically walk out of here,' said Marshall.

James Cawley laid back and stretched out his damaged leg.

'The treatment we have received is appalling,' said Marshall.

'Not really!' replied Cawley. 'They expect that we can cope with pain and heal as quickly as they do.'

'Do you think they will kill us?' asked Marshall anxiously.

'I don't know,' replied Cawley, 'but they won't eat us'.

They were paid almost no attention until after sunset, when a young woman silently brought them some food. This consisted of some grilled dried horse, some fresh lightly cooked ganimantj, a small bundle of root vegetables and some baked ground seedcake. The pair ate well and rested until darkness.

Marshall looked seriously at James Cawley.

'Perhaps I should escape and bring back a rescue party for you,' he said.

'As you please, sir,' said Cawley, 'but believe me, you would not get a mile out there before they killed you. If we have any chance of survival, it is here. I know something of these people, and they are reasonable'.

'Perhaps so,' said Marshall gruffly, 'but they have been influenced by the likes of this African slave and William Knight. I do not share your confidence, lad'.

'Do as you see best, sir,' said Cawley as he made himself comfortable and prepared for sleep.

At sunrise two older women removed the bark splint from Cawley's leg. They examined it carefully, and then made a bed of various leaves for his leg. They then completely covered it in more leaves, and finally wet down the whole mass. About an hour later, the leaf bed became quite warm. By noon much of the pain had left his leg.

Marshall became rather more adventurous and began to wander about the camp. Except for one small girl who followed him everywhere, no-one spoke to him or even seemed to take any notice of him.

Marshall observed that the Bidjigals were poorly housed compared with the coastal groups. The only housing in the camp consisted of simple shelters built out of single sheets of bent bark. The coastal people built houses in which seven or eight people could live. These people were nevertheless well clothed, with large, well-tanned fur cloaks and other clothing. His wanderings took him deeper into the camp, where a couple of more substantial shelters had been built.

'Looking for a lady, Mr Rum Corps?'

Marshall was astonished.

Staring at him through a small opening in one of the larger shelters was a middle-aged European woman wrapped in an Eora cloak.

'Hope Pemulwuy kills you, you bastard.'

'Madam, what are you doing here?' said Marshall, astounded by the woman's presence.

'Doing better than you are, redcoat,' she laughed, 'a Bidjigal camp in New South Wales ain't no place for a bloody redcoat'.

Lieutenant Marshall stood before the woman in his bedraggled uniform. 'I had heard of some English girl supposedly living with the natives, but do I understand right, madam? Are you living by choice with these savages?'

'Compared with your lot they are a bunch of angels. Get away from me before somebody gets the idea that I know you. That young woman you spoke of lives in another camp and you would do well to keep away from her as well.' She turned away but continued speaking, 'there are quite a few white people living among the Eora, white children, orphans and deserted children as well. They are better looked after here than in Sydney'.

Marshall, still bewildered, returned to tell James Cawley of his find.

Cawley was quite excited and begged Marshall to return and ask the woman if she could get a message to a man called Awabakal. Marshall returned, but the woman had gone. Later in the afternoon, the same young woman who had brought them food returned. Cawley asked and she told him that her name was Burungaroo. Cawley did his best to engage her in further conversation, using his very limited Eora vocabulary. This girl was very cooperative, and after some time he learned that the European woman's name was Silky.

Silky Donovan, Cawley told Marshall, was a convict woman who had killed a soldier. She was to be hanged, but had escaped about a year ago. Cawley said that she had accused the soldier of repeatedly raping her.

'Is this happening?' said Marshall, 'convict women escaping and joining the natives and neglected children?'

'I don't really know,' replied Cawley, 'perhaps so'.

That night, Burungaroo returned and told them that Pemulwuy was in the camp. They waited in expectant silence for an hour. Finally Marshall spoke.

'Do you have any idea what will happen to us?'

'No, but I can't imagine that they mean us well,' muttered Cawley. Burungaroo had built a fire close to the two Englishmen, and Marshall continued to tend it. It was around midnight when Pemulwuy appeared before them. He was wrapped in a cloak and carried no weapons.

Marshall struggled to his feet, but Pemulwuy said: 'We'll not talk tonight'.

'Do you know Awabakal?' he asked Cawley.

'Yes.'

Pemulwuy turned and walked away.

'So that's him.'

'Yes, that's Pemulwuy.'

'Strange character.'

Early in the morning Awabakal appeared at the Englishman's camp. He was delighted to see James Cawley and embraced his friend, who was now sitting up with his leg still embedded in the compost heap.

'It is almost four years,' said Cawley. 'I thought that you had gone home until I heard recently that you were with Pemulwuy'.

'It seems that we must be attacked by a horse in order to meet.' Both men laughed.

'Ah Jimmy, many things have changed,' said Awabakal, 'you see,' he said pointing proudly to his missing front tooth, 'I am now a man in the Eora way'.

'Is that the same for Koori people?'

'Not exactly,' said Awabakal shaking his head, 'but it will have to do for now'.

'How do you know him?' Marshall demanded as he returned to their camp tree.

Marshall had got up early that morning, washed himself and done the best he could to make his ragged uniform presentable.

Marshall, who had remained aloof till now, entered the conversation.

'Private Cawley, who is this man?'

'We knew each other before the fighting,' said Cawley. 'We spent some time on patrol together.'

'You mean he is a deserter?'

'No, he was a kind of press-ganged scout. As a matter of fact that was when we both first met Pemulwuy. He comes from far north of here, a lake called Awaba. It is the same place that we call Coal River, about one hundred miles north.'

'I see,' said Marshall, obviously disturbed by the closeness of the two men, who seemed unaffected by the present situation.

Marshall looked thoughtfully at Cawley and said. 'Ask him what his leader intends for us'.

'Ask him yourself,' replied Cawley, 'he speaks perfect English'.

Marshall bristled at the hint of insubordination in Cawley's manner, but decided not to pursue the matter at this point. He turned to Awabakal and addressed him quite formally.

Awabakal answered with sour disdain.

'You will be taken before the *alodim* in the afternoon.' 'Alodim', Awabakal said to Cawley, 'is a kind of council'.

'How, may I ask, is such a 'thieves' court to be conducted?'

A hard, brutal look swept across Awabakal's young face.

'You Rum Corps speak of thieves,' he said deliberately, 'keep your insults for Pemulwuy. He will likely kill you for it'.

James Cawley was struck dumb by this exchange. Awabakal looked sharply at Cawley.

'You should pick better friends, Jimmy.' Awabakal turned and walked away.

'Who the devil do these people think they are?' said Marshall to Cawley who looked sadly after Awabakal.

Cawley turned to Marshall. 'Awabakal may be the only friend we have in this place,' he looked hurt, 'you turned him away'.

Marshall swung around and put his hand on the tree that had been their home here.

'How do you expect me to act, man?' He paused. 'I am an officer and a soldier of the King...do you expect me to beg favours?'

'He came here in friendship,' Cawley said half to himself.

'For God's sake man, can't you see...he's a soldier...a warrior...whatever. He is the enemy.'

It was late in the afternoon when Marshall was called to the meeting. Cawley was told that he would not be taken to the meeting. Lieutenant Frances Marshall of the New South Wales Corps walked down the short slope between two armed Eora. The meeting, he saw, was composed entirely of males, spread out in a wide double ring. Everyone was seated on the ground, and Marshall was invited to do likewise. He complied with as much dignity as he could muster.

He found himself facing Pemulwuy, who for his part sat partially turned away. The others faced the centre of the ring. Marshall did not recognise the men sitting on either side of Pemulwuy, but he recognised Caesar and Knight. There was another European, very bronzed and in Eora garb, sitting close to Pemulwuy. From the frequency with which the others used the word when they referred to him, Marshall guessed that the man's name was Gurrewe. The entire group bristled with Eora weaponry and there were some muskets. However, they were not as menacing as the English captive had expected. Nothing was said to him for a minute or two, and so Marshall decided to take the initiative.

'I assume I can speak in English,' he began.

But he was immediately interrupted by Pemulwuy, who thrust forward a large, rigid, rectangle of flattened, smooth, stringy bark.

'Look at this, Englishman!' he said.

The bark had been painted with a variety of local pigments. It appeared to contain the forms of animals interspersed with symbolic patterns. It had no meaning at all for Marshall.

'It's a map, Rum Corps man,' said Gurrewe, he spoke savagely, with a deceptively soft Irish lilt, 'have you lost the art of reading since coming to New South Wales?'

Marshall realised that this must be the Irish convict, McDonough, whom he had heard talk of. He stared at Gurrewe with deliberate contempt.

Then he looked at the bark. It was indeed a map, but there were no English names on it. Some other names were written in the Latin alphabet, but he did not recognise them.

CHAPTER 18

CONFLICT AND INTEREST

Yenowee, who was sitting next to Pemulwuy, reached over with his right leg and pointed with his toe.

'We here,' he said in clipped English.

Pemulwuy then addressed Marshall again in clear but slightly mannered English.

'The Rum Corps builds towns now in *Arrowanelli*,' he said, pointing to the area of the upper Georges River, 'and also in Waun, which is the Parramatta River district'. He stared hard at Marshall, his turned eye oddly absent, as if searching his ranks to one side, 'what is the purpose of this?'

Marshall swallowed hard. There was no secret about the settlement plan.

'To...develop and protect the fertile land for farming,' he said slowly.

'What kind of weapons will be used in these towns?'

'I don't know. That's not my responsibility.'

The Irishman leapt to his feet and moved threateningly towards Marshall, waving a club.

'Let me beat it out of him,' he bellowed, 'like the bastards did to me!'

'No!' Pemulwuy restrained him sternly. 'You'll make yourself a savage like he is!'

Gurrewe glowered, but he gave in to Pemulwuy's authority. It was clear who was in charge here, thought Marshall. His life—and perhaps Private Cawley's too—almost certainly depended on this outlandishly imposing black man's whim.

'Men suffer pain for a special purpose,' Pemulwuy snapped at Gurrewe, 'using it to torture people as the British do is weeree'.

Marshall had little understanding of what was being said, but he caught enough to feel compelled to defend the British position.

He got to his feet. 'You call the British savages,' he said loudly, 'yet we offer you protection, civilisation and Christianity! We try to show you how to use this land properly!'

'Civilisation!' Pemulwuy shot back fiercely. 'You are a people who build your world on the suffering and misery of other people. Your means of exchange is the rum,' he paused, his face dark with anger. 'Your religion has no strength,' he snarled, 'it does not punish evil people. You are a sickness that has arrived on our shores'. Pemulwuy pointed a long, sinewy arm at Marshall. 'You came simply to steal our land!'

Marshall could not contain himself. 'You don't use it productively!' he insisted.

Pemulwuy seemed to become ominously calm. 'We use it to obtain food,' he said. 'What will you use it for?' Then he stood up. 'This is wasting time,' he said, turning his back on Marshall.

'Kill him!' Caesar, the black American snarled.

There was a brittle silence. Marshall could hear his own heartbeat. Pemulwuy turned back, and stared at Marshall keenly.

'Do you wish to die?' he asked.

'No, of course not, I…'

'Then put your leg out in front of you,' Pemulwuy demanded.

Marshall felt his body prickle with fear, but he obeyed. He had no choice. He stretched his right leg out in front of him. Then Pemulwuy moved so quickly that, although Marshall instinctively tried to withdraw his leg, it was too late. Pemulwuy broke the metatarsals of his right foot with a single stroke of his club.

The pain was blinding.

'Leave when it heals,' said Pemulwuy solemnly. He signalled to Awabakal and another to carry the Englishman away.

Marshall vomited noisily when he arrived back at their prison quarters. He lay beside Cawley in a state of shock. The private did his best to comfort him while the lieutenant's broken foot swelled, and the dazzling vision of pain was finally enveloped in darkness.

Late that night, Caesar told Awabakal and Gurrewe of Yella Mundi's story about Yanada and the moon. Neither of the men could puzzle out the answer to the riddle. The American took a gulp of rum belonging to the stolen store from which he alone was allowed to drink in the camp.

'Another thing I don't comprehend,' he said, his deep voice echoing in the balmy Australian night. 'Why couldn't Yanada get with child after she had been cast out of her own land?'

Gurrewe smiled. Caesar's strange accent, half-American drawl, half whaler's jargon, fascinated and amused him.

'Ah,' he said, 'I understand that,' he paused thoughtfully; then stabbed the air with one finger. 'The Eora believe, so far as I can tell, that the spirit of a child comes from the land, usually from water, into a woman's body. If she is not on her own land, she either cannot conceive, or she takes the risk of conceiving a wrong spirit of some sort.'

Caesar grinned lazily. 'What about *yanga*?'

'I think they reckon the joys of the marriage bed play a part, but don't lead to the actual conception. I can't say I really don't know.'

Caesar seemed satisfied. He pondered for a while, staring out at the night.

'Another thing,' he said to the Irishman then, 'something that puzzles me. At first, like most people, I thought these fellows didn't know nothin' about money and trade, but they do. They maybe use some kind of credit.'

Awabakal, who had been idly listening to the conversation, intervened eagerly: 'wea li nunga wea fowinid ninnga!'

'What the hell does that mean?' growled Caesar.

'It works something like when you give presents,' said Gurrewe. 'You become beholden. It's a kind of dealing in beholdenness.'

For a while, he and Awabakal tried to explain the idea in terms the American could understand. They were relieved when Pemulwuy arrived and gave them an excuse to break off.

The Eora leader sat down and talked directly to Caesar in English.

'I have been thinking about your muskets,' he said. 'I agree that you should use them. I can get powder for you. They will be very useful against the fortified towns.'

Caesar nodded but also frowned, as if he was pleased to hear Pemulwuy's approval but was irritated at needing to have it in the first place. 'But the Eora must continue to practice their spear and shield fighting and use it at all times,' Pemulwuy added. 'I have noticed that when a man has a musket, he will not fire it until he can see his target and aim. This is not good. A prepared man with a spear throws by instinct.'

Gurrewe helped him. 'Yes. He does not need to see the target the way a musket soldier does.'

There was a pause. Caesar looked away. Pemulwuy brooded for a moment; then turned to Awabakal as if he had just remembered something.

'Tell your Rum Corps friends to leave as soon as they are well enough, or I will kill them,' he said. 'In any case they will fight no more.'

CHAPTER 19

A SUMMER OF REGRETS

Around mid-October in 1793 the camp in which Marshall and Cawley had been living moved to the bank of a tributary of the Hawkesbury River. It was a long painful journey for the two of them and they estimated it to be between eight and ten miles. Cawley's leg was still bound up in a kind of cast made from fine strands of bark and cloth embedded with yellow clay. Marshall's foot had been similarly encased. His was a bandage made from a loose woven cloth impregnated with the same clay. Both had made themselves useable crutches and under the circumstances were remarkably mobile. They gathered their own firewood and did a bit of food gathering, but were still completely dependent on the Eora people for the products of hunting. Even with vegetable foods, they were always afraid of eating something poisonous. Marshall had grumbled frequently about witchdoctors, but confided in Cawley that he believed his foot was healing reasonably well.

'Well, sir, you are luckier than I,' said Cawley.

'Why is that, lad?'

'It's the way the Eora set the break,' said Cawley. 'Did you notice that woman who showed us how to find the tree grubs we eat?'

'Yes,' nodded Marshall, 'she seems to have one leg shorter than the other'.

'It's the way they set it,' said Cawley. 'It heals strongly but you have a limp.'

'Have you measured your leg?'

'Yes. It seems about half an inch shorter than the other leg,' said Cawley.

'Good Lord! Strange practice,' said Marshall. 'Well it's the end of the army for you, my boy.'

After some weeks the woman known as Silky Donovan had become more friendly and helpful, particularly to James Cawley. She still tended to regard Marshall as the enemy, but as the time passed and his uniform started to fall to pieces, he began to appear less a part of the Rum Corps. Marshall had become sufficiently friendly to ask if she could tell the camp people to look out for some britches or shirts. She laughed.

'Not be Rum Corps gear, but maybe a set of slops.'

Marshall grinned, 'be better than what we have'.

Long talks with Silky revealed that in coming to live with the Eora she had found a dignity in her life which she had not found in the colony of New South Wales or in London.

'My only regret is me children I left in the old country,' she said.

She had been accepted among the Eora people, and during last winter had become the willing second wife of a gentle old man *Bian Benu.* She said that the Eora people needed to work about five hours a day to supply themselves with all they needed in this place.

'I intend to spend the rest of me days here,' she said. 'It's not paradise, but I have certainly escaped from hell. I ask these people to keep a watch on convicts coming in, just in case one of me babies arrives. Then I will bring them here,' she paused and sniffed, 'I only wish that they were better cooks and built better shelters like the coastal people. This camp is horrible in the wet'. She paused again—then went on, 'that little girl you asked about, Milli. She was an orphan and the only work she could find in bloody England was prostitution. She got sent here for stealing a gentleman's cup when the bastard would not pay her. Then she was placed with a farm settler who used her as a whore until that footpad Knight rescued her, but she's doin fine now and she has some powerful women friends among the Eora. She never did settle for Knight although she is grateful to him for bringing her here'.

'That woman could talk the spout off a tea pot,' Marshall said later to Cawley, 'terrible gossip, but a great source of news'.

As time went by Marshall became more and more morose. The stolen convict issue britches and shirts didn't help. James Cawley, on the other hand, appeared to be enjoying himself among the Eora. He even had an almost constant companion in the form of Burungaroo; she was taken by his blue eyes. Jimmy and this friendly girl joined in with Silky in the affairs of the camp, taking an active interest in the gossip and particularly the joking. He found the Eora camp full of humour, although he had to accept that he became the target of some of the amusement. This was the way of it.

Marshall, on the other hand, failed to take any enjoyment from their situation. He felt that his existence was nothing more than totally wretched. Marshall considered that he was the most unfortunate of human beings. First he had been posted to New South Wales Corps, as the result of a minor insubordination in Britain. No sooner had he arrived in the accursed colony than he had been taken prisoner by these strange people. He felt he had been severely ill treated; crippled at the whim of the madman, and accused of being a savage and a thief. Marshall was the product of a genteel British family. Many of the ideas and even the very nature of what was good about English society was being challenged here by the Eora, and even by the two Europeans in whose company he found himself.

One day when they were fishing Marshall said to Cawley, 'if Pemulwuy would let you, you could live here with these people, couldn't you?'

Jimmy said nothing.

'You would bed down with that little girl that trails around after you at the camp, and live like Silky.'

'I could think of worse,' said Jimmy at last, 'but Pemulwuy will have none of that, I reckon'.

Late one evening Awabakal arrived at their campsite. He had come to remind them that they must leave the camp as soon as they were reasonably mobile. James Cawley told Awabakal that he had heard from Silky and others in the camp that it was extremely dangerous to do so. He said that the British were still looking for them, making it more likely to get them killed. Worse than this, he said that the young excluded men would use anything that looked British for spear practice.

Marshall, who had made some degree of peace with Awabakal said: 'We are virtually defenseless in such combat. They will not return our own weapons, and we have no skill with Eora weapons. Besides,' he went on, 'we are not sufficiently recovered to fight'.

'I understand that,' said Awabakal, 'but you must rest and prepare yourselves for your journey back to the British'.

'What's the hurry?' asked Cawley. 'Is Pemulwuy coming back here?'

'No. It's Gro Mok,' said Awabakal very seriously. 'Gro Mok men can be very dangerous. They may even enter the camp to kill you.'

Although questioned closely, Awabakal was not prepared to explain the full significance of Gro Mok, except to say that it was a secret society used by the Bidjigal people to force other groups into supporting them in matters of vengeance. He went on to explain that among the Eora people it was the Kamergal group who were responsible for calling major meetings to do with ceremonies. This also applied to matters of vengeance. The Bidjigal and, of course, Pemulwuy, were not in a position to do this. He went on to explain that to gain this sort of power Pemulwuy had invoked the use of Gro Mok.

'So that's the trick,' Marshall said. 'We wondered how he managed to hold so many tribes together in this conflict,' he shook his head, 'clever bugger'.

The next morning Awabakal bid them farewell and said that he would return in two or three weeks. He suggested to both, and particularly Cawley, that they might give some thought to the idea of joining an Eora group.

James looked up surprised. 'Pemulwuy would not allow that.'

Awabakal smiled secretly, 'he would if I asked him'.

Awabakal returned in just over a week and told them that they must leave the place urgently. He said that there was a great tension growing between Caesar and Pemulwuy and that Eora people everywhere were getting to the point where they would kill an Englishman on sight unless he had become part of an Eora group. He asked Cawley again whether he had considered joining the Eora. There is a family in this group that has a daughter who fancies you, he told him.

'I have, Awabakal,' he said, 'but I am full with the whole thing. Your people have now made it possible for me to return home,' he pointed to his plastered leg. 'It's over for me,' he said, 'England is home, and that's where I'm going if I can'.

Awabakal said that he understood. He told the pair that he had a fairly large and substantial canoe in which they would be able to go down to the mouth of the Hawkesbury River. There was a British settlement near the opening to the sea. He sat down and drew a map of the river and the location of the settlement.

'Awabakal, that's the place where we first met,' said Jimmy Cawley.

Awabakal smiled.

'Yes, that's where I mean.'

'Are you going to come with us, Awabakal?'

'No, no, I can't come. It is best this way Jimmy. It's over for you and me. It's best you go to your place. I must fight your people now and it will be a bad fight; it's best that you're not here.'

As they were about to leave, a young European female strolled up to them. She was quite an apparition, green-eyed, bare-breasted and with a shock of red hair partly covered by an odd looking hat of local construction. Awabakal introduced her, and Cawley said that Silky had told them about her. She carried a rum flask which she handed to Marshall, who seemed mesmerised by her.

'It is not rum,' she said with a shy grin, 'but you will need a water container on your voyage'.

At this point Marshall spoke up.

'Madam!' he said gallantly, while averting his eyes from Milli's breasts, 'you are welcome and should come with us. You are an English woman'.

Milli laughed. 'What! Arrive in Sydney town with a couple of rummies newly released from Pemulwuy. I would finish up on the end of a piece of rope and most likely, so would you.'

'God help us! Has it come to this,' Marshall said aghast.

'It has, your 'honour.' Go with haste and think yourselves lucky.'

Milli dropped the flask and left, leaving Marshall quite distressed.

'You're a good fellow, Awabakal,' said Marshall. 'There is absolutely no need for this ridiculous bloodshed. It is clear to me that the Eora have the basis for being sensible. We should be learning to live together, not trying to kill each other.'

Awabakal sat on the ground and looked up at him sadly.

'It's too late. People like Jimmy and I and Milli, or even Gurrewe and Nargel and Silky, could live together and maybe even you, without fighting, but the people of the Rum Corps and Pemulwuy!' He shook his head, 'that's different. They must fight and die'.

'But, Awabakal, His Majesty is determined that you shall live as protected British subjects; that we will all live together in this place in peace.'

'No, Frances,' said Awabakal, 'it's true what Pemulwuy says, you're not trying to live with us. You're just trying to steal our land. If you take our land we will all die anyway. We must die fighting you for it'. Awabakal shook his head sadly.

After dark, Awabakal led the two Englishmen, slowly and painfully for Cawley, to the bank of the Hawkesbury River tributary. They launched a bark canoe of some sixteen feet in length. The canoe carried two paddles, one for each. Awabakal then loaded the boat with a large piece of dried ganimantj, two spears, a string bag full of yams and the rum jar filled with water. Jimmy Cawley held Awabakal by the arm, he had tears in his eyes and his voice trembled.

'I shall always remember you Kiraban-Awabakal,' he said. 'This time here has been the making of my life.' He embraced Awabakal, 'I shall always dream of you and your land of stories'.

Awabakal smiled tearfully and pushed the canoe away from the shore. He watched it glide down the stream then waved a last farewell. It was for him a farewell forever to the only real and unconditional friendship that he had found with one of these people from the other side of the world.

Tedbury and Awabakal were still relatively young in the world of Eora. They had nevertheless greatly grown in status through their activities within the Gro Mok. They quite often wore the colour of the Gro Mok openly and a bone ornament through the septum of their noses. Even these two were split on the issue of massed attacks, however. Tedbury tended to support his father's view, leaving Awabakal caught between the two. Yenowee was also clearly a Pemulwuy supporter on this issue and would not even engage in private discussions with the others about it. This left Awabakal in *Weuong*'s camp. Weuong was of a more open mind, but still different although not as different as Awabakal who came from another people and this seemed to make Weuong cautious. The only other close dissident was a young man called *Gomil*, but he was a very secretive person. Awabakal began to feel himself alien among the Bidjigals.

He often wondered how a man from so far away as Gurrewe managed to live with a Bidjigal wife. He thought that he would not want a Bidjigal wife, at least not one of the spiky ones like Nargel or Coleleu or even Millicent. He smiled to himself and thought, Coleleu and Milli had even taken to riding horses sometimes. But then, he thought Milli was not Bidjigal or even Eora. Awabakal shook his head. He thought that by comparison, Koobee and the Kamerigals seemed such a simple and sensible lot.

A large group of Eora people gathered, consisting mainly of Bidjigal, but also now including other Eora, some Daruk, several Englishmen and the African.

In the alodim, arguments flew backwards and forwards about the issue of massed attacks. Gurrewe now tended to support Caesar and Knight in their views of this strategy along with Awabakal and Weuong. Pemulwuy was prepared to concede that some new strategy would have to be devised if they were to deal with fortified towns, but he remained convinced that a massed attack against a musket position would be disastrous.

While the issue of massed attacks was the centre of most arguments, there was another bone of contention among these groups. Many believed that they should immediately attack Parramatta and the new fortified towns. Pemulwuy was again unsure of this strategy, and after the day's meeting held private talks with Gurrewe, Yenowee and Weuong.

Pemulwuy told the group that shortly he would have to go away to engage in private religious activities associated with an important site belonging to his father. He said that during that time he would think about the things that were discussed at the meeting and when he returned they would attack the British.

He pointed out that they were now very strong and had many weapons. If they attacked carefully, then the British expansion could be stopped by the end of summer.

Pemulwuy, Yenowee and Gurrewe talked and argued long into the night. Gurrewe remained convinced that only massed attacks would yield victory, but Pemulwuy refused to accept that logic.

Finally Pemulwuy ended the argument.

'Bulumna,' he said, 'there is much yet that you do not understand about the Bidjigal. Victory for us is different from the British. We must not go beyond our way'.

This left Gurrewe completely bemused and deeply disturbed.

'There is an edge to Pemulwuy that no-one will ever understand,' he thought.

The next morning Pemulwuy left.

Some meetings in the camp continued until it was generally decided that another meeting would be held at the end of the year. Tedbury left with Pemulwuy and Awabakal was left alone.

These were the times when Awabakal longed to be home in his place. He felt that his father and mother would be very worried that their son must seem lost to them. He was their eldest son and, like Tedbury, there would be things that he should be doing with his father.

The next day he felt much better since his father had come to him in a dream. In the dream he told Kiraban that he knew what he was doing in the land of the Eora and approved of it.

It was early December before Marshall and Cawley arrived in Sydney. Their trip down the Hawkesbury was largely uneventful. Awabakal had left them well provisioned but had warned them to stay on the water and not land. They were glad to have the water container that Millicent had given them. Cawley was quite surprised to find that Marshall was also deeply affected at their parting from Awabakal and the Bidjigal people at the camp.

'I want you to know Cawley,' said Marshall, 'I appreciated your loyalty and help back there. If you have the opportunity I would like you to pass on my regards to that young man Awabakal, Burungaroo and the English girl and the others that assisted us,' he paused and looked away, then said seriously, 'I shall see that you are properly treated when we return James Cawley'.

On their arrival in Sydney, Marshall and Cawley were greeted with much excitement. Marshall became quite a celebrity in better social circles. He wrote the usual dry non-committal military report for the Corps as was expected of him. Then he spent many hours talking to Collins about his experiences. Even Grose had entertained him at dinner. However, it was Collins who pumped him for information about life among the Bidjigal. Many of these discussions were done with Watkin Tench present.

'What about the lad Cawley?' Tench asked.

'Oh, I dare say he has quite a tale to tell,' Marshall replied, 'always loyal to me, but I believe that he fell for a delightful native girl who looked after us while we were captive. I must say she was a great help to us during our convalescence'.

'What about during your escape?' Tench asked enthusiastically.

'Well, yes…actually we were assisted by a few people,' Marshall was himself puzzled about why he concealed their association with Awabakal or Millicent and felt ashamed that he was being disloyal to the Crown. He later told Collins about Millicent privately, but he told no-one about Awabakal.

Collins tended to dismiss his report about the Gro Mok, but Tench did not, and pursued it. He said that he had come across the same sort of thing in India and mentioned some Papist secret societies that he knew of in Ireland.

'Fanaticism! Puts heart in the troops,' he said.

Things had not gone well for Tench during the interregnum and he was eventually appointed to command the remaining Marines which would be responsible for the security of Sydney.

Private James Cawley received an honourable discharge from the New South Corps in 1794. He was promoted to corporal and offered a position as an overseer on a property granted to an Officer of the Corps. His status would be that of a free settler with his own small grant of adjacent land. He declined all offers and left the colony without ever telling his story. Perhaps James Cawley was unsure what story he had to tell or to whom he should tell it.

Marshall found Sydney almost an alien place after his return. He dreamed often of the wilderness of his capture. He thought of the gentle Eora people, who he could not help but compare to the dissipation and vice in which he found himself in Sydney, and of that of his life in the regiment.

Sometimes he thought of the young English woman Millicent. He thought of her now in memory. Her delicately freckled and tanned breasts he saw in hindsight as flowers upon her chosen land. He had fancies of going back and finding her in that wilderness. Her brilliant green eyes would make that easy. Yet, all he had to remember her by was the rum flask which he had brought back to Sydney with him. He set it before him in his quarters. His only material memories of the whole thing were that flask and his painful foot.

He realised in time that he must cast the flask away; and, after all, he had only known the woman for a short time. But he also realised that in that fleeting moment he had fallen in love with her. He felt that he would love her all of his life. That simple powerful emotion flooded over him and filled his life now.

Frances Marshall even imagined life in the wilderness with this woman.

In his mind's eye, he saw their children, tanned like her, understanding this strange land as he never could…and comfortable with native children like those he had experienced in the camp. Millicent would have taught their children fluent Bidjigal. He would of course, ensure that they spoke the King's English and perhaps he could learn Bidjigal himself. After all he could also speak French. But then, so could Pemulwuy. He thought of tender nights in the scented land with this green-eyed beauty…of fishing in the sparkling waters of her adopted land, and then hunting to feed them.

In imagination he went further. He thought of a farm upon a land grant.

But then it would always be on someone else's land. Perhaps with Milli in tow who seemed to be accepted as Bidjigal, the Eora would accept this. He thought that perhaps Pemulwuy would accept them. He knew that to join her in what had now become to him an idyllic enchanted wilderness, he would have to accept the protection of Pemulwuy.

He now knew that it was that protection that had allowed Cawley and he to sail down the Hawkesbury unmolested. He even tried to think better of the crow. He was, after all, a successful soldier in his own way and perhaps with age he may become more statesman-like. Not now of course, surrounded as he was by ruffians and miscreants. But with time he thought, men like that Awabakal would become his advisors and things would change.

Marshall sat quietly and drank at least a half a bottle of awful but intoxicating wine.

So be it. He realised that he was probably the only Englishman in New South Wales who did not fear Pemulwuy now. He thought Cawley and Silky Donavan could recruit Awabakal to take him to see Pemulwuy. This was not a matter of war. This was a matter of the heart, of a woman of his own kind. Yes, he knew enough of the Eora now. Pemulwuy would this time receive him differently. In fact he thought the boot would be on the other foot. He could not be accused of stealing anything. He was simply claiming a woman of his own race who was somehow attached, for want of a better word, to the Bidjigal. From his experience, he believed that Pemulwuy was at least an intensely honest man. He would happily hand over this woman. In fact this would seem like some sort of victory to him. Make him almost a civilised man. He took another gulp of the bad wine.

Another alternative was that he could find the girl, marry her and take her back to England. But what if she rejected him? He laughed! She may have become over civilised by the bloody Bidjigal. Those women all seemed pretty independent and strong willed, but then he was an officer and a gentleman.

He thought that Jimmy Cawley would have been well advised to go back and claim that lovely little girl who had taken such a shine to him. God knows, if Pemulwuy wins this war he could promote Cawley to a sergeant, even an officer, and he deserves it. Mind you, he thought if I were to join them, he would likely make me…even a General Officer.

For God's sake, this is all ridiculous and treason, he thought. In any case, imagine arriving home with a convict wife. He knew that he did not have the courage for that.

'I would be better off taking home a Bidjigal wife, some fierce dark thing like that Coleleu, whom he had met once with Silky, she was naked and riding bareback on a stolen horse,' he chuckled, 'she could speak perfect English and would stand English society on its ear, but imagine trying to live with such a wild woman,' he thought, but then his mind drifted back to Millicent. 'God, but this love thing is a strange business.'

In his mind, he saw again the beautiful green eyes of his Millicent—eyes that belonged to England. He finished off the last of the bad wine, stood up and thought that, like Cawley, the time had come for him to go home.

CHAPTER 20

THE SECOND LOSER

Pemulwuy and Tedbury returned from their pilgrimage late in December. Pemulwuy disbanded the meeting in Waun and said that he would reconvene it when the flowers bloomed on the coorijong trees. This would be late in January.

Caesar was angry and let the world know it. Pemulwuy walked among the Eora as though he had discovered a great secret. He instructed a small group led by Yenowee to report on the situation around Brickfield, near Sydney.

Pemulwuy himself went with Weuong and Awabakal to the Botany Bay area. Tedbury stayed in the Waun region, while Koobee went fishing.

As Koobee left the meeting, William Knight, who was slowly mastering the ***boomerang***, asked him: 'What do you call the kind of *boomerang* that does not return?'

Koobee looked up with a grin. 'A stick,' he said.

Knight was not amused and went off to join Caesar. He found him talking to Gurrewe.

'How the hell does he expect to win a war? He releases a British officer, calls a meeting of hundreds of people and then walks off!'

Caesar fell silent, threw a piece of wood on the fire. Then he said, 'the man refuses to use muskets'.

He pointed a long black finger at Gurrewe.

'I'm going to plan my own war and Pemulwuy can do as he likes.' Gurrewe stood up.

'This is stupid,' he said. 'We have others to fight besides ourselves. I must talk to Pemulwuy.'

Gurrewe walked away. Caesar followed him. 'What is it with you and Pemulwuy, Irish?' he demanded.

Gurrewe turned quickly. 'It's not me and Pemulwuy, Caesar, it is you and Pemulwuy.'

'What do you mean?'

'Pemulwuy belongs here…this is his place. Caesar, you don't belong anywhere,' Gurrewe said.

'The hell I don't,' responded Caesar. 'My people come from Africa.'

'I know that, but you said yourself you don't know where. You are an American black man, kind of everybody's black man. Pemulwuy is Eora—he is the spirit and the soul of this place.'

'Ah, shit!' exclaimed Caesar. 'Listen, Irish, you are everybody's white bird, the white bird, you fly around with no place to land.'

Gurrewe drew out his knife. Caesar glared at it then turned away.

'Put it away, Gurrewe, before I kill you,' Caesar said, and walked back towards the fire.

Gurrewe left camp early in the morning, but by the time he caught up with Pemulwuy it was evening and Pemulwuy was camped on the Parramatta River. Pemulwuy welcomed him.

'Gurrewe, come and join us.'

'Pemulwuy, I have not come to stay, but you must listen to me.'

'Tonight we sleep, tomorrow we talk,' said Pemulwuy, and began to sing quietly.

Gurrewe slept fitfully and woke very early in the morning. He joined Yenowee by a sweet-smelling ti-tree campfire. McDonough thought this was risky and mentioned it to Yenowee.

'Muskets can't kill Pemulwuy, Gurrewe.'

Gurrewe shook his head slowly as Pemulwuy came up to them.

'Gurrewe, we shall talk now.'

He seemed in excellent spirits. Even his turned eye seemed to be focusing unusually well.

'Pemulwuy,' began Gurrewe, 'I must warn you about the…'

Pemulwuy waved his hand and shook his head.

'I know what you have to say,' he interrupted. Then he sat down and extended his arm in front of him, marking the sandy ground with his finger.

'Let me tell you the answer to the riddle.'

Gurrewe frowned. 'What do you mean?'

'Yanada.'

'Oh, the secret in Yella Mundi's story.'

'It is not a secret, Gurrewe,' murmured Pemulwuy. 'It is the third part of truth.'

'I don't see what that has to do with it, but anyway, what was her secret?'

'Yanada conducted herself into madness,' said Pemulwuy. Gurrewe let his words sink in for a minute. Then he said quietly, 'she planned it to get herself out of the trouble with the two men. She pretended that she was mad. So that was it!'

Pemulwuy held Gurrewe by the shoulder, 'that is Yanada's third part of truth,' he said. 'Go back now, tell Caesar and Knight. You must all know what your own truth is.'

Caesar refused to attend the January meeting at Waun in 1794, but William Knight went along. Pemulwuy told the group that the most vulnerable place in the British domain was Sydney, but Tench and Carpenter had set up a perimeter defence.

Pemulwuy said that they must attack Sydney. They were ready to attack Brickfield. This was the simplest way to weaken the British resolve to continue their expansion into the Western valleys.

'Send them back to defend Sydney. That will send them running back to the place where they came onto our land.'

He told them that the attack would take place in four days, and they were to make their way to the attack meeting place separately.

The attack strategy was fairly simple: frontal attack on the military base and two flanking attacks across the small village and farms behind it. Pemulwuy had agreed to experiment with a surprise mass attack, which would be led by Gurrewe. This surprised everybody, especially Awabakal and, for that matter, Gurrewe. Pemulwuy would lead one flank attack and Yenowee the other.

The others left camp and headed towards the sea. Gurrewe went to Goman camp with William Knight to find Caesar. He desperately wanted to resolve the conflict that hung thick in the Eora world. They reached Caesar's campfire at dusk. Caesar sat alone, softly singing a plaintive American song.

'You hear me, Gurrewe,' he said, breaking off from his song, 'Follow the Drinking Gourd'.

Gurrewe said, 'yes, it's about freedom'.

He smiled sadly, 'ain't that what we're all wanting?' said Caesar.

Gurrewe shook his head slowly.

'Surely, it's what brought you into the bush here with Pemulwuy?' Caesar asked.

'I don't know,' said Gurrewe, 'but I did find out about the riddle'.

'So did I,' said Caesar, 'Yanada's secret... It is a strange way the Eora have,' he paused. 'But they have never been slaves.'

Knight sat down and said nothing, but Gurrewe remained standing. He shook his head. 'And they never will be. They own this place, this is their land. The Africans aren't slaves in Africa.'

Caesar laughed softly, 'some are, even there'.

Gorrewe looked down sadly at Caesar. 'So what will you do, Caesar?'

Caesar looked up at the Irishman. 'We fight the same war. Pemulwuy will fight his way and I will fight mine,' he looked into the fire.

Gurrewe said sadly, 'but maybe it is not even the same war'.

Gurrewe's group assembled on the night of the twenty-first day of 1794 about two miles from Brickfield. There were close to sixty people in his force. Runners told Gurrewe that each of the other forces consisted of at least thirty men.

Pemulwuy sent a message at about midnight telling them not to attack until the following evening. The attack was now to be made at sunset.

This was a big problem for Gurrewe. How did he disperse and hide such a large force so close to Sydney, and then reassemble them in daylight?

Gurrewe called the group together and told them to hide until morning. They were not to paint up until one hour before sunset.

Gurrewe took Nargel and hid on a small rise that overlooked the rapidly expanding township.

From there he watched the town come to life. He saw the world of the Europeans before him—their farms, their livestock, their dreams. A great bitterness grew inside him. Nargel watched him hurt, and she held his hand and whispered, '*mangan alli*'.

Gurrewe touched her hand and smiled. She and her people were the only dream he knew now. But there was once another dream.

An hour before sunset the Eora forces assembled. They attacked as the sun touched the mountains.

The garrison station was a collection of about twenty tents. The Eora warriors had to run across one hundred yards with no cover. They did this with remarkable success and were almost on top of the garrison before the British became aware of them. At about thirty yards the attackers launched a single volley of spears and musket fire.

Amid the chaos and disbelief in the British camp, they managed one disorganised musket response, but their adversaries were among them before any serious resistance could be mounted.

The British fell back in disorder, straight into the flank attacks of Pemulwuy and Yenowee.

The plan called for Gurrewe's force to fall back quickly to cover the retreat of Pemulwuy and Yenowee. The disorder of Gurrewe's group during the retreat was puzzling both to Pemulwuy and Yenowee, but the British were in no condition to take advantage of it.

The retreat was successfully accomplished. By midnight the bulk of the force was on the other side of the harbour and well out of British reach. By dawn Pemulwuy knew that Gurrewe had been killed.

Lieutenant Carpenter was with the southern group that had been hit in retreat by Yenowee's group. In all there were about sixty men in the encampment at the time of the attack. Less than twenty could still walk at the end of the attack. When Tench arrived, they had counted fourteen Eora and thirty-six British dead. Tench was shocked. He had been no more than two miles away, with a force of fifty men on patrol.

'It's incredible,' he said, shaking his head, 'they're not going to hit the fortified towns first'. He stopped and wiped his forehead, 'they're going to concentrate their forces and strike at Sydney!' He looked up at Carpenter. 'How many were there?'

Carpenter could only guess. 'About two hundred.'

'How the hell did they get across that clearing?'

'I don't know. They were all painted up. I think the men were mesmerised.'

Tench stood stunned as he gazed across his forward garrison post, surveying the carnage of the recent attack. 'He has beaten us,' he said almost under his breath, 'he has beaten us. If he has enough people with him now, he can end this war: force negotiation or worst evacuation'.

Major Paterson of the New South Wales Corps unceremoniously relieved Tench of the perimeter command and sent Macarthur scurrying back to Parramatta. Paterson set about preparing Sydney against further attacks.

Orders were given to shoot all Eora people on sight. The local population had sensed the impending doom and, except for a few drunks, had scattered to the four winds. Despite this, three Eoras were shot that night.

Carpenter wondered how Tench could have been so completely wrong about the massed assaults and the tactic of diversionary attacks. It was true that their casualties were relatively small, while the Eoras had lost a significant part of their force, but it was still a great victory for Pemulwuy and a disaster for the British. Carpenter failed to see how Grose and the New South Wales Corps could keep this event from London.

Collins was searching the rocks area for Tench or Carpenter but instead found Francis Marshall who greeted him stoically.

'What's all this I hear about evacuation Lieutenant? Has the Corps lost its balance?'

Marshall was very cautious and responded carefully. 'I don't believe that is a view held by the Corps.'

'Well it certainly is a rumour rife in the civilian population. I mean where would one evacuate to? England, New Zealand…where?'

'I agree sir, but the rumour that I have heard proposes Botany Bay; some see that as a more defendable position.'

'For God's sake man, that amounts to abandoning the colony!'

CHAPTER 21

A BALANCE OF WEAKNESS

While Pemulwuy's party had been painting up for the Brickfield attack, Caesar and Knight, with forty men, had attacked the halfway-fortified position at Rof's farm.

The attack was a simple, massed frontal assault. It was successful, and by sunset the installation had burnt to the ground.

Caesar lost ten men. The British casualties were not so heavy because the bulk of the garrison had turned tail and run. Caesar's losses would have been greater had Macarthur led his forces into the action at Rof's farm.

Macarthur had, however, received a variety of garbled messages, the most startling of these being that Sydney was under heavy Eora attack. Halfway to Sydney he received another message saying that the outer defences had failed and Pemulwuy was in the streets.

Macarthur's mounted unit arrived at Brickfield two hours before dawn, just after Carpenter had received news of the other simultaneous attack.

By the time the raiding parties had reached Waun camp, nobody dared go within ten yards of Pemulwuy—he was in a rage. Caesar was completely confused by Pemulwuy's state of mind and confronted him.

'What the hell is wrong with you?' he bellowed. 'It's a great victory! British are crawling into hollow logs! There are fifty of them running around the bush that we can pick off in the next few days!'

'How do you count your victory, Caesar?' barked Pemulwuy, 'in Eora dead? In one night, African, you and I have filled this place with angry spirits. Look at the blood on the heads of the women: *Panera*!'

'This is war, Pemulwuy. This is what it's all about.'

Pemulwuy leapt into the air and shouted.

'You speak like Irish! He lies dead; his spirit has nowhere to rest. His people, like yours, are slaves to the British. Is that the victory you plan for the Eora?'

Caesar picked up an Eora club and shield.

'I am no slave, you bastard! And I won't follow a madman like you!' he growled menacingly.

Pemulwuy screamed out, and then fell silent and inert, his shoulders askew, his head leaning to one side as though his neck was broken. His cloak had fallen around his feet, his painted naked body had the appearance of a crippled bird; a *currawong*. The people in the camp had been drawn to the scene. They now watched in silence, horrified and spellbound. Suddenly Pemulwuy leapt into the air again and sprang around Caesar in long, insect-like, weaving movements.

Caesar held his ground and watched carefully. Pemulwuy darted to one side then the other. He tossed a club and shield up into the air with his feet.

He caught first one, then the other. He stopped, crouched, and then leapt at Caesar. There was a clatter of timber weapons, and a scatter of onlookers.

Then the combatants parted again.

The duel became a terrible death ritual. These two terrible dark warriors circled each other, lunged...attacked and withdrew. They were like great lithe beasts from some mythical other world. At each attack their ferocity was desperate. Their battle was lit only by firelight and the light from the watching stars.

The two opponents began to circle each other more closely now. The audience drew closer, but none would dare to interfere. Suddenly an encounter, Pemulwuy was struck to the ground, his shield smashed to pieces... Caesar attacked... Pemulwuy was on his feet again.., a great slicing blow from Caesar's club…and this was his error. Pemulwuy moved inside the blow, his own club moving in a sharp arc that seemed to bounce off Caesar's skull…and it took his life.

Caesar staggered backwards and collapsed. Pemulwuy walked a little way into the darkness and fell to the ground, his forearm broken and blood seeping from his mouth and ear. Watkin Tench smiled bitterly. 'They killed each other!' he repeated incredulously for the tenth time that morning. ' They held victory in their hands and simply threw it away.'

'So the rumour goes.' Carpenter murmured.

'Well, it's of no further interest to me,' said Tench none too convincingly. 'I sail for England in April, my friend. For me it is over.'

Carpenter said nothing, but let the Captain talk.

Tench fell into a brooding silence, a glass of wine clutched in his hand. Then suddenly he looked at Carpenter and his eyes were wild.

'I don't believe he's dead,' he said, 'I've seen him crawl off like this before'.

'Come,' Carpenter objected feebly, 'the man…'

'But for me it is over,' Tench repeated, as if to himself. 'I have lost to a worthy enemy. I cannot blame it all on the Rum Corps, on the intrigues or on Grose's incompetence. Pemulwuy had the match of me. He knew how to use the terrain, knew our weaknesses,' he shook his head gloomily. 'Remember this when I am gone, Carpenter. In this place called New South Wales, it is not our strengths that we pit against each other, but our weaknesses!'

'And what is Pemulwuy's weakness?' asked Carpenter softly.

Tench shrugged, 'if only I knew. One day he will show it…'

'Sir, you fought with your hands tied!'

'Perhaps,' Tench took a gulp of sherry, 'but my opponent was too damned clever'.

Carpenter frowned, 'Collins may well be right. We should perhaps consider some sort of agreement, a treaty no less.'

Tench considered his words, but was unconvinced. 'No, Pemulwuy will never agree or give up, no matter how great the pressure on him. He believes us to be rogues and thieves.' He managed a wintry smile. 'In part he is right. Nonetheless, it is the white races that have the will and determination to master nature. However, I must say that we have done poorly in this place. We cannot even hunt game to feed ourselves. You know I've not seen more than half a dozen kangaroos brought down with a musket, yet elsewhere we hunt buffalo and even the lion with them.'

'Pemulwuy uses his wooden weapons so effectively in hunting and in war,' he paused, 'but in the end choice—and the choice of the other primitives—is to become as the horse, a well-cared for servant, or be driven to extinction. It is the way of the world'. He reached out and touched Carpenter's arm almost sadly. 'If it were not us here, it would be the Dutch or the Spanish; the French, revolution or not.'

'Sir, the day will come when this land will be truly British, I shall do my utmost when you are gone,' said Carpenter, his voice heavy with emotion.

'I'm sure you will,' Tench said, 'and in the meantime I leave in admiration of Pemulwuy. If I were him, I would do as he has done, except for the stupid fight with the African'. He paused. 'We had in ancient Britain a warrior like Pemulwuy. A Queen, called Boadicea. She was like Hannibal and Vercingatorix for that matter. They were great soldiers in their time, but Rome prevailed, as England, the new Rome, must. God, but history is brutal and filled with ironies.'

There were duties to attend to. Carpenter walked thoughtfully back to barracks.

He wondered idly if the Roman forces in Britain had been as corrupt and inefficient as the Rum Corps. He looked out across the broad bay of Tuhbowgule, shimmering in the humid heat, and it occurred to him that perhaps one of his own ancestors, seventeen hundred years before, might have died at the hands of a Roman. He hoped it had been quick and clean, in battle with a worthy opponent. The fate of the natives in New South Wales, he thought, would be much more slow and agonising—gradual strangulation by Macarthur, Abbott, and the rest of the Rum Corps.

If Pemulwuy was dead, he had chosen his moment well, and died in triumph and with dignity, he thought.

Major Francis Grose resigned his post around the time that Tench left the colony. Reasons of health were given. Paterson took over as Acting Governor of New South Wales. At no time was any report forwarded to London regarding the attack on Brickfield. A casual reference was made to the death of a certain native troublemaker, but the circumstances were not described in detail. So far as London was concerned, all was quiet in the antipodes; the stage was set fair for a continuing policy of coexistence with the natives.

Such was the beauty of illusion from twelve thousand miles away. And who was going to spoil the Colonial Office's dream?

A long winter of silence hung heavily on New South Wales. Nobody really believed that Pemulwuy was dead. In fact many British and Eoras believed that he could not be killed.

The sharp chill of the westerly winds swept into the land of the Eora.

These were the Aboriginal winds gathered from the cold hinterland of the huge continent, set to roam across the great silent deserts of *Terra Australis.*

They descended from her blue mountains and scalded with cold the tears of her mourners.

Narewe pulled her cloak close around her against the chill. The mourning cuts on her head had long healed, and her sorrow had turned to bitterness. Awabakal, Milli and Coleleu had watched and restrained her from taking a personal revenge against the British, but they did not understand the depth of her loss.

Narewe knew and understood the great capacity for violence and cruelty among the Europeans, but she had also known a special secret about them. Buried within their violence and will was a tender and passionate love, almost a thing of the mind. Now the people who brought it to her had taken it away.

Even in the chill of this winter, her rage would well up and blind her for days. Poor Awabakal and Coleleu, they tried to console her, but their simple acceptance of Pemulwuy's truth enraged her more. She found some solace with Millicent, but whatever war was, it seemed always to end in death. The stupid British did not seem to care about that. Dying to them seemed some grand thing to do. Why did they not go and do their dying somewhere else, and leave the Eora world alone? But then they had brought her Gurrewe, her great clumsy, soft, beautiful Irishman, but they had spilled his blood on her land.

There was no more rage now. Nargel had found her own truth to it all. In her womb a child moved and it would live after Pemulwuy and the British were long dead.

CHAPTER 22

TERRA NULLIUS

No-one was more pleased than the Eora at Grose's resignation and the accession of William Paterson as acting Governor. This change, and Pemulwuy's attack on Brickfield, meant a setback to Macarthur's plans for headlong expansion. Paterson, for all his brave words to the departing Phillip two years earlier, quickly decided on a policy of caution. The extent of the Brickfield disaster had been diplomatically hidden from London, but he could not risk more fiascos on the same scale. The Grose-Macarthur plan was shelved. Paterson agreed that established settlements like Parramatta and Toongabbie should not be abandoned, but he ordered that farming only be carried on within a fortified area one mile beyond the perimeter of each town. Stage two of the old Ross plan was also to be adopted. It proposed close settlements of the land between the Parramatta and Georges Rivers, with easy water access.

Paterson's main aim was that the place should look shipshape. He was an ambitious man, and even at this stage he may have believed that a period of good housekeeping might encourage the government at home to leave him in acting command of the colony, or even to appoint him Governor.

Macarthur, Abbott and the rest of the Rum Corps went along with the plan. There was growing anxiety that Phillip, known to be making mischief in the corridors of power in London, might encourage the British government to dispatch another regiment of troops to the colony, breaking their military and economic monopoly. This prospect was horrifying. It could even end in American type treaties with the natives. If there was one thing on which they agreed, it was that New South Wales should be viewed as *Terra Nullius*, a country in which no-one had exercised sovereignty or owned land before the British had arrived. The *Terra Nullius* doctrine, based on the (to alien eyes) hopelessly primitive native way of life, treated Australia in all practical terms as an uninhabited continent.

The early emancipists, proponents of freed-convict settlement, such as Lord Cable and Underwood, had little liking for the jailers of the Rum Corps, but they readily supported *Terra Nullius*. Most were anxious to ensure title to the new land being opened up to the north and west.

Pemulwuy had been the great barrier to that expansion. This united Rum Corps potentates and emancipists alike. The Eora victory at Brickfield, followed by the news of Pemulwuy's death, meant days of high drama for the colony.

The British camp was not, however, united. Some considered Judge Advocate Collins a danger to Rum Corps rule. He advocated an idealised, enlightened British rule. Collins was not in principle opposed to *Terra Nullius*, but he could not support the kind of brigandry being practised by prominent officers in the New South Wales Corps. His aim, the gossips said, was not the acquisition of land but high office—perhaps the colony's highest.

There were even dissident voices in the Rum Corps itself. The inconvenient Lieutenant Frances Marshall, despite his harsh experiences at the hands of Pemulwuy, had been heard to declare that the idea of Australia as an empty continent was absurd: the natives were clearly the owners of the place. Even worse, he was known to spend a lot of time in the company of Carpenter, who in turn had been influenced by Tench's notions of 'legitimate conquest'.

The colony of New South Wales was, in short, a hotbed of gossip and intrigue. Alliances and enmities were petty and personal. Huge the continent might be, but its destiny was in the hands of a population no bigger than that of a fair-sized English market town, and the power-brokers were a tiny group of men without clear central direction, and very little in the way of decent ideals or intellectual capacity.

Nevertheless, the Rum Corps barons seemed to have plenty of reason to congratulate themselves. There was suspicion that Tench's motives for leaving New South Wales with an uncharacteristic lack of resistance did not bode well for the Corps. Some claimed that he intended to join forces with Phillip and Bennelong when he returned to Britain and make trouble. For the moment, however, the important thing was that he was out of the way. And, of course, Pemulwuy was supposed to be dead.

The rumours that Pemulwuy had not been killed persisted, but by the beginning of 1795 there had been no reliable reports of his whereabouts or health. The British again grew confident that the threat to their declared sovereignty had passed.

Collins, meanwhile, had turned his attention to the rum trade, which had expanded under the acting governorships of Grose and Paterson.

'It's a scandal,' he told Carpenter. 'On some evenings, I swear half the population is in a state of intoxication. Children are neglected, women abused. It's worse than Gin Lane!' He stopped in mid-flight, and then added, 'there are orphaned children all over the place. The only care they receive is from native families who adopt them. The situation is intolerable'.

Carpenter shrugged. 'What did you expect, Mr Collins? The New South Wales Corps are nothing but a pack of brigands and pirates. They have become more powerful than any governor. Soldiers who are a disgrace to the flag….'

Collins and Carpenter continued to seek each other out for nightly talks over a glass or two of wine. One evening, Carpenter seemed disturbed.

'I have it on good authority that a *Yoo Lay* ceremony is to be held at Port Hacking,' he told the Judge Advocate. Like him, Collins was aware that at this ceremony young Eora men entering adulthood had a front tooth removed. It was a major event in the Eora calendar. 'More importantly, though, sir,' he added, 'I am also told that Pemulwuy is alive and well and will be attending the event'.

Collins started. 'Impossible! He would not have the gall. Besides, if he were still alive, he would have showed his ugly face somewhere by now.'

'I believe he would indeed dare attend, sir. Such outrageous and provocative acts have always been his speciality. I believe that the reason that no-one has seen the man is that nobody is prepared to go out at some risk, to look.'

'Then you believe your information to be accurate?' said Collins.

'I do,' Collins looked thoughtful. 'I would suggest, Mr Carpenter, that you do not divulge this news to anyone else, especially any member of the New South Wales Corps. I trust you have not already done so....'

'No, sir.'

'Good. What is your intention?'

'To lead an expedition to the place and observe the ceremony discreetly.' 'Even better!' Collins smiled, 'I should very much like to accompany you on the expedition. As you may be aware, I made sketches of such an event some years ago, but I should be glad to confirm the actual method of avulsing the tooth'.

Carpenter, if he was honest, failed to understand Collins's interest in such things—he personally considered his expedition more of a prudent military measure—but Tench had told him that the Judge Advocate was keen to gain recognition in British learned circles for his first-hand studies of the New South Wales primitives.

'It could be dangerous, sir,' Carpenter said doubtfully, 'I shall be taking a leaf out of Pemulwuy's book and moving my men in small, highly mobile groups, assembling them at agreed points'.

'Works, does it?' said Collins.

'In the bush it proved very successful.'

'Even if Pemulwuy should by chance appear, he would surely respect the interests of scientific research,' said Collins.

'Er...I suppose he would, sir,' said Carpenter, but thought that, for a scholar, Collins had a lot to learn.

Nargel gave birth to a son in December 1795. He was a remarkably big infant, and Narewe had considerable difficulty in delivering the child.

The child was very fair, almost the colour of his deceased father at the height of his suntan. The two women with her were appalled. Milli said that the child had a beautiful colour. The others were unconvinced. It was no wonder she felt such pain; she had given birth to an alien child. Narewe argued that his skin was not as white as the British and Milli said that English children were born red. But the old women insisted that he was the product of some odd spirit and should be killed.

Coleleu was near at hand and sought Yenowee's intervention. Both Yenowee and Koobee went to see the child.

Yenowee stared uncertainly at the strange infant. In all parts he was like an Eora child, but the colour of his skin was different. Yenowee had always been concerned that the British had not dealt with the Irishman's corpse properly. Now he feared that instead of being the Irishman's child it might be a terrible creature re-infected with its father's spirit. Koobee was also worried about this.

Koobee pointed out that the child, unlike the British, had a foreskin on his penis, as did Eora people. This observation surprised Yenowee.

'Did you not know that the British mutilate their children's genitals?' Milli said, 'it is to do with their religion'.

She did not know why. Koobee said nothing, simply brushing the pierced septum of his nose.

Then Koobee and Yenowee entered the more promising argument that the child was the product of two good spirits; one Irish, one Eora.

Finally Koobee picked up the infant in his arms.

'He is a beautiful child; not half of anything. He has a new spirit and it comes from two lands. You should call him *Boolayoo*.' This was a constructed word which meant, more or less, 'belonging to two things'.

Millicent kissed her friend and said quietly. 'Nargel, wherever the British go they build castles like where Gurrewe died. Here they built their castles at Tuhbowgule. One day your baby will inherit them.'

That ended the matter. From now on, nobody dared challenge Narewe or her child.

The military technique borrowed from Pemulwuy worked very well. Carpenter successfully assembled a force of fifty men at a vantage point overlooking the place at Port Hacking where ceremonies were normally held. They began to move in on the supposed gathering.

A small family of Wanegal people were terrified to find themselves suddenly surrounded by the military might of Britain. Once they had calmed down, they told Collins and Carpenter that the ceremony had already taken place. It had been held a week before on the south shore of Botany Bay, and Pemulwuy had been there.

'We were duped, by God!' exclaimed Carpenter.. 'I confess I'm beginning to believe that Pemulwuy is alive. This is typical of him!'

'A wild-goose chase….' growled Collins. He had travelled on horseback, but it had nevertheless been a long and arduous trip from Sydney.

Carpenter shrugged, 'we'll cross the Georges River further up, then follow the road back to Parramatta. There is no point in wasting time here'.

Collins decided that, at least for him, the expedition would not be wasted. He proposed to Carpenter that he be given a small military escort. He would proceed along the coast towards Botany

Bay. That way he could gather samples of the beach coal, which had become of considerable interest to the colony as a source of fuel. Carpenter reluctantly gave him two men from the New South Wales Corps, both corporals.

After leaving the main party, Collins and his escorts travelled slowly down the coast. He planned, once they reached the fortified position on the south side of Botany Bay, to leave the soldiers and the horses there and head back to Port Jackson by boat, thus giving him further opportunity to inspect the patterns of the beach coal deposits.

About five miles short of the bay, they came upon a small beach that appeared to be very rich in coal. Collins dismounted and handed the reins of his horse to one of the corporals.

'Wait here,' he said, 'I shall have a closer look'.

Eager to inspect the beach, he climbed quickly down to the sea's edge, and within moments he was out of sight of his two companions. Then there was an agonised scream from the beach.

The two corporals leapt from their horses and raced down towards the sea. Collins came into view at the foot of a small, sandy slope. He was lying on his back about forty yards away with a spear sticking out of his left thigh. Near to him stood an Eora man holding another spear. He turned to look almost curiously at the two soldiers. They fired their muskets simultaneously. The balls either completely missed their target or—as one man later claimed—passed clean through him.

'By Christ, it's Pemulwuy!' said one of the men.

'I could swear I hit him.' the other muttered.

They started to move forward again gingerly, keeping an eye on the black man, who did not seem to be paying any attention to them now.

Then there was a snort and a scuffle from the scrub. They turned round only to see their horses disappearing into the bush. Before they could move, they were hit with a hail of spears.

One of the corporals was virtually pinned to the ground by a spear in his side. His companion dragged him over the rise into a small dip in the sand. 'Can you reload?' he hissed.

'I can try.' Another volley of spears, but this time no injury.

The unwounded man succeeded in reloading a musket, readied it and gave the other to his injured comrade to prime. Meanwhile, he put his head up cautiously but could see no target in sight. Collins was now alone on the beach. His assailant had vanished as mysteriously as he had appeared.

'How are you, sir?' he called out.

'Get this spear out of me!' was all the Judge Advocate could find in himself to say.

'Is it bad, sir?'

'It hurts badly. That's all I know!'

It was some minutes before the corporal dared make the run across the sand to Collins. The sight of the spear impaled in Collins's thigh almost made him vomit.

'Corporal Johnson's been hit. I have removed the spear. It caught the bottom of his ribs, I think,' he told Collins.

'Get this thing out of my leg, corporal.'

The corporal cut away the surrounding clothing. Collins, still lucid, though in great pain, told him to cut the shaft of the spear off and pull it through. It was a difficult operation, performed with the tip of a bayonet, and took almost half an hour.

When the spear was finally removed, Collins fainted and the corporal bound the leg tightly to prevent bleeding.

The two wounded men were made comfortable on the beach and left with a musket each. The fit corporal took Collins's pistol and set off through the bush to Botany Bay to fetch help.

CHAPTER 23

THE DAY OF THE FOX

'There is no doubt about it. It was Pemulwuy. The musket balls did not pass through him. They missed him by a mile.'

Collins lifted himself up on his elbow and repositioned the pillow.

'He is a bloody madman!' he said. 'He stepped out of nowhere and asked me if I was looking for him. I said I was and told him that I was unarmed. The animal then speared me without provocation.'

It was almost a fortnight since David Collins had been brought into the hospital in Sydney. He had been very ill, and the surgeon had predicted that he would lose the leg.

For a week he lay in a critical condition, but slowly he began to recover. Carpenter was his first visitor, and though Collins was weak he was anxious to tell his story.

'They say that you may not be able to walk for months,' said Carpenter. 'I suppose you know that Paterson appointed that drunkard Atkins to act as Judge Advocate.'

Before Collins could answer, they were joined by Lieutenant Marshall.

Collins retold the events of his wounding.

'He did almost the same thing to me once,' said Marshall, 'sometimes, he is completely out of his mind'.

'Mad as a fox,' interjected Carpenter, 'mad as a fox!'

'There was a time when I thought better of the man,' said Collins, 'but he is simply a savage and that's an end to it'.

The three discussed the future. All agreed that the present approach adopted by Paterson would make things very difficult for any renewed activity on Pemulwuy's part. Incursions into the two western valleys had eased. The fortified perimeter farms would make things very hard, even for an old fox like Pemulwuy.

As Carpenter and Marshall were leaving the hospital, Carpenter turned to Collins.

'If only Pemulwuy knew how close he is in forcing us to negotiate.'

'Captain Tench believed that he was close to forcing evacuation before the fight with the African', said Carpenter.

Collins laughed with a touch of hysteria. 'That's possibly true,' he said, 'but nobody can even talk, let alone negotiate with that madman.' He paused and became serious, 'kill Pemulwuy, gentlemen, and we may yet find a better way to start New South Wales, a respectable way'.

Under Eora law and the adopted relationship between the Irishman and Pemulwuy, Nargel became a wife to Pemulwuy. Tedbury's mother Boorea did not particularly like Nargel, although she had to put up with her. As a result of this, Nargel and her son spent a good deal of time with Koobee's family. This was a good arrangement and Pemulwuy approved of it.

Koobee's people had suffered greatly from a smallpox epidemic in 1789. In early June that year an outbreak of measles among the remaining Kamergal took the lives of both of Koobee's children. Strangely, Narewe's child, Boolayoo, seemed completely resistant to the disease. Milbab was inconsolable and resented Boolayoo. The little boy had grown to love Milbab and could not understand her change in attitude. He spent many nights in tears.

After three weeks Milbab weakened and became affectionate again towards the child. Narewe understood the situation and decided to leave the child at the camp for a while. She joined Yenowee, Weuong and Gomil at a camp some six miles north of Parramatta where they were waiting for Pemulwuy. Pemulwuy arrived a week later with Awabakal and Tedbury. After the African's death, William Knight had drifted into Daruk country and was said to be living with a group near the foot of the mountains. Millicent Copley remained with a Bidjigal group with Nargel. Koobee and others joined the group a few days later and an alodim began.

They discussed the much tighter approach that had now been adopted by the British. Koobee told them that a new British Governor was to come the next summer. He also told them that the ordinary soldiers in the Rum Corps were drinking very heavily and appeared less and less able to fight.

Pemulwuy was puzzled that the British had not adopted any form of new armaments, such as shields, to deal with the Eora. He was keenly interested to hear of the new Governor. He insisted that they attack the western towns before he arrived.

It was agreed that they must carefully examine the Parramatta perimeter.

The idea of attacking Parramatta did not impress Koobee and Yenowee, but Tedbury and Awabakal were delighted with the prospect.

It was mid-July when an American whaler anchored in Sydney Cove, carrying an auxiliary cargo of whale oil and South American rum. The ship brought a letter addressed to Lieutenant Carpenter. Carpenter's excitement grew when he realised that it was from none other than Watkin Tench:

Lieutenant James Carpenter

Dear James, I write to you in great haste and therefore with brevity. The captain of an American whaler bound for New South Wales with a cargo of rum has agreed to deliver this letter. We are anchored together in the Bay of Islands in New Zealand. I urgently wish you to know that I have realised Pemulwuy's weakness. The fact is that he cannot justify heavy casualties, no matter how glorious the victory. Both the natives' religion and their natural disinclination to large-scale warfare put them, and Pemulwuy, at a grave disadvantage. We, on the other hand, can bear almost any level of casualties in the cause of victory. I admit that this comparison of two races' attitudes gives me cause for some sadness. Who knows, but Pemulwuy's inhibition is not the mark of a superior spirit! Nevertheless, we are British soldiers and there is a war to be won. Use this information with care. I shall write again when I reach England...

My best regards

Watkin Tench
Royal Marines

Carpenter immediately decided to consult Collins, now convalescing at his cottage and gradually beginning to take a more active part in the colony's affairs once more. 'Sir,' he said, 'this could be of vital importance don't you see?'

Collins sat back in his chair, resting his leg on a low stool. 'Yes, yes,' he said. 'I realise that there may be truth in our friend Mr Tench's observation and I suppose it bodes ill for Pemulwuy in the long run. But, short of our deliberately encouraging the spilling of native blood—which would put us on the level of barbarians—I cannot see how we can exploit this weakness'.

'Well, sir,' said Carpenter, 'there will be those willing to do that very thing'.

'But not our new Governor,' Collins told him. 'I have information that the peace party in London have argued successfully. The Colonial Office wants tranquil relations with the natives, not bloodshed, and for all my horror at the behaviour of creatures such as Pemulwuy, I continue to sympathise with that point of view'.

Carpenter nodded. 'Time will tell.'

It was only a few days later that attacks on the perimeter farms to the west of Sydney began. Initially there were just sporadic raids on livestock, but on 22 July a farmhouse was attacked and set on fire.

Macarthur pleaded with Paterson for more troops to guard the perimeter. Paterson, who was close to panic, refused, saying that he feared another attack on Sydney. The colony's forces were already seriously overextended.

From 26 July to 2 August, Pemulwuy and his warriors rampaged around the whole perimeter, burning and looting—and always keeping a step ahead of the Rum Corps' patrols. The Bidjigals avoided any close combat, being satisfied with distant spear attacks, stealing livestock and burning.

Carpenter, pinned down at Sydney, observed that it was some sort of terror campaign—and it worked.

Finally Macarthur was forced to evacuate the settlers to Parramatta. On 4 August, a patrol of twenty men were ambushed at a heavily fortified farm on the Parramatta Road. The battle raged for about half an hour until the farm stockade was destroyed by fire. The British defenders steeled themselves, fixed bayonets, and waited. Nothing happened. A relief group arrived just after noon; still no attack was mounted. Macarthur prepared himself for an all-out assault on Parramatta, but once again nothing happened. No attack came.

Macarthur was summoned to Sydney, leaving a Lieutenant Palmer in command. At the residence, an emergency meeting was convened by Paterson, and Carpenter was among those invited.

'I am convinced,' Paterson told the conference, 'that Pemulwuy intends to attack Sydney again. If such an incursion were to succeed, even partially, I could never forgive myself, or explain it to London, for that matter'. He looked hard at Macarthur, who simply pursed his lips and stared at the ceiling. 'I believe that these raids on the western farms are half-hearted affairs designed to draw our very limited forces away from Sydney, thus exposing us to an attack. Your opinions gentlemen?'

Macarthur made no move to push for reinforcements.

Carpenter decided it was time to say his piece. 'Sir,' he began, 'while agreeing that Sydney is indeed vulnerable, I would dispute that the raids on the western settlements were no more than feints. Human casualties have been low—though we cannot say the same of livestock loss, which is considerable. I must, however, remind you that the damage done to the actual defensive works has been serious. In fact, it would not be an exaggeration to say that the perimeter defences lie in ruins'.

'But we cannot leave Sydney defenseless, man!' said Paterson testily. 'If we were wrong and Pemulwuy attacked us, it would be a scandal of the first magnitude, a disaster that would profoundly undermine the British position in this land.' And your own reputation, thought Carpenter.

'I am firmly convinced that Pemulwuy will not attack Sydney,' rejoined Carpenter, keeping his temper firmly in check, 'from a military point of view as we understand it, he undoubtedly could attack Sydney. But, because of the traditions of his people, he could not risk the high rate of casualties that such an attack would certainly involve…as it did last time. For so many of his men to die violently outside their own land, where their spirits must supposedly reside in some way after death—I believe that such a thing would be unacceptable to Pemulwuy'.

Abbott was grinning broadly, as was Macarthur. Carpenter had been careful not to mention Tench's name while developing his argument, but everyone in the room knew that the opinion he was expressing had to be Tench's. 'Thank you for that short religious discourse,' said Paterson dryly, 'do you have any practical suggestions?'

Carpenter reddened, 'yes, sir, in practical terms the only sense I can see in Pemulwuy's recent activities point to his softening our defences in preparation for an attack on Parramatta itself. I am aware that this too might cost him dearly, but it is possible, even probable, that such is his intention.' He fell silent.

Macarthur shook his head. 'So, my dear Carpenter, first our Pemulwuy is a shrinking violet, frightened his boys might get hurt, and then he is a military genius again.' He threw up his plump hands in mock despair. Then his eyes narrowed. 'The native mentality is little better than that of a pack of dogs,' he snapped, 'they simply attack where they think there is plunder to be had'.

'If dogs are all they are, they have given us a damned bad time!' Carpenter retorted hotly.

Paterson called them to order. Macarthur continued in more measured tones.

'I grant that Pemulwuy must conserve his forces where he can,' he said. 'And I propose two things: first that the defensive positions around Parramatta be strengthened and extended. It is essential that farm land be kept in production. Second, I propose that Mr Carpenter be put in command of a substantial mobile force, and that he be charged with clearing the recalcitrant natives from the area around Parramatta,' he smiled wolfishly, 'he obviously believes he has the measure of these blacks. I am only too willing to let him prove he is right!'

This was a deception; he expected Pemulwuy to attack on the other side of the perimeter and was secretly preparing to meet the attack. The second rumour was spread deliberately by soldiers to convicts. Somehow, once information had got to the convicts it was always passed on to the Eora.

CHAPTER 24

NORTH ONE MILE

Carpenter felt all the loneliness of a prophet unheard. Sometimes it seemed he was the only European left in New South Wales who had any real understanding of the threat Pemulwuy represented. Paterson had sent him out with a force of fifty men to patrol the Parramatta perimeter farms. Naturally, Pemulwuy never came near him. As for Macarthur, using his position as autonomous baron of the colony's western marches, he was constantly pressing the reluctant settlers to return to their recently evacuated farms, which made Carpenter's task difficult, if not impossible. As soon as a farmer returned, he became a target, and there were simply not enough resources to guard every farm. Carpenter greatly admired the courage—or foolhardiness—of these colonists, because the Eora never left them alone. As more settlers returned, Carpenter was faced with the prospect of splitting his forces and playing into Pemulwuy's hands.

Pemulwuy did not attack the township of Parramatta itself. Carpenter felt that it was the existence of his force that deterred any direct attack on the town. And unless Pemulwuy did attack a fortified position, there was no chance of inflicting serious losses on the Eora... The result was a stalemate occasionally broken by hit-and-run violence.

Carpenter had another fundamental problem. The Eora's intelligence network was extraordinary. They had precise information on every move Carpenter and his detachment made. Eventually, in his frustration, Carpenter was led into a desperate manoeuvre that was very nearly successful.

A small detachment of the New South Wales Corps was bringing some provisions out to a perimeter farm originally known as Macalister's Mistake. It had recently been dubbed North One Mile Depot. Carpenter, aware that his every order was being leaked to Pemulwuy, announced that his force, divided into two sections, would meet the shipment. This was, in fact, his intention. However, he spread another rumour—that the order was a deception; that he expected Pemulwuy to attack the other side of the perimeter and that he was secretly preparing to meet that attack. Carpenter had found that the rumour path was from soldier to convict to the Eora.

Pemulwuy and Yenowee compared the rumours.

'I think that Mr Carpenter is trying to trick us,' said Yenowee. Pemulwuy agreed, but was uncertain about what he was up to.

'It's simple,' said Yenowee, 'we have enough men to attack both positions'.

'No!' said Pemulwuy. 'We will attack Parramatta.'

'But you have always said it would cost us too many people.'

'This will be a trick attack to create confusion among the British.'

Pemulwuy carefully outlined the plan. Whatever Carpenter intended to do, Pemulwuy would wait until he was well clear of the town, then personally lead a diversionary attack on the town. This would draw Carpenter away from the North One Mile and Yenowee would attack it with a large force. Meanwhile, the people should evacuate Waun camp and move further down the north side of the harbour. There Awabakal, Tedbury and Koobee would prepare and attack the settlements the British called Lane Cove and Kissing Point.

Pemulwuy and Yenowee would withdraw northward after their attacks. If Carpenter tried to go down the north side of the harbour to Lane Cove, both Pemulwuy and Yenowee would attack him. The country would provide an excellent situation for distant spear attacks.

Carpenter's force divided just outside Parramatta. One rode to the east and one to the west. About half a mile out, they swung north. Carpenter was with the western group when he received an urgent message that Pemulwuy was attacking Parramatta in person.

The lieutenant leant against a tree, his smooth face suddenly heavy with despair.

'There's no end to the bastard,' he said. 'He has outfoxed me.'

He gave the situation some thought, and it occurred to him that Pemulwuy might be planning to draw him back to Parramatta while the Eora attacked North One Mile after all. He decided to take a risk.

'Tell Captain Macarthur that I shall return with all haste,' he told the waiting dispatch-rider.

The messenger turned his horse for Parramatta. Carpenter got together his remaining section, ready to follow, but deliberately sent no message to stop the eastern detachment from homing in on North One Mile. As he expected, there was no sign of Pemulwuy when he reached Parramatta. Two buildings were on fire. The raid had been swift and superficial. The really startling news was that Pemulwuy had been shot in the head.

Apparently the Eora leader had headed the attack and cast the first burning spear. A settler had loosened off a shot at him and claimed that he had seen him topple to the ground, then get up and run away, clutching his head.

Carpenter made a desperate attempt to persuade Macarthur to combine his garrison forces with his and to intercept any attack on North One Mile. Macarthur refused point blank to leave Parramatta. A bitter, desperate Carpenter wheeled his horse once more and led his section back towards the original rendezvous point.

Yenowee's original attack on North One Mile was successful, inflicting heavy casualties on the mixture of Rum Corps troops and settlers at the depot. He was about to disengage when Carpenter's eastern force, heading for the rendezvous with their commander, attacked him from the rear. The first musket fusillade did not take a heavy toll, but Yenowee could see that his forces would be cut to pieces if they tried to retreat. In desperation, he led his men in a Black Caesar-style massed attack on the musket section. Fifteen of his men were killed in the fighting, and Yenowee was himself wounded by a bayonet in his chest and shoulder. The battle that followed was waged savagely on both sides. Both the settlers and the Rum Corps men from the depot joined in the fighting and suffered heavy casualties.

By the time Carpenter arrived with his other section, after a headlong ride from Parramatta, the Eoras had effectively broken out into open country, at enormous cost. He tried, by more hard riding, to cut them off to the west, but there he met a heavy barrage of spears from Pemulwuy's group and had to make a hasty retreat.

When Carpenter counted the Eora dead, he was sure that by tragic accident he had won a significant victory over Pemulwuy. Eora casualties had been very heavy, and the Eora would be crippled by grief when the morning came.

Macarthur would hear nothing of victory. He considered that Carpenter had bungled the entire operation.

'I hold you personally responsible for the lives of the settlers killed in this incident, lieutenant!' he said, 'and I shall ensure everyone knows it!'

Carpenter, exhausted and still horrified by the carnage, came close to violence.

'Macarthur, had you had the courage to leave Parramatta and join in the rescue of North One Mile, lives would have been saved and a crushing blow dealt to the natives! You are a coward, sir!'

'I shall write a report!' blustered Macarthur.

'That you will not, sir. Such a document might find its way into the hands of a real British soldier, and that is a risk you could never take.'

Macarthur stamped out of the room. He would have to travel to Sydney himself and settle the thing.

Then, in the middle of the night, as the British licked their wounds in Parramatta, a messenger arrived to inform Macarthur that Pemulwuy had not rested. After the North One Mile incident, he had proceeded to attack both the Lane Cove and Kissing Point settlements. Reinforcements were on their way by water from Sydney, but more immediate help was desperately needed.

Macarthur summoned Carpenter to his house.

'As your superior rank, I order you to take a force down the north side of the harbour and attack the enemy from the rear,' he said coldly.

Carpenter could not believe his ears. 'With what? I would be lucky to get twenty able-bodied men under arms! To march down the wooded north side of the harbour with such a small force would be both suicidal and futile.'

'That is an order!'

Suddenly Carpenter's anger left him. He felt a strange calm, a certainty that Macarthur might well be sending him to his death. So be it. If he survived and got back to Sydney, he would find a way of breaking this conspiracy of silence before it cost more Englishmen their lives. The colony must either fight Pemulwuy with all its resources, and destroy him, or make peace. The present situation, neither war nor peace, suited only land-hungry brigands such as Macarthur. And, of course, a guerrilla leader like Pemulwuy.

He offered no resistance when Macarthur gave him ten men. At dawn he and his tiny force marched out of Parramatta.

In fact, they reached Lane Cove without even sighting an Eora. All the signs showed that the natives were busy disposing of their dead. He had been right. Almost inadvertently, he had won a major victory over Pemulwuy.

The Lane Cove and Kissing Point settlements had been attacked simultaneously. Casualties had not been high—perhaps the edge had been taken off Pemulwuy's bloodlust by the North One Mile deaths—but the settlers' properties had been severely damaged. Almost all their stock had been killed, houses had been burnt, and tools and provisions and gunpowder stolen.

Lieutenant Marshall had already arrived from Sydney with a cutter and thirty men. He and Carpenter immediately decided that the remaining settlers must be evacuated to Sydney without delay. Kissing Point would be abandoned and a garrison left at Lane Cove.

The two officers sat down together in one of the intact cottages. Both were grey-faced with fatigue, and Marshall's foot was causing him some pain. Carpenter was more bitter and disillusioned than ever before.

'But still, they will not call this a war. Still there is no mention of Pemulwuy in dispatches to London, still no demand for reinforcements from home,' said Carpenter, 'too many men here have an interest in secrecy and land. Sometimes I think that Pemulwuy is right about the stealing of land'.

Marshall remembered sadly that the last time he had heard a statement like that, it was in a Bidjigal camp and it was made by a man called Awabakal. He shrugged and unbuttoned his tunic.

'I can only offer one morsel of hope,' he said. 'It seems that Captain John Hunter's appointment as Governor has been confirmed. He is already on his way to New South Wales and is expected in about two months. Perhaps the colony will now have a strong, honest guiding hand.'

'Not a day too soon,' Carpenter muttered.

He knew of Hunter, and also knew of the ship he had lost, the *Sirius*. Four years before, Hunter had been close to disgrace. However, the fact that he was being sent out as Governor did not necessarily bode well—a failed ship's captain to a failing colony.

'Ah well,' Carpenter said, not wanting to disillusion Marshall, who seemed a decent type for the Rum Corps, if a little wet behind the ears, 'I shall be most interested to hear what Captain Phillip has told him about the situation here'.

They spent some time discussing the future, trying to instill a little optimism. Then Marshall changed the subject.

'By the way,' he said casually, 'I found a curious reference to a meeting between Phillip, Ross and Grose in which they discussed something called galgalla. Do you have any idea what the word means?'

Carpenter frowned. 'Not exactly, I believe it is an Eora word. I once heard Captain Tench mention it—some kind of sickness. He was rather guarded about it, I must admit.'

And so they sat in the cottage by the river and rested as best they could. Perhaps Pemulwuy would leave them in peace until a new governor came, and perhaps that new governor might bring hope to this tormented place.

CHAPTER 25

COMING HOME

Koobee and Awabakal stood on *Garrangel*, the north headland, at dusk and watched the tall ship arrive. This was the ship that carried the new British Governor to Sydney. A stiff nor'easterly wind had her cut down to topsails. He watched her laboriously tack as she set herself to enter the harbour.

Neither man spoke. Two weeks had passed since Pemulwuy had sent them on this vigil. After dark they would cross the harbour and confirm the event. Sydney was far too dangerous to be anywhere about in daylight.

Awabakal wondered idly what this new governor would be like. Another Phillip, he imagined. He went to speak to Koobee; then changed his mind.

Koobee had been so depressed since they arrived at Kayumy, his old home. Nobody lived there now. The Kamergal either feared British reprisals in response to Pemulwuy's activities, or else the few who had survived the smallpox epidemic had died from one of the new sicknesses.

'I suppose there will be more fighting and dying now.'

Awabakal was surprised at Koobee's statement.

'No. It might not be so,' said Awabakal. 'Remember the last governor, Arthur Phillip. He always said that he wanted us to live in peace.'

'Oh yes, I remember,' said Koobee. 'He was the one who sent Tench out to take six Bidjigal heads. He was the one who started it all.'

'I think that it was the Rum Corps, really,' responded Awabakal. 'Remember, *Bacoolong* speared Phillip and he was still friendly.'

'Perhaps you're right,' Koobee kicked at the ground, but what Pemulwuy says is still true. They are stealing our land.'

'But perhaps the new governor will stop them and take the sicknesses away, too.'

'Perhaps.'

The two men walked to where the canoe was hidden and began the long and arduous harbour crossing. They were in no hurry, for they knew that the ship would not dock until the following morning.

The British really turned it on for their new master. Their scrubbed white faces were tinged with pink in the morning sunlight. Awabakal was amazed at the variety of clothing worn by the women. Even the Rum Corps looked respectable, after a fashion. Sergeant Weaver, a notable drunk, stood painfully to attention with his shapeless red nose twitching in the light breeze. A group of manacled Irish convicts squatted behind him, looking quite unimpressed.

The Governor, accompanied by an entourage of aides and Marines, stepped ashore and was saluted by Major Paterson. Awabakal thought that he must learn his name, and he told Koobee he intended to sneak up and ask one of the convicts. He stood up and then quickly dropped to the ground.

'It's Bennelong,' he said in disbelief. 'Bennelong has come back. He was on that ship.'

Koobee peered carefully from their hiding place.

'You go and tell Pemulwuy all that we have seen. I shall wait and make contact with Bennelong,' he said.

Awabakal and some of the other young Bidjigal men had developed a technique of running and resting that allowed them to cover more distance in a day than a man on horseback.

The running became an almost unconscious process. His body selected the footings and guided his steps, while his mind moved across the land in another way. In the eye of his mind the land became alive; its spiritual essence moved and shimmered about him. The sky was not fixed and touched the earth at will. Awabakal now followed a clear path marked by this firmament. He listened to voices that whispered and sang from a thousand mouths in the land. He listened until the sound of his heart stilled the magic land and made him rest.

Pemulwuy still carried the bright scars of the buckshot in his forehead, but the sharp pains in his head had now long passed. Awabakal told him that it was not Arthur Phillip who had returned. It was a stranger, accompanied by Bennelong.

Pemulwuy asked if Yennerawannie had also returned, but Awabakal did not know.

'Bennelong must know much about the place of the British,' he said.

It was well into the night before Koobee felt that it was safe to make contact with Bennelong.

Bennelong was overcome with joy to meet his old friend. He had been very concerned to find almost no Eoras in Sydney and was anxious to hear from Koobee all that had happened in his absence. They talked on into the early hours of the morning. Bennelong was very upset with what he heard, and at the end of Koobee's stories they both went to sleep. Bennelong said that he had much to tell Koobee the following day.

The sun was high in the morning sky when the two awoke. Bennelong informed Koobee that he intended to go out and talk to Pemulwuy.

'He will kill you straight away,' said Koobee.

'Not when you tell him what I have to talk about.'

Bennelong lit a fire in his hearth and prepared something to eat. 'Now let me tell you about England, Koobee,' he said.

Bennelong began by explaining to Koobee that the new governor had been charged by the King to make peace with the Eora.

'Reconciliation,' said Macarthur, 'with a mad dog like Pemulwuy!'

'The Governor is clearly charged by His Majesty to reconcile the natives and that is the fact of the matter.'

Paterson leant forward in his chair.

'Let me assure you that Phillip had all but talked them into sending a regiment of Highlanders out here with Hunter,' he paused, 'Bennelong is to be assisted in every way to open a discourse with the Bidjigal'.

'Well that solves that,' interjected Captain Abbott, 'Pemulwuy will kill him on sight'.

'Gentlemen,' said Paterson amid a general mumbling from the officers of the Corps, 'it is pointless taking an opposed attitude. We are now under Vice-regal direction to get on with this business'.

Koobee met Awabakal halfway back to Pemulwuy's camp. They walked slowly together, retracing Awabakal's footsteps. Koobee carefully repeated the essential facts of Bennelong's amazing adventures in England.

Koobee went through the same procedure at the alodim. There was much discussion and a good deal of relief registered by the older men. Pemulwuy agreed that he would meet with Bennelong at a place on the northern shore of the harbour. Bennelong must come alone.

Within a few days, the news of Bennelong's return and Pemulwuy's agreement to meet him had spread from the Hawkesbury to the far south of the *Tharawal* country. The more important news was that it was being said that the new governor had put an end to the war between the Eora and the British. At first a few black faces of Wanegal and Kamergal gingerly appeared about Sydney. They then disappeared to the point overlooking *Wanun*, to Bennelong's cottage. By the evening of the first day there were thirty or forty people gathered about Bennelong's place. Hunter sent food, wine and two of his domestic staff to assist Bennelong in entertaining his visitors.

Collins noted that no Bidjigal people had appeared, and certainly none of Pemulwuy's known comrades. Paterson ordered the New South Wales Corps not to interfere in any way.

Late that evening Collins reported that Koobee had arrived; and Hunter issued an invitation to both Bennelong and Koobee to join him for afternoon tea the following day.

Bennelong was very pleased to see that Hunter had restored the formality of his office, and he proudly escorted Koobee into the Vice-regal presence.

Bennelong had offered Koobee English clothes and a razor. Koobee had rejected these. He wore a large Bidjigal cloak in Pemulwuy's fashion. Since he was a Kamergal, the large cloak made him look quite small, and his beard lacked the bushy spread of the Bidjigal people. A decorated bone piece through his septum and a similar piece in his hair gave him, however, the newly characteristic look of an Eora soldier and a lieutenant of Pemulwuy.

Koobee walked into the Governor's reception room with Bennelong, who seemed quite at home in the place. He saw a tall, pale man in an impressive-looking uniform which he recognised from their vigil at the harbour. This was the man they called Hunter, who had come from England to rule the British in New South Wales.

The man seemed amiable: less stiff and stern than he had been in front of the military reception committee at the harbour. Koobee noticed that he spoke English differently.

'This gentleman's name is Koobee, Your Excellency,' said Bennelong, pushing Koobee slightly forward.

The Governor smiled and bowed. Koobee made an attempt to imitate the perfunctory movement from the waist, which caused the Governor some amusement. He offered them a seat. Koobee sat down in a strangely soft but stiff-framed chair. To think Englishmen sat for hours in these things! He did not know where to put his limbs, and he could not get his back comfortable.

'So, Mr Koobee, you are a friend of Pemulwuy's, with whom I believe there have been some...misunderstandings. Well, you need have no fear of me,' the Governor said. He had a pleasant voice, with a sound of rolling consonants in it.

'Your voice is different from other Englishmen. Did you also have to learn their language?' Koobee asked, a polite half-joke.

Hunter laughed, and his eyes twinkled as he looked to his aides for support.

'Aha, Mr Koobee. That is because I am not an Englishman. I am a Scotsman! We are different, and we speak differently, but we have the same king and the same God. And so we live together in peace...as I hope you and we can also!'

Koobee was puzzled, but he knew he had to be polite. He asked about the kinship relations between the English and the Scots, and again Hunter made a remark about their king.

'And Mr Pemulwuy, is he in good health?' the Governor asked then, giving up on the complex subject of the United Kingdom.

'He is...well,' said Koobee. This was all getting to be a bit too much. The Governor seemed well meaning, perhaps too much so. It would be hard to explain all of this to Pemulwuy. He felt relieved when, after another few uncomfortable minutes, the interview was over.

'Please tell Mr Pemulwuy that we must talk. There must be a way we can live together, it is what my government wishes,' concluded Hunter as they bid their farewells.

Bennelong escorted Koobee out to the back verandah and said that he had some more business in the residence. He would not be long.

He walked back into the building. He could hear embarrassed laughter in a reception room, where the Governor and his aides were discussing the meeting with Koobee. Hunter was comparing his own Scottish accent with Koobee's clipped English, and his officers were joining in the joke. Collins emerged. He had agreed to have a word with Bennelong before he left.

'Well Bennelong. That was, on the whole, a success. They tell me you are going to visit Pemulwuy and parley with him. Tell him of your experiences in England, and attempt to convince him of the government's good intentions.'

'Yes, but first I shall talk to others—Kamergal and Kardigal. Then I shall talk to Pemulwuy.'

The Judge Advocate had already told Bennelong of his encounter on the beach and his wounding. Bennelong said that Koobee had told him of the attack and he tried to explain to Collins that Pemulwuy had no intention to kill him. He said that that kind of wounding was for a very different reason. Collins would hear none of it and fixed Bennelong with a stern gaze.

'That man is a killer. I hope you realise that. I fear that he will murder you on sight. Will you be able to protect yourself?'

Bennelong smiled. 'I have learnt a lot in England, Mr Collins,' he said, and reached into his pocket, producing a small, delicately worked silver pistol. 'This will easily kill a man at twenty paces, and it is so small that he will not even notice it.'

Collins nodded, 'then good luck, my friend. The peace of this colony and our people's wellbeing depends on you'.

Governor Hunter's quest for peace had begun, and Bennelong was to be its instrument.

CHAPTER 26

PEACE, BROTHER

The Governor offered Bennelong horses for himself and Koobee and an escort of Marines. Bennelong jokingly pointed out that he would spend most of the trip to Pemulwuy's camp picking Koobee up off the ground. He went on to explain more seriously that he would dress and travel as an Eora man. He said it was important that he be seen by his people as one of them. Hunter was impressed by this and left Bennelong to make his own preparations.

Bennelong prepared himself for the journey by first going with Koobee to visit and attend a meeting of Kamergal people at a place near Kamay called *Cronulla*. He removed his clothes, donned a ganimantj hide pubic shield and placed a stick ornament through his nasal septum. He and Koobee walked to Kamay. His skin had become very much lighter, but any concerns Bennelong may have had about the kind of reception that he would receive were swept away by his welcome. The Eora were certainly sick of Pemulwuy's war, and Bennelong told them that it was over. He said that their concerns over the land would all be settled at a big peace meeting after he had spoken with Pemulwuy.

Bennelong sat with the Eora on the sandy shores of Cronulla, where he listened carefully to all that the people had to say. He watched the sea sweep up the beach, spend itself; then retreat from the land. The sea seemed to wash his mind clear of the sadness he felt over the death of Koobee's children. It took his uncertain memories of Tench and Pemulwuy out into the deep clear water and sterilised them under the burning Australian sun.

Koobee and Bennelong camped that night at Cronulla and next morning began the walk back to Sydney. Bennelong felt strangely sore all over. He could not bear to insert the stick in his nasal septum and his feet hurt. Nevertheless they began the journey. By the time they had reached halfway, Bennelong could barely walk. His feet, softened by the wearing of shoes, were cut and blistered. They stopped and Koobee made him some makeshift shoes out of ganimantj hide. The two men struggled on to Sydney, and by the time they had reached his cabin, Bennelong was in great pain and could not bear Koobee to touch him. Koobee wanted to fetch a cardigan, but Bennelong insisted that the Governor's surgeon attend him. The English surgeon was very amused to find that Bennelong had a severe case of sunburn.

It was a week before Bennelong felt able to undertake his journey and the meeting with Pemulwuy. He decided, on second thoughts, that he would accept the Governor's offer of horses. Bennelong had become an accomplished rider while in England. He suggested that Koobee learn to ride one of the animals before they left. Koobee was pleased with the opportunity, but this led to a further three days delay. Koobee felt insecure at having a saddle between himself and the horse and insisted on riding bareback. The result of this was that he severely hurt two rather delicate parts of his lower anatomy. He could not walk for one day and felt barely recovered by the time they left. Bennelong maintained his determination to wear Eora clothing. This time however, he took with him a large Eora-styled cloak which he had had made from wolf skins while in England. In the late Australian summer it was unbearably hot, but it was, Bennelong thought, a protection against sunburn.

It was a slow trip because Koobee refused to ride and led the horse that he been given. This very much annoyed Bennelong, and he said angrily: 'Why did you bring the damned thing?'

'I can always eat it,' Koobee replied nonchalantly.

The welcome at Goman camp was somewhat restrained, but Awabakal was delighted to hear of Koobee's adventures with the horse and he spent a good part of the afternoon trying to encourage other men to try to ride or at least to pat the horse on the rump.

Pemulwuy sat down with Bennelong and shared some cold ganimantj which Bennelong had not tasted for a long time. Bennelong talked about England and Pemulwuy questioned him intently. Towards dusk, Bennelong stood up and addressed Pemulwuy.

'I bring you a gift from England,' he said.

He handed Pemulwuy the small silver pistol. Pemulwuy was most impressed. The two were joined by Yenowee, Gomil and some others. They spent the next hour blowing bits of bark off a blue gum tree. Pemulwuy was amazed at the power of the tiny machine. He turned to Bennelong.

'We will all come to your peace meeting in Sydney. We shall talk of it tomorrow, and then he ordered a feast of ganimanti and a variety of other foods and later in the night there was dancing and painting up.

Late in the night, some of the young men introduced Bennelong to new game that they had invented, called *monoe.* The game was played by placing a little hot water in a rum flask. Someone then put their big toe over the entrance to the flask while cold water was poured onto the flask. If the toe was withdrawn at a certain time, it made a great hollow sound and everyone shouted out.

Bennelong was not terribly impressed and tried twice without any success. Pemulwuy then tried the game. He left his toe there just a little too long, and his toe was drawn firmly into the flask. Pemulwuy let go a howl of pain and leapt into the air, flask attached. In the ensuing struggle to free his toe, Pemulwuy's sense of humour completely deserted him. The young men cleared out and Bennelong thought that the peace meeting was in jeopardy.

The next morning Pemulwuy had regained most of his composure. He assisted Bennelong in rescuing Koobee's horse from being the main course for the evening meal. Pemulwuy sternly told Koobee that both he and Awabakal would ride it back to Sydney. Awabakal went pale at this prospect and promptly disappeared. Yenowee volunteered, but Pemulwuy said that he wanted Awabakal to accompany him. Pemulwuy and Bennelong formally concluded their business by the afternoon, and Bennelong turned his mind to more serious matters.

Bennelong sought news of the woman *Goniana*, who had been promised to be his bride before he left For Sydney. He discovered that she was now the wife of a man called *Yerrinibee* and that Goniana now had two children. This very unsatisfactory state of affairs was repaired in part by Goniana's family's promising her younger sister Gnooroin to Bennelong as a wife. This would take a great deal of further negotiation and could only be concluded by a certain type of meeting with Yerrinibee. Yerrinibee was not present, and Bennelong said that they should meet in Sydney.

Captain John Hunter was very pleased with Bennelong's tidings.

'Did he place any conditions on these talks?' he asked.

'None whatsoever,' Bennelong replied.

Paterson found the situation quite unbelievable. Worse still, he could find no way in which he could take any of the credit.

The New South Wales Corps was ominously silent about the whole affair and Carpenter strutted about Sydney with his new-found marine colleagues. Macarthur left Sydney soon after hearing of the proposed peace meeting. It was rumoured that he was headed a long way up the Georges River. Relations between the locals and the British had improved remarkably. Many of the townspeople had taken advantage of the lull in hostilities to open up trade relations with the Eora. Fresh meat began to appear for sale in all parts of the town. The British were surprised to find that they had acquired an Eora name '*Gubba*'. David Collins thought that it was drawn from the word the Eora used for musket. The Eora discovered that some other language changes had occurred during their cessation of relations with the British. The Eora word for women, 'Djin', had degenerated to 'gin'. This was, in fact, the Awabakal term for woman. The word now referred exclusively to native Australian women or mixed race women. The Eora word for tame dog, 'tungo', had become 'dingo' and referred to the native wild dog the Eora called 'worragul'. The mysterious word 'kangaroo' still persisted, and even some Eora had begun to use it to replace 'ganimantj'. Ganimantj sold as kangaroo was thought by the British to taste better. British merchants claimed that it tasted like English deer if properly cooked.

The peace meeting was planned for the first week of May in 1796.

The week before this, Pemulwuy had imposed some conditions. He wanted the meeting to be held at *Balgowla*. Balgowla was on the north side of the harbour, near the mouth of what the British called Middle Harbour. It was, at this stage in the colony's history, neutral ground. Pemulwuy further insisted that the Governor must be present in person; and that, apart from the principals, no more than ten others from each side should attend. All must, he said, be unarmed, and the meeting place itself must remain secret.

Paterson was now very concerned for the Governor's safety, and strongly advised Hunter against such an isolated location. After some argument between the emissaries from each side, it was agreed that the meeting take place on a beach in a small, sandy cove near Balgowla that the Eora called *Weeaggi*. To allay the Governor's fears, Pemulwuy agreed that an armed ship could be moored off the cove.

Hunter was by now somewhat exasperated, but he assented to the compromise.

Then, with the day of the parley approaching, Abbott warned him that Bennelong had speared an Eora and that the New South Wales Corps expected trouble among the natives.

Bennelong was officially carpeted before the Governor. He walked into the reception room at the residence to be confronted by Hunter, Paterson, Abbott, Marshall, Carpenter and Collins. Bennelong, far from being contrite, was oddly defiant.

'Bennelong, you are a civilised man,' said Hunter, peering down his aquiline nose at the Eora man, 'how can you, who have put so much effort into these negotiations, then jeopardise them by wounding one of your own people?'

Bennelong had been a little late for the meeting due to a clothing change from Eora cloak to jacket and hose. He felt that he should wear the clothes of the wolf when he hunted with the wolves; and those of the dog when he was to play tame.

'I used a dooul on Yerrinibee,' he said firmly. 'He is only wounded in the leg'.

The British officers exchanged worried glances.

'Why did you do it?' Collins then asked.

Bennelong looked aside at him with an expression that was close to contempt. '*Murra murrong*,' he muttered, 'you sir would say: A matter of honour'.

Eager to show off his knowledge, Collins turned to Hunter. 'A dooul, Your Excellency, is a light, sharp, unbarbed spear used in these ritual matters. I was speared with one,' he said, then relaxed a little. 'I believe that the whole thing is something to do with a woman,' he added with a wry smirk. 'It is a kind of duel.'

The Governor nodded. Well, at least that was explicable. Hardly a duel, he thought, more like a matter of fisticuffs, a situation common to the taverns of Portsmouth as well as the New South Wales bush. He remained stern, however.

'Bennelong,' he said heavily, 'you are retained in His Majesty's service, and it behoves you to act accordingly. I am absolutely appalled that you would compromise your position by involving yourself with some local gin.'

Bennelong's eyes flashed briefly.

'Your Excellency, it was a matter concerning my wife!'

The Governor seemed not to hear. 'If this act of yours causes difficulties at the forthcoming meeting with Pemulwuy, I shall hold you personally responsible,' he said, wagging an admonitory finger, 'now leave my sight, please!'

Bennelong left the residence feeling much aggrieved. He could not win. He was truly an outsider in both his own society and the one he had adopted.

'Civilised, are they,' he thought sourly, thinking of the officers at the residence, 'I offer them friendship and help, but the only thing they really respect is Pemulwuy's violence'.

There was rum at his cottage. Rum quietened doubts, stilled fears and eased pain.

CHAPTER 27

THE TRUCE

The time of day of the 'secret' peace meeting arrived. Balgowla must have been the most densely populated place on the east coast of Australia. Carpenter estimated that there were close to a thousand Eoras in the Balgowla area.

The British responded by mooring the ship *Gloucester* off Weeaggi so that she was broadside on to the landing. A camp of some two hundred soldiers and hangers-on came onto the beach. Paterson and Grose were appalled at the situation. In Sydney they were betting even money on either the Governor or Pemulwuy leaving the meeting alive. Local gossips claimed that Carpenter had marksmen positioned in the trees to shoot Pemulwuy when he showed up. Others had it on the best authority that Pemulwuy planned to put a spear into the Governor's chest when they met. At the other end of the scale it was rumoured that Sergeant Weaver was planning revenge on the Eora for having skinned and eaten his cat.

It was just after noon on the day of the meeting when Pemulwuy appeared at the rear entrance to the Governor's residence. A bewildered female servant sought to enter the Governor's drawing room, where Hunter was engaged in earnest last-minute conversation with Paterson, Grose and Abbott before his planned departure for Balgowla by water.

'What on earth is it now?' asked the Governor irritably.

'Excellency…it's Pemulwuy,' the aide stammered, 'at the back door. He says that he wishes to begin the meeting here and now'.

Four well-bred jaws dropped. There was a rush of brass to the back door. Hunter was at the head of the group as they moved through the door into the open air. There he had his first view of the men with whom he was duty bound to make peace. In a small, tight circle sat most of the elite members of the southern continents, Australia's first military forces—Pemulwuy, with Yenowee, Tedbury, Gomil and Koobee, all watched over by two anxious sentries.

Hunter did his best not to be shocked by Pemulwuy's bizarre appearance. He sat with a ganimantj cloak drawn about him. His wandering eye and air of wiry ferocity always created a presence of power and danger. For a moment Hunter was lost for words, and it was Pemulwuy who initiated the conversation.

'Good afternoon, Governor Hunter,' he said. 'Will you join us so that we may have this meeting?'

His English was fluent, if slightly stilted, with an almost 'literary' flourish that was probably a deliberate affectation. Hunter stood and looked at him, fascinated. How was it possible that these men, known to be dangerous, had gained such entry to the Governor's residence? He finally asked the Eoras to come into the house. After some discussion, they said they preferred to be outside. They did not get up.

'Well, to meet here is probably a wise move, Mr Pemulwuy,' Hunter said carefully. 'Would you like me to arrange some refreshments?'

Again, the offer was politely refused.

'I am pleased that you have sufficient confidence in my goodwill to come to Sydney,' Hunter continued, putting a brave face on an awkward situation.

'Governor Hunter,' said Pemulwuy crisply, 'I believe that those who intend to murder one or the other of us are mostly on the other side of the harbour'.

Hunter quickly changed the subject and suggested that they conduct the meeting in English, since all of the Eora spoke fluent English, and of the officers present, only Abbott had so much as heard Bidjigal spoken. Pemulwuy agreed, though remarked quite pointedly that in time he hoped Captain Hunter would indeed be able to conduct future meetings in the language of the people of this land.

By now Hunter had realised that Pemulwuy was not just a formidable warrior, but a careful negotiator, perhaps even a statesman of sorts, he thought.

Hunter called for chairs, and when settled, began his opening preamble. He was very much aware that the Eora would examine carefully every word and gesture. Nevertheless, he made a good job of explaining to the Eora leaders that he had been charged by the British government with bringing about reconciliation with the native people of the country. He then suggested that Pemulwuy might wish to outline the grievances that had led to the recent conflict.

'Governor Hunter,' said Pemulwuy simply, 'your people have come here uninvited and unwelcome and have stolen part of our land, this is why we fight'.

Hunter pursed his lips and nodded. Patience was needed.

'Even now, as we meet, Captain Macarthur is forcing the settlers back onto the farms that surround Parramatta,' Pemulwuy continued, 'I believe that he is also planning to take land from the Tharawal people as well'.

And so it went on. Hunter listened politely, without interruption, to the catalogue of injustice.

When Pemulwuy had finished, he acknowledged him with a slight bow and began his own justification.

'First I must tell you, Mr Pemulwuy and gentlemen, that this country is no longer in isolation from the rest of the world. People everywhere else in the world talk to each other; they trade goods and sometimes settle on each other's land to do this.' He paused and wiped his neck. The sun was hot, and his naval uniform was not designed for noon encounters in the New South Wales summer. 'The settlers to whom you refer are using this land to produce the food that we all need. They are not thieves. They found the land empty and untilled and there is plenty of it.' He paused. 'How can they be thieves under these circumstances?'

Pemulwuy said nothing for a moment, apparently uncertain whether the Governor wanted an answer to his questions.

Then he frowned. 'It is easy to be a thief, Governor Hunter,' he said grimly. 'You take something that is not yours. You don't have to know who owns it.'

Hunter coughed and whispered with Major Grose. Pemulwuy waved his hand to indicate the area around them.

'None of this land ever belonged to the British,' he declared. 'You say that you come from a place far away.'

Hunter took some whispered advice, this time from Paterson.

'Mr Pemulwuy,' said the Governor, 'you must realise that the peoples of the world are forming themselves into a number of empires. You are fortunate enough to have been selected to become part of the British Empire. You are, in fact, protected by us'. Another swift exchange followed between Hunter and his attendants. 'You could have been much less fortunate and fallen into the hands of the French or the Spanish,' he said.

Pemulwuy was unmoved. 'Could they do worse than kill us and steal our land,' he demanded. Hunter responded testily: 'We are not getting very far with this, are we?' He drew up to his full height, staring straight at Pemulwuy. 'You realise that if you continue to fight, there will be much suffering, you will be wiped out,' he said.

Pemulwuy got to his feet and stood full-square facing the Governor.

'Governor! Captain Phillip left this place because he could not do as his leaders over the sea bid him do. He offered us his civilisation and what we saw was drunkenness and people beaten. He offered 'protection' and his soldiers hurt and killed us. Then he began to steal our land.'

He stopped and gazed intensely at Hunter, his strange eyes bright and burning with an unrelenting hostility. Then suddenly he looked at the ground. 'He failed here and so will you!' Pemulwuy said. He waved his arm to the countryside and when he continued, it was like a chant. 'This land will hate you. Even if you kill us, this land will despise you. It will never be your country. It will starve you and make you thirst. It will kill your animals and poison your spirits, burn you, you will become the ugliest of people!'

There was real hurt and shock in Hunter's face,

'This is madness,' he said hoarsely, 'I have made no threats to you, and you place a curse on us'. He spread his fingers out in front of him. 'If you walk out of here as you are, you will commit your people to a terrible struggle that you must lose. Surely Bennelong has told you that we have many many more people in England to replace any of us that you kill?'

Pemulwuy slumped back to the ground.

'So that's the end of it,' he said in a quite different, despairing voice.

The Governor seized his opportunity. He moved towards the Eora party.

'Mr Pemulwuy,' he said gently, 'there is another way, and that is peace'.

Pemulwuy's reaction was again unpredictable. He tipped back his head and laughed.

'I have now had some experience with this thing you call peace,' he added quietly, as if to himself. 'The trouble with this peace is that it is made by soldiers.'

'At least it is not war,' coaxed Hunter.

'But how can two soldiers make a peace for those who are not soldiers?'

'Soldiers can make a truce, I am afraid that is all we have,' Hunter said. He became pleading—'Do you think I would not reverse all that has happened here if I could? But I cannot, and neither can you. All you and I have to offer is a soldier's truce, and that is better than the way things are'.

Pemulwuy stared at him for a moment, then turned and spoke rapidly in Bidjigal with Yenowee and the others. After a while he addressed the British again.

'Is there anything beyond a truce?' he asked.

Grose attempted to hiss some advice at Hunter but was waved aside.

'Yes!' Hunter said quickly, 'we should discuss reservations of land for your people'.

'What does that mean?'

'We have part of the land for our farms and settlements, while you may hunt and live undisturbed in others.'

Pemulwuy laughed, 'such a thing could have been done long ago. In our way, people from a different group can always arrange to make use of another's land in a proper way'.

Hunter seemed very surprised.

'I was unaware of that,' he said.

Pemulwuy began another discussion with his companions.

'This reservation thing was done in America with the native people and it proved to be a happy solution,' Hunter intervened.

Pemulwuy looked suspiciously at him for a moment; then rejoined the Eora debate. When the talk was concluded to the Eora's satisfaction, Pemulwuy stood up and addressed the whole group.

'We agree,' he said, 'a truce now. We must talk about this other 'reservation' thing with all Eora'.

He made his arms into a circle, then stopped and listened to something Yenowee said in Bidjigal. Pemulwuy nodded.

'Your people must stay where they are now,' he told the Governor, 'no more new farms until we talk again'.

It was now Hunter's turn to consult his colleagues. He spoke mostly in English, but switched briefly to French when addressing Paterson. Paterson shook his head, listened a little more; and then nodded. Pemulwuy followed the conversation intently.

Hunter formally addressed the Eora.

'It is agreed as you say. There are to be no acts committed on either side which break the truce. Your people will not attack or interfere with us, and we shall not interfere with you.' He paused and took a breath. 'We accept this state of affairs until another meeting is held here in the spring.'

'September,' said Paterson helpfully, in case the Governor had not yet adjusted to the southern hemisphere's seasons.

Pemulwuy nodded, turned to his fellow Eora and said in English: 'When the goanna comes out'.

From then on, the meeting was guardedly friendly. Pemulwuy and Hunter shook hands, and the other Eora joined in, rather awkwardly shaking hands with any Englishman in the group.

The Governor ordered wine in celebration, and Pemulwuy and his supporters took a glass with the British. Pemulwuy said, '*Weda*,' and raised his glass. Hunter awkwardly said the same strange word; then raised his glass.

The Eora left about an hour before sunset, just before the multitudes from the north shores descended on Sydney.

CHAPTER 28

A SOLDIER'S PEACE

It was not until the early afternoon, when Bennelong noticed that Awabakal and some other people close to Pemulwuy had gone that he became suspicious.

He spoke to Carpenter. 'Go back and stop the Governor coming,' Bennelong implored. 'I believe there is something wrong.'

Carpenter remembered something of Bennelong's past premonitions and was not inclined to place much credence in the warning. By three o'clock, however, he was worried. Apart from the question of Hunter's safety, he was concerned that there might be violence on the beach unless something happened soon.

He had just ordered the withdrawal of the British contingent from the beach when a small boat arrived, confirming that Pemulwuy had tricked them. The meeting was taking place in Sydney.

Carpenter steered clear of Bennelong until all British forces had been evacuated from Weeaggi. He then informed the Eora intermediary that it was up to him to deal with the situation.

'Pemulwuy outwitted us,' he said. 'The meeting was held in Sydney. I leave it to you to keep the peace here.'

Bennelong was angry, but he was also frightened. Some of the waiting Eoras had become impatient and had pressed forward onto the waterfront, eager to see what was happening. Bennelong decided to keep his own counsel until dark. Then he would slip away in one of the many canoes lying on the edge of the beach. Yet again, he told himself, experience had taught him to trust neither Pemulwuy nor the British.

'They deserve each other,' he said half aloud.

Bennelong felt distraught and betrayed as he waited for evening, still issuing bland assurances to the Eora crowd. He decided that he must find a way to kill Pemulwuy.

Then, at the pinch of sunset, Weuong appeared beside him with a message from Awabakal.

'Bennelong,' he said, 'tell these people that the meeting has been held and Pemulwuy and the Governor have agreed that there will be no more fighting until the goanna comes out. Then there will be another meeting'.

Bennelong felt an even greater sense of betrayal, but there was also a feeling of relief that nothing worse had happened. He called the Eoras to a meeting, built a fire, and did his best to retain what dignity he could under the circumstances. In his heart, he quietly made a vow that he would become more cunning. Neither Hunter nor Pemulwuy would ever humiliate him again.

Unseasonable rain had turned the entire township of Sydney into a quagmire. It always remained a mystery to Lieutenant Marshall how earth that was baked so hard in the sun, could so quickly be reduced to slush with rain. He picked his way past the headquarters' building on his way to his own quarters. He noticed that Captain Macarthur's grey stood forlornly tethered in the rain. The mud seemed to find its way into every part of the Corps buildings, no matter what barriers the convict labourers tried to create. Abbott, Macarthur and Greville sat sipping fortified wine while they awaited Grose's arrival.

'I must say that I'm amazed that the truce has held even this long,' said Greville.

'That red spot brigade of Pemulwuy's seems to wield great influence, for better as well as for worse,' Macarthur retorted.

'I say, do you really think there's something in it?' asked Gosford. He was something of a fop, the younger son of an English noble family, and even by the standards of the Rum Corps, none too bright. 'I mean, surely it's just black mumbo jumbo.'

Macarthur laughed dryly. 'Well, of course it is that too. But I can also assure you that that fellow Pemulwuy uses it for political means that would put a Borgia to shame.' He licked his lips. 'Ah... the joy of real Spanish sherry on a winter's day, such as it is.'

Major Grose stepped into the room, having handed his cape to a waiting servant. He dried his hands with a small yellow napkin.

'Beastly weather,' he announced to no-one in particular. Then he saw the wine. 'Just the thing!'

He was handed a glass, and then sat down and stretched his boots out in front of him.

'Well, gentlemen,' he said: 'What is to be done?'

He waited, taking a long draught of the liquor. The sweet, heavy wine made a pleasant glow as it travelled down into his well-padded stomach.

'I take it, sir, that there has not as yet been an official report on the matter?' said Macarthur.

'Certainly not,' replied Grose. 'I think even the Governor himself is a trifle embarrassed at his own success. What he has conceded so far is partition or near, dammit.' He shrugged, sipping at his sherry, 'mind you, he takes his commission seriously, and it is explicit in the matter of dealing with the natives. Peace at just about any price'.

'But surely it says nothing about partition,' Macarthur objected, 'not, of course, that the Governor has used the word, but it's what the agreement amounts to. Words like 'reservation' can't change the reality'.

'No,' Grose said, 'his orders spoke in terms of reconciliation'.

'Reconciliation, eh?' said Macarthur. 'It actually uses that word, does it?'

'Well…, yes, as a matter of fact it does.'

Macarthur looked thoughtful. 'So Phillip had his say.'

'And Bennelong and that fool Tench I'm sure,' chipped in Abbott.

'If the Colonial Office is using that term, someone must have implanted the notion that there is a real conflict here,' said Macarthur.

'And if news of a truce should get to London,' Gosford said, 'I hate to think of the consequences'.

Grose sighed, 'there has been no report to London yet. Hunter doesn't want to raise false hopes and end up with egg on his face. Should the government get to know, however, the consequences could be serious. A namby-pamby policy established in New South Wales. Still, you can't expect anyone in London to understand these people or the situation here'.

'So what is to be done, as you yourself asked but a few minutes ago?' said Macarthur.

Grose shifted position in his chair. 'Paterson is right, I believe,' he said. 'Hunter's soft underbelly is sovereignty. This whole business clearly puts into question the legitimacy of British sovereignty in New South Wales and we must press him hard on that point, both here and through our friends in London.'

'It will not be easy,' said Gosford. 'The Governor seems to have fixed on Pemulwuy as some sort of noble savage. Won't hear a word against him.'

Grose laughed. 'He will learn, as others have. Just give him time.'

Macarthur and Abbott said nothing. Time, they had already decided, was something they didn't have a great deal of.

It was only a few hours later that Bennelong received a summons to join Captains Abbott and Macarthur in Abbott's quarters. Bennelong used to delight in such invitations, but since the Weeaggi affair, he had come to feel that all the British benevolence that he had once enjoyed was just a trap. They regarded him as little more than a pawn in their game with Pemulwuy. Nevertheless, he accepted the invitation.

Abbott lost little time in coming to the point.

'Bennelong, my dear fellow,' he said, 'we have a saying: one's enemy's enemies are one's friends.'

He and Macarthur told Bennelong that, 'in all truth', the old Eora order must change. Recent events were, however, leading to an agreement between the British and the Eora that could hold up the march of progress, with all the benefits that such progress might bring for the natives—and particularly for men such as himself, who had welcomed the British. They reminded Bennelong that he was, like them, a prospective landowner. Already he had possession of a cottage on the point, which in future would be a valuable property.

'The only barrier that really stands in the way of a successful outcome to all our endeavours is Pemulwuy,' said Abbott.

Bennelong made a skeptical gesture.

'I would probably have to agree with what you say, but the only way to discredit Pemulwuy now is for him to break the peace,' he said gloomily.

Abbott glanced at Macarthur, 'such things can, of course, happen. They can even be arranged,' he said. 'Peace, after all, is only the interval between wars, my dear Bennelong.'

Bennelong got to his feet. 'What Pemulwuy says of you is true,' he howled, 'there is no end to your trickery'.

Macarthur put a restraining hand on Bennelong's shoulder.

'This is a soldier's peace, Bennelong. Leave those matters to soldiers. In this case, Pemulwuy is a master of trickery. He practised some on you very recently—and on me also.'

'Yes, that is true,' said Bennelong, wincing at the memory. He sat down again. 'If I was allowed to deal properly with him, I would win. I have been educated in England. I read books—I know things that Pemulwuy has not heard of.'

'Ah! But trickery is something you don't learn in genteel English society.' Bennelong thought about that. 'In that case, I don't see what my part in any scheme of yours might be.'

Abbott smiled, 'good Lord, man! You didn't go to England for nothing!' he said. 'You are the obvious leader of your people!' He let the compliment sink in. 'You have all the good sense and understanding to lead your people in dignity to become a proper part of the British Empire. White and black alike, all partners in progress and prosperity.'

Bennelong peered at them suspiciously.

'Fine words,' he murmured, 'but look at how I was treated at Weeaggi. Carpenter left me in the lurch'.

'Carpenter is a nobody...a leftover marine!' said Abbott.

'That meeting with Pemulwuy should never have taken place without you,' Macarthur added, 'the Corps will ensure that nothing like that ever happens again'.

Bennelong was far from convinced.

'You take the land and I become a landless nobleman except for a cottage at Warrun...'

Macarthur laughed. 'You did learn a thing or two in England, after all,' he said, 'but you are quite wrong, my friend. There is plenty here for everyone, if all cooperate'. He reached out and poured Bennelong a glass of wine. 'You have seen England, her cities, her ships, her army, her power.' He said, 'you know it is pointless to oppose such power'.

He waited for Bennelong to drink his wine.

'My friend, there is absolutely no question as to who shall own the land of New South Wales. We all shall! You and your people, as British subjects, can own a share and be just as prosperous as the rest of us!'

'But the Eora do not know how to farm land,' said Bennelong.

'Then teach them, Bennelong. Make them aware that there is an alternative to Pemulwuy,' said Macarthur.

Bennelong walked home deep in thought, despite being a little tipsy. The proposal was similar to the dream he and Phillip had shared. And, after all, this thing they called progress did seem inevitable. Bennelong realised that after his travels and experience in England, he was different. He had imagined that things here would be very different when he returned, but they were not. He thought, if only he could grasp all this properly, things could still become better for him. He recalled that someone in England had once suggested that he might become the King of New South Wales. He shook his head. He did not want such a thing… in reality he wanted to be nothing more than Pemulwuy was now… he thought that Pemulwuy had achieved that by killing people. He coughed, and walked on. These dammed British seemed to admire that…all of them.

He looked up at the dark sky, 'you could never seem to make real friends with any of these British,' he thought despairingly. They never really accepted him as an equal, although they talked about this equality idea a lot. Now that he thought about it, he realised that the English really did not like anybody. They detested the Irish and the French who lived nearby and many of them now lived in England. They were suspicious of the Scottish and even of each other. Even here, Bennelong felt quite sure that Carpenter and Macarthur would murder each other if they could get away with it. What hope, he thought.

Bennelong ached for the kind of affection that Pemulwuy seemed to bear for Koobee and Awabakal who were different, and even the Irishman who came from far away. As his lonely cabin came into view in the darkness, he wished that he had never left the Bidjigal to come to Sydney, and wished that he had never gone to England too. He sighed…but all that was too long ago now.

CHAPTER 29

THE DOUBLE-HEADED COIN

Pemulwuy moved very quickly. He scattered his men to the winds to inform the Eora carefully of what the truce meant. Koobee felt badly about leaving Bennelong out on a limb, but he thought that he understood Pemulwuy's reasons.

Koobee regarded the outcome of the peace meeting as very good. Being Kamergal, however, he objected to being a simple messenger for Pemulwuy.

'This is not Gro Mok business,' said Koobee, 'an *alodim murray* must be called by the Kamergal. It is their place to do so. These things shall be decided then'.

Pemulwuy made no objection to Koobee's demands. In fact, he encouraged him and sent him home with good wishes. Nargel watched Pemulwuy closely, and she sensed that there was more to his intentions than met the eye.

Nargel watched Pemulwuy walk around the camp like a caged worragul. She believed that some time ago Pemulwuy had engaged a gogaruk to sing her. Why Pemulwuy should involve sorcery against her she did not know. She had confided her fears to Awabakal who dismissed them out of hand. Awabakal in fact scolded her, saying that she had not dealt properly with the loss of her first husband, and that it was she who was spiritually disturbed, not Pemulwuy. Awabakal's counsel moved her, but not sufficiently to abandon her feelings about Pemulwuy. Nevertheless, she now doubted that she was any longer the target of Pemulwuy's mischief. But, unlike Awabakal, she continued to believe that there was darkness to Pemulwuy's mind. She watched him secretly and carefully.

The unusual late winter rains caught the camp unprepared. People were struggling about with complaining children in the mud and wet, seeking and preparing better shelter. During this period Nargel lost sight of Pemulwuy, and by the time she realised the fact, he was gone.

A week later Milbab ran up to her and said that Pemulwuy had taken Boolayoo down to the escarpment.

Nargel raced through the light scrub, her feet barely touching the ground. She stopped in full flight when she heard singing. She listened, and it was Pemulwuy. She peered uncertainly at a rock ledge. Pemulwuy sat naked, singing, and the child sat before him quietly playing with some stones. Nargel stood in silence for a minute; then she said, 'Boolayoo'. Boolayoo looked up and called out to his mother. Pemulwuy continued the chant and did not move. Nargel listened and realised it related to her past husband. This made it very difficult for her. It was absolutely improper for a woman to intervene or even be present for such men's business. She stood breathless and undecided for a minute. Finally she steeled herself, walked over and sat in front of Pemulwuy and the child.

Pemulwuy's eyes were closed and he continued to sing. Nargel reached out to pick up the child. Pemulwuy's arm restrained her. She sat quite still, her heart pounding; then quite abruptly Pemulwuy stopped. He looked at her and smiled.

'Take your child now.'

Nargel swept Boolayoo into her arms, looked down and stood up, then stopped. Pemulwuy looked up at her. Nargel's eyes were ablaze.

'If you harm him, my husband, I will kill you.'

Then she was gone. Later that night a Wanegal man from Sydney came to visit Pemulwuy. They talked late into the night.

After these two incidents, Pemulwuy seemed to change again. He became affable and statesmanlike. He took his place at the head of the Goman camp of the Bidjigal people and led them to the alodim murray in the country of the Kamergal. There were between a thousand and twelve hundred people at the meeting. Such an unscheduled meeting caused a great food problem. The meeting had to be very short so that the people could move away quickly to find better sources of food. Later in the winter, such meetings were usually convened to coincide with some especially plentiful food source, such as a stranded whale or some bountiful vegetable crop.

On the first day, Koobee and Yenowee spoke for a time. The older men of all groups then convened separate meetings that went on long into the night. Next morning they all assembled again.

The first issue to be dealt with was the subject of partition. The discussion moved to the question of farming. Pemulwuy was asked to speak. He stood up.

'I do not want to be a farmer,' he said in English. He paused—then mysteriously added: '*Tyerabarrbowaryaou*'.

Perhaps no-one but Pemulwuy completely understood the concept described by this complex Eora expression. Awabakal, who was not a native speaker of Eora, translated the term simply as 'I can never be a white man'.

About an hour later, Pemulwuy was asked to speak again about the increase in the British population. Pemulwuy spoke for a while on this subject. He said that Bennelong would talk to them in the afternoon and knew more of these things. He did say that any agreement must limit the British population, for it caused a great drain on available food supplies. He concluded by saying that their population increase made them hungrier and more inclined to steal land. It did not make them stronger.

'To beat us they must kill me, and they cannot do that unless I let them,' he said.

Later in the afternoon Bennelong spoke to the meeting for some two hours. He pressed all those present on the need to have decided what they wished to do before the spring. He stressed at great length that the Eora should be very careful not to break the truce.

Late that night, Pemulwuy told Koobee that he had heard Macarthur intended to break the truce. He also said that Bennelong knew of this or was suspicious of Macarthur. Koobee said he had heard of many rumours, but he did not believe them.

Koobee walked away sadly. He did believe that Macarthur intended to break the truce, but he also believed that Pemulwuy intended to break the truce. Koobee was determined that he would think about the situation tonight and confront Pemulwuy with his conclusions in the morning.

That night Pemulwuy met with Yenowee, Weuong and Awabakal. He told them that while he believed that Hunter was honest in what he had said, he had no such respect for the people of the Rum Corps. He said that they would use the truce either to expand their farmlands, or to plant the seeds that would produce their food in the summer. Some argument ensued as to whether this amounted to a breach of the truce. Yenowee thought that it did break the truce, but that he did not believe this was a sufficient act to claim that the truce was broken. Pemulwuy was inclined to agree.

Weuong claimed, however, that clearing the land of trees constituted a breach of the truce. Awabakal pointed out that the British might claim that the Eora winter burns could also be called a breach. Pemulwuy agreed with this, but thought that it would be almost impossible to prevent this ancient tradition of burning off the old summer vegetation. Besides, if they did not, it would increase the risk of dangerous summer bushfires. Finally it was decided that burning off was also not a sufficient cause to break the truce.

Awabakal was then invited to expound a Karegal idea for partition which he claimed to have understood. He said that the Karegals had noted that when the Europeans made gardens many animals came to eat them and grew fat. The Karegal therefore proposed that the Europeans should farm the valleys and the Karegals stay in the highlands and enjoy the well-fed animals from the European's farming. The condition had to be that no fencing could be permitted. Yenowee said that the Borogegal wanted the British to let their new animals run free and then they should hunt them side by side.

'Bennelong is going to tell the Governor about all these things.'

Pemulwuy smiled, 'I am sure that the Governor will be pleased'.

The meeting began to break up the following morning. Koobee came troubled to Pemulwuy's camp and sat down beside Yenowee. Pemulwuy was away farewelling others leaving the alodim.

'Koobee, you're unhappy,' said Yenowee.

'Yes,' Koobee hung his head, 'I think that the Kamergal are happy to see the British partition in Borogegal country but not their own country. They want the British here, but not too near them'.

'You think the peace is no good?'

'I think that Bennelong tells lies about it,' said Koobee.

Pemulwuy returned. He was in high spirits.

'Ah, Koobee,' he said, 'how are your mareemy?'

Koobee had almost forgotten his misfortunes on the back of a horse. He was more curious as to the reason why Pemulwuy used a Karegal term for his injured parts.

'Improving,' he said. 'Why do you use a Karegal word?'

'We must get used to the British peace, speak one language, all be farmers, and call the Governor 'Excellency'.'

Koobee looked sadly at Pemulwuy. 'You don't intend to keep the truce, do you?'

'Koobee,' said Pemulwuy placing his face close, 'you have listened to the alodim murray. Do you believe that the Eora want to live like the British?'

'It may be better than dying,' said Koobee, 'no matter how we have to live'.

'Koobee,' Pemulwuy said seriously, 'we may yield and still die. The British brought with them a secret way to kill us...come, we must talk to the old men and to Bennelong'.

This all left Koobee rather bemused. He followed Pemulwuy and Yenowee across the camp to a small gathering of mostly grey-haired men. This was an alodim gaeray—a meeting of further or conclusive business.

Bennelong was addressing the group when the others arrived. He hesitated a moment and then went on. Bennelong was explaining that heavy work could be done by horses and that these animals could also be used for hunting and rapid transport. Pemulwuy's opinion was asked on this matter and he agreed with Bennelong. As time went by, it appeared that Pemulwuy seemed to be supporting most of the things that Bennelong was saying.

Bennelong always found this situation disturbing. He really enjoyed Pemulwuy's support, but the cost was always so great. He realised that in his strange, quiet way Pemulwuy was either challenging him or laying a trap. It did not surprise Bennelong that Pemulwuy had not exposed his real position at the alodim murray. This present meeting was the proper forum for such admissions.

The old men also sensed the contest. They watched and listened carefully. They asked their questions but made no speeches. Long speeches were for the alodim murray.

'Just what advantage would you think that their ships give us?' An old man asked the question of Pemulwuy.

'You could travel to distant lands.' Pemulwuy paused. 'More importantly, your sons could go to England and return fine fellows like Bennelong.'

Bennelong picked up the sarcasm, and took the floor.

'Horses and ships could allow us to travel quickly to meetings like this, to ceremonies at any time, and to bring much food from distant places. I have seen them do this in England.'

The point was won.

'And the farms can produce this food quickly and in great abundance,' proposed another.

'But Pemulwuy does not want to be a farmer,' laughed another.

'Pemulwuy does not have to,' said Bennelong. 'We can train the young men.'

'Then who will hunt the ganimantj in the tomorrows?' said Pemulwuy.

'The British will work the seed farms; we shall have the animal farms. We shall still hunt, but there will be more and new animals,' replied Bennelong.

An old man nodded thoughtfully.

Where was Pemulwuy's barb?

'But who shall judge all this to be just?' Old Yella Mundi spoke for the first time. 'For the British, the Governor, for the Eora, a council...a special alodim…you and you shall be able to talk to the King of England,' said Bennelong.

Not even a mutter from Pemulwuy.

'But what if the British Governor is not just?' said Yenowee. 'How shall we talk to this King?'

'We shall have our own ship,' said Bennelong.

Pemulwuy's eyes were on the ground. 'At the spring meeting we should insist on this.'

There was something sinister here, Bennelong thought. He must attack. 'But this is all for nothing if the truce is broken,' he said.

'If a young man breaks it, we will punish him,' said Yella Mundi.

'What will you do if Pemulwuy breaks it?' Bennelong said at great risk.

Bennelong stood up as he spoke and took hold of the dagger in his belt. Pemulwuy still did not move. There was absolute silence. No-one moved. Then Yella Mundi stood up.

'We shall be responsible,' he said, 'Pemulwuy *tamira yanoong*'.

Pemulwuy did not look up; he only reached out his hand. Yella Mundi's expression referred to the voluntary binding of the hand to signify the making of a promise. The consequence of breaking the promise was death brought about by spiritual influences.

Bennelong completely failed to understand this total submission on Pemulwuy's part.

Pemulwuy stood up with his hand still outstretched.

'I will make this promise,' he said solemnly, 'I will not break the truce unless the British break it'. He turned to face Bennelong, his hand still outstretched.

'The British can break the truce by killing us with muskets, with bayonets, with swords,' he said. 'Or with their sicknesses,' he added with a cynical smirk, 'the galgalla'.

And that was the barb!

Bennelong jumped to his feet; 'How do we know that they are guilty of making the sickness?' he yelled.

'The galgalla is in the jar,' said Pemulwuy with a triumphant smile on his face. 'We have seen the jar and know what was hidden inside. The British would never talk to us about it even if we asked. It was always a secret.'

Pemulwuy fixed the old men with his strange gaze. 'But now they may not use it, then the truce will hold unless the British break it some other way. We will know all this when the goanna comes out.

CHAPTER 30

THE DIE IS CAST

Bennelong galloped his horse most of the way to Sydney. When he arrived at the headquarters of the New South Wales Corps, he leapt from the exhausted animal, rushed into the building and literally flung himself upon Captain Abbott. The plump officer pacified him as best he could, meanwhile sending a message for Macarthur to join them.

'Galgalla!' Bennelong kept repeating. The truce will be broken by smallpox! The sores in a jar! He was still breathing with difficulty when Macarthur walked into the room.

'You knew...you knew that Pemulwuy knew....'

'I haven't the vaguest idea what you're talking about, my dear fellow,' Macarthur said. He put his hand on Bennelong's shoulder. 'This is ridiculous, now, pull yourself together and tell us what irks you, man!'

For the moment, all Bennelong could do was repeat the accusation. 'You gave Pemulwuy a spear and let him strike my heart!' he gasped finally, 'I am betrayed again'.

Abbott took a grip on his other shoulder, and together the two officers forced him down into a chair. Macarthur handed him half a tumbler of rum and told him to drink.

Bennelong almost choked on the rough spirit, but as it coursed through his system it had a settling effect. His anger dwindled slowly into a morose despair.

After fifteen minutes or so, Abbott and Macarthur managed to wheedle an account of the alodim out of Bennelong.

'So, did he actually use the word 'smallpox'?' asked Macarthur.

'No,' moaned Bennelong. 'He used 'galgalla'. It's a new Eora word, but it means the same thing.'

Macarthur nodded solemnly.

'Bennelong,' he said, 'I can only assure you that I have had nothing to do with any plan to infect your people. You must believe me on that score'.

Bennelong stood up a little unsteadily. He pointed his finger at Macarthur and then at Abbott. 'There is something to it, or Pemulwuy would not have said it,' He paused and drew a long breath, 'and if any of the new sicknesses kill Eora people, then the truce is over and Pemulwuy will blame the British'.

He turned away, made for the door. He stopped on the threshold and faced them once more. 'It is over for me,' he said sadly. 'Pemulwuy is too cunning and the G*oorunganegal* is never enough.'

Then he was gone.

The two officers looked at each other.

'What in hell does that word mean?' Abbott asked.

Macarthur sat back in his chair, smiling crookedly. 'Goorunganegal?'

'Er...yes.'

'Something like a bribe, or more accurately, payment in advance. I suppose what he means is that anything we or the Governor offers will never satisfy our friend Pemulwuy.'

'You are well informed since you took over Parramatta. I didn't realise you had such close contact with the natives and some command of their language.'

'I don't,' said Macarthur.

His grin broadened. He leaned forward confidentially.

'You see,' he explained, 'I have a man named Barrington who, as a convict, was servant to that wretched fellow Macintyre, the so-called gamekeeper murdered by Pemulwuy years ago. I picked up on Barrington, who had a lot of useful knowledge about the blacks. He's a free man now. Acts as my factotum and constable. Full of useful information about native customs and what passes for their morality. A formidable chap, not to be trifled with. Luckily, he's under my thumb'.

'And what about this smallpox in the jar?'

Macarthur's face became thoughtful, even sly as he considered his response.

'I have heard of such things,' he said. 'It concerned a new method of controlling the disease. A fellow called Jenner invented it, the surgeon Balmain told me about it. The idea is that if you give people a mild dose of the pox, they will become able to fight the more severe form.... Science, old boy. Naturally enough, the natives don't understand it, and they think it's part of a conspiracy to wipe 'em out.'

'Well, is it?' Abbott asked.

'Not so far as I know,' said Macarthur easily, 'hardly necessary, in any case. The fact is that civilisation brings with it diseases that primitives simply cannot bear as we can. A cold that would merely lay you or me low for a few days can easily kill them. A fact of life. Their bodies are not resilient. Pemulwuy knows that full well. The rumour of the fatal jar is useful to him. It adds a touch of drama. But in a sense he is right. Disease is our invisible weapon. Our sicknesses will cut a massive swathe through the natives' ranks as we move through this continent, settling it and converting it to useful cultivation. The natives are doomed'.

'And there's nothing we can do?'

'Nothing. We are the fitter, more resilient race. We shall inherit the place. Pemulwuy or no Pemulwuy. What we cannot achieve by force of arms, disease and the joys of rum will do for us,' said Macarthur with grim satisfaction. 'A weak race is extinguished; a strong one takes its place. Read your history, my dear Abbott, and you will know that this process is as old as time. Nothing your namby-pamby do-gooders in London say or do can alter the fact.'

'Then Pemulwuy shall have his fight, eh?' said Abbott, then added, 'I would like to know how Pemulwuy knew of all this?'

Macarthur shrugged, 'he spent a lot of time with the bloody French and the Russians when they were here'.

More likely from a damned British seaman, Abbot continued, 'I recall there was some sort of fuss in India at one time about this sort of thing'.

Macarthur rang a hand bell for a servant to bring them refreshments.

'The man will have his fight,' he said comfortably, 'and so will Hunter. A manageable little war will but hasten the process of white settlement. So long as we play our cards with determination and skill, and that we most assuredly will sir. You and I, even former convicts like Barrington, all know that this place has more to offer than jailhouses and stinking kangaroos'.

The Governor had spent a long, troubled night in close consultation with the surgeon, Balmain. After Balmain left him, he had sat up late into the night reading reports alone and waiting for the dawn. By ten o'clock the next morning he had before him Major Grose, Major Paterson, Captain Collins and the hapless Lieutenant Marshall whose old leg wound always gave him trouble in the morning.

The pale and drawn Hunter began the meeting by briefly describing the new and sinister ingredient in the political potpourri of New South Wales that had now come to prominence—galgalla. Bennelong had reported the matter before disappearing on a drinking bout. More importantly, there was evidence from Lieutenant Marshall. It seemed that information had been conveyed to him by one of Pemulwuy's henchmen, a man with whom Marshall had become acquainted during his captivity and who had assisted his escape; he is a local but the Lieutenant does not recall his name, quite understandably.

'Easier communication is another advantage of having a truce, as well as fresh meat,' Hunter said, 'this man provided a supporting account of the meeting in question'. He now called the meeting to order.

'Gentlemen,' the Governor began, 'if I seem a little slow to you this morning; it is because I spent most of the night awake. I spent a good deal of the night in discussion with the surgeon and some of his colleagues, and the rest of the night reading what I could of Governor Phillip's notes and records'. He cleared his throat. 'Let me first of all ask you the question that burns before us here.' He paused, more out of weariness than any desire to create effect. 'Do any of you have information regarding a jar said to have contained matter from smallpox sores?'

Both Paterson and Grose expressed great consternation, while Collins sat passively. Finally Grose came to the point.

'Excellency,' he said, 'I have heard of such things, and, in fact, I recall making some investigations at the time. I found there to be, however, no substance in the rumour'.

Hunter nodded absently. It was the kind of bromide that he had come to expect from Grose. In the past months, he had learned the limits of his Governor's powers when faced with opposition as slippery and ruthless as the Rum Corps. It was best to deal, where possible, only with men he could trust, though they were precious few. With no-one else willing to respond, the Governor then went on to explain that he had questioned Balmain very closely, and as a result he believed that it was common practice for physicians to remove matter from lesions associated with smallpox. This, his informant claimed, was in case the physician needed to seek a colleague's opinion in order to properly identify the disease.

'Balmain told me that there is some sort of theory these days,' Hunter continued, 'that if left in the jar for some time, the infectious material from smallpox sores can be administered to the skin to produce a mild form of the disease which renders the recipient immune to the more virulent forms occurring naturally. However, he said that he had heard rumours of such experiments being carried out in India with disastrous results; started an epidemic he understands. He also tells me, however, that to the best of his knowledge, no such experiments have been carried out in this colony.' He paused, 'but he did admit to me that smallpox traces were collected in some jars during the 1789 outbreak, and he does not know the present whereabouts of those samples. He believes that the material was most likely disposed of by burning.'

He let the statement hang. There was quite a long silence. Then Grose spoke up again.

'Your Excellency,' he said, 'there has never been any truth in the suggestion that the disease was deliberately released among the natives. During the interregnum, the colony abounded with rumours of all sorts, and these quite often became common currency among the natives, who are great gossips and tend swiftly to turn rumour into fact. Pemulwuy has obviously picked up some such talk, but I must assure you that it has absolutely no substance'.

The Governor squinted slightly and pursed his lips.

'If that is the case, Major Grose,' he said, 'then I would like some clarification of the word 'galgalla'. As Mr Collins tells me, the expression refers to an evil contained in a jar, an invented Eora word'.

Collins hastily intervened, saving Grose's bacon.

'Your Excellency,' the Judge Advocate said, 'I have further considered that question overnight, and I have come to the conclusion that the natives may well be referring to the physicians' practice of drawing matter from a boil with a heated bottle. I am informed that some sort of entertainment or game has developed among the Eora, using just such a bottle'.

Hunter nodded. 'It is clear to me in the light of this discussion that we can safely consider the matter closed. I can see no good reason for making an official report to London on the matter.' He looked hard at the Rum Corps contingent. 'Should I, however, find evidence that I have been deceived in this matter, then I can assure you that I shall take severe measures against those responsible.'

He referred to the papers on his desk, turned a page or two, and then looked back at the assembled officers.

'And now we must consider this ploy—for ploy you believe it is—something that Pemulwuy has dreamed up. He has given us to understand that any deaths the Eora people attribute to unfamiliar diseases will be regarded as a breach of the truce. I need hardly say that this puts us in an extremely difficult position.'

Paterson nodded vigorously.

'Excellency, the entire situation is quite impossible. The natives suffer terribly from the commonest of diseases. The man is playing with us! As for smallpox, we have no evidence that the disease was not already in New South Wales before our arrival and hence the Eora word.'

The Governor blew his nose, leaned his chin in his hand. His face was ashen with tiredness.

'I quite understand that,' he said with a hint of despair, 'and it seems we are innocent parties—provided that this business about the jar of scabs is indeed a rumour, or else the disease was here before we arrived, as you say'.

Paterson said, 'you have our assurance your Excellency'.

There were nods all round the table. Even Collins joined his assent. Only Marshall seemed reluctant.

'Excellency, I certainly did not master the Bidjigal language during my incarceration. However, the local words for other illnesses did not sound anything like galgalla, but then it could be a word from one of the more distant languages.'

'Very well,' said Hunter, 'nevertheless, we must be cautious. If there is an outbreak of disease, I must be notified immediately. And we must do what we can to educate the natives—incorrigibles such as Pemulwuy apart—regarding this matter. So far the truce has held up remarkably well. Let us hope that if it is broken, we are not to blame'.

'Thank you, gentlemen.'

The Governor stood up and asked Marshall to see him in his study. This seemed to alarm the others, but they all filed out silently.

Marshall was apprehensive when left with the Governor. But as it turned out, all the Governor wanted to say was that he should keep his lines of communication with the natives open. Marshall was tempted to offer to travel to the Bidjigal camps to improve this communication, and perhaps to see Millicent Copley again. However, he thought better of this as he realised that even this harmless meeting with Hunter had raised suspicions. He also knew that even an accidental meeting with someone like Awabakal was on the edge of treason.

An hour later, Grose had Abbott before him in his quarters. The normally phlegmatic Major was close to anger.

'First Macarthur leaves Sydney, without so much as a by-your-leave! Then this damned galgalla business!' he barked, 'I fail to understand why you did not come to me with this story when you heard it from Bennelong!'

Abbott shifted position uncomfortably. Macarthur had indeed left early on horseback for Parramatta, and he had been in a hurry. He covered up for Macarthur as best he could.

'Neither of us took the chap's ravings very seriously,' he said. 'You, yourself are aware of Bennelong's notorious unreliability in such matters. England and all, the man is still nothing more than a savage.'

'Quite so, but what is Macarthur up to?'

'He has simply returned to his post, so I believe. It was clear from Bennelong's account that Pemulwuy might well be up to something. Over the veracity or otherwise of the detail, Macarthur is the commanding officer of the Parramatta district, he would never forgive himself if Pemulwuy had, say, launched a surprise attack.'

There was little Grose could say to that. He salvaged some of his pride by ordering Abbott to join with Carpenter and set up a system of patrols around Sydney forthwith. 'There must be no repetition of the Brickfield fiasco.'

Then he dismissed Abbott and summoned his clerk. In the damp heat of midday he began to dictate a stiff letter to Captain Macarthur.

Captain Hill took the ultimate responsibility for the action that broke the truce, although later he insisted that it was a Lieutenant Lancing who was actually responsible for the killing of two Eora and shots fired at others. Whatever the truth of the matter, all reports agreed that a small group of Eora stole a bag of flour from a farm some two miles north of Toongabbie.

The farmer promptly reported the theft to Captain Hill, who was responsible for patrolling the Toongabbie area. Hill, it was said, swiftly tracked the group down and caught them red-handed with the flour, still in its unopened bag in their possession. The little party of Eora consisted of two men, three women, and a number of children. The adults were tied together by their necks and led on foot towards Parramatta.

A mile and a half from Parramatta, the patrol and its prisoners stopped to rest. It was then, the reports claimed, that one of the Bidjigal men attempted to club a soldier to death with a large rock. The man fired in his own defence and killed him. The other Bidjigal man, who had somehow managed to free himself, ran towards the bush and was shot between the shoulder blades before he reached cover. On seeing all this, the women and children also made a dash for the bush. A number of shots were fired at them, but none of them seemed to have been hit. The two dead Eora men and the bag of stolen flour were brought into Macarthur's headquarters approximately one month before the goanna came out.

None of the reports mentioned that a certain Constable Barrington had also accompanied the fatal party and stayed close to the prisoners at all times. After all, it had been the soldiers who had done the actual killing.

Pemulwuy's reply was swift and brutal. On the night of the second day after the bodies had arrived in Parramatta, he swept down upon the fortified settlement at Lane Cove and literally drove the small garrison into the sea with an attack of extraordinary ferocity. The settlement was set on fire. The glow in the evening sky was visible from Sydney, and all knew quite clearly that the truce was over.

CHAPTER 31

THE FALL OF TOONGABBIE

Bennelong walked carefully into the Governor's presence. He bowed politely, then stooped down and placed a small handful of hairstring bindings on the floor.

'Your Excellency,' he said, 'these are the bindings from Pemulwuy's hand. He says that this is the end of the truce, it is broken by the British'.

'I have taken action concerning the incident at Parramatta, justice will be done,' Hunter said, smarting from Bennelong's unspoken accusation.

Bennelong looked at the floor. 'It is over, Excellency. Pemulwuy only needed that excuse. You will have to kill him now if you can.'

The Governor took a step towards his erstwhile companion.

'Bennelong, don't talk such nonsense,' he said, 'Pemulwuy has made an unprovoked and savage attack, and he will be brought to justice for it, like any criminal. Let me assure you that I do not hold the Eora people in general responsible for his doings. You are yourself witness to and proof of that'.

'Your Excellency,' Bennelong answered slowly, 'I believe that Captain Macarthur ordered those two men killed near Parramatta to provoke Pemulwuy. Also, he did not want you to find out the truth of the smallpox jar'.

The Governor's eyes widened with anger. The normally gentle Scottish burr became an ugly rasp.

'Bennelong I have thoroughly investigated the affair of the jar, and I find the rumours untrue. I have done all in my power as a representative of the Crown, and my conscience is clear. If you truly wish to do good for your people, you will help to squash these absurd rumours—and you will tell the well meaning majority of your people to separate themselves from Pemulwuy. Now, get on about your business!'

Bennelong left the residence as angry as the Governor and determined to write to Phillip in England. As he walked towards the road, he saw Carpenter approaching. The lieutenant attempted to call him over, but he quickly disappeared into the bushes, pretending he had not seen him.

Later that day, Carpenter sought him out at his cottage on the point.

'Bennelong, I want your help,' he said. Bennelong looked at him suspiciously and waited for him to explain. The great letdown of Weeaggi still rankled with him.

'The fact is,' the officer continued, 'I have persuaded His Excellency to give me what I believe will be sufficient forces to deal with Pemulwuy once and for all. I want you to be my guide and advisor.'

Bennelong still said nothing.

'Well, man. What d'you say? Surely you wish to have that troublemaker brought to justice every bit as much as we do.'

After a long silence, Bennelong said, 'you will not find him. The Rum Corps will stop you. If they don't kill you, Pemulwuy will'.

Bennelong would not budge. Carpenter was shocked by Bennelong's prediction, but only slightly discouraged. He went back to Hunter that evening. It was agreed that he would command a force totalling two hundred and fifty men. He would have the lame Lieutenant Marshall with him. Surprisingly…even Paterson supported the exercise.

The plan was to divide this considerable force into two parts. One, commanded by Marshall, would patrol the north side of the harbour. Carpenter's, a smaller, more mobile unit, would operate closer to Pemulwuy's known haunts and attempt to match his movements.

Carpenter's reasoning was that if Hunter restrained immediate new settlement to the south side of the harbour, and kept things tight in the Parramatta area, Pemulwuy would attack either the north side of the harbour around Lane Cove and Kissing Point, or the Parramatta area itself. If Marshall's substantial forces were guarding the north shores, then Pemulwuy would be more likely to concentrate his attacks in the area that Carpenter patrolled.

Pemulwuy did indeed turn his force towards Parramatta, and Macarthur steeled himself for a major assault. But Pemulwuy contented himself with a few minor attacks on the perimeter farms before fading back into the bush.

There was some resistance to any further activities among the Eora, particularly from the Kamergal group. All supported Pemulwuy's reprisal attack on Lane Cove. They were reluctant, however, to be committed again to a full-scale conflict as before.

Koobee warned Pemulwuy that Bennelong's tantalising vision of cooperation with the British was causing a great reluctance among all the coastal people. Koobee believed that even Gro Mok was unlikely to sway them. He went so far as to suggest that the Kamergal, the Borogegal and the Karegal might attempt to make a new separate peace with the British.

Pemulwuy remembered the Irishman's warning of 'divide and conquer'. Curiously, his warnings of disease had worked on the British, but because no recent outbreak had occurred, he had failed to secure firm allies beyond Eora country. Pemulwuy was also worried about Carpenter's newfound support. He met with the Bidjigal and *Ramedigal* stalwarts.

'Carpenter is our only dangerous enemy,' he said. 'We shall spend the summer creating other enemies for him.'

Pemulwuy did this most effectively. From October until the end of January in 1797, Pemulwuy's attacks were small, isolated, simultaneous and mischievous. They ranged from Middle Harbour to Castle Hill, with occasional strikes as far as Kamay. The attacking forces were never more than twenty strong and usually much smaller. The raids occurred at dawn, dusk, or in the night. Occasionally provisions or animals were stolen, but usually the aim was to burn houses, fodder or crops, and to kill animals or people from a distance.

Carpenter's divided approach proved totally useless. The only action Marshall saw was in a bushfire, where he lost two men. The fire was apparently lit by accident. Macarthur, now recovered from his part in the breach of the truce, resumed his criticism of Carpenter. He organised delegations of settlers and emancipists to petition the Governor to remove him from command of the expeditionary force. Even Collins and Marshall were losing patience with Carpenter's efforts.

Carpenter was recalled to Sydney and confronted successively by Grose, Paterson, and finally Hunter. The Governor informed the unfortunate lieutenant that he felt impelled to place him under the command of the New South Wales Corps. He even went so far as to suggest that his tour of duty in New South Wales ought to be coming to an end and that he should consider returning to England.

Carpenter went to see Collins at his house. Collins provided little consolation. In fact, he strongly supported the idea of returning to England. He intimated that he was considering such a move himself.

'Pemulwuy is beyond the resources of a soldier. Leave him to the Rum Corps. One way or the other they will strangle him, even if it takes them twenty years and a thousand British lives.'

Collins caught Carpenter's arm in confidential, comradely style, 'even Tench saw that in the end, old chap'.

Carpenter left Collins's house in a mood of deep despair and walked down to the waterside. He had spent little time in the docks area in recent months. Now that he gave it his attention, the night time atmosphere of the place was impressive, even exciting. A substantial ship was pulled up at the new quay, its bare yards black against the liquid pearl of the still moonlit harbour.

He thought of England. Like so many who had volunteered for service in New South Wales, he had come to escape personal problems at home. Those problems seemed petty now, and in any case they must surely be buried by the years. He felt a surge of nostalgia. In England it would be winter, with a crisp hint of snow in the air, and no Pemulwuy. Then his stubborn obsession welled up inside him.

He shouted, 'God! Please let him attack Parramatta!'

In the early days of March in 1797, Toongabbie was the first British town to fall in battle to the Eora.

Toongabbie lay some four to five miles to the west of Parramatta, and by late 1796 it had become an independent centre for the surrounding farms. Parramatta was fast turning into a hellhole of vice and drunkenness as the western hub of the rum trade. The tight-knit western farming communities much preferred to do their socialising in Toongabbie.

Pemulwuy moved a force of some one hundred warriors, unseen, between the farms. At dawn on 22 February they launched a determined and sustained attack on this early British town. When the farmers became aware of the attack, they barricaded themselves inside their houses and some were able to watch Toongabbie burn. Pemulwuy's casualties were very few. The British suffered greatly. By half noon there was no more resistance.

Pemulwuy's forces ransacked and pillaged everything in sight and by noon were gone. Carpenter's wish had almost come true.

CHAPTER 32

PEMULWUY'S CHANT

The attack on Toongabbie stunned all of New South Wales. Even Collins was impressed with the skill of the operation. Although he now considered Pemulwuy nothing but a wild man, he admitted that this amounted to a serious military action.

Macarthur could stand the tension no longer. The situation in Parramatta was impossible. The place was full of horror stories from the Toongabbie refugees, and he got almost no cooperation from the local settlers. This time he was seriously anxious about the possibility of an attack on the town. He placed Lieutenant Palmer in command of the garrison and hightailed it For Sydney with the cry: 'Where is Carpenter?'

Carpenter fared very well out of the Toongabbie disaster. He was put back in charge of his expeditionary units and dispatched with all haste to Parramatta.

'Pemulwuy is bound to attack Parramatta,' Carpenter said brusquely when he met Lieutenant Palmer. 'He must not have another victory.'

Palmer glowered back, stung by Carpenter's seemingly officious arrogance.

'For God's sake, man,' he snapped, 'we are talking about a no-account savage who's had a bit of luck, not some serious military commander'.

'You think so?' said Carpenter with mild amusement. 'The bloody man has had substantial success against us for more than seven years.'

'Besides, the perimeter attacks we've had so far, have been nothing more than minor skirmishes,' Palmer persisted, 'and there's a vast difference between Toongabbie and Parramatta'.

Carpenter was having trouble keeping his temper in check. 'Sir,' he said through clenched teeth, 'you have a timber stockade. Therefore you are vulnerable. Pemulwuy could attack and burn the village at night and then starve you out of the barracks if he so chose. He is obviously sufficiently well organised to pick off reinforcements that come along the Parramatta Road, as they must'.

'Is that what you expect?' demanded Palmer, still trying to keep his end up, but becoming more uncertain by the minute.

Carpenter rested his chin in his hand.

'No, actually I don't,' he said more calmly. 'I believe that he will do all he can to split us and draw part of the force away from the town. Then he will attack. It has been his way in the past.'

He shrugged. Everything was speculation. Best to get down to known facts he thought.

'Have you any accurate idea of the size of the force we face?' Carpenter asked Palmer.

'Reports suggest between two and three hundred.'

Carpenter shook his head in wonderment.

'Dear Lord,' he said, 'he has really done it! Collins had told me that he is using some religious device to draw the Kamergal, Bidjigal and Karegal together. It's obviously true!'

'A foreman named Lewis claims that he saw Daruk and Tharawal men with the group as well,' said Palmer with a grave nod.

'The whole Eora world and some,' said Carpenter, 'and no doubt a few Irish as well'. 'Quite true. It's certainly an absurd situation.'

Carpenter smiled coldly, 'the Irish are your problem. Pemulwuy is mine'.

He drew up a chair and sat down. Palmer had a thorough dislike for Marines of any sort, and Carpenter in particular. He clasped his hands behind his back and faced Carpenter, thinking 'sarcastic bastard'.

'Do you intend to take the expedition out, then? Are you going to look for him?' he asked.

'That would be futile,' Carpenter answered crisply, 'the military risk would be too high, and in my experience it's a waste of time scouring the bush'. He waved a hand towards the west, 'he is no ordinary rogue, this one,' he added.

Palmer returned the compliment with a faint smile.

'Well, you should know, Mister Carpenter,' he said. 'He has, I understand, run you and Captain Tench from one end of the colony to the other.'

'That he has, Mister,' Carpenter responded grimly. His thoughts wandered for a moment to Tench and England, old promises and old loyalties, 'but sooner or later I shall have him'.

'You seem to think this is some kind of bloody adventure,' scoffed Palmer.

Carpenter was unperturbed. 'It is certainly bloody, and indeed, is not all this—this continent and this colony—a rather stupid adventure of some sort?'

Palmer was speechless. The veins stood out on his forehead. He recovered and merely said, 'this is a British colony'.

'Yes, of course,' said Carpenter cheerfully. He stood up once more, 'but, to go back to the matter at hand. I believe that he will attack, but with a relatively small force. Then he will withdraw swiftly. If he does so, I shall pursue a live trail—but not with all of the expeditionary force. I think he will try to double back and attack you here'.

'The stockade!' said Palmer. 'That's preposterous!'

Carpenter shook his head. 'Not so. He has the smell of our blood now...and confidence...he is already starving us out.'

The marine officer gestured towards the window.

'Where are your perimeter farms Captain Palmer?' he asked. 'You can't mount an armed guard on every farmhouse in the colony. He has effectively prevented us from taking meat from the land, and now he is stopping the planting of crops.'

He turned back on his heel to face Palmer. 'It is him or us, Mister! Him or us!'

They were joined by two younger members of the Corps: Lancing—who had been involved in the truce-breaking—and Cowlishaw. Carpenter explained his plan.

If and when Pemulwuy attacked next, he told them, a limited expedition of thirty or forty men would pursue him. The same number would leave in the opposite direction. Neither would go far. Carpenter expected that Pemulwuy would then double back and attack the settlement. At this point, he would have a substantial British force before and behind him. Pemulwuy would be quite aware of this situation. He would then have to choose between attacking a military formation in open country or attacking a fortified town.

'Whichever he chooses to attack, he faces musket fire,' said Carpenter. 'If he attacks Parramatta, I shall be forewarned by you and attack him from both sides and the rear.' He paused. 'It will cost him heavy casualties, and this he cannot bear.' He paused again. 'It is the wisdom of my experience that to cause Pemulwuy a heavy cost in blood is the way to his defeat.'

The plan seemed attractively simple and likely to be successful. Palmer gave his assent, and two mobile expeditions were prepared. Once this was done all they could do was wait. And wait they did—for almost a week.

Early in the afternoon on 16 March 1797, Pemulwuy attacked. There was a strong smell of rain in the air. The attack was substantial on both the western and northern sides of the settlement. The two attacks came about ten minutes apart, with the eastern attack first. There were two British casualties from spear wounds and a wagon ransacked on the northern side. The entire operation lasted no more than fifteen minutes, and then they were gone. Carpenter's two forces set off, one to give chase and the other in the opposite direction.

About three miles away from the settlement, Carpenter's detachment came upon a small group of Bidjigal men with some of the contents of the wagon. They fled at the sight of the British. At this point Carpenter stopped, moved back to within two miles of Parramatta and waited for Palmer's signal. A day later he sent a runner back. Two days later, late in the afternoon, Carpenter abandoned his plan and set off reluctantly for Parramatta once more. He felt an acute sense of defeat. Tench, he recalled, had almost lost his life at the hands of this demon, and even Collins had begun to believe that he was beyond defeat. It was as though he could read minds.

It was almost sunset when the party came within sight of Parramatta. Carpenter was very much aware of the shambling disorder of his troops after two nights in the bush. He halted the group and proceeded to restore order.

The harsh calling voices of the soldiers echoed in the silent land. The hawk, disturbed, rose upon his wings and watched the British patrol become ant-like. As he ascended, the dusty road healed into a dark thread which lost itself in the vague geometry of the embryonic alien town of Parramatta. The sun touched the mountain range and shed a pink pile carpet for his flight home.

The smell of eucalypt fires welcomed the weary band to Parramatta. The dusk had awakened the oil lights of the town. The group assembled; anxious to be dismissed. A few of the townspeople and their dogs wandered over to hear the company's news. Carpenter dismounted and stiffly saluted the waiting, disappointed Lieutenant Palmer.

A woman's scream split the twilight.

Carpenter and Palmer ran past the stunned soldiers towards the source of the outcry and stopped in total amazement.

Pemulwuy stood like a burnt tree less than thirty yards away on the roadway. His face was in shadow, his back to the west, a cloak about him and his right arm bare and free. In that light it could have been any Eora warrior, but it was Pemulwuy. Pemulwuy yelled at them. Carpenter drew his sword, and a dark shaft appeared in his chest. Carpenter fell to his knees. Palmer staggered backwards and for an instant he watched Carpenter die. Palmer shouted: 'Fire!'

The night exploded in musket blasts and shouting. A hail of spears and seven more Marines joined Carpenter on the ground. Palmer became what he could of a British officer. He stood stiffly and shouted close orders. The company surgeon ran up to him, shouted something, and died as a musket ball ripped through his left lung. It was a catastrophe. There was a fire and great commotion in the south of the town. The air was full of screams and musket fire.

'Regroup! Regroup!' bawled Palmer.

'Carpenter was right,' he thought as the nightmare unfolded. 'England is at war with these damned savages.'

He stood up, screamed out the pattern for retreat, and some order prevailed.

Palmer tried to see ahead into the darkness.

'Dispatch patrols, investigate, report,' he shouted and a sergeant scurried way.

Things had quietened down considerably. With the cessation of the musket fire, some of the light returned. At least two houses appeared to be ablaze in the south, but the civilians had become silent and hidden. There seemed to be only soldiers visible. There was the smell of burnt powder and burning timber, the sounds of the dead and dying. The only thing missing was the enemy.

It appeared that as the company had charged towards Pemulwuy, they had been attacked on both forward flanks by spears cast from a distance of at least thirty or more yards. Altogether twenty-two of the company had been injured. Five at least were dead from spears and some three or four from musket wounds received from their comrades or townsfolk in the confusion.

The township had also been attacked from the rear by a party estimated between forty and fifty men. One civilian had been killed, nine wounded, and four buildings set on fire.

By the time darkness had fallen, all of the Eora forces had withdrawn, but a strange waiting silence pervaded the night.

Palmer and Lancing were the only officers present when the time came to take stock of the situation. Lieutenant Cowlishaw was missing, and Carpenter was dead. The remaining sections of the expeditionary force, plus the Parramatta garrison, numbered some one hundred and sixty in all. The main problem for the two British officers was that they had no idea of the strength of the Eora force. The accuracy and devastating power of the spears under these circumstances gave muskets little advantage. Even men with minor spear wounds were a burden to their comrades.

The civilian population, meanwhile, was in a state of panic. They were also armed, which was a mixed blessing. Palmer feared they were just as likely to shoot British soldiers as Eoras if it came to the chaos of street fighting. Palmer knew that from a military point of view, he was paralysed. The entire initiative lay with Pemulwuy out on the perimeter, and all he could do was sit and wait for the next blow to be struck.

The loss of Parramatta before dawn was a real possibility. Palmer shuddered. For himself, and for Britain, it would be a crushing humiliation.

Carpenter was at last beyond success or failure. Ironically, he had been right, this last time. It had cost him his life. He had totally underestimated the sheer boldness, cunning and violence of which Pemulwuy's forces were capable, and he had paid a soldier's price for such a miscalculation.

The silence in the bush finally ended with mournful, piercing chants. The sound went on for some ten minutes, and then the perimeter went quiet again. The British waited anxiously, primed their muskets. But nothing happened.

About an hour later, there was another short spell of chanting, followed by a hail of spears and an attack, led personally by Pemulwuy, on the eastern side of the stockade. This time one Eora man was shot dead and one Englishman speared. It was a classic Pemulwuy hit-and-run attack. Some fifteen Eoras, supported by a larger group of spear-throwers, rushed a house, set it on fire, and then withdrew. By eleven o'clock that night, the moon was at its fullest and shed a brilliant light over the besieged township. Two more minor attacks had been mounted, and Eora weaponry littered the dusty streets of Parramatta. Still no major attack, but all this activity had the feeling of a softening-up process. Palmer knew he must be prepared for a major offensive before dawn.

If the Eora were to move on the settlement in force, the cost of defending the perimeter would be too high, Palmer decided reluctantly. Solemnly, his face a grim mask of humiliation, the young commander ordered the entire population to withdraw inside the stockade. He gave the town to Pemulwuy.

Two hours after midnight the town was occupied by the Eoras. Sentries at the stockade could now easily see the Eora people moving about the town. No more fires were lit, with the exception of a bonfire at the front of the makeshift church. The British waited.

An hour before dawn a meeting was held in front of the church. There were some twenty Eora men gathered around the fire, wrapped in skin cloaks.

'We must attack before dawn.'

'Tedbury is right.'

The second speaker was Yenowee.

'We have the weapon of fire and we must use it before daylight.'

Pemulwuy sat motionless and said nothing for a time. The others waited.

'I do not want their town,' he said at last.

Tedbury jumped to his feet.

'Woyan, this is the way of the British. Towns are their strength,' he answered.

He turned to the others. 'It must be ours tonight!'

'And what will you do with it, my son?' Pemulwuy's voice was restrained. Then he stood up and spoke loudly, 'build a Sydney for the Eora!' He moved his hand in a birdlike fashion, 'drink the rum!'

Pemulwuy, half bent, glared at the ground. Still in this stance, he thrust one arm towards Sydney. 'You want to be English; then go to Sydney. Join Bennelong!' Still holding one arm out, he thrust out the other, pursed his lips in the direction of his hand and said, 'our power is in the earth'.

Pemulwuy continued to hold this strange pose and there was silence.

It was difficult to tell whether the light still came from the moon, or whether dawn was beginning to break. Nor could any of the sentries clearly say when the figure first appeared, but it was Pemulwuy.

Palmer rushed to the parapet, accompanied by the ex-convict, now constable Barrington. Lieutenant Lancing stood transfixed by the apparition in the half-light.

The three of them and the sentries watched fascinated. The bizarre, one-eyed warrior stood motionless in his fur cloak, staring towards the stockade, unfathomable.

'It is the bastard!' said Lancing, turning to Palmer.

Barrington moved forward, his sharp face and keen eyes in the image of hawk.

'Sure it be 'im sir,' he confirmed. 'I haven't seen that face since Mr Macintyre was murdered. But I'll never forget it.'

Lancing, who had also clambered up to the parapet, looked around nervously.

'There must be two hundred out there, at least. But no fire. I don't understand.'

Palmer said nothing. For a moment longer he peered at Pemulwuy, measuring the distance—some forty yards. He caught the eye of Barrington, who gave him the ghost of an understanding smile. Palmer turned, reached out.

'Give me a musket!' he hissed, 'primed'.

He stood up to his full height, clear of the protecting wall, checked the priming and took careful aim. The report rang out, and the flash of powder cleared the darkness for an instant. The vision of Pemulwuy was frozen in the light of the discharge. Then darkness descended again.

Palmer leapt down from the parapet and the rest of the troops rushed to their positions. But nothing happened.

The wait until dawn was agonising. Still no movement beyond the stockade. No-one dared venture out of cover again until the sun was already quite high. When they did, they found themselves peering incredulously down at the prostrate figure of Pemulwuy. He lay where he had fallen in the hours of the night. There was red blood on his cloak and his dark skin. He looked very human.

'He is clearly shot dead,' said Palmer. 'A ball in the chest.'

He paced the parapet, considering his next action.

'Mr Lancing, do we have the powder to withstand any large-scale attack for long?' Palmer asked.

Lancing shook his head.

Palmer peered into the dawn light, 'I feel they are gone,' he said and turned to the soldiers below. 'Sergeant!' he bellowed as he came to a decision. 'Go retrieve that man's body!'

The small detail of Rum Corps soldiers went about their fearful task watched with dread by their comrades inside the stockade.

It was midday. Pemulwuy lay bleeding and breathing faintly in the midst of the British. Palmer had sent patrols out to scour the settlement.

'I can't be certain, but I think that man is close to death.'

This diagnosis came from a civilian of doubtful medical ability who was their only help since the death of the garrison surgeon during the fighting.

'As a matter of fact,' said the man, standing up, 'I can't understand how he can still be alive, sir. The ball seems to have passed right through his heart'.

Palmer nodded thoughtfully. 'Leave him. If he dies, he dies. In the meantime it is an advantage that we have him alive.'

He beckoned Lancing to his side. 'Mister Lancing, arrange a military escort. I shall take the prisoner to Sydney personally, be he dead or alive.' Palmer paused, 'and send a rider ahead. I want to be met by reinforcements from Sydney'.

Palmer swung around on a well-worn boot heel, shaken and exhausted, but knowing that he could be a proud soldier of his King once more. Almost as an afterthought, he said: 'I shall take Carpenter's body with me as well. He was a good soldier. Perhaps now they will promote him.'

The journey to Sydney, with the barely living Pemulwuy laid beside the body of his old enemy, was uneventful and painfully slow. At every turn they expected to be attacked by the Eora. The only surprise was that Palmer and his detachment were met less than four miles out of Parramatta. Somehow, Sydney had been made aware of the attack. When intercepted by Lancing's messenger, the reinforcements were already halfway to Parramatta.

By the time Palmer reached Sydney, he had mentally constructed a glorious account of the whole attack. The hundreds of screaming savages assaulting the thin, red line. How the native leader had been laid low with one, well-placed shot. Unfortunately for the lieutenant's hopes of a victor's laurels, he was met by his direct superior, Captain John Macarthur. Macarthur quickly took charge of the situation and conducted him into a very different world from the horror and confusion of the night of Pemulwuy. Macarthur was, of course, all smiles and approval. He seemed to know all the details of the fighting already.

'Believe me, I appreciate the job you did. Must have been quite an experience!' he told the young officer.

Palmer sat ill-at-ease in a chair.

'But you, after all, are the hero—not Pemulwuy,' Macarthur continued. 'You must not forget that. Yours was the extraordinary part in the action.'

Abbott arrived to join in the debriefing. In front of these two worldly-wise, older men, Palmer felt bedraggled and lost.

'We can, after all, hardly describe this as a military operation, a battle even.'

Macarthur glanced at Abbott, chuckled as if the very notion was ridiculous. 'A police action, perhaps, in which a young officer showed quite exceptional courage.'

He paused, beaming at Palmer encouragingly.

The lieutenant was speechless for a moment. 'But...how do you explain the casualties in Parramatta?' he stammered, 'it's impossible to…'

Macarthur shook his head, grasped Palmer by the shoulders almost tenderly, like an exasperated father, and said; 'Believe me, I understand these things.' He stood back.

'Seriously, Captain, to speak of war with a few hundred obscure primitives,' he shrugged, 'don't you see, this thing is getting quite out of proportion, to the point of absurdity'.

Macarthur worked his way back over to Abbott's desk and sat down heavily.

'What we have here,' he said, 'is another treacherous raid by a notorious band of savages'. He put his forefinger to his lips, 'our forces were taken by surprise; there were, of course, some minor casualties, including that damned marine. Lieutenant Palmer took charge of the situation and brought back the leader of the group to face British justice'.

Abbott nodded vigorous agreement. Palmer's face still wore a look of stunned disbelief, but he was under Macarthur's spell, like a rabbit with a wolf. Macarthur stood up again, and looked away from Palmer to stare out of the window, rocking gently on his heels.

'Lieutenant Palmer, you will, of course, be mentioned appropriately in my report. Lieutenant Carpenter will naturally receive full military honours. Now let's have done with the matter!' He turned back into the room and smiled. 'You should prepare yourself, dear fellow. We have some important news to report to His Excellency the Governor...'

Captain John Hunter stood in stony silence while the surgeon examined the pathetic figure of Pemulwuy. The Eora leader lay spread-eagled on the small bench in the jail. He was manacled by both feet.

Finally the surgeon stood up and addressed the Governor. 'Your Excellency, I cannot tell if his lung is pierced, but it is certainly collapsed,' he said. 'There seems to still be a good deal of bleeding in the chest cavity, and his heartbeat is very slow and feeble. He will die.'

'Is he conscious?' asked the Governor.

'Certainly not,' said the surgeon. 'It is unlikely that he will regain consciousness before he expires.'

The Governor sighed. 'So be it.' He looked down on the body of the man to whom he had tried to extend his idea of the hand of friendship. 'I wish to be notified the minute he dies,' he said.

The Governor turned on his heel and left the room, closely accompanied by an aide and Captain Abbott.

Macarthur lingered a while. He stood staring down at the prostrate figure before him—lifeless, but still surrounded by an aura of danger.

'Pemulwuy,' he whispered, 'your name means earth... God! Have we actually made an enemy of the earth itself!'

'He is to remain under guard,' said Macarthur with a nod to the soldier by the door, 'under strict guard, in irons, hand, foot and neck…iron shackles'.

By the end of the first day in the jail, Pemulwuy did indeed appear certain to die. His breathing seemed suspended, and he was comatose. There was no detectable heartbeat, but his body remained strangely warm. The surgeon examined him carefully, but would not declare him dead.

Petty Officer James Thomas, the Governor's aide, spoke quietly with Hunter on the evening of that first night.

'She is an Eora woman named Narewe,' he told Hunter. 'She has been at the jail all day, demanding to see the prisoner. She says that she is a relative and will not go away, no matter what the guards do.'

'Is she an associate of Pemulwuy?'

'Who knows, your Excellency. She seems harmless and has no weapon.'

'Did she say why she wishes to see him?'

'No, your Excellency. These people never do. Abbott and Macarthur are against it.'

The Governor frowned and rose from his armchair.

'Nonsense!' he growled, 'the wretched man is in chains, under guard, and at the point of death!' A shadow of a painful smile passed over his face. 'And it could well be in our interest to broadcast the news of his impending passing, Thomas,' he said. 'She is to be admitted for a short time…five minutes.'

The guard beside Nargel felt the chain in his hand grow cold. He changed his grip. The whole room seemed tense and poised as though Pemulwuy was about to die.

It seemed an age that Nargel stood there. Then she leant over, touched Pemulwuy, and began to sing softly to herself.

'Take her out,' said the other guard, 'she gives me the spooks'.

Nargel's song had developed into a definite chant by the time she stood under the southern stars. Those stars seemed to reach down and touch her and carry her lament into the wind.

By midnight the chant murmured along the whole of the Parramatta River. Sometimes it could be heard with clarity of diction; in other places, almost as a dream. By midmorning on the next day the chant had reached the Hawkesbury River in the north. It never stopped. It never changed its theme. The Eora world sang for Pemulwuy. By the fifth day the chant had become maddening. On the night of that day it stopped and Pemulwuy was gone from the British.

CHAPTER 33

THE CONSPIRACY OF SILENCE

Pemulwuy's mysterious escape from Sydney had a more profound effect on both the British and Eora communities than any of his military victories. He had been seriously wounded, locked in a cell, in chains, under guard...and he had simply vanished! From this time, neither the British nor the Eora regarded Pemulwuy as an ordinary man.

Sydney became a town of rumours. There were wild stories that Pemulwuy had become a crow and escaped. Someone reported that he was seen walking through the air beneath the full moon. Even the seats of power were not immune to him, his mania, or his magic. One evening in April, a frightened servant girl came rushing out of the Governor's drawing room, gabbling that she had seen Pemulwuy standing bold as brass on the Governor's terrace. So convincing was her terror that Hunter, two of his aides, and a sergeant-at-arms carried out a search of the terrace and the surrounding area.

The first reliable report that Pemulwuy was actually alive came soon after, from none other than Lieutenant Marshall, the New South Corps officer, who had earlier been a reluctant 'guest' of the Eora leader.

Marshall had been sent down to Botany Bay with a small detachment to investigate rumours of rum-smuggling in the lower reaches of the Georges River. Making the trip from Sydney by boat, he landed in the bay of Kamay and set up his first camp on the northern shore of the river mouth.

A naval officer, Matthew Flinders, had carried out a detailed survey of these waterways just the year before, accompanied by a surgeon named Bass and an Eora boy, Bungaree. Flinders had reported the natives to be friendly and helpful. Predictably, given the reputation of the New South Wales Corps these days, Marshall's reception had not been nearly as welcoming.

Not long after the landing, two of Marshall's men had come to him in a state of some anxiety, bringing tales of native sorcery in the neighbourhood. They had suggested to their commander that they move camp as soon as possible, since they were a small force and vulnerable to sudden attack. After some thought, the equally nervous Marshall had ordered them to shift camp about a mile further upriver. There they took over one of the huts left from the earlier settlement, grateful for the measure of security provided by its sturdy walls. The plan was to lie low and use this vantage point to report on any suspicious river traffic.

No smugglers came. Perhaps someone, somewhere, had spread the rumours to put the forces of law and order on a false trail. Soon time began to drag. The entire expedition was beginning to feel like a fruitless exercise, and there had been no sign of hostile natives either. The lieutenant had taken to wandering alone around the pleasant, sandy landscape immediately behind the camp. His damaged foot still gave some pain and he limped slightly. This late afternoon, in the course of his 'constitutional', Marshall discovered a discarded umana. It was a beautifully made implement and he examined it with keen interest. By all appearances, it looked as though it had been used for some purpose which had damaged the barb to which the spear was fitted for throwing. Marshall was still idly musing on his find—a suitable souvenir of this godforsaken place, perhaps—when a shadow spoke to him from his far left.

'Is that something of value to the Rum Corps?' asked a sardonic voice in the distinctive clipped accent of the native-born Australian.

Marshall turned and felt his chest tighten with fear. There was Pemulwuy, no more than twenty feet from him, perched like a crow in the low branch of a dead tree. He had a large cloak draped around his powerful shoulders, and his turned eye caught the fading daylight in an eerie fashion that reminded Marshall of the goblins who had haunted the fairytales of his English childhood.

'Do not call out,' Pemulwuy said quietly.

He had no spear or any other visible weapon, but Marshall knew better than to think his enemy was defenseless. The lieutenant did not move a muscle.

'Tell me,' Pemulwuy continued pleasantly: 'Is the Governor displeased that I escaped his jail?'

Marshall took a deep breath. He was, after all, a gentleman and an officer of the King. He must maintain his dignity this time...although he was overcome by a cold fear.

'The Governor, like the rest of us, is completely at a loss as to how you did it,' he answered with a casualness that he did not feel. Marshall remembered what had happened to Captain Collins when he had met Pemulwuy on a lonely beach.

Pemulwuy said nothing—just watched him expectantly—like a cat pausing in its play with a mouse.

'And ... how is your health?' Marshall stammered. He immediately felt foolish. To speak this way to this mysterious dark spirit-like creature, who had so damaged his foot during his captivity! Enquiring after his health, as though Pemulwuy were an acquaintance met while out riding in the park. Marshall gritted his teeth and asked: 'How is Awabakal and the English girl Millicent?'

'They are well; I shall tell them that you asked.'

'I would be pleased if you would,' Marshall replied, amazed at the surreal nature of this strange conversation.

Pemulwuy threw back his head and uttered a strange cackling laughter.

'And tell the Governor I am very busy building him a ship to take him back to England!'

With that, he slipped down from the tree and moved forward a few paces. Then he sidestepped and disappeared noiselessly into the bush.

Marshall stayed rooted to the spot for some time, staring stupidly at the empty branch. This was a strange, strange country. Had he really seen the living body of his enemy? Or had it been some apparition? A figment of the heat or a creation of his fear! And as it turned out, Marshall found it no easy matter convincing anyone of his encounter when he got back to Sydney. At that time, the easiest way to cast doubts on your own sanity was to claim that you had seen Pemulwuy somewhere. It was only after he had talked things through with Collins and, with his support; he succeeded in convincing the Governor that he was sane and had seen Pemulwuy.

Governor Hunter sat with William Paterson in his drawing room, each nursing a glass of sweet wine. Their surroundings were comfortable, but hardly redolent of vice-regal splendour. As for the Governor himself, he was a troubled man, conscious of his precarious and isolated position in the colony. Despite all the impressive powers conferred on him by the Colonial Office, and the high hopes with which he had arrived in New South Wales, his stewardship had been something of a failure. The New South Wales Corps had him over a barrel—and a rum barrel, at that. These days there were very few officers he could trust, but the man with him now could be reckoned at least halfway reliable. Hunter was more dependent on Paterson's company and advice than he would have cared to admit.

The Governor took a sip of wine and sighed.

'I find it quite extraordinary,' he said slowly, 'this business of Pemulwuy. I have been attempting to find out more of the details of his rise to notoriety. But, God help me, there's not a single mention of the man's name in any official records that I can lay my hands on'.

Paterson looked at his superior and smiled warily.

'I see, sir…'—he left the sentence hanging.

'And yet he has been involved in the affairs of the colony one way or another, for more than ten years,' Hunter pressed on, 'and he has been an active opponent of our interests for at least eight of those...'. He made a languid gesture of disgust. 'It appears that there has been something of a conspiracy of silence.'

Paterson cleared his throat. 'I must admit it is rather strange,' he said, 'though I confess I hadn't quite seen the matter in that light'.

'Phillip left some notes relating to the murder of his gamekeeper, Macintyre,' Hunter said. 'Those notes clearly indicate that Pemulwuy perpetrated the crime. And yet the official record does not name him. Astonishing! Not at all what I would have expected. Captain Phillip was usually a most thorough administrator.'

'I see your point, sir,' Paterson said reluctantly. 'Be that as it may, however, it could be argued that...ah...we have come a little far to be introducing the fellow to the world now. I would humbly submit that it would look even odder if he were suddenly to figure prominently in our records and dispatches.'

Hunter refused to take the hint. He had spent most of his life commanding a ship of the line, not playing politics. Paterson winced as the Governor suddenly thumped the arm of his chair and snapped.

'My good man, lives were lost in the so-called incidents at Toongabbie and Parramatta! I cannot ignore that fact. And yet, I have had the utmost difficulty in prising any details out of the officers involved—and especially any admissions that this fellow Pemulwuy played a leading part in the disasters. This can't go on! Palmer's report reads like a complete fabrication!'

'Sir——'

'For God's sake, I was here in Sydney, I know what happened—and I have a pretty good idea of the casualties.' There was an uneasy silence. 'It is obvious to me that there has been a concerted attempt to keep Pemulwuy's existence and activities hidden.' Hunter continued in a calmer voice, 'furthermore, if I don't enter his name in my reports I shall, in effect, be joining your conspiracy to conceal the existence of a very cunning and troublesome enemy of the crown. I'd wager we're not finished with him yet!' He paused thoughtfully, 'I have still not received any sensible explanation of how he escaped from detention'.

Paterson choked slightly on his drink, but covered up his discomfiture quickly.

'Sir, I must protest,' he said, 'if there is indeed a conspiracy—and I don't believe that this is necessarily so—then I am no part of it. While acting Governor, I made numerous notes of the man's activities in my diary, as did Captain Collins. There is ample evidence…'.

'Then I must ask you to help me, William,' said the Governor, cutting him short in his gruff naval manner. 'I want you to get to the bottom of this. And I want to obtain the names of those natives said to have been involved in those attacks.' He paused thoughtfully. 'Perhaps, to avoid embarrassment, we could simply name Pemulwuy along with those of his henchmen, without special prominence.' Hunter smiled sourly and suddenly felt a long way from home. 'God knows, most Englishmen would have considerable difficulty pronouncing them, let alone summoning up any interest in their identities. But we must try, we must try....'

There was no avoiding it. The next day, Paterson began his enquiries. Or at least he got as far as speaking to Collins. Both men did a polite little dance around the issue at first. Both expressed their surprise at the Governor's suspicions. A conspiracy? Collins was clear that he personally had included Pemulwuy's name in a number of his reports. If the native leader's name had not subsequently appeared in any official documents forwarded to the Governor, it was certainly no fault of his.

'Of course, of course,' Paterson agreed hastily. 'The Governor does, however, demand some sort of explanation. The question must remain.'

Collins could only nod. 'It must indeed. I can't imagine he would make a lot of fuss about nothing. Curious!' His pink forehead furrowed with thought, 'except, of course...I mean, it would be understandable if the officers responsible at the time had been reluctant to make a hero of Pemulwuy. I mean, it is one thing to turn in reports of scattered native resistance, and so on. It's quite another to—shall we say—place undue importance on a single individual leader. Then it begins to look like a full-scale rebellion and questions start to be asked in high places. At least, that's my experience.'

'Good Lord, are you saying there might have been something going on?'

'Of course, one can't be certain. I am only thinking aloud, William. Trying to help.'

Paterson nodded. Collins's house, like all the dwellings in the young colony, was built on British lines without many concessions to the local climate. He was sweating, and he was very tired after staying up half the night being polite to the Governor through several bottles of wine. He grabbed at the opportunity that presented itself. He had to give the Governor something, and perhaps Collins was the man to get it for him. At all costs he wanted to avoid getting his fellow officers in the New South Wales Corps into hot water. He might not approve of the way they played politics, but if he let them down, he would end up an outcast. Far better to leave the dirty work to Collins. Collins disliked the Corps, had no ambitions as a rum merchant, and had a well-known bee in his bonnet about Pemulwuy.

'Nevertheless,' Paterson said smoothly, 'I suppose we should follow every lead, however unlikely. And as a resident of the colony of some ten year's standing with many informal friendships and acquaintances—not to mention experience of local conditions—it is possible that you could pursue this matter more effectively than I. Do you believe Pemulwuy to be an important leader, and his blacks a danger to us?'

Collins' face darkened. 'Upon my oath I do! He is a madman. He holds these otherwise innocent people under a spell and urges them on to violence. I myself was the victim of his uncontrollable bloodlust. Were we to kill him, New South Wales would benefit beyond measure.'

'An interesting point of view. I must bow to your superior knowledge. Would it be too much to ask you to make some enquiries?'

Collins looked at Paterson, then shrugged ruefully, realising that the other man had neatly passed the card on.

'Very well,' he said. 'I'll talk to some people. Unofficially, of course.'

'Naturally, and thank you.'

Paterson had been right. Collins had ten year's experience of New South Wales, and he knew that his task would not be an easy one. No-one he spoke to, and especially the officers of the New South Wales Corps, showed much interest or desire to pursue the subject. Their rum monopoly had turned these officers into businessmen, a state within the state, and Collins knew it. Nevertheless, he could not push too hard without going beyond the bounds of etiquette, which he had no power to do, and for their part his brother officers and officials fobbed him off with a casualness that was almost insulting. The plump Abbott's response was typical—a subtle guarded manner, hidden beneath a facade of affable banter.

'I suppose you could say we have a problem, old boy,' he told Collins, 'you could even stretch the point and say those blacks are challenging our sovereignty. But I don't think we can invest one particular savage—say, this Pemulwuy character—with any special powers. Unless you believe all this poppycock about sorcery. The fact is, the blacks are far too disorganised for that sort of thing.

It's quite understandable that the reports don't give the chap too much prominence. Wouldn't make sense to do that.'

'I believe that Pemulwuy is a rabid dog,' Collins said, momentarily losing his composure, 'I also believe that he is, in his way, a cunning and ruthless opponent of our authority and quite capable of leading a full-scale rebellion. In fact, without him there would be no 'incidents' as you choose to call them. What do you say to that?'

'Aha! You're getting like old Tench with his 'black Hannibal' notions, Collins,' Abbott chuckled. 'That won't get you anywhere. Look what happened to him!'

Collins could not help but rise to the occasion. 'Regardless of what might or might not have become of Captain Tench, this man Pemulwuy has very effectively opposed us here. He has taken many British lives to the point of threatening our sovereignty on this land, and he has done this for a decade. I can well understand the Governor's concern. Worse still, there must be many others who know of this and the future will hold us responsible.'

At that point Collins gave up on Abbott and he left.

Eventually Collins made a visit to Lieutenant Marshall, the only officer to have seen Pemulwuy alive since his escape from Sydney. The man was clearly lonely and suffering from the privations of colonial life and the continuing problems with his injured foot from when he was detained by Pemulwuy. He looked sallow and exhausted, even ill, when they met, and his distress became even more marked when Collins explained his purpose.

'I really don't feel I'm qualified to judge, sir,' he said at first, 'perhaps there are people more experienced'.

'We've both had the dubious privilege of meeting Pemulwuy. We have discussed the fact that he is obviously a serious threat, and never mind what Macarthur and company say, be frank with me, for goodness sake, Mister. In reality, you have had the closest contact with him of anyone.'

Marshall nodded vaguely. 'Pemulwuy is very dangerous.'

'Then why this reticence about him? If he represents a threat to our control of this region, why has he not been identified and dealt with appropriately? Why hasn't the Colonial Office been informed?'

'Sir, I am a junior officer without much experience.'

'Come, man! You've got eyes in your head; you've got ears to hear with!' Marshall swallowed hard and toyed with a paperweight on the table beside him.

'Of Pemulwuy and his people I cannot tell you very much,' he murmured, 'no more than I have ever been able to tell you already. As a prisoner I was for the most part an observer and only saw the man once or twice. There was a man who might have been able to be more help.'

'Who?'

'The private soldier who shared my captivity. A man named James Cawley. A simple soul, but with a brain in his head and a big heart. I think of him often now that he is no longer here.'

'Is he dead?' asked Collins impatiently.

'No,' said Marshall with a wry smile. 'He broke his leg. It was mended native fashion, so that it healed but remained slightly lame. The wretched fellow was sick for home and the life of sorts he could make for himself there. He was offered both a land grant and a position on an officer's holding but he refused both. He obtained an honorable discharge from the Corps, a promotion to corporal and passage home. He was a loyal comrade during our captivity, and he understood the natives well. Far better than any of us educated creatures.'

'I seem to recall the name…'

'And, like all the rest of us officers and gentlemen, you did not see fit to record his impressions of life with the savages of New South Wales. Well, he knew much about Pemulwuy and his cohorts. Now that he is gone, and he can no longer be called a traitor, I will confess on his behalf; he rather admired them. After all some of them arranged our release and our passage back to Sydney. I must admit I was especially grateful to the fellow who directly assisted us.'

Collins frowned. 'I see, and you?'

'Sir, I do not have Cawley's simplicity. To me, as an officer of His Majesty, they remain enemies, these natives. It is with that in mind that I agree with you; whatever their admirable traits, they are fierce and determined enemies of England, to be taken very seriously.'

Marshall paused, his eyes tired. He put a hand to his forehead.

'Looking back now I have come to form an opinion that we could somehow have done better than we did at the time,' he paused again thoughtfully, then went on, 'those who deny the nature of Pemulwuy's war have only their own interests at heart'.

Collins asked, 'and who are these people who deny the danger from Pemulwuy and might wish to conceal the facts?'

'Sir—I wish it to be clear that I cannot criticise any of my superiors or brother officers by name,' Marshall said slowly, 'do I have your assurance that this will go no further?'

'You have my assurance. This is not an official inquiry.'

'As you know,' Marshall began, 'the position of the New South Wales Corps in this colony is quite unusual. We are all of soldiers, jailers and administrators. This role is in some ways taxing, in another potentially advantageous'.

'You are referring to officers' involvement in the rum trade?'

Marshall nodded, 'and the ways in which certain officers of the Corps are able to...set themselves up in a splendid, even nabob-like style of life. Then there is the question of land grants, from which those same officers are in a position to profit mightily, with the added advantage of cheap convict labour to work their estates'.

'This is all common knowledge, regrettably,' Collins murmured with a frown. 'What has it to do with Pemulwuy?'

'If...and this is only a theory, sir...London realised the scale of native unrest, it might do two things: First, inquire into the causes of that unrest, second...'—Marshall paused uneasily, 'the government might see fit to send reinforcements fresh from the home country—forces under the command of officers who would probably object to the way in which business is conducted in New South Wales under the present military administration. Do you follow me, sir?'

Collins understood immediately. Unfortunately, the young officer refused to discuss the matter in any more detail or name names. He had already gone further than he had intended. So far as Marshall was concerned, all he wanted to do was to serve his time and get back to England's green and pleasant land, where there were proper courts, freedom of a sort, no snakes or spiders—and certainly no chilling, goblin-like black assassins like Pemulwuy hiding in the trees.

'Well, thank you Frances, you have been very helpful. I have one more favour to ask of you. There is a lady, few enough such creatures out here, who wishes to speak to you about your time when held by Pemulwuy's people.'

'Who is she?'

'Her name is Penelope Reid. She is a writer of some sort and the daughter of Edward Reid, the timber merchant…owns a brig and imports timber from New Zealand.'

'Yes, I think I've heard of him, also deals in some sort of live stock.'

'Yes, that's the fellow. Actually, he breeds heavy horses, draught horses you know.'

Marshall nodded, 'I will be happy to assist the lady'.

Collins walked slowly back towards his own house, pondering on what Marshall had told him, realising that he had found a very good reason why Hunter's underlings were playing down the native resistance. But why had Pemulwuy's name been virtually expunged from the records? Collins was too much a product of his own culture and time to share Tench's vision of Pemulwuy as a 'modern Hannibal'. But there was no doubt of the man's importance among his own people, or of the threat he represented to the colony of New South Wales.

'But why not name him?'

After a short rest, he went in search of Bennelong. Bennelong had always explained so much in the old days and they had shared Governor Phillip's friendship. Perhaps he could explain this oddity further. It took Collins an hour's tramping around the dusty roads of the settlement before he found his mark. Bennelong was sitting in the shade near the fish markets, staring at the passing scene—the gangs of convicts, the shopkeepers, the casual strollers, the officers out riding—and he was rotten drunk on rum.

Collins stared down at him with mingled sadness and distaste. The lively intelligence, the nobility of the early years was gone. Here was a derelict human being in European rags. His upper lip had been split and there were angry bruises on his dark skin.

'Good God, man,' he murmured. 'What have you been doing to yourself?'

Bennelong stared at him hazily. 'My life is bad, Mr Collins, very bad. The government stipend...is not enough for food or good clothes.'

Though sufficient for gut rot rum, thought Collins, but he said nothing.

'And my health is also bad.' Bennelong rambled on, 'in the town everything costs so much. If the Governor would only...'.

Collins leaned over, pulled the man to his feet, and inspected his injuries. The cut was inflamed, possibly infected.

'How did you get that?' he asked sharply.

'I fell, Mr Collins.'

'And who pushed you?' Collins gripped the tatters of the man's coat and looked at him sternly.

Bennelong kept up the pretence for a moment more. When Collins continued to hold him, he gave a crooked smile and mumbled: 'A fight, my own people. Since Pemulwuy escaped from the jail, I am no longer popular with them.' He seemed to think for a moment, then said strangely, 'you tried so hard to kill him, but you killed me instead'.

The bitterness in Bennelong's voice was both chilling and pathetic. So Collins' investigation into the conspiracy of silence ended in a riddle. Collins hadn't the heart to upbraid him for his drunkenness, and he needed something much more. As for his task for Governor Hunter, he never even penetrated the first part of the half truths.

'Come on, old chap,' he said with a sigh, taking Bennelong's arm. 'You're coming home with me.'

It was a strange progress back to Collins's house—the tall, erect officer with a pronounced limp with his arm around the ragged Eora man, half supporting, half dragging him along the road under the curious gazes of the townsfolk. Finally they reached home. Collins called for his convict servant to fill a bath for their guest.

After Bennelong had been bathed and scrubbed, Collins cleaned up his wound and put surgical spirit on it to inhibit the infection. Bennelong had sobered up enough to be both sullen and watchful, his eyes searching the living quarters for more alcohol. Recognising that Bennelong's cooperation had its price, Collins poured himself and Bennelong a glass of claret each.

Bennelong drank gratefully, and on the second glass he became more communicative, until Collins put his leading question.

'I have a problem,' he told Bennelong. 'It seems that, despite his prominence among the native troublemakers, Pemulwuy's name does not occur in the official records. You were Governor Phillip's friend. You have been in the bush with military expeditions. You hear what people say. I want you to tell me why you think Pemulwuy's name is never mentioned.'

Bennelong had appeared quite cheerful. As Collins moved towards his question, Bennelong's face began to cloud over. There was a silence while he drank some more wine.

'I don't know anything about Governor Phillip's records,' he said then, 'the Governor was an honest man and a good friend to me. That is all I know'.

'Then you have no explanation?'

'Not that you would understand, Mr Collins,' said Bennelong softly, with a kind of mysterious sadness.

'Nevertheless, tell it to me,' said Collins, moving to refill Bennelong's glass. He decided to let Bennelong drink if it helped him to talk. He could always sleep it off later. A bed could be made up for him somewhere.

'Ah...you must know, Mr Collins, that among my people the name of a person who dies is never mentioned again.' Bennelong continued 'maybe many, many years later it can be said. The name goes in the secret language. And if the person's name is like some other word—a word for food, water, meat—then we must find a new word. Perhaps we will take it from some other language, or create our own new word...'.

'That is all very interesting,' Collins interrupted him impatiently, 'but Pemulwuy is most certainly alive!'

Bennelong's eyes were hooded as he stared at the Englishman.

'For you, for the British, perhaps he is not. Perhaps for you he is dead, not a human. Perhaps that is why you cannot mention his name.'

CHAPTER 34

GALGALLA

Because Milbab had become ill in the winter of 1797, and Koobee spent a lot of time with her, Boolayoo had been sent back to his mother at Waun.

'Now that will keep your tail down for a while, then,' said Kate Donovan.

Nargel looked up with a grin. Nargel was in her mid-twenties now. She looked very youthful, but usually resented references from older women about her wayward girlhood. Silky was an exception. She teased Nargel further.

'The child is looking whiter each time I see him. I think that it is English that Milli should be teaching him.'

Nargel hugged her somewhat oversized five-year-old. He resisted, disengaged himself and ran off to join a group of other children.

'To be serious, Silky, I suppose that you are right. He should learn English.'

'The little devil does not even speak Bidjigal well. You would think his father, bless him, was Kamergal instead of a fine Irishman.'

'You teach him English, Silky.'

'Goodness. I don't speak the language so well myself.'

Nargel laughed.

'Well, you don't speak Bidjigal at all.'

'Now that's not true, my girl,' said Kate Donovan. 'If you listen closely you will find I have a kind of Irish-Bidjigal.'

They both laughed. 'Milli is the one to teach the boy.'

Then Kate asked Nargel about her relationship with Pemulwuy.

'You know what that sort of second wife is among our people,' Nargel said.

Kate agreed that this might be the case for herself, but Nargel ought to have considerably more in the way of charming a man and getting his blood up.

Nargel laughed. 'I think that the last time Pemulwuy had yanga was when Boorea produced Tedbury.'

'But I saw you swimming in the river with him one time.'

Nargel laughed again. 'I'd not do it now,' she said, 'he has so many musket holes in him, he would sink'.

'And that's a strange business,' said Kate. 'Do you believe that he can't be killed?'

'No,' Nargel answered with great seriousness. She then horrified Kate by laughing and saying, 'he is already dead'.

Boolayoo came running up to his mother and told her to come quickly. Kate and Nargel followed the child to where a group of Bidjigal people were looking at a very sick Kamergal visitor. Kate examined the prostrate man.

'It is smallpox, I think,' she said.

Nargel stood up and signalled the others back.

'It has come,' she said. 'It is galgalla.'

The Kamergal man died the next morning and the campsite was abandoned. Kate Donovan insisted that nobody touch the body, and the whole campsite was set on fire.

'Fire is the only protection against the accursed thing,' said Kate, 'we must burn every place where we know it to have been'.

The disease moved slowly through the winter and, at Kate's insistence, Pemulwuy burnt out all of the Waun district and most of the Hawkesbury area. Kate and Pemulwuy fought incessantly about this. She usually won and the Bidjigal people spent most of the winter and the spring far out of reach of the disease and the British.

The strange disease reached epidemic proportions among the coastal group and particularly the unfortunate Kamergal, who had suffered badly with the early smallpox epidemic. Milbab died, and Bennelong told Hunter that only Koobee and two others remained alive from this entire group. 'We were at the point when it seemed possible to separate the coastal groups from the troublesome Bidjigals; Pemulwuy's prophecy of galgalla had been fulfilled. There is not a native in New South Wales who will trust us now. That includes Bennelong,' said Marshall.

'Can we not help them in any way?' asked the Governor. Balmain said that there was nothing that they could do. He confirmed that the disease was smallpox. It had also appeared among some of the Europeans, but the practice of isolation and quarantine contained it.

'Pemulwuy's people seem to be faring well,' said Balmain. 'I believe there is some old convict woman immune to the disease who is advising the Eora.'

One morning in mid-October a furious argument broke out between Kate, Nargel, Boorea and Pemulwuy. Pemulwuy's brave lieutenants, Yenowee and Weuong, ran for cover and Milli with them.

Koobee had remained in the infected Kamergal country, mourning his dearly beloved Milbab. Both Nargel and Boorea had pressed Pemulwuy to bring him into the safe Bidjigal lands. Pemulwuy sympathised with his wives' concerns, but he refused to allow Bidjigal people to become exposed to the galgalla. A mouthful of abuse from Nargel had resulted in her being knocked to the ground with a bleeding nose. Nargel had in return attacked the great warrior and bitten him ferociously on the calf of his leg. Boorea had also attacked him, and it was Kate who, in a sense, rescued Pemulwuy from his furious wives.

Kate agreed in principle with the two women, but she also agreed with Pemulwuy. There was only one solution. She and Pemulwuy would go and see what could be done for Koobee.

It was an odd couple who began the dangerous journey down the north side of Tuhbowgule in the early summer of 1797. Pemulwuy walked unchallenged through the Australian bushlands, his great cloak hung about one shoulder. His face was decorated with two white vertical marks, he now always wore his hair up in a forehead band, and he had a wide bone ornament through his nose. He had bent the might of Britain in the antipodes; he had defeated or killed the best warriors that Britain had pitted against him. He was probably the greatest warrior that ever walked the continent of Australia. Trundling along behind him was Kate Donovan, a heavy ganimantj skirt draped quite gracefully about her waist and a string bag over one shoulder. Her greying reddish hair, almost waist long, flowed and tossed about her bare sunburnt back and breasts. Kate was the involuntary, unsure—but the ultimate—European adventurer. The two made camp in a pleasant, though exposed, clearing on the edge of the great harbour.

'Silky,' said Pemulwuy, 'if we both die of the galgalla, what will become of the Eora?'

'It won't kill me,' said Kate, 'and there is nothing the British have that could kill the likes of you'.

'I am immune to muskets,' said Pemulwuy. 'Ah, you have a healing thing about you,' said Kate. 'I saw that wild wife of yours tear a piece of meat out of you that would have made an Irishman lame for a month. You healed in two days.'

Kate Donovan dropped off to sleep early as the night darkened. Pemulwuy waited until the night was deep. He then slipped away and carefully circled the camp. Finally he found a comfortable spot some thirty paces from their campsite and there fell into the half sleep of the universal soldier.

Pemulwuy and Kate arrived at Kayumy late in the afternoon. Pemulwuy had carefully reconnoitred each human group they encountered. Kate on the other hand was becoming less certain of the situation as she examined each dead body they found.

They found Koobee lying alone in his house, deathly sick. Pemulwuy had looked inside first and came out to give his verdict.

'It is too late Silky, he is dying,' he announced sadly.

Kate pushed him aside, entered the dwelling and kneeled down beside Koobee. She awakened him and stared at his feverish moist eyes. Then she took the cloak off his naked body. Her own liquid green eyes swept over his dark skin.

'How long, Koobee?' she asked.

He held up his hand and stretched out five fingers. 'Is this the same as for Milbab?'

Koobee croaked a painful 'yes'.

Kate stepped outside to where Pemulwuy stood like a black archangel.

'It is not galgalla. I suspected it was something else.'

She swept her skirt about her.

'The poor devil is half starved.'

She jerked her thumb over her shoulder.

'Your bloody highness, go and catch us some fresh meat and some plant food.'

Pemulwuy cursed this white witch that fate had attached to him—and proceeded to obey her wishes.

'Be quick!' she shouted as he disappeared into the bush.

Hunting and gathering was difficult for Pemulwuy in this part of his world, so he did his vegetable gathering first and returned.

'This is woman's work, Silky,' he said angrily.

'Having children is woman's work, your majesty,' she replied. 'Feeding a sick comrade is everybody's work. Now get us some meat.' It was getting dark and Kate's task weighed heavily upon Pemulwuy. The only thing that he could easily catch hereabouts would be a British soldier. Perhaps he thought old Silky would not notice the difference between a Rum Corps' hindquarter and a piece of ganimantj.

'Eating a *Djeraba* would not really be cannibalism,' he said to himself. Nevertheless, he arrived back well after dark with two possums. Koobee was sitting up, having eaten a broth that Kate had made from a selected portion of the vegetables that Pemulwuy had brought earlier.

Kate would not let Pemulwuy come too close to Koobee while she baked the possum. Koobee ate some of the meat, and then went to sleep again.

'What is the sickness?' asked Pemulwuy.

'It is a cold of some sort, I think, but certainly not smallpox.'

Pemulwuy recalled that he had been very sick from a cold once when he was living in Sydney.

'I was here in '89 when these people were hit hard by the pox,' said Kate. This sickness looks a bit the same, but it is not your galgalla.'

'But he was dying,' said Pemulwuy.

'Of starvation, I think', said Kate, 'a few days and we can take him back'.

They had to travel very slowly with Koobee on the way back. Kate insisted that they travel further into the Kamergal area so that she could confirm to herself that the disease afflicting this group was not the dreaded smallpox.

Many days later, they brought Koobee into Bidjigal country. There was rejoicing that their disaster-prone brother had this time avoided the worst.

The war could continue. The legend of galgalla had now become a powerful ally.

CHAPTER 35

A DIFFERENT KIND OF WAR

Whatever the disease was that affected the coastal people of New South Wales in 1797, it served Pemulwuy's ends well. Any immediate threat to his authority disappeared. The Kamergal group were decimated by the disease and were thereafter neither able to contribute to nor oppose Pemulwuy's activities.

Hunter did his best to debunk the smallpox scare, but to little avail as far as the Eora were concerned. Not very many of the British believed him either.

Pemulwuy had more or less a free rein in the Parramatta and Georges Rivers region. He attacked at will, but was finding that his destruction of the resolve and effectiveness of the Rum Corps had created a new enemy—the settlers themselves. These determined and hardy people, living within sight of each other, were well armed and becoming difficult targets. A number of leaders had arisen among them. One such man was called George Barrington, the tough ex-convict whom Macarthur had made Chief Constable of Parramatta.

In the first six months of 1798, Pemulwuy lost as many warriors to the settlers' guns as he had in the last two years to the Rum Corps and the Marines.

It remained a puzzle to the more intelligent British officers why Pemulwuy did not attack the individual farms with larger forces. Collins was among those who were bemused by his strategy—or apparent lack of—though he could still fall back on the explanation that Pemulwuy was at heart no more than an irrational savage. He had become more concerned, even fascinated, by another aspect of the situation.

One night Collins wrote of Pemulwuy, referring to a conversation with the now much-respected Chief Constable Barrington:

'A strange idea was found to prevail among the natives respecting the savage Pemulwuy, which was likely to prove fatal to him in the end. Both he and they entertained the opinion that from his having been frequently wounded he could not be killed by our firearms. Through his fancied security, he was said to be at the head of every party that attacked the maize grounds and it certainly became expedient to convince them that he was not endowed with any such extraordinary exemption.'

Expedient or not, there was nobody in New South Wales capable of teaching Pemulwuy other than what he chose to believe. It appeared that both David Collins and Pemulwuy had a common enemy in the Rum Corps. Collins' expressed opinions, and his enquiries into the conspiracy of silence, finally caused his transfer. The Rum Corps leaders succeeded in getting rid of Collins in 1798. He was sent to set up the new penal settlement in Van Diemen's Land. Doubtless they would have liked to have been able to send Pemulwuy to the harsh southern island as well, but this was far more difficult.

Collins had not been completely correct in his assertion that Pemulwuy was at the head of every attack. Yenowee led some of the 1798 operations, and Nargel herself led a raid on a hut on the Georges River, in which one Englishman was killed and Nargel was wounded by buckshot in her left thigh.

Nargel's action did not have Pemulwuy's approval—and, admittedly, her place at the head of that war party was the result of unusual circumstances. Awabakal had planned to join a group led by Yenowee in the upper part of the Georges River. When they arrived at the crossing, they found that a hut had been built on the opposite bank by settlers determined to prevent the Eora using the crossing as an escape route. Nargel, who was with the group, suggested that she should make the crossing alone and engage the people in the hut in conversation. While she was doing this, she said, Awabakal and his people could swim the river underwater to attack the hut from upstream.

All went well until one of the swimmers hit a submerged log and was forced to surface. The two men from the hut fired on the unfortunate swimmer. Nargel signalled the others to rush the crossing. Due to her position, she ended up in the forefront of the attack, showing all the ferocious courage she had revealed in her rescue of her Irish husband from the British all those years ago. Pemulwuy was not at all convinced that Nargel or any of the others had his immunity to musket fire. He was shown to be only too right when Yenowee was killed in a raid on a farmhouse at Prospect Hill.

Simultaneous attacks at different locations had kept the Rum Corps in a state of constant confusion. In late August, Yenowee led what was to be a hit-and-run stock-killing raid. The farm was one of four, fairly closely located about a small wooded rise. Yenowee and eleven men made their way onto the rise at midnight. At dawn they speared a number of animals; then retreated across a cleared paddock in a neighbouring farm. Somehow, however, a warning was given, and people from a third farm moved quickly and cut off their retreat. The group came under heavy musket fire. Yenowee decided that the only thing to do was to retreat back to the rise. This they did successfully. The settlers, now fully alert and numbering about sixteen, set themselves up on opposite sides of the rise so that it was well covered. Muskets were a great advantage in such an open situation.

Yenowee settled in and waited until the settlers drew closer. He planned that one part of his group would act as if they were going to make a break from one end of the rise, and draw the settlers' fire, while the bulk of the group escaped from the other end and attempted to outflank the settlers, using their nearby crops as cover. The first group would then try to escape.

The first part of the scheme worked well, but the outflanking movement, however, came unstuck. Three of the group were wounded. Yenowee became desperate, and he and three others made a mad rush on the settlers. The outcome was that the first group got away, but Yenowee and his companions were killed by remarkably accurate musket fire.

When the settlers realised that they had killed so many of Pemulwuy's group, including Yenowee, they lived in literal terror of fearful reprisals. Barrington told Macarthur that the settlers believed, like the Eora, that Pemulwuy could not be killed. Unless military protection was provided, they planned to leave their farms. Military protection was provided, but to everyone's surprise Pemulwuy did not attack. At least not then.

Pemulwuy was deeply grieved by his friend's death, but he refused to carry out any immediate reprisals. He had come to realise that these farmers were more dangerous than the military. Pemulwuy made no further raids, and withdrew his people well clear of the farms.

A small alodim was held high up on the Georges River in late November. Pemulwuy told all the groups of his concern about the loss of life they were suffering at the hands of the settlers. He said that a new method of dealing with these farmers was necessary. They needed a new weapon.

Pemulwuy told the Eora that attacks on the dwellings were becoming more difficult because of surrounding areas of cleared land and the fact that the settlers were reasonably well armed and had become very capable of using the firearms they had. They had little livestock left, so any kills were of no real value.

After much thought, Pemulwuy decided that the settler's weakness was the crops at the height of the summer. They would set them all on fire. He then explained a plan involving a sequence of burnings. One force would start at Prospect Hill and the other at Castle Hill. They would both converge on the farms closer to Sydney and then move back to Parramatta.

Weuong and Tedbury would begin at Castle Hill, while he and Awabakal would take Prospect Hill. Pemulwuy reminded Weuong and Tedbury to keep their groups' size to twenty or less. The uncomfortable truth was that the Eora had found that the hard countryside could not support a group any larger, if they had to live off the land. However, they had been pleasantly surprised to find that hunting well fed animals near the farms was very good.

The general plan for crop burning was to station groups at two or three separate points according to the wind. The fires were then to be lit at different intervals, so as to draw the firefighting forces from one point to another and so ensure the escape of the raiding parties.

Pemulwuy and Awabakal arrived at the Prospect Hill area in mid-December. They headed straight for the collection of farms about the small rise where Yenowee and his comrades had perished. Awabakal and the others knew that this was to be the long-delayed revenge.

They watched the location for three days—then moved into action. The group was split into three, but unusually two of the sections contained only two people each. These two were to light fires at intervals of about half an hour, a quarter of a mile apart. The rest of the group would penetrate the grain field nearest the first intended fire at night and lie in hiding in the grain.

Just after sunrise the first fire was lit, and within ten minutes the flames had produced a great pall of smoke. Farmers came running from two different directions to the fire. The largest party comprised some six men and came towards the fire from the west.

When Pemulwuy stood up, spear in hand, less than twenty yards from the nearest man, the settler knew that he was about to pay with his life for the life of Pemulwuy's lieutenant.

By the time the second fire had started, five of the farmers lay dead in their burning maize. Some of the women and those who had escaped the initial attack barricaded themselves in their farmhouses, where they fired at the Eoras. Pemulwuy retreated. He watched the crops burn until nightfall, then successfully set fire to two of the farmhouses and left the place.

From January 1799 until April of that year, the British grain crops were systematically burnt. The technique remained the same throughout. Where possible a bushfire was started to windward, usually at about midday. This initial lighting was followed up by several others at varying intervals. When firebreaks had been cleared around the crops, the bushfire was started first and the crop set alight later. Poor results were obtained only when low wind conditions allowed the fires to be brought under control. On only two occasions were spears thrown at firefighters, and on only one occasion did a military patrol manage to put a fire lighting group to flight.

Some farmers managed to harvest the crops before Pemulwuy burned them, but it was clear that the grain crops of New South Wales were not going to feed the colony that winter. Pemulwuy had devised an effective strategy to deal with the militant farmers. This he had done with very little risk to his own people. He had struck another blow at the existence of the colony. He had found his new weapon. It was a hot but very successful summer for the Eora.

CHAPTER 36

SOME MOMENTS OF TRUTH

Pemulwuy's groups assembled at a place south of Port Hacking in Gweagal country. This was considered the best spot for a winter rest. Hunting was good. The Gweagal people had never really recovered from the early smallpox epidemic and placed very few demands on their land; it was rough country, well away and protected from the British settlements. Pemulwuy called a meeting.

It was a strange, expectant gathering, a time to account. Pemulwuy was in a distant mood, and this heightened the expectancy. As well as this, two old Tharawal men had arrived with William Knight and the Daruk band that had joined Pemulwuy. Pemulwuy convened an alodim, and etiquette demanded that the Tharawal group should speak first. The two old men felt some embarrassment at this meeting. Two years before, Pemulwuy had warned the Tharawal that the British would also want to take their land. He had invited them to join with the Eora, but the Tharawal hierarchy had thought better of it and graciously declined.

The first of the old men spoke in remarkably good Bidjigal. First of all he said that he brought good wishes and congratulations from the Tharawal to the Bidjigal, exalting Pemulwuy for his victories against the British. He carefully acknowledged the Bidjigal's Ramedigal allies and the Kamergal, represented solely by Koobee. He finally switched to the Gweagal tongue and thanked their two rather pathetic representatives for being so hospitable in their land.

'One of the last of the great Tharawal diplomats,' said Weuong quietly to Awabakal, 'they once had a great reputation for this sort of thing'.

The old man then went on to say that some 'little' time ago Pemulwuy had invited them to join the Bidjigal in defeating the British. The Tharawal had thought about this carefully and now saw great wisdom in their joining forces.

'Lying old bastard,' whispered Weuong in English. 'Macarthur is up there making another town called Camden and taking their land.'

The old man said that they had tried to open friendly relations with the British but this had failed. The Tharawals, like the Eora, were now attacking the British.

'And getting the *boongas* beaten off them,' added Weuong quietly.

The old man then suggested that the Tharawal and the Eora should join forces to defeat the British. He ended abruptly and sat down.

Pemulwuy then began to speak. He went through the whole necessary preamble; then said: 'The Eora must concentrate their winter effort in the Kamergal area, since while the Eora have been concentrating on the Parramatta and Georges Rivers area, the British have spread out again at Lane Cove and at the Hawkesbury.'

He said, however, that he would accept the Tharawal offer to fight on their land (an offer they had not actually made). Further, he would send two experienced Eora warriors to show the Tharawal how to fight the British.

'I will send you Weuong and Awabakal,' he said.

Both these men were quite shocked at this announcement, but very honoured.

After dealing with the Tharawals, Pemulwuy asked William Knight to tell them of the Daruk situation.

The Daruk, said Knight, had a great respect for the Bidjigal. They had always contributed young men to Pemulwuy's forces, although they saw no real threat from the British. They considered their wild rugged country west of the Hawkesbury sufficient defence. Last year, however, they had been hit badly by some sort of respiratory infection, and many had died. Knight had told them that this sickness was a weapon of the British, hoping that they would be encouraged to join Pemulwuy en masse. Sadly, he said, it had had the opposite effect, and they had become quite reluctant to expose themselves to such dangerous things.

Knight concluded that all groups he had spoken with in the west were very concerned as to why the Bidjigal had not taken Parramatta from the British. Knight said that Toongabbie was regarded by the Daruk as simply a big government farm. The same was said about Lane Cove and Brickfield. Therefore the Eora had still not taken a substantial British town, although they had held Parramatta in their hands in March of 1797. This latter point also remained a puzzle to the Eora. When Pemulwuy went in alone, he had made his lieutenants swear to withdraw if he was killed. When he was shot down, they had indeed withdrawn, without understanding why. Tedbury had defended his father's actions, saying that he had a secret motive. And his spectacular escape from Sydney had seemed to verify this.

Pemulwuy stood up.

'We had won the battle of Parramatta,' he said, 'we could easily have taken the town from them, but if we had done that many people here now would be dead'. He tipped his head back and forwards, 'what gain would we have for these deaths?' He stopped and thought for a moment. 'I understand about the British and towns,' he said. 'If you have towns, you must have farms to feed the people who live there. We are not farmers, so what value are the towns?'

Then Tedbury shocked everybody by standing up and asking the question that all knew was a contentious issue between them.

'My father,' he said, 'if we are not to have towns, how shall we ever defeat the British? No matter how much we attack them, they simply retreat within their towns and come back out again after we leave'.

Pemulwuy did not get angry as everyone expected. He spoke quietly. 'I said that to live in towns they need farms to feed them. We shall destroy their farms as we have done this summer.' He paused. 'This winter they will depend on their ships to bring them food from other places.' He stood up. 'Next summer we join with the Tharawal and Daruk and destroy their farms again and again and again. Eventually they will have to leave and find another place or go home.'

This seemed to satisfy everybody, and the meeting broke up about an hour later. Only Koobee remained somewhat unconvinced and as pessimistic as ever.

Pemulwuy thought this morose condition of Koobee's was due to his sickness and the loss of his family. He decided to talk to him. That night Pemulwuy went to the camp of Koobee and Awabakal. This visit was ostensibly to brief Awabakal on his impending mission to the Tharawals. Koobee was a fisherman, and his people built substantial comfortable dwellings. The Bidjigals were hunters, they lived in miserable shelters by Kamergal standards. The thought of a winter with the Bidjigal did very little for Koobee.

'Besides,' he explained to Pemulwuy, 'I am sick of fighting, I have never liked it'.

Pemulwuy placed his hand on Koobee's shoulder. 'You have always been a reluctant soldier, my old friend,' Pemulwuy said with real tenderness, 'but you have always been a good fighter and a loyal ally. Now you need to rest'.

Koobee shrugged his shoulders.

'Where?' he said.

'Why don't you go to the Tharawal with Awabakal?'

Koobee shook his head. 'Pemulwuy,' he said looking directly at him, 'how can we win? We are at least half of us dead from their sicknesses. We burn their farms, but every year they build more and increase their numbers while we become less. They already outnumber us many times.' He stopped and looked down at the ground.

'To avoid us killing their animals, they go to the Tharawal land. Next, maybe, to Awabakal's land. Other people do not know how to fight like you.' He paused and looked up again. 'Pemulwuy, you have beaten their soldiers, but not their people.' Pemulwuy was listening and drawing on the ground.

'Koobee, it was their diseases that were their greatest weapon,' he said, 'but we are strong now. We move in small groups and we do not die so much from them.' He stood up. 'I have heard that wars are not won, you must make your opponent lose'. He paused, 'they have done their worst to us and we have not lost. Now they can only lose'.

CHAPTER 37

FAREWELL TO THE RELUCTANT SOLDIER

Early the following morning, Pemulwuy sent for Awabakal and Koobee. As they walked towards Pemulwuy's camp, Awabakal thought over the conversation of the night before. It was true, he thought, that diseases had severely decreased the Eora population. Pemulwuy's persistence in attacking the British farms had forced them further afield into other people's land, and in doing so provided the Eora with more allies. He was now about to guide and assist one of these allies.

When they arrived at Pemulwuy's camp, they were met by a new white face. William Knight introduced them to a convict newly escaped from Parramatta called Kenneth Wilson.

Wilson, a forceful bull of a man informed them that he intended to join up with Thomas Thrush, another escapee, and become bushrangers. They did not want to join Pemulwuy so much as to work with him against their common enemy. While Milli Copley was pleased to see other white faces, she did not seem to like these two very much, although both Coleleu and Nargel tried to encourage her to be nice to them and were puzzled at her reluctance.

'I seen plenty of roughs and scruffs like them in London. I don't intend to wind up with one here.'

Further, Milli told Pemulwuy that these two reminded her of Caesar. The following morning, Pemulwuy met again with the two Europeans. He was curious about the gossip of the British, and he wished to pursue this idea of the bushrangers.

Wilson delighted Pemulwuy with the rumour that Governor Hunter was to be sent back to England and reprimanded for his failure to deal with the problems of the new colony. Pemulwuy was also curious to know of Collins, but Wilson knew nothing more of him since he had left for Van Dieman's Land which was across the sea.

The most important news was that Macarthur claimed to have outwitted Pemulwuy by shifting his grazing operations out of Eora land into the Tharawal country. Collins had apparently told Macarthur that Pemulwuy would not carry out raids in another group's land. Wilson spread out a map he had stolen in Parramatta and showed the new settlements at Camden.

'So that was what Macarthur was up to during the truce,' said Pemulwuy, 'taking all their animals into Tharawal country'. He was annoyed with himself for not having understood this.

Pemulwuy turned to Weuong. 'He may have outwitted himself. He has drawn the Tharawal into the fight where I could not.'

Pemulwuy sent Weuong off to look after the two old Tharawal men and to tell them that he wished to talk to them further. He then turned his attention to Wilson and Knight.

Pemulwuy asked the two men to sit down with him. He said nothing for a time, while both Wilson and Knight sat somewhat ill-at-ease.

'Tell me,' said Pemulwuy at last, 'why do the British call you bushrangers'.

The two Europeans looked at each other. Knight said, 'I suppose because we move about in the bush'.

'You steal from the British?'

'Yes...like you do.'

'I don't steal from the British,' replied Pemulwuy carefully. 'This is our land; everything here belongs to us.'

'No,' said Wilson quickly. 'I don't mean like that.'

'Is this what you did in England?' Pemulwuy asked without looking at either of them.

'No...but people do.' Wilson said. 'They are called highwaymen...sometimes footpads.'

'Why do they do this?'

'To live..., if they have no money,' Wilson replied.

Pemulwuy looked thoughtfully at the two. 'It is a strange world you English have,' he said. 'Does Bennelong know all of this?'

'I don't know,' said Wilson. 'I think that he only listens to gentlemen,' he added awkwardly.

'Why are some English gentlemen and others like you, these other things?'

Wilson was at a complete loss. Knight simply said, 'it should not be...but it's the way of it.'

'Has it always been so?' Pemulwuy asked.

Wilson now tried again, 'if a man can get away and make his fortune elsewhere, then he can become a gentleman,' he said. Pemulwuy's sharp change of expression made Wilson wish he had kept his mouth shut.

'Is this fortune thing made by stealing from people in other lands?' asked Pemulwuy.

'Yes,' said Knight, throwing caution to the winds. 'That is what the Rum Corps are trying to do here.'

'But we have no fortune here,' said Pemulwuy.

Knight glanced at Wilson. 'You have land,' he said.

Pemulwuy looked down at the ground. 'And do you also want our land?' he asked without looking up.

'No!' said Wilson quickly. 'We only need to take some food from the land as the Eora do. It is your help we need.'

'How can the Eora help you?' asked Pemulwuy.

'By warning us of British movements—and by hiding us from the government when we need to escape,' answered Wilson.

Pemulwuy nodded and said, 'and by not killing you'.

'Yes, indeed, sir,' said Wilson.

Pemulwuy got to his feet, nodded to signal his assent. 'It is agreed, then. We help each other to fight the same enemy differently.'

Wilson and Knight smiled with relief.

Later in the morning, the two Europeans and the Daruk left. When Koobee joined him, Pemulwuy, who had been giving the matter a lot of thought, said that it would be good to have many other convicts take up the profession of bushranging. Perhaps, he thought, they should release those wretched people when they had the chance.

'That may not be any good,' Koobee said. 'These people will be no good out here for a long time. Remember how long it took Irish to learn to live out here.'

Koobee's main concern was to tell Pemulwuy that he planned to spend some time in Kamay. Pemulwuy dropped the intriguing subject of bushranging and said: 'This is good, Koobee. You must spend the night here with us.'

He paused, 'in the morning I shall walk with you as far as the river'.

Koobee agreed and left to prepare for his journey.

Pemulwuy then joined Awabakal and Weuong with the Tharawal men. He talked to them for some time, assuring them that the Bidjigal were now very interested in assisting them. He said that after Awabakal and Weuong had been with them for a time, he would come and join them as well. The Tharawal men were very pleased, and were anxious to leave with the good news.

Pemulwuy bid his two lieutenants farewell. Awabakal was now a fine young man close to his twenty-eighth year. Pemulwuy thought idly, as he watched them leave, that he must give some thought to Awabakal, and perhaps think about a wife for him and for Weuong.

When he returned to his camp Nargel asked if she and her son could come with Koobee to the river. Pemulwuy thought that this was a good idea and left Nargel to arrange it.

Pemulwuy sat down alone to give some thought to the whole situation. A curious balance of wins and losses had appeared. He felt that he had defeated the Rum Corps, but the settlers, who were determined and courageous, had become more of a problem. He had now found a way of dealing with them and preventing the British from producing food, so forcing them to rely on shipping. Diseases had severely cut back the Eora population, but they had survived and their numbers had again begun to increase. The British had cunningly occupied land of an adjoining people to prevent Eora attacks on them. But this had eventually caused a joining of the two peoples against them. Overall, it seemed that the balance was on the Eora side, but somehow they still seemed to be losing. He decided to sleep on it.

Early the following morning Pemulwuy, Nargel, Boolayoo and Koobee set out for the Georges River crossing. The breath of winter had touched the wind which swept the troubled summer from their minds. They walked easily in the cold morning. Boolayoo played about them, spending his childish energy on Pemulwuy's heels and his mother's skirt-tail. Nargel leant on Koobee's arm, scolding and chattering as they walked.

Boolayoo took little notice of his mother's good-natured scoldings and even less of Koobee's. Koobee finally yielded his spear and umana to the child, then picked him up and placed him on his shoulders. Now, in this enchanted morning, Boolayoo said that he was taller than Pemulwuy.

A musket ball ripped through Koobee's heart beneath him. Koobee tumbled to the ground with the child. A second shot rang out and Nargel swept up her child and rolled to one side of the track. Pemulwuy did likewise on the other. Pemulwuy regained his feet like a cat, spear at the ready. He could not see Nargel or her child, just Koobee released in death, staring sadly at the Eora sky.

A spear flashed from the undergrowth. It was Koobee's spear, thrown by Nargel. A cry indicated that it found its mark some twenty yards ahead.

Pemulwuy screamed out, threw his weapons into the air and bounded forward. Still shrieking, he leapt scrub five and more feet tall. One of the Europeans fired wildly as this fearsome apparition descended on him, but if the first attacker had been struck by the spear of the she-worragul, the second had the teeth of the man-worragul himself at his throat.

For a few seconds the bushlands were split with a hideous duet of screaming that echoed and chimed through the trees. Then silence.

Nargel ran forward with shield and club and came upon the attack site. One European lay with his head almost torn from his body, the other with spear stab wounds all over his chest and the broken shaft protruding from his throat. Pemulwuy lay between them, his face covered in white foam exuding from his mouth, his hands red with the blood of his enemies. He lay between the new dead, writhing in an agony of violence and madness.

The child had listened and watched in hidden frightened silence. Now he ran and cast himself on the prostrate body of his old companion, Koobee. His tears fell onto the earth. When the winter rains came they carried the child's tears, with the blood of that day, along the channels and corridors of the forest and into the river. They flowed together down to the sad, grey waters of Kamay.

THE THIRD PART OF TRUTH

'...the secret truth within each person'.

CHAPTER 38

THE AMBASSADORS

The old Tharawal men travelled slowly. It was a long three day's walk to the camp the Tharawal called *Wingikara*, about eight miles south of the British settlement of Camden. The camp lay in the base of a small blind valley open to the north. It was situated on the banks of a large waterhole surrounded by lush vegetation.

Both Awabakal and Weuong were impressed with the soft, green country of the region. They were, however, far too much Bidjigal warriors to feel comfortable camping in a blind valley surrounded by high ground. Once they had crossed the southern dreaming lines into Tharawal country, the two old men dropped Eora languages and immediately switched to a Tharawal tongue. Weuong knew this language reasonably well, but for the first two days it might as well have been *Pitjantjatjara* as far as Awabakal was concerned. Once in the camp, Awabakal found some younger men and, more importantly, some younger women who spoke some Bidjigal. Awabakal was most surprised to find one young woman who spoke reasonably good English. Awabakal soon discovered that the Tharawal were very interested to learn this new and strange language and were delighted to find that both he and Weuong were fluent speakers of the language.

Tharawal people went to more trouble than the Bidjigal to house themselves, and while their dwellings were nowhere near as substantial as the Kamergal, they were a much better winter abode than their Bidjigal equivalent. Their weaponry was similar to the Eora, except that they used boomerangs more. They had smaller shields and used much longer, heavier spears.

Both Weuong and Awabakal became aware of how much the Bidjigal spear had changed over the last ten years. Both men carried three or four short, light, and generally iron-tipped spears. Their shields were larger than the Tharawal equivalent and made of lighter timber. They were clearly designed to be impaled on bayonets rather than defend against a club. Neither of the Eora men carried boomerangs but both carried long iron knives. These were the weapons of a soldier, thought

Awabakal, and certainly not designed to bring down the huge grey ganimantj that roamed these parts.

Awabakal and Weuong were patently armed and organised to hunt men, and the Tharawals held them in awe.

There was much singing and ceremony with their arrival. Many people came to the camp and there was much dancing and eating. The Tharawal were clearly good hunters and very affluent.

The celebrations gave the Bidjigal men a great opportunity to introduce themselves properly. They danced and sang of the battles of the last eight years. They demonstrated in dance the technique of disarming British bayonets and the rapid flat crawling to avoid musket fire. They showed them how the short Bidjigal spear could be thrown from a prostrate position, and how a second spear could be launched before the first had found its target. At one stage a big Tharawal man challenged Weuong to a duel using clubs. Weuong wandered up casually, deflected a club blow with his shield, kicked the man's feet from under him, and knocked him unconscious with the lightest tap of his club.

Awabakal thought that the Tharawal were brave and determined, but they were hunters not warriors. Both Awabakal and Weuong agreed secretly that a force of fifty Bidjigal warriors could wipe out the entire Tharawal people in a month. This thought hung strangely on the two.

The same strange thought seemed to be transmitted to the Tharawal. Soon their excitement and awe of the two Bidjigal warriors changed to uncertainty and suspicion. The Tharawal had never experienced anything like these two, and properly so. These Eora warriors would probably have been among the best close combat fighters in the world at that time. They had been trained and blooded in eight years of successful combat against part of the most powerful military force on earth.

Social life for both Weuong and Awabakal was nevertheless very good. While the Tharawal men became uneasy with the Eora, they were the idols of the women, and Awabakal said jokingly to his companion that Weuong would have to return to Pemulwuy alone.

'I doubt that,' was Weuong's reply, 'the old crow is going to come and get us'.

After the welcome, the Tharawal had a big meeting in which Weuong, being the older of the two visitors, made the running. This was the first time these two men had had the opportunity to operate out of the shadow of Pemulwuy, and they grew with it. The meeting seemed to go very well. Notwithstanding the Tharawal concern about the new two-edged nature of the alliance they were being offered, their confidence in dealing with the British rose greatly.

A week after they had arrived, on the evening of Yanada, Weuong and Awabakal heard about the death of their old Kamergal companion. Weuong fell to the ground, beating it with his hands. Awabakal flew into a great rage. He smashed a spear on a tree and then smashed other things around the camp. Weuong became most alarmed when Awabakal shouted out his dead friend's name again and again.

'Koobee! Oh, Koobee, Koobee! my father's brother.... Oh, Koobee.'

So great was the ferocity of the mourning that the nearby Tharawal cleared out and did not come near the Eora for days. The Tharawal feared that not only might their guests bring them physical harm, but they might also call an angry spirit down upon them.

Awabakal and Weuong consoled themselves to some extent with the tale of the terrible revenge taken by Pemulwuy and Nargel. Weuong embellished this tale slightly later and further terrified the Tharawal. He told them that Pemulwuy and his wife had torn their friend's killers to pieces with their teeth and made the Georges River run red with blood.

Following on their experience of these two Eora warriors, the very thought of Pemulwuy's impending visit was terrifying. Many of the Tharawal believed that they were probably better off to accept their lot with the British than have such terrible friends. Weuong became sensitive to this and thereafter put on what Awabakal called 'his best guna-eating grin'.

This helped a little, and the two Eora were able to get down to the more serious business of reconnoitring the new British settlement. They moved about with four Tharawal men.

This settlement was indeed different to the settlements in Eora country. The country was much more open and the British dwellings further apart. They seemed to be more concerned with grazing animals than with farming. The hated fences were, however, still apparent.

Pemulwuy had warned his two lieutenants not to attack farms before he arrived. As a result of this, Weuong and Awabakal spent the time gaining a good understanding of the district and training as best they could with their Tharawal comrades. To the delight of the older people at Wingikara, relations between the groups began to improve. But two events unfortunately set this process back again.

Yanada had left the sky after her recent pregnancy and all with concerns of love in their hearts awaited her return. One such person was Weuong. He had become deeply infatuated with the berringen, *O'some,* who spoke English. These two lovers whispered to each other in the moon's dark shadows in the language of Shelley and Shakespeare. O'some discovered that even the dreams of love with this new, fierce kind of man born of *Terra Australis* were different. There was a new physical passion and possession to it. The Tharawal understood something of the fierce reputation of Bidjigal women, but these two Bidjigal men were something well beyond that in everything that they did.

Awabakal could see the storm coming and tried to warn Weuong that O'some was promised to someone else. Weuong responded by telling Awabakal: 'You are like Pemulwuy. You have about as much understanding of women as a dead black fish.' Awabakal wore this, but he persisted in warning Weuong that without appropriate relations about, there could be only one end to the situation.

The end came rather sooner than expected with a challenge from O'some's paternal line. Weuong refused to yield his claim and pressure was brought to bear on Awabakal. It was awkward, sensitive pressure. The Tharawal felt that the two Eora men probably had the power to carry out the claim. They did, however, remind Awabakal of the network of reciprocal responsibilities that existed between the Bidjigal and the various Tharawal groups.

Awabakal was appalled at all this. He was not even Eora, and yet he was being pressed to carry the responsibility of a Bidjigal elder. He decided that he must take Weuong in hand.

'I have fought the British for ten years and have asked for nothing,' Weuong protested to Awabakal. 'I did this for the Tharawal as well as for the Eora. I am five years older than you and have not yet a wife.' He sat down beside Awabakal. 'I will end my days like Yanlarree,' he said.

'Yanada's lover?' asked Awabakal.

'Yes' said Weuong. 'He went in search of Yanada.' Weuong paused solemnly, 'this is a secret part of the story. The rainbow was angry and Yanlarree became the brown snake. He moves on the earth and cannot find Yanada, he is forever alone'.

'But you are not Yanlarree,' said Awabakal.

Awabakal told him he was acting stupidly. Awabakal said that if Weuong wanted two Bidjigal wives he could arrange it within an hour of their return and he said, 'you know that is true'.

Weuong would hear none of this, and the two became quite distant.

Awabakal confided his difficulty to the older Tharawal people. They said that Awabakal must be sure to be present at any incident that might occur as a result of this. Awabakal agreed reluctantly.

Awabakal decided that they should make a trip to the far north of the British settlement. He used Pemulwuy's instructions to them as an excuse. Pemulwuy had told them to examine the method by which this distant settlement was supplied. As they were about to leave, Weuong was challenged.

Awabakal stood beside Weuong. A frightened but determined young Tharawal man faced them some thirty paces away, holding a shield and a spear fixed to an umana. There were perhaps a dozen other people standing around. Awabakal could see O'some wrapped in an opossum skin cloak, turned away crying against a tree behind the challenger.

Weuong fitted a spear to his umana and shouted in response to the challenge.

Awabakal went cold all over. He could see that Weuong was not going to be content with any ritual solution. He was possessed of love and of his own power and intended to kill the challenger.

Both men shouted at each other. Weuong said that he was in a propriety relationship with O'some and his right beyond that lay in his right arm. This was terribly dangerous. Awabakal was at a complete loss as to what to do.

At this moment, one of O'some's brothers rushed up and tore the cloak off her. Another struck her but was quickly restrained, and O'some stood naked in the cold, crying loudly. Awabakal knew that Weuong, consumed by passion would easily kill ten of them. Now he could clearly see the girl's bare buttocks some thirty paces from him.

Next to Pemulwuy, Awabakal was probably the most accurate with the Bidjigal spear. In the growing shadow of the impending conflict, Awabakal lifted his spear without the umana, took careful aim and flicked it into the air above the heads of the prospective combatants.

In order to accomplish this difficult task, Awabakal had to throw the spear with a little more impetus than he would have wished. The head of the spear pinned the skin of two cheeks of O'some's posterior together and knocked her to the ground. The only thing better judged than the flight of his spear was his decision to cast it. Weuong dropped his spear and attacked Awabakal with a club, smashing his shield in half. Awabakal fell to the ground, watching Weuong carefully.

Weuong threw his weapons to the ground and marched off into the bush. An old man walked up to Awabakal, helped him to his feet, embraced him and said: 'The Eora have such great wisdom and skill, in such young men'.

Weuong's challenger stepped forward. Honour had been satisfied in a proper way, and the challenger could now regain his status with the ethic of generosity.

He shouted. 'I give her to Weuong. I withdraw my right. She shall go away and heal and then Weuong shall take her to the Eora's country.'

Meanwhile someone had removed the dooul from O'some and stopped the bleeding from the light flesh wounds. She was lying on her stomach and Awabakal walked over to her. She looked at him in joyous tearfulness.

'I knew a woman who was like you once,' he said in English, 'be what you have to be and you now have our protection for all the days of your life'.

He found Weuong in the forest on the hillside. He touched him on the shoulder and said in English and Bidjigal.

'If you don't mind a djin with a few more holes in her boonga, you have a Tharawal wife.'

Weuong leapt up and threw his arms around Awabakal.

'You will be after Pemulwuy,' he said as tears streamed down his face.

It was the second unfortunate event that occurred in the land of the Tharawal for which there was no traditional solution. It affected Awabakal for the rest of his life.

One of the things that upset the Tharawal was that both Weuong and Awabakal seemed to accept and encourage women to use the weapons of men. Awabakal and Weuong discussed the matter and Awabakal thought the Tharawals justified in their concerns. He felt that he and Weuong were influenced by the peculiar example set by Narewe. Weuong would not accept this. He said that his own mother could throw a spear as well as his father. He said Bidjigal women had a tradition of men-like activities, so the issue remained at an impasse.

Awabakal had eventually persuaded Weuong to undertake a northern excursion. They arrived with six Tharawal comrades quite close to the dreaming division between the Tharawal and Eora, but still in Tharawal country. The British had developed a path wide enough for their wheeled vehicles, and they hid and watched one such caravan pass to the south.

Weuong decided that they should wait and record the amount of traffic on the track. On the following day a four-wheeled vehicle drawn by a horse came into sight. This vehicle was driven by two people and appeared to have a good deal of cargo in the open back of a vehicle the British called a buggy. Awabakal knew that when drawn by two horses it was quite fast. The vehicle was accompanied by two soldiers on horseback.

The entourage was no more than a hundred yards away, passing through fairly open, lightly wooded land. The sight of the soldiers caused Awabakal's mind to cloud again with the sorrow of his lost friend. He watched quietly for a while and then said: 'Weuong, this is near Eora land. Let us show the Tharawal how to kill the British.'

Weuong was somewhat taken aback, but the enthusiasm of the young Tharawal men pressed him to agree.

Weuong turned to the Tharawal men.

'Let us see how good you are with those long Tharawal spears,' he said. 'Kill the horses and we shall show you how to kill British soldiers.'

The Tharawal men were quick to take up the challenge and positioned themselves a little further along the road on a small ridge.

Two of the big spears brought the horses to the ground and the buggy to a stop, smashing its pole. The other two horses were also hit and fell to the ground. One regained its feet and shook the spear from its chest.

Weuong and Awabakal attacked across the flat ground, rolling on the ground, dodging musket fire and projecting spears as though from catapults.

Both the soldiers were hit and knocked to the ground. The two Eora men then concentrated their attacks on the civilians, who were firing from behind the damaged buggy. One of these two, a woman, caught hold of the horse that was still on its feet, climbed into the saddle, and turned to gallop away.

Awabakal stood up at great risk. He took careful aim, judged her movement and threw a spear. The throw must have covered the best part of fifty yards. The head of the spear hit the escaping figure between the shoulder blades and she toppled to the ground. The remaining man behind the buggy could have killed Awabakal but failed to reload. He stood up and begged for mercy. Weuong killed him with a club.

Neither of the soldiers were dead. Weuong and Awabakal dispatched them with clubs, just as the European woman that Awabakal had killed might have rid her garden of snails.

This was all too much for the Tharawals. They would not even come to gather the spoils of war from the vehicle.

At the time of the incident, Awabakal thought no more of killing the woman than he would feel of someone killing Nargel in battle. She was a combatant fleeing to warn other British. Weuong, on the other hand, thought that it was a wrong thing to do and said so.

He made sure that only an Eora spear was left to identify the raiders. They took the two horses that were able to walk. He had learned diplomacy well.

The Tharawal camp was even more concerned at the event than was Weuong. But it was Weuong who told them that if they had no heart for war, then they should become like horses and pull the British ploughs. Relations again deteriorated.

Pemulwuy arrived at the time of the next moon's darkness. The Tharawal were pleased that he had arrived and again put on another great welcome. It dwindled out rather quickly, however, and even the women seemed terrified of Pemulwuy.

Pemulwuy sat between his two emissaries at a meeting of the Tharawal elders. The discussion was abstruse and led nowhere. Pemulwuy ended the meeting, saying that he would talk again later. He stood up and signalled his two comrades away.

CHAPTER 39

THE DAY OF THE WARRIORS

Awabakal and Weuong quietly accepted Pemulwuy's berating.

'They tell me that you two behaved like Worraguls.' After some time he eased their pain by telling them that he expected no better from the Tharawal. He laughed and slapped Weuong on the shoulder. 'If you had not come, the Tharawals would have laid down for the British. Now they will have to fight.' He then turned sharply and spoke to Awabakal in an intense way. 'If the white djin had stayed and begged you for mercy, would you still have killed her?'

This question took Awabakal by surprise.

'I...I don't know,' he said.

'She shot at us with a musket,' said Weuong. 'We have white djins living with us. They tell us that if the British capture them they will be killed by hanging with rope. I think that Silky would be hard to catch and Milli is safe while she runs with Nargel and Coleleu.'

'We don't have to do as the British, but I asked Awabakal a different question,' said Pemulwuy to Weuong.

Awabakal shrugged his shoulders.

'It is done.' Pemulwuy then assumed a more matter-of-fact attitude. 'Your attack was excellent, and the Tharawal now know what they have to do when they fight. True, the killing of the woman has left every Eora and Tharwal woman terrified of British reprisals. But not the Bidjigals.'

He stopped again, thought—then made a dismissive gesture. 'But, as you say, this one fought like a soldier,' he added, 'if women are to be soldiers then they must expect to die like soldiers. Bidjigal women expect that, but most other Eora don't and I am sure that the Tharawal don't.'

Pemulwuy stood up and told Weuong and Awabakal that he must go and talk again with the old men. He said that they would leave tomorrow after the sun passed the top. Almost as an afterthought, he turned and said to Weuong.

'Don't forget to collect your berringen.'

The three Eora men and the Tharawal woman left Wingikara in the late afternoon.

They headed east for about three miles, then cut back south, circled Wingikara camp and headed north towards Daruk country.

They camped that night by a waterhole in some rough country west of Camden. Weuong built a separate camp and withdrew with his hard-won bride. Pemulwuy and Awabakal settled down by their fire and talked into the night.

'Why did you leave the muskets we captured and bring these damned Tharawal spears?' asked Awabakal.

'And two of their umana?' said Pemulwuy.

'Yes. Why?' Awabakal asked. 'The muskets are too heavy and we must be able to move quickly.'

Pemulwuy laid back, placed his hand behind his head, and said: 'The Tharawal will not join us in our war unless they have to Awabakal. I hope that you can throw these Tharawal spears, for we must make the Tharawal fight their own war. After this at least some of the younger men will join us.'

Awabakal laughed. 'That's a good plan, but what of Weuong's wife? She is no Bidjigal woman. She will never keep up.'

'Weuong must return quickly to Goman. The determination of the Eora is also weak.'

They talked late into the night, and Pemulwuy told Awabakal that he had another mission to attend to when they returned. The British had brought some Awabakal men to Sydney and Awabakal must find out what the British were up to.

Awabakal was overjoyed at this news. It was as though some part of his life that had died was suddenly alive again. He had great difficulty sleeping that night and kept waking to practise the language that he had not spoken for so long—his own language, Awabakal.

In the amber mist of the morning they bid farewell to Weuong and O'some. Pemulwuy and Awabakal watched the two as they walked in their new-found joy towards the lands of the Eora.

When they were out of sight, Pemulwuy and Awabakal picked up their weapons, looked at each other for a moment, laughed, and ran down the slope towards the British settlement. Awabakal walked on a hidden carpet beside Pemulwuy. They talked and laughed together, the sense of power and freedom that surrounded them echoed and sparkled in the bright spring morning.

They hunted the British with the great clumsy Tharawal spears. They rolled in the deep green grass with the musket shot. They struck at will and left a trail that no-one ever believed was Tharawal, but the Tharawal paid for it.

CHAPTER 40

COME HOME, SOLDIER BOY

Arranging a meeting with his people in Sydney was very difficult for Awabakal. He was now well known to the British, and it had occurred to him that the Awabakals might well be bait in a trap.

He discovered that these Awabakal people had been brought to Sydney from Coal River, so that a new missionary, whatever that was, could learn their language. They lived in a small hut close to Reverend Marsden's house, near the harbour. It took the best part of a week and considerable influence to persuade some locals to arrange for the Awabakals to be taken on a fishing expedition to *Waroama*, called Cockatoo Island by the British.

Awabakal planned to meet them when they landed on the island. He arrived some hours before the fishing party. The waiting was beyond him. He walked about and watched the sea anxiously. Then suddenly the boat was in sight. Awabakal thought that his heart would stop beating.

When they landed on the island, Awabakal marched down the beach to meet them. He recognised the shapes of Awabakal faces, Awabakal clothing, and the smell of the sea. He must return with them, he thought. The time had come.

The Awabakal group, already disturbed by the fearsome tales they had heard of Bidjigal warriors, cringed in terror at the sight of this battle-scarred and dangerous looking creature now approaching them.

Awabakal was shocked to see their reaction and stopped. He threw down his weapons and called to them in Awabakal, a language he had not used for ten years.

'I am Kiraban, son of *Bintunkin*. I am Koori.'

The group stared in stunned amazement and disbelief. One lifted a fish spear, and for a moment Kiraban thought that he would throw it.

'Who are your father's brothers?' the man asked.

'*Kakuya* and *Bunkillikan*.'

'I am *Murrorong*!' shouted the man, and ran forward and embraced Kiraban. 'Baido told me about you long ago. We thought that you must be lost forever!' he said.

Kiraban's heart sang in the warm familiar embrace. He closed his eyes hard against the joyous sting of his tears, which washed the years away.

There were in fact two close relations in the group, and they sat on the rocky shore and talked away the great time that had separated them.

The British had indeed come to the land of the great lake *Awaba*, but had not at first stayed there. They went further north to the place they called Port Stephens. Later they returned to the river, that they called Coal River. They camped near the river mouth at *Mulubinba*. They did not take the land but collected great quantities of the substance they called coal. Kiraban realised now what the familiar smell was in Sydney—the fire stones.

They told Kiraban that the British were kindly, gave them things, and wanted to teach them about their religion. They had also offered them clothes.

Kiraban told them that he had fought with Pemulwuy against the British for ten years. He told them that the British were not to be trusted; that they would be nice to them for a time and would then take their land. The Awabakal said that they would think about all this and that Kiraban should now join them fishing. They all boarded the boat and paddled to the other side of the harbour.

The boat was pulled up on the beach in a small sandy cove. The Awabakal men then began wading out in the water with their multi-barbed fishing spears. They gave one of the spears to their lost son.

Kiraban had not done this for years. He had fished in these waters, but the Awabakal technique was different. In the smaller rivers and creeks the Eora used nets more than spears, or else lines and hooks. There was, however, little shallow water with sandy bottoms about Tuhbowgule and the Eora hunted fish from bark canoes. They cast food scraps into the water to attract fish, and then speared them with single-pronged barbed spears. Around Lake Awaba there were many extensive sandy shallow waters. The Awabakals walked in circular patterns raising sand with their feet. Sea creatures so disturbed, were then speared with light hand-held multi-pronged spears. Kiraban was as much in the way as he was useful, but he persisted. After about an hour the others had a substantial feed of fish, including a large ray.

They returned to the beach, where Kiraban could show them that he had not lost the Awabakal art of lighting a fire. They cooked their fish and joked with Kiraban, saying that when he came home with them he would have much to learn again. There was a great beauty and pleasure to those few hours that they spent together. Their reunion was interrupted by Kiraban, who sensed the approach of others. He gathered his own weapons from the dinghy just as two Europeans, both holding muskets, appeared from the bush behind them.

'Put down your weapons or I will blow your black heads off!' shouted one.

The others did not understand English, but Kiraban dropped his spears and signalled to his companions to do the same.

'Now, what are you doing with that boat?' the armed European snorted.

Kiraban answered in English, 'the missionary gave it to us to fish'.

'You're a bloody liar,' said one of the Englishmen, and walked down the beach towards them.

The other remained behind with his musket levelled.

Kiraban felt strangely sad as the man approached. He knew what he had to do. As the first man reached him, Kiraban stepped in front of the boat. The man lifted the gun barrel as if to strike him.

'Get out of the way,' the man growled.

Kiraban kicked the gun from his grasp and dropped onto the sand by his spears. The European swung away from Kiraban, trying to recover his weapon, and got an Eora spear in his back just below his ribs. The other man was surprised. He hesitated, then, as he fired, a spear was already in the air. The musket ball raised a spurt of sand beside Kiraban, and, although the man instinctively ducked away from the spear, it caught his hip. He fell down, dropped the musket, pulled the spear from his hip, regained his feet and plunged awkwardly towards the cover of the trees.

Kiraban had to handthrow a second spear. It took the man in the base of the spine at about the third vertebrae. He stumbled to the ground just two feet from a tree. He rolled over on his back, screaming in agony as the spear shaft twisted in him. The man near him was also still alive, semi-conscious, breathing heavily. Blood was running from his mouth.

The other Awabakals were standing in shocked amazement. The whole event had lasted only seconds. Kiraban looked quickly at the man on the sand beside him and then ran over to the other. The Awabakals heard the wounded man scream out as Kiraban approached him, then silence. Kiraban returned to find that the man near the boat had died. He tried to speak to the Awabakals but they drew away.

'This is what I am,' Kiraban said in desperation. 'This is what they have made of me.' He flung his arm towards the two dead, 'they are a savage, brutal people'.

Murrorong stepped forward and took Kiraban's hand. 'This is a terrible thing you have done, but you are my brother's son. Come back with us to Awaba. Leave behind this terrible thing.'

Kiraban embraced him, smelling fish and sweat and home. He stood back, tears flowing from his eyes.

'There is no place for me in Awaba now,' he said. 'Tell my father that I have learned to kill the British. Tell him what you have seen here. Tell him that I shall fight them until they leave.'

He hung his head.

'Tell my mother to watch the moonflowers where I was born.'

Kiraban fell to the ground and covered his face. The others stood awkwardly. Then one of the younger men came to him.

'Kiraban, we did not know how to help you,' Kiraban looked up and smiled. 'It may be better that you never learn.'

He got to his feet. 'You must leave this place now, quickly,' Kiraban said. 'The British will revenge themselves on you for this.'

'But the missionary?'

'He is only their servant. He can give no protection. You must return home.'

'How can we do that?'

Kiraban looked at the boat.

'It is strong and big enough.'

He pointed towards the heads.

'You must go home in this.'

'What of the Eora man we left on the island?' asked Murrorong.

'He will be all right.'

'How far must we paddle this boat?' 'You must paddle north to the other side of a great River,' said Kiraban. 'Paddle all day and camp on the beach at night. If you see a British ship, paddle ashore and travel across the land until you come to Awaba.' He stopped. 'Now go quickly.'

'But what of you?' Kiraban laughed. 'I am like Pemulwuy,' he said. 'I shall go where I wish and I will come home when the British are gone'. Then he remembered something, 'but you will fight.' he said. 'I saw it in a dream. It will be beside a koori man with a name very like mine.'

It was just on sunset when the little group set off. Kiraban watched them fade into the closing twilight. He gathered up his weapons and set off into the bushlands. Within an hour the new moon had risen and Kiraban looked up at her and smiled sadly. Like the night bird and Gurrewe, Awabakal had learned the last secret part of his own truth.

CHAPTER 41

THE BUSHRANGERS' PARTY

Not only did the Tharawal suffer the British reprisals, but two weeks after the Eora had left, the Tharawal around Wingikara suffered an epidemic of influenza. The Eora heard that one of the British raids was upon a small family group in which all were killed—men, women and children.

Awabakal faced a silent censor wherever he went. Outwardly he passed it off by saying that the first victim of the British he had ever seen was a young unarmed woman, murdered by Macintyre and Tilmouth. Inwardly he cringed.

The Tharawal made some pathetic retaliatory attacks, but with little effect. If it were true that the Eora had learned how to fight the British from the British, then it was equally true that the British had learned to defeat the Tharawal from the Eora. However, as Pemulwuy had said, many young disillusioned Tharawal men joined the Bidjigals.

Weuong, Awabakal and Gomil all tried to tempt Pemulwuy to make some raids on Tharawal country, but he was unmoved. He carefully watched the young crops grow about Parramatta and waited.

The bushrangers, Knight, Wilson and company, had not fared so well. They were now joined by another European, Thomas Thrush. They had seven Eora men with them, plus horses and muskets. After a few successful hold-ups, all worthwhile supply groups were found to be accompanied by up to twenty mounted soldiers. Pemulwuy thought that the bushrangers were using second-rate British techniques against the British.

Late in November, the bushrangers had applied some European logic to their operations. Anywhere else in the world, they decided among themselves, they would steal money. In New South Wales, therefore, they must steal rum and use it to increase their power and influence as money would. Early in January, after a fierce gun battle, they succeeded in escaping with some thirty gallons of rum.

Rum was a rather special sort of currency devised by the New South Wales Corps. The bushrangers found that it was nearly impossible for them to make use of it to their advantage. In any case it was also a temptation, and their level of drunkenness was slowly rendering them incapable of doing anything.

Towards the end of December in 1799, they decided that the best thing to do with the remains of their catch was to celebrate the turn of the century. So they invited Pemulwuy and his group to a party.

Pemulwuy had become progressively more irritable with the onset of summer. He was appalled at the collapse of the Tharawal, and remarked to Weuong that the Eora and the Tharawals had done better when they faced worthy British soldiers like Tench. He could sense the power of British society itself growing with their numbers. Their pressure to expand was almost tangible. Pemulwuy saw them burying their roots in his land like a cancer. He needed something else now.

On 30 December 1799, Pemulwuy and ten of his group arrived at a pleasant camp on the upper reaches of the Hawkesbury River. They were heartily welcomed by Knight and Wilson, who introduced their newest recruit, Thomas Thrush.

Pemulwuy realised very soon that Thrush had more or less assumed the leadership of the bushrangers.

Thrush was a stocky, swarthy Londoner who spoke English in yet another way. Knight told Pemulwuy that he was originally from Tyneside, whatever that meant. He had been transported for burglary. He seemed intelligent and ruthless, and had learned the rudiments of bush craft. To Pemulwuy's fascination, he found that this rough man's name was identical to that of an English songbird that was said to sing exceptionally sweetly. For all that, Thrush also possessed a great deal of commonsense in his English fashion. Pemulwuy could talk to him once he had learned to understand his English.

Pemulwuy's two wives accompanied the group, as did O'some and Milli. Weuong and Awabakal were to go hunting so that there would be ample food. Pemulwuy's first reaction to the place was that it was too dangerous to have such a camp on a river. Besides it was too isolated, too distant from the bushrangers' targets. Pemulwuy made these points to Thrush. Thrush agreed that he did not like the river location, but then it was absolutely necessary to have water for the horses. The horses, he said, enabled them to cover great distances and so operate from distant places.

'We're just ordinary English folk, for better or for worse,' said Thrush. 'We can't run all bloody day like you folk. You were brought up to it, so that's all right for you.'

'But these horses, they take so much looking after,' Pemulwuy objected.

Thrush shook his head. 'Not if you're a bit organised,' he said in his strange, strong accent. He went on to say that if Pemulwuy used horses, he would also need to find suitable locations for operations. Then Thrush thought it over and elaborated for Pemulwuy's benefit: 'I mean, if you're organised for this line of work'.

'Do you hunt on your horses?'

'Yeah,' replied Thrush. 'But we don't hunt much,' he added with a rueful grin.

'Well, how do you live?'

‘Oh, we steal from the farms. We steal sheep, cows, flour.’ Thrush looked at Pemulwuy with a touch of reproach. ‘You lot spend too much time killing the farmers and destroying the crops and property.’

Pemulwuy said nothing. Thrush licked his lips and continued, ‘with your style of operating, and all the power you’ve got, you could use our way of doing things—drive the government mad and live like a king back west, out of reach...’.

The discussion didn’t last long. Pemulwuy left the bushrangers, wandered around the camp for a while, then went to the river and sat staring into the water. It was quite clear that he wanted no more conversation.

It was almost sunset when Pemulwuy heard a familiar voice. ‘And where is himself?’

He stood up and grinned from ear to ear, ‘Silky, what are you doing here?’ The Irish-Eora woman smiled back at him.

‘Ach,’ she said. ‘Did you really think I’d let you be drinking all that rum by yourself? Now let me look at you.’ Kate Donovan stood back admiringly. ‘You look a picture, me darling. Those two beautiful wives of yours must be looking after you well.’

At that moment, Nargel landed around Kate’s neck, joined straight after by Boorea and Millicent. They all embraced and wept a little. Kate looked at Pemulwuy again.

‘Tis a sad thing about our old friend Kamergal,’ she said, careful not to mention the name of their departed comrade.

On the other side of the camp, keeping close to their precious horses, the three English desperados sat that night listening to the singing of old Australia. They drank a little rum, smoked, and talked.

‘Well, I suppose this kind of music could grow on you,’ said Thrush, ‘but I’ll tell you something: a good, lively tune on the fiddle will go a long way in this place.’

The others laughed.

‘And a handsome girl who’d dance a jig all the way to bed—and keep jigging when you got there!’ said Knight.

No-one was going to disagree with him on that score. They all knew they could never go back to the remembered rough-and-tumble pleasures of home, only too brief and maybe not so wonderful though they might have been at the time. Their memories of good times were now turned fantastic by twelve thousand miles and the passage of years. What awaited them here was a rough life in the bush, an existence of sorts secured at pistol point—and, if they were caught, death at the end of a rope. A mood of relative sobriety descended on the trio.

Thrush jerked a thumb towards where Pemulwuy was singing with the others.

‘You know,’ he said, ‘I find it darned hard to imagine that bloke over there can kill two or three rummies armed with muskets—just like that!’

‘You can take it from me he can—and his best men likewise,’ Knight said. ‘I’ve seen them do it in a fight.’

He mimed the speed and dexterity with which Eora warriors could cast their throwing-spears, whistled through his teeth to show how they flew through the air.

Thrush nodded, and took some more rum.

'Well, do you really reckon he can't be killed by musket fire?'

Knight sucked in his cheeks, and thought for a moment. 'I don't know,' he said at last. 'All I'll say is, he's got more buckshot in him than a coachman's whip.' He shook his head slowly, 'he's a strange one, and that's the truth of it.'

'You know something else,' said Knight. 'The old bugger brought six or so ladies to the party, some white and some black. Here they come now, half naked and all.'

Thrush smiled broadly at the sight of the approaching women. 'A man could get used to that. I bet you that Irish biddy at the front knows a few ditties, damn shame we don't have a fiddle. Besides she would soon teach the younger ones a dance or two, specially that redhead with the rough cutty sark about her.'

The next morning, Pemulwuy sought out Kate Donovan and asked her to talk with him. He explained to her that he was concerned at the way young Eora men and women were living here with the bushrangers. Kate looked at him almost pityingly. 'Pemulwuy,' she said gently, 'there is little else for them. The British will not let them be, and for the most part they are not up to fighting like you'.

'Do you think that they still want to, Silky?' asked Pemulwuy, strangely humble.

She looked away for a short while. 'I don't know,' she said.

'And tell me, Silky,' said Pemulwuy quizzically, changing tack, 'do people live in England like this?'

'Oh yes. They are called highwaymen.'

'So I have heard,' Pemulwuy nodded. 'It is just another part of British life, then.'

'In the end,' said Kate, 'it may be the only place left for the Eora and the rest'.

Their conversation was cut short by the arrival of the hunting party, loaded with a great catch and the women had prepared a big fire. It was what the British called New Year's Eve, and celebration started forthwith.

'Here is rum,' Thrush announced. 'We'll all have to get our own drinking cup, since we've not enough to go around.'

Milli walked up with Coleleu and handed out a half dozen metal cups removed from some farmhouse.

'Now there is a smart girl,' said Wilson.

Milli laughed, 'I am pretty good with nicking cups, that's how I come to be here in the first place'.

They all laughed, and then Weuong called out. 'Pemulwuy, will you drink the rum?'

'Yes,' he replied, 'I must learn of the effects of this rum among friends'.

The rum keg was breached and Thrush brought Pemulwuy a metal cup of the brown, pungent liquid.

Kate Donovan said; 'Let me introduce you to a British custom,' she lifted her cup, 'a toast to the King's man: to Governor Hunter who returns to the devil's island in disgrace!'

There was a great shout of agreement. Then Kate turned to Pemulwuy.

'To me old black friend, who sent him home after Arthur Phillip. *Weda*!' Pemulwuy stood up at this point and drank from his cup. He was cautious, but even then it took away his breath for a moment.

Awabakal, Nargel and Milli gulped at the common vessel they were sharing. Nargel's eyes nearly popped from her head, and Awabakal fell to the ground in shock. Milli stood up a little breathless herself and laughed at them. Both Nargel and Awabakal were joined by several others in a plunge into the river. Kate made a new toast to them.

'Weda! To nature's virgins, God love em!'

Nobody much understood her; but by then, nobody cared much either. They burnt their hands on the hot food and their throats with rum. They danced and they sang away the eighteenth century.

Pemulwuy drank quietly and was delighted to watch the Europeans dance. This he had never seen before. Then quite suddenly he joined Awabakal in a deep sleep from which they both awoke in the nineteenth century.

CHAPTER 42

STRANGE BEDFELLOWS

Pemulwuy had been sick in the early hours of the morning. At sunrise he arose, squinting and supporting a great headache. He noticed some movement at Awabakal's camp and walked towards it.

Awabakal was sitting by his resurrected fire, silently bearing his hangover. Weuong was noisily complaining to O'some about the condition of a swollen cheek. Awabakal offered no sympathy, saying that he ran into a tree. Weuong would not accept this explanation, and was quite sure that someone had struck him. He could not remember who, but was concerned that whoever it was had taken a great advantage of his drunken state. He had also burned himself on some hot meat. Pemulwuy sat down amid the evidence of disaster and commented that they looked and smelled like a detachment of the Rum Corps.

Awabakal's camp, no matter how bad, remained the only real sign of life. They were soon joined by a number of others, including Thrush and Wilson. It was a bad morning for allies to talk. At first things went quite well, because the two Europeans brought with them a handful of dried herbs from which the Eora made a kind of tea. They also brought a metal vessel in which to make it. They could find no sugar anywhere, but the hot, strong black substance improved the entire company. Pemulwuy said that his group would move out as soon as they had properly recovered. He hoped that would be shortly after midday. Thrush said he had hoped that they would have more time to talk about some common problems.

'I must talk to you about powder and shot, as this is our greatest weakness,' he said.

Pemulwuy said that they had gathered quite a few muskets of recent times for the bushrangers and would give the weapons to them gladly.

'Oh, yes, we are grateful for that,' said Thomas Thrush, 'but, as you well know, muskets are quite useless without powder'.

Pemulwuy shrugged his shoulders. 'I have always argued this way,' he said. 'If you use the weapons of the British, you become dependent on the British.' He put some more tea in his cup. 'The weapons we use come from this land, so there is nothing the British can do to cut off our supply. We take our food from the land, and we take only what we need...we even use the land as a weapon,' continued Pemulwuy, 'it carries the fire that burns their plant food'.

Thrush reached down and picked up one of Awabakal's spears. He pressed his thumb on the metal tip and turned to Pemulwuy.

'And where might I ask, did this come from, if not from the British?'

Awabakal, headache and all, joined in at this point.

'This is different. Once you have the iron, you can use it over and over again. It is not burnt up like powder.' He opened his hands to indicate an explosion.

'It's still British material,' said Thrush, who was stubborn this morning.

Pemulwuy looked at him sharply.

'This material does not belong only to the British,' he picked up the spear head. 'I first saw this metal on a French ship.'

Thrush seemed to realise that he was pushing his argument too far and put the spear down.

'All right Pemulwuy, you have made your point. But we can't fight the British without muskets and powder. We can't use those spears like you do.'

Pemulwuy stretched out his legs. There was a distinctly uncooperative air about him.

'You also need horses to create this whole thing you do. Then you must also have Eora and Daruk people, and they must live differently to our ways.'

Pemulwuy stopped and stared at Thrush, his strange eye shifting across his face. 'All this you do just to steal from the British, and then you live here and you are just another kind of British.'

Pemulwuy looked intensely at Thrush. 'Thomas Thrush,' he said, 'you do not fight our war'.

Thrush could see this situation deteriorating fast. He quietly cursed himself for raising these matters with a man who had a heavy hangover. Wilson joined the conversation.

'Pemulwuy, everything you say is true,' he said, 'but remember one thing: we fight the way we do because it's the only way we know. We fight because, like you, the British have made us fight. We do not steal your land; we are your friends, we are your allies. What is most important Pemulwuy—we are the only people besides you that are fighting the Rum Corps'.

Pemulwuy reached over and placed his hand on Wilson's leg. 'You are right, Kenneth,' he said more reasonably. 'We are strange friends, but we are allies and we fight the British together, each in our way. I cannot fight them in your way and you cannot fight them in mine.'

Pemulwuy turned, looked at Thomas Thrush and smiled at him.

'Well, Thomas, what is it you want us to do for you?'

Thrush relaxed visibly and returned Pemulwuy's smile, showing yellowed, uneven teeth.

'First, I'm very sorry about your headaches.'

They all laughed. Then Thrush went on, 'whatever attacks you make, be sure that you always take the powder. The shot is also important, but the powder is what really matters'.

Pemulwuy nodded in understanding. 'Yes, we will do this,' he said, 'but you must remember that the soldiers do not attack us very often now, nor do we attack them. Our problem is now with the settlers. They are different. They do not fix bayonets. They fight something like us and they are not stupid and frightened like the Rum Corps'. He paused and looked towards the east. 'I have observed that this summer their crops are different. They leave empty spaces in the wheat to stop the fires. They have also formed what they call wheat protection squads. These are groups of armed men who patrol about the bush. I think if they see us they will shoot us on sight.'

Wilson became intensely interested in all this. He was a quiet man, and when he spoke it was in well-considered words.

'Pemulwuy, you are quite right,' he agreed. 'They are more dangerous than the soldiers. It is more difficult to know where they are. But they have a weakness: they have houses and families and they have things to lose. Remember that.'

Pemulwuy nodded. 'Yes, I know this, but then we also have families and we have our land to lose. For us, that is our strength.'

'I hope it is,' said Wilson, 'but be careful it doesn't become your weakness too'. He sighed. 'There's plenty more of these whip-cracking settlers where they come from. That's the difference.'

Pemulwuy's group left the camp in mid-afternoon. From now on, the bushrangers intended to alternate their attacks between the road linking Parramatta and Camden and the road linking Parramatta to the new Hawkesbury settlement. When the going got too tough, Thrush said, they would shift their attention further down along the north side of the harbour towards Lane Cove. Pemulwuy said he would still maintain his attacks on the grain fields of Parramatta and Toongabbie.

'We must not let them feed themselves.'

Pemulwuy began destroying the wheat in late January. He organised simultaneous attacks in the far west of Toongabbie and to the south of Parramatta. This time they avoided setting fire to the bushlands around the wheat fields. They felt the bush was their protective shield, and it could be used later in the summer when its fuel burden was greater. By mid-February the fight was really on.

The wheat patrol squads had been run from one end of the Parramatta district to the other. They were all mounted and armed, and shot virtually anything that moved. Pemulwuy laid out a careful intelligence network so that he knew of their position almost from hour to hour. Using this technique, he was able to burn almost fifty per cent of the crops by the beginning of March.

Casualties on Pemulwuy's side were relatively small, although during that summer six men were lost to musket fire. Only once during the whole period did Pemulwuy attack a patrol squad, and this attack he led personally.

Pemulwuy's approach was, as usual, to kill the horses first. As soon as one of these squads was attacked, their agreed strategy was to turn and charge straight in the direction of the spear-throwers. Pemulwuy had come to know this, and he had made sure that the bulk of his men were in bush land where a horse was of little value. He attempted to lead the squad into an ambush. The settlers had also learned a few tricks, however. When they saw what Pemulwuy was up to, they retreated again to the flat, open ground, from where they then tried to entice Pemulwuy to attack them in terrain favourable to their style of fighting. Pemulwuy simply waited and allowed the darkness to approach. The settlers on patrol were only too aware of what he planned, and soon they galloped off, carrying their wounded comrades, as night overtook the battleground.

The bushrangers had not done anything like as well on the supply routes. Their problem was that they had not the advantage of the same sort of intelligence network that Pemulwuy had. Pemulwuy passed on any information he had to them, but did not supply them with close intelligence for their attacks. As a result the British had been able to devise plans for dealing with their new highwaymen. In one attack, on the Parramatta/Prospect Hill Roads, they kept a group of soldiers back along the road just out of sight of a wagonload of supplies. The bushrangers successfully captured the supply wagon, only to be overtaken and badly mauled by the following soldiers. Two of the new Irish recruits were killed, and both Thrush and Knight were wounded.

Pemulwuy had become aware that the British were searching the upper part of the Hawkesbury River, looking for the bushrangers' camp. He managed to warn them in time, but now they shifted their camp westwards even further. They had reached the limit of horse borne operations.

At the end of March Pemulwuy made his way to this new camp, called *Gittigitti* by the locals, which in Eora means to tickle. The camp's drawback lay in the fact that it was surrounded by tall grass, the seeds of which were able to penetrate the woven clothing of the Europeans and cause great discomfort to their legs. Pemulwuy was also concerned as to where the British intelligence was coming from which had led them to search for the first camp. When he arrived at Gittigitti, he found the camp quite depressing. Knight had received a very severe wound in the hip which seemed to be refusing to heal. Thrush, on the other hand, had largely recovered from a wound in the shoulder. The camp was open and bare and there was a definite feeling of failure about the whole enterprise.

Pemulwuy told them that they looked as though they needed a success, and so he invited Wilson and any of the Eora or Daruk people who wanted to accompany him to the Hawkesbury settlement. He said he was going to give them a good burning before winter and that there might be some spoils of war available.

Six of the bushrangers, including Wilson, left Gittigitti with Pemulwuy and proceeded down the Hawkesbury River towards the settlement.

A day after they had left Gittigitti, Pemulwuy's scouts told him that there was a military patrol some four or five miles ahead, about a mile to the west of the Hawkesbury River. Pemulwuy turned to Wilson who, like him, was on foot. Pemulwuy refused to take horses.

'Here we may be able to get you some new horses, plus powder and shot,'said Pemulwuy. 'By Christ, this is what we lack: your knowledge of the country and the way your people can tell you what is going on around you,' Wilson exclaimed.

During the next day they followed the army contingent at about a one mile distant. The group consisted of about ten men, all mounted and moving towards the east. Pemulwuy's group caught sight of the British soldiers at midday and followed them unseen until they made camp that night.

The British were very cautious and set sentries, but they had no feed for the horses and therefore had to allow them to graze. The horses were hobbled, one belled, and two men minded them throughout the night. The Eora waited patiently until the two horse guards settled down and, in fact, one of them had gone to sleep. The unsuspecting soldiers were struck down as though attacked by black snakes. The Eoras caught the horse with a bell on its neck and removed it. One of the raiding party sat for the rest of the night clanging the bell from time to time while the others took the horses away.

Just before dawn Pemulwuy released a volley of spears into the camp, and amid screams of agony the remaining soldiers sought cover and fired off a few rounds. The camp was surrounded by fairly open ground, and the Eora could not get within forty yards of the British without exposing themselves.

Pemulwuy waited for about a quarter of an hour. Then he called out to the British: 'Soldiers of your King,' he bellowed, 'is Watkin Tench among you?'

Except for the groans of the wounded there was a stunned silence among the soldiers. Then one of them said: 'Jesus Christ, it's bloody Pemulwuy! What's he talking about? That fellow Tench has been gone for years!'

Pemulwuy's voice pealed out again through the awakening bushlands: 'If he is not with you, then you have no chance of escaping me alive!'

Their reply came swiftly.

'Captain Tench has gone to England. We are three walking and three wounded. Give us quarter!'

Pemulwuy's reply came equally as swift.

'So end it, then. Throw down all your arms and walk out clear of your camp. Carry the wounded out with you. If one of you harms my people, I will kill you all.'

The soldiers discussed the situation quickly. Pemulwuy had never been known to show mercy—he had never taken prisoners, he had never given quarter. It was a great risk, but obviously no greater than the risk of opposing him.

One of the wounded called out from where he lay. 'We came out tracking bushrangers and ran into Pemulwuy. Surrender. We don't have any choice except to die.'

The surrender was carried out with no problems whatsoever. It astounded both the British and Pemulwuy's own people, but Pemulwuy had his reason. He even gave the British two horses on which to carry their seriously wounded comrades. Two others had died. He allowed them sufficient food to get them as far as the Hawkesbury settlement and turned them loose.

After the humiliated British had gone, both Wilson and Awabakal turned on Pemulwuy.

'Why did you do that?' They demanded in angry chorus.

Pemulwuy smiled and told them that it was fortunate the soldiers had found him and not the bushrangers, for they would now look no more for bushrangers here.

He chuckled heartily and waved a hand in the direction of the defeated.

'My friends,' he said, 'the Rum Corps do not want to fight Pemulwuy anymore!'

CHAPTER 43

THE LOSERS' LOSERS

When Samuel Marsden arrived in Sydney in 1793 he was probably the nearest thing that New South Wales had seen to a European intellectual. He was a man of God, who had failed a degree at Cambridge.

When Bennelong returned from England in 1796, he took little interest in Marsden. In fact, it was some two years later before he even spoke to him. Bennelong had developed a deep distaste for these Englishmen who spent their time trying to be big fish in little pools—usually British colonies. As time went by, however, and his fortunes fared not so well, he began to reassess the size of both the fish and the pool.

Close up, Bennelong couldn't stand a bar of the pompous, dour Marsden, or for that matter, his sanctimonious religion. Even after his stay in England, Bennelong found Christianity confused and superstitious. It was a religion easily used for political purposes. Nevertheless, like Pemulwuy, he was finding that hard times make for strange bedfellows. After his initial fall from grace among the British military establishment, he found it not all that difficult to become something of a darling among the missionary set in Sydney.

Language, Bennelong had found, was about the only thing of value that he still had which was of any interest to the British. These days, even that resource was mainly of interest to missionaries and their armchair supporters. These people were eager for 'contact' with the natives. They needed to have access to their language before they could get on with the urgent business of saving their poor benighted souls, and as even Bennelong thought now, stealing their land.

Marsden sensed Bennelong's dislike for him and was therefore inclined to steer the colony's 'civilised black' into the arms of his lesser acolytes. One of these unfortunate men of God had been responsible, with Bennelong's help, for bringing the Awabakal people to Sydney. He felt deeply responsible for the disastrous event that had occurred on the beach on the northern shore of the harbour.

Bennelong had been completely deceived by the Eora over the affair of the disappearance of the Awabakal people along with the missionary's boat. He knew absolutely nothing of the fishing trip.

Nevertheless, it signalled the end of his love affair with the evangelicals. Afterwards he was held in great suspicion; he found himself rejected by the missionaries in general and by Marsden in particular. This left Bennelong in almost complete social isolation in Sydney.

Like the participants in the bushrangers' party at the Hawkesbury camp, Bennelong also had a great hangover on the first of January in the year of 1800. The intensity of his headache was increased dramatically by 'getting ditched' and leaving New South Wales- A New South Wales Corps soldier told Bennelong with a cruel relish that he was unlikely to retain his ownership or even the access to his cabin on the point.

Bennelong was very much out of touch with events in Sydney. The news that he would lose his cabin completely took him aback. He had been aware that Hunter had not been as successful as he had hoped in New South Wales, but he had not expected this. He rushed around furiously, trying to obtain information from anyone who was prepared to talk to him. Finally, unable to unearth a reason that satisfied him, he put it down to the actions of Pemulwuy. In desperation, Bennelong begged an audience with the Governor. It took him the best part of a month to obtain it, but he persisted and eventually stood before Hunter.

The Governor did his best to look busy, but Bennelong simply stood quietly before him and eventually Hunter had to ask him to sit down. They were an interesting pair, these two: If there was a competition for losers in the Australian adventure; it might well be won by one or the other of them.

John Hunter had originally arrived in New South Wales in 1786. In 1792 he was returned to England for losing a ship at Norfolk Island. In 1793 he had applied for the position of Governor of New South Wales. There was not much else offering for someone with his kind of reputation and record. After he arrived in September of 1795, it became clear that his appointment as Governor had done nothing to improve his luck. Hunter had been notified that he was to be replaced and would leave the colony sometime in the spring.

'Excellency,' said Bennelong, 'I am told you are to return to England. Tell me, please—is this true?'

Hunter nodded warily. 'It is true.'

'Why, your Excellency?'

'Oh, my time is up, Bennelong, and I must return home,' said Hunter. 'I don't want to stay here until I die, you know.'

Bennelong looked crestfallen. 'They say that when you go the government will take my house.'

The Governor looked at him sharply, 'this cannot be so! Who says this?'

'A Corps officer told me.'

Hunter coughed and looked away. 'I shall, of course, ensure that this will not happen,' he said none too convincingly. It was obvious that his thoughts were elsewhere.

Bennelong did not pursue the matter of the house. Soon Hunter would be far away, he thought grimly. What had Phillip been able to do once they had got back to London? Where was Phillip now? Instead, he raised the question of relations between the settlers in the west and an increasing geographic range of the colonial population, and especially the continuing problem of Pemulwuy. A vague discussion took place, but Hunter showed no sign of wanting to pursue the matter. For him, quite clearly, the time for action was past, and he was merely serving out his term, a tired and disillusioned man.

'Excellency,' said Bennelong desperately, making dramatic gestures with his hands. 'I have a plan that will save everyone! Solve the entire problem! I beg you to listen!'

Hunter looked at him with a flicker of interest mingled with a stab of guilt. Bennelong wore the remnants of some decent British clothes, and some attempt had been made to wash them, but somehow the dirt had become ingrained. They were creased, and in places torn. The man before him still bore an unfortunate scar on his lip, the remainder of a brawl with others of his race years ago. Bennelong was, for all the world, the living image of everything about the past of this place that John Hunter would one day be happy to forget. Nevertheless, he felt he should listen.

'Very well,' he said heavily, 'proceed'.

'Excellency,' Bennelong began, 'you must know that very few leaders remain among the Eora. So few indeed that they would take up no room on one of your ships. My plan is simple,' he paused excitedly, '...when you return to England, you must take me and these important men with you. We will again speak to the government in London. This time there will be a peace agreement that will last!'

The silence that followed was short but total.

'Bennelong, my good man, that is absolute nonsense!' Hunter boomed. 'I must remind you that you and Yennerawani, rest his soul, were in England for four years discussing such matters. Things have been much worse since your return! I can have nothing to do with such a harebrained scheme. It would be horrendously expensive, and certainly a mere embarrassment.'

It was then that Bennelong broke down and cried. He told Hunter of the accusations made about him after Awabakal had stolen the missionary's boat and fled Sydney, leaving behind two British corpses. He moaned as he described the conspiracies against him hatched by the New South Wales Corps and others of his own people living in Sydney. He was a British subject, he said, and he had the right to live where he wished. And he could no longer bear to live in New South Wales, or anywhere else in this land. Finally he fell on his knees before the Governor and begged him pathetically to take him back to England when he left.

The Governor was, in his way, moved. He felt sadness and guilt at the plight the man was in. 'Bennelong, Bennelong,' he soothed, 'I see your point'. He reached down and touched the man's quivering shoulders. 'If it were simply my whim, I would take you with me. But don't you see that there is no value in your returning to England?'

'What can I do?' Bennelong wailed.

Hunter thought furiously. 'I believe that you can do something,' he said after a while. I believe that you should gather together some leading members of your people and take up a land grant. One will certainly be made available to you! What you have failed to achieve for your fellow natives through diplomacy and negotiation, you may well attain by simply acquiring farming land on which you may all live happily...'

Despite his disappointment, Bennelong found himself taken by the idea. He left the Governor's residence and, as he made his way down to his cottage, he decided that he would drink no more rum. Within the next few weeks, he would go out and speak to some local people and tell them of his plan. He would then arrange for Hunter to make a grant of land for him. He knew that this must be done before the Governor left for England.

The following day, Bennelong dressed again as an Eora man. Except for his fine fur coat, which was long gone in exchange for rum, he vaguely looked the part. He had decided that he would talk to some of the people from Kamay.

He set off at about midday and on the outskirts of Sydney ran into two Wanegal people. He stopped them and []told them about his plan to obtain land grants from the Government. They were amazed that Bennelong would suggest such a thing. One of them said that if he did this, Pemulwuy would simply come and spear him and that would be the end of it. Most other people Bennelong tried to talk to about the issue simply avoided him, or at least the subject. After about a week of fruitless trying, he decided that he would go ahead alone and seek a land grant. He arranged another audience with Hunter.

This time the Governor saw him at short notice. He was generally disappointed that Bennelong had made no progress in obtaining support for his land claim. He was, however, unimpressed by the idea of a sole claim. He thought this could cause more trouble than it solved and told Bennelong so. Bennelong agreed to try a little longer to obtain other support. After he left, Hunter realised that Bennelong was fighting a losing battle. He did not particularly want to face the embarrassment of a weeping Bennelong at dockside when he left, so he arranged for Bennelong to be provided with an improved stipend of rum which would keep him effectively out of the land of the living until Hunter was well away.

Penelope Reid was no beauty, but she had a refined look about her, particularly for a seaman's daughter. She was perhaps six years older than Frances Marshall, and obviously quite wealthy. She was certainly the lady that Collins had described and asked him to speak with. Penelope Reid joined Lieutenant Marshall for lunch at the Corps Officer's Club, which was located near the so-called 'Rocks' barracks close to the quay. In fact this part of Sydney was becoming quite fashionable, and since the attacks on Brickfield it was considered safe.

He learned that Penelope Reid's mother had died of some ailment in New Zealand and she had been brought up by her father and his brother and a Maori partner of their business. All worked in the timber industry there. Her father had come to New South Wales as the demand rose in the colony for light easily worked timber for boat building and furniture. Now they were examining the new found softwoods from the Coal river region and further north. They had a depot in Sydney and a small horse breeding property, both of which Penelope managed. Marshall mentioned that he had observed that her father's vessel was a topsail schooner rather than a brig as he had been told, but nevertheless quite a substantial vessel and ideal for the Tasman trade apparently.

'Actually she was built in America,' Penelope said, 'as a brig, and sailed to New Zealand. She is probably still registered as such'. She told him that her father and uncle had virtually rebuilt the vessel there.

She smiled and explained. 'Her hull is built of American Douglas fir, a light very strong timber, but now, everything else including her rigging and spars is built of New Zealand Kauri pine'.

'Are there no suitable shipbuilding timbers in New South Wales?' Marshall asked.

'There is,' Miss Reid replied. 'We have set up a small *pit mill* here, and export some Spotted Gum to Russell for boatbuilding. It is very strong and ideal for steam bending for ribs,' she explained. 'We are presently investigating an interesting cedar from the north coast, and there is an excellent pine now found in Van Deiman's land which we hope to import here and to New Zealand in the future,' she said.

'Madam you are well informed.'

'Well, that is if there is going to be a New South Wales in the future.'

'Madam I can assure you…. I hope…'—Marshall searched for words.

Penelope smiled, 'my dear Lieutenant, I did not come to dine with you to argue politics….I apologise'.

Marshall regained his composure and smiled.

'No please, it is I who should apologise. In this place one seldom gets the opportunity to discuss anything with an educated lady.'

Penelope laughed too loudly for an English lady, even in New South Wales.

'Sir, I am a British subject. I understand ships and timber and I can keep accounts. I speak English and Maori and am literate in both. I speak reasonable Karigal and some Awabakal. I know some Pacific history and I play the piano a little. Not bad for a sailor's daughter, but hardly an educated lady sir.' She smiled.

Marshall sprang to his feet, even seemed to click his heels, and he bowed.

'Madam, I admire your achievements, 'but what can you possibly seek from a junior officer of the British Army in this colony?'

'Lieutenant—you have met Pemulwuy and survived. Sir you have been there, I would not have such courage and I doubt that many men would have.'

Penelope smiled in admiration. She explained that her father wanted her to write an account, or some sort of book of their antipodal life as a kind of memory of her mother.

Marshall had assumed that Penelope would be mainly interested in learning more about the native situation in the Sydney region and in particular about Pemulwuy. This he thought was why she had sought him out. After all, it was well known that he, a serving New South Wales Corps officer, had indeed been held captive by Pemulwuy and had survived.

She was certainly interested in all that and compared it in their discussion- with the native contact in New Zealand. However, she seemed to believe that the situations were dissimilar. The

Maori were much more a warrior people like the British, whereas with the exception of the Bidjigal people, the native people of New South Wales in general were not. However, after his grilling by Collins, Marshall only offered a fairly careful account of his experiences as an unwilling guest of the Bidjigal. Then the conversation changed. He was completely dumbfounded when he learned that the lady's prime interest concerned the mysterious and, as she described her, beautiful young English woman Millicent Copley, whom she believed was living with the natives. She had learned that Marshall had met her.

Marshall thought that his confidante, Collins, had been a little loose with this confidential information. He made a mental note to be more circumspect in future.

'Well,' he stumbled, 'I wouldn't quite describe her as beautiful; at least when I met her. She was sunburnt and freckled… somewhat the worse for wear… as a result of the rough life that she lived half naked, in the bush'.

'Did she have no clothes?'

'Only a sort of kangaroo skin skirt… and a ridiculous hat of some sort.'

'Would you describe her as ugly, you know unattractive?'

'No! I…suppose with a good bath and decent clothes…she could have been quite...yes—even beautiful.'

Penelope drew out a small journal from her bag; Marshall noted that her eyes were almost violet.

'The girl had quite remarkable green eyes,' Marshall said…'and a pleasant personality'.

'Did you offer to bring her back to Sydney?'

'Of course…but she was afraid to come with us…she is an escaped convict you know.'

Penelope wrote something in her journal.

'What was her crime, so young?'

Frances Marshall felt tears come to his eyes and looked downwards.

'She stole a tea cup from a house in London I believe.'

Penelope looked searchingly into Marshall's now moist grey eyes. 'This seems like a bitter sweet tale sir.'

Marshall pursed his lips. 'Madam much of what happens here is that.'

Penelope smiled wistfully and said, 'incredible! You fell in love with her Lieutenant'.

After Pemulwuy had released the soldiers from the Hawkesbury patrol, he and the others moved forward quickly and, through ways unknown to the British, they arrived on the outskirts of the new Hawkesbury settlement some two days later. Even with horses, the soldiers would still be a full day reaching the place. They watched the place carefully for about half a day. It had certainly grown: the farms had spread deep into one valley and across the rise into another.

Wilson asked Pemulwuy whether he intended to make an attack on the settlement. Pemulwuy said no; what he was doing here was something quite different.

He turned to Wilson and smiled. 'I want to see how well they burn, and what they do when they are burnt.'

They waited until dusk, when a nor'east wind came from across the river and blew the grass seeds into the air. They then moved close to the edge of the central settlement area. They lit a very small fire in the grass, damped it down and watched the smoke rise and be carried by the wind. By eight o'clock that night the wind had changed to the south and swept in across the settlement. Pemulwuy then instructed his people. They lit a horseshoe of fires on the border of the settlement and then stepped back behind them. Within an hour the forests on the Hawkesbury slopes were blazing and the furious infernos swept towards the settlement.

'Now what?' said Wilson.

Pemulwuy was standing on a ridge watching.

'Now we watch,' said Pemulwuy without looking towards Wilson.

The Eora watched the ridge farmers evacuate their houses quickly in the face of the fire as it raced down the slopes. In order to see exactly what was going on, the Eora people had to hazard infiltrating the pathways left open between the fire heads. The farmers down in the valley brought up water from the river on carts. They also tied sacks to sticks and began to beat at the grass fire. Pemulwuy watched them very carefully and he learned what he wanted to know.

On the way back towards Waun, Pemulwuy explained to Wilson that he intended to take his advice. He said that as well as this wise advice, he had observed that the settlers' weakness was their concern for things. It was not so much family, but their things—their property and possessions—that they were determined to protect. The people only seem of value to fight the fire. They are so different to us, I wish that I had understood this earlier,' he said.

'The forest will heal, for us it is the people and the other creatures that must escape. Pemulwuy shook his head slowly. Pemulwuy said that if he were to destroy the Parramatta region farms this summer, then he must first of all prevent the wheat protection squads from being effective. Secondly, he must make the fires large enough so that they were outside the control of the farmers.

Pemulwuy told Wilson he now believed that he knew exactly what to do. He also explained that he would prevent the Eora all over the Parramatta district from firing the land as they normally did this winter. The purpose was to create sufficient fuel burden so that his plans for the British settlers the next summer would have the best possible chance of being effective.

It was impossible to tell whether Wilson had made his decision before or during the expedition with Pemulwuy, but on the way back to Waun the laconic bushranger informed him that he wished to give up robbery-underarms and join Pemulwuy. Pemulwuy was, to say the least, surprised. 'Our life is very different to what you have known with the bushrangers. Surely that is more like the way you Englishmen like to live?' he said.

Wilson grimaced. 'There's not a lot to that,' he answered.

'I do not care. The fact is, I wish to fight the government. I have seen the evil it does, how they oppress my fellow men, and this robbing and thieving is not up to much in a place like this. A foolish game that achieves nothing, the only thing of value to steal in New South Wales is rum. That is of little value elsewhere.'

Pemulwuy nodded gravely.

'To fight with you would seem useful, sir,' Wilson continued. 'I have come to feel for your people,' a little gleam came into his eye, 'and I reckon you're a better bet in the long run if a man wants to stay alive'.

Pemulwuy had no objection, although his mind wandered to a very different European who had made a very different commitment to Pemulwuy's cause a long time ago. Perhaps, thought Pemulwuy, there was a real difference between the Irish and the English.

Francis Marshal felt both left behind and in a sense deserted. He was indeed the left over marine. He was to have left with Hunter. That was the agreement he had made with Collins. Now both Collins and Hunter were gone, Hunter back to England and Collins to Van Deiman's land. Marshall was stuck with the last of the marines...an unhappy bunch at the best of times.

Marshall flopped into the only decent chair in his quarters. His room had been cleaned but still had about it a dank smell. This had just begun to complete his misery when he noticed something different—something quite special—a letter.

He also couldn't help but notice that the only other thing on his table was that confounded empty rum jar—the one Millicent Copley had given them when they left the Bidjigal camp For Sydney. He thought sadly that it was the only souvenir he had of her, or of the whole place, for that matter.

'I should have got rid of the damned thing ages ago,' he thought. His mind clouded over with an exquisitely painful memory.

Marshall stood up and searched around the room for something to open it with; he settled for a bayonet and opened the letter. Any letter received in New South Wales usually came from someone else living in this accursed place—but this was different. It smelled of the sea...of ships perhaps. Once opened, the letter even seemed to have a woman's scent about it. Marshall read it carefully.

'My Dear Lieutenant

You will note that I am back in New Zealand.

I think of you often and the short time we spent at the Officer's Club in the New South Corps lounge.

I hear bits of gossip from New South Wales—really a sad place. I had not written to you earlier because I understood that you were about to return to England. What on earth are you still doing there?

Please write

Penelope'

Marshall grinned or rather grimaced: 'What indeed?' He thought. 'Penelope Reid, she or her family—whatever...they had made themselves part of these antipodal domains—he had not...and perhaps never could.'

In his mind's eye he could see her face still—her strange violet eyes. He immediately thought of Millicent Copley—her scarlet hair and her delicately freckled breasts and dreams of what might have been.

He felt his eyes fill with tears.

'For God's sake he had been through all this before. It was not so much something that was over—it was something that had never really begun', he thought, and then stood up.

'Rum—he should go out and get some rum and get rid of that old rum flask that contained such painful memories', he said to himself.

Wilson had left them halfway along the track and went on to Waun, and then to Gittigitti, to tell his other friends of his decision. He rejoined Pemulwuy's group at the Goman camp about a fortnight later. Some six weeks later, Thrush, Knight, four Eora and two Daruk rode into the camp. They were greeted cordially by Pemulwuy and invited to join him at his camp to meet. Thrush said that he wished to talk to him about something very important. Later in the night they talked for several hours. Thrush told Pemulwuy that with Wilson leaving the whole bushranging operation was getting to seem pointless. He said that under present conditions the only way bushranging would be any use was in close connection with what Pemulwuy was doing.

Thrush finished the conversation by saying: 'When you left me last time I asked you to get powder for me. This time I'm asking you: What can I do for you so's you'd let my group work closely together with yours?'

Pemulwuy thought about this for some time. He said he would give them an answer the next day.

The next day Pemulwuy climbed on the back of one of Thrush's horses and rode with him some distance into the forest. As he rode, Pemulwuy outlined a proposal that would allow them to operate together. The two groups would live separately, at some distance apart. Pemulwuy felt that it was necessary for the bushrangers to maintain their mounted capacity, and therefore they needed one permanent, distant camp where a change of horses could be kept and looked after. The essential thing that Pemulwuy insisted on was that both groups operate under his command. During that day there was a lot of consultation among the bushrangers, and even a little among Pemulwuy's group.

By night they had agreed. Together they planned their strategies for the summer of 1801.

On 28 September 1800, Captain John Hunter, one-time Governor of New South Wales, sailed for England. He left his name on the Coal River that runs into the Pacific Ocean, ninety miles north of Tuhbowgule. It passes by the silent lake of Awaba.

CHAPTER 44

A WAR OF WORLDS

Pemulwuy followed Wilson's advice carefully. His forces spent the spring and early summer of 1800 terrorising the settlers—and more importantly their families. The Eora would wait patiently until all or at least some of the adult males were away from the homesteads; then attack it. These raids were aimed strictly at inspiring terror—spears through thatching and windows, firing sheds, stealing supplies, and all done with much noise and fuss. The attacks usually lasted less than an hour, and then the Eora were gone.

This was hardly what Pemulwuy would have called war, but it destroyed the cunning and dangerous wheat protection squads. They became too afraid to leave their families and other possessions. Pemulwuy did not set fire to the wheat in 1800. He was poised for the summer of 1801, the year of Governor King.

Pemulwuy had Wilson write out for him a message to the new governor. It was written on a piece of ship's canvas with charcoal and hung from a tree on the outskirts of Sydney. It read:

Governor King you are not welcome here. You have come
like Phillip and Hunter to steal our land for your masters.

The response to Pemulwuy's offer was very simple and quickly delivered. Pemulwuy must surrender himself to the authorities in Parramatta where King and the New South Wales judiciary would then consider his future with some leniency.

Pemulwuy's reply was equally swift. He set fire to virtually all of the country west of Toongabbie. This was again part of the strategy. Pemulwuy had found that the threat of a bushfire sent the protection squads home. Burning wheat on its own brought them onto the offensive, but once preoccupied with a serious bushfire the crops were easily burned.

The skies above Sydney remained black and grey with the smoke from the burning of the New South Wales forests. The huge fuel burden from the last summer and winter now kindled a wall of fire that swept down on Parramatta and Sydney. The Eora people had been warned well in advance. Not only did they move from the path of the fire, they placed themselves in suitable positions to hunt the fleeing fauna. The British settlers, on the other hand, had no way of dealing with these horrific fires. They seemed so well placed that all believed that they had been deliberately lit. When Pemulwuy's warriors started appearing from the flames and smoke, setting fire to everything that had not burned, they were sure. The Eora rode the flames like surf, assisting them to jump the firebreaks, lighting them anew when they went out.

While Awabakal and Weuong burnt out Toongabbie and Castle Hill, Pemulwuy set fire to Prospect Hill. By April the whole Parramatta district was a black, bleak mass of charcoal. The wheat and maize crops were virtually a total loss. Looting and minor raids picked the bones of the corpse of this latest British adventure.

Late in April the fires started to move down the north side of the harbour towards Lane Cove, but they were stopped by rain. The summer offensive ended.

The British were in complete disarray. Pemulwuy had at last found his perfect weapon. The grain crops had failed, and they were now burdened by refugee settlers. Their old enemy of eleven years had unleashed a weapon against which they had no defence. The dreams of these determined adventurers lay in the ashes of New South Wales.

A meeting in Sydney of senior officers of the New South Wales Corps had almost ended in a riot. Lieutenant Marshall had finally cracked, physically attacking Abbott and Macarthur and calling them rogues and scoundrels.

King stepped in.

'We have a colony facing its gravest threat and you fight among one another like unruly children!' he scolded.

He gave the Rum Corps an ultimatum:

'Drive the natives from the Parramatta region or abandon all the inland settlements.'

This did, indeed, send the Corps scurrying back to their posts. Not only had Governor King threatened their own holdings, but he had now given them a direct order to take the land from the Eora. The age of the peacemakers, Phillip and Hunter, was finally over.

Under this new policy, the approach of the New South Wales Corps was simple: take a large force, attack all known Eora campsites, and kill everybody found there.

Wilson argued bitterly with Pemulwuy. 'They are using the same method against you,' he insisted. 'Your only advantage is that your people are mobile. You must continue to attack their houses.'

Pemulwuy reluctantly agreed. He pursued a desperate war of attrition. No-one will ever know how many people were killed in New South Wales in that winter of 1801. Both societies were devastated, and when the green grass grew in the blackened valleys of New South Wales in September, there were few British or Eora families to welcome it. If Pemulwuy had not been alive, the Eora nation would have given up in that spring of 1801.

Pemulwuy's power among his people remained undiminished, but the Eora, like the Tharawal, had lost the heart to fight on. The spring brought with it an epidemic of influenza, which swept through the weakened Eora groups like Pemulwuy's summer fires. This particular epidemic also hit the settler families hard and weakened their resolve to return to their burnt and wasted farms. The pressure from British society to return was, however, very great. If one family failed to return, another would quickly step into their shoes. This fierce competitive spirit among the Europeans was something that the Eora could not even imagine, and certainly did not possess.

The bushrangers were in high spirits. They saw their ally Pemulwuy as achieving a brilliant victory over the British.

'One more summer,' Thrush said to Pemulwuy, 'and we will have them in the sea'.

Pemulwuy smiled, but most of his face showed no emotion whatsoever. Pemulwuy was very concerned at the ability the Rum Corps and their police had shown in locating Eora camps that winter.

'I must leave for a while,' he said, 'special business!' In mid-September Pemulwuy left his group and walked to his secret place—a dreaming site of his father's.

The site was not very imposing. It lay on the side of a hill in a sandstone outcrop. This site had been continuously maintained by Pemulwuy's paternal line for thousands of years. Pemulwuy entered a small, shallow cave. Its walls had been marked by men so distant and mysterious in their antiquity that the question of what the marks were never crossed Pemulwuy's mind.

Pemulwuy touched the rock walls with his fingertips, closed his eyes and sang a soft, melodious chant. The cave slowly filled with the song, which deepened in timbre. The song floated down to the face of the rise and fulfilled its meaning and purpose. Its meaning was the land; as it had always been. Its purpose was renewal: renewal of the spiritual communion of the Eora people and this land their source of life.

When he had done with the site, Pemulwuy climbed to the hilltop and sat with his chin on his knees. He looked across this countryside as he had with his father. He could see nothing but the forest, but he had a vision of open space and farms. He struck his head to put the vision away, but it persisted.

He cried out: 'What is it I must do?'

The voices of the land swept up the slope in answer; there was an urgency in them. They gave him warning, but had no special form; no words on which to form action, only sadness.

Pemulwuy sat down. He looked up at the sky and said quietly: 'Is it over?'

Over recent months Pemulwuy's own group had absorbed Eora people from sick and damaged family groups. They had come to him for protection, and he offered it readily. Now that the bushrangers and he had joined forces, his camp contained both sorts of Eora society. There were those who, with Pemulwuy, drew their strength from the ancient traditions of Eora society. The others were all kinds of social refugees. Perhaps, he found himself thinking, one day that was all there would be of Eora society.

CHAPTER 45

THE HEART OF DARKNESS

With all the shadows that crossed his mind, Pemulwuy felt renewed as he left the site. He wandered thoughtfully through the late afternoon, his feet on the earth. He pondered the future of the war, seeing it as though he were a distant observer.

He could see the British inevitably crawling back to their farms. There was no tinder to burn them out this summer, but next summer and for a thousand years he would meet them in this terrible, cleansing catharsis. Even when he was gone, the fires of the land would meet them year after year. He would never win, but neither would they. It would be an eternal losing game and they would all play it forever.

Pemulwuy plucked a large twig of new blooming golden wattle born anew from the burnt blackness of the forest that Pemulwuy had used as a weapon to protect it. He pressed the blossoms to his face and felt the soft blooms on his cheeks. Then he saw Boorea, a tiny dark speck through the wattle blooms.

Boorea ran to him and threw her arms about his neck. Her eyes were full of tears and anger, he had never seen in her before.

'They have killed Narewe, O'some, Weuong and the children,' she wept.

Pemulwuy lifted Boorea from the ground. His face was ablaze.

'Who did this?'

Boorea tipped her head to one side.

'Pemulwuy, they knew where we were. There were soldiers and settlers, many of them.'

Pemulwuy took his wife upon his back and ran for two miles. He met Thrush and Knight, running in horror and panic through the bush. They added Wilson to the list of dead.

'How did this happen?' screamed Pemulwuy.

'I don't know,' panted Thrush. Tedbury and Awabakal were at our camp. They told us you intended to move closer to the sea. Then Gomil came in wounded and said that your camp had been attacked. We came as quickly as we could, but they were gone. Awabakal and Tedbury are on their tracks now.'

'And where are our dead?' asked Pemulwuy.

'At the camp.'

'Then leave me and follow Awabakal.'

'But Pemulwuy,' Thrush caught his arm, 'they may have come back and be waiting for you there'.

'Let that be true!' he snarled, 'take Boorea to somewhere safe!'

He turned away and was gone.

Knight took Boorea in his arms and said to her. 'Don't worry; I believe that he could kill the whole British Army if they were there this night.'

Pemulwuy stood silently in his camp. The fires still smoked and the trees stood as silent, blind witnesses to the massacre. The campsite was strewn with Eora dead. He walked about trance-like until he found Narewe. He knelt down beside her. She lay on her back with her legs caught under her. Her eyes were closed and her lips slightly parted. There was a great red hole in her chest and a spear in her tiny, slender hand.

Pemulwuy picked up Narewe, carried her to a clear place in the camp and laid her on the ground. He found Weuong with O'some lying across him. Weuong had been killed with gunshot. O'some had her head crushed in by a musket butt. He picked the two bodies up together and laid them beside Narewe. Next he found Wilson, the back of his head partly blown away. He laid him beside Weuong and whispered, 'you wanted to join us. Now you will sleep with us forever'.

Pemulwuy worked his way slowly around the camp. The men, the women, the children; he carefully laid out each body. He then set about gathering wood and methodically built a funeral pyre over his dead. Finally he picked wattle blossoms and cast them on the top of the pyre.

He stood silently for a while; then began to sing. It was a long, slow sobbing chant and it carried all of the earth's burdens and its tears.

It was dark when he finished. Pemulwuy then lit a fire. He picked up a burning bough and called out in English;

'Gurrewe! If you are still one with your spirit, take Narewe to your island before I set her spirit free in her own land.'

Pemulwuy cast the bough into the fire. In a few minutes a great blaze reached into the sky and Pemulwuy was gone.

Somewhere about mid-afternoon of the next day Pemulwuy found the bodies of three soldiers. He looked quickly at them. This was the work of Tedbury and Awabakal, he knew.

Pemulwuy continued to track the attackers. Their tracks were now followed by those of Tedbury and Awabakal. The group seemed to number about forty-five, all mounted. The three dead must have been a forward scouting party. About a mile further on, the group split. Tedbury and Awabakal had followed the larger group towards Parramatta.

Pemulwuy followed the other group. About a mile from a lighted farmhouse he saw two soldiers riding towards him. Pemulwuy stood; spear poised on umana, in the centre of the carriage track.

The soldiers were almost on top of him before they realised he was there at all. One got a spear through his cheek into his skull and the other pulled his horse to a jarring halt in time to receive a second spear through his stomach.

The first fell from his horse, and the other's horse bolted with the soldier clinging to its back. Pemulwuy left the man on the ground dead and walked on towards the farm.

As Pemulwuy walked towards the house, the darkness seemed to follow him like a great descending shadow. A dog barked, and died, as he approached the house. One man walked out with a musket, and he died with a spear deep in his chest. But he cried out as he fell, and the others locked the door. Pemulwuy leapt onto the roof like a huge black spider and screamed out curses. He heard a woman scream from inside the house, then a man's voice.

Pemulwuy slid down a wall and put a piece of timber against the rear door. He then sat down, carefully made a fire, and proceeded to set fire to the house. He retreated almost fifty paces, and called out 'I am Pemulwuy! I am alone! Come out and die as my family died, or burn to death!'

He waited as the building began to burn. He heard the cries of a frightened child, and thought of the children who had died under musket butts, one day past.

At last the door opened and three figures ran out, a man first, carrying two muskets. One woman ran to the right, and one to the left carrying a child. The man fired both muskets, but Pemulwuy killed him with a spear. The woman on the right was brought down with a hand-thrown spear in her hip.

As Pemulwuy ran forward, the woman was crying out in pain. The other woman joined her and knelt beside her, still clutching the child. Pemulwuy suddenly stopped, frozen. The second woman was Eora. He ran up and threw her to the ground with the child screaming in fear.

'What are you doing in the house of the djeraba?' he shouted.

'Kill me, Pemulwuy,' she said. 'Kill me and kill my baby!'

'What are you doing here?' he screamed at her.

'This white woman is my friend,' she replied, now crying, 'she looked after me and my baby. My men are dead. You have bled us to death Pemulwuy. Kill me and kill her!'

Pemulwuy turned and walked away into the darkness of his bleeding land.

Boolayoo had escaped the massacre at Pemulwuy's camp, along with four other children and some twelve adults. They all joined the bushrangers with Awabakal and Tedbury.

Tedbury left the camp to try and find his father. He returned a week later, having been unsuccessful, but he also brought back a piece of paper with a printed message on it.

'It has something to do with you,' he said to Thomas Thrush, handing him the paper.

Thrush spread it out carefully. Since he could not read, he had to get Millicent Copley to help him.

Milli read the paper as best she could. The gist of it was that the Governor on 25 October had offered a reward for the capture, dead or alive, of Thomas Thrush and William Knight. The reward consisted of seven gallons of spirits.

The two Englishmen were quite flattered; although Thrush pointed out that he had stolen ten times that much rum from them.

On 17 November the reward was increased: 'For a prisoner for life or fourteen years, a conditional emancipation; to a person already conditionally emancipated, a free pardon and a recommendation for a passage to England; to a settler, the labour of a prisoner for twelve months; to any other description of person, twenty gallons of spirits and two suits of slops.' .

Thomas Thrush and William Knight were described as escaped convicts and vagabonds who were, it was suspected, living among the natives and assisting them to commit many acts of violence on the settlers.

On 22 November 1801, Governor King finally committed Pemulwuy's name to an official record. He was included in the order outlawing Knight and Thrush. On that day Pemulwuy joined some interesting company among future Australians.

CHAPTER 46

THE JUDAS TOUCH

The Rum Corps were certainly delighted with Chief Constable Barrington's successful attack on Pemulwuy's camp. Astonishingly, not only had he located the camp, but somehow he had got his force past Pemulwuy's intelligence network and his lookouts.

There was no doubt in the British mind that the attack was devastating. Except for one fairly minor reprisal, nothing had been heard of Pemulwuy or his group for a month or more. It was now late in January and it looked as though 1802 was not going to have a summer of fires.

King was quite affected by the eventual death of the woman involved in Pemulwuy's attack on the farmhouse. It was this that moved him to give Pemulwuy the status of an outlaw. Any legal status at all for Pemulwuy worried the Rum Corps, but they decided it was better than allowing him the status of a military enemy—a position they had successfully resisted for eleven years.

Pemulwuy was, however, not that easily put to rest. The legend of the man was immense and even at this, his lowest point, there was a rumour that during the attack on the camp, Barrington had fired at him twice point-blank without bringing him down. This rumour was fed by the fact that none of the very substantial number of claimed dead had actually been brought in. In fact, the reason was that once the attackers had found that Pemulwuy and Awabakal were not in the camp, there had been something of a panic. They had expected an attack from the rear. Even the steely-nerved George Barrington had regarded discretion as by far the greater part of valour.

It had come to a point where Macarthur himself was disturbed by the persistent rumour of musket shots having no effect on Pemulwuy. Barrington swore before witnesses and God that he had not laid eyes on Pemulwuy. Macarthur, however, was forced by frightened settlers to make Barrington perform his oaths before the Governor.

King was quite satisfied with Barrington's explanation of why no scalps were brought in. He was nevertheless very curious as to how Barrington had managed to accomplish such a feat where all others had failed.

'It was accomplished by artifice, your Excellency,' said the Chief Constable of Parramatta with a humourless smile. He went on to explain that he had placed pressure on one of Pemulwuy's associates to betray him.

'Accomplished by bloody artifice' growled Captain Abbott. 'I saw how Hill tried that method years ago with Bennelong!'

'True,' said Macarthur, 'the Judas touch. But the time now is more conducive to such approaches, and Barrington is just the man for this. After all, he was a pickpocket'.

Pemulwuy had not been seen by anyone since the attack on his camp, and Awabakal and Tedbury had more or less taken joint command of the remaining forces. They had also joined company with the bushrangers, who were presently camped near the mouth of the Hawkesbury River.

With Pemulwuy known to be still alive, it had not taken Awabakal and Tedbury long to locate the Judas. In fact, there were two of them. Their story was that Barrington had captured their families and had threatened to kill them unless they led him to Pemulwuy. They said that they had agreed to do this, believing that they could lead the group into Pemulwuy's hands. Awabakal was inclined to believe one of them, but not the other. He had known him to be dishonest in the past. Thrush insisted that they must make an example of them. They discussed this for a while with the two- bound accused, lying in front of them. Finally the two Eora leaders told the Europeans that this was Eora business and would be dealt with by them alone.

Awabakal and Tedbury tied the two to a tree on Parramatta Road, and then concealed themselves about forty feet away. The two traitors were told that if they raised any alarm they would be killed immediately. If they did as they were told, then they had only to hide themselves among the British to avoid Pemulwuy, who would certainly kill them.

About an hour after this, two constables rode up. They stopped to examine the situation, and the two bound Eora stood in silence while their would-be rescuers were speared. One died immediately, and one raced towards Parramatta carrying a spear in his body.

Both Thrush and Knight were impressed with the Eora solution, but still held reservations about not killing the pair on the spot. Awabakal looked seriously at the two ragged Englishmen. 'They have been sung,' he said. 'They are finished.'

One evening early in February, Pemulwuy appeared at the camp. Everyone had been somehow dreading this, although Tedbury said that his father was simply mourning. Everybody was concerned about the mental condition in which Pemulwuy might arrive.

But, except for being somewhat vague, he seemed in fairly good spirits. He was particularly pleased to find that Boorea was looking after Boolayoo.

Awabakal and Tedbury explained the results of their investigations and the fate of the traitors. Pemulwuy showed little apparent interest.

Pemulwuy told them that he intended to go a long way south into Tharawal country—to see what the British were up to and to visit other possible allies. He warned the group that their present position was very dangerous and they should go to Gittigitti and operate from there.

The following morning he was gone. Boorea said that Pemulwuy also wanted Awabakal to see what was happening in Sydney. Tedbury and Gomil should watch the situation among the Eora.

Thrush and Knight went with them to Gittigitti and then said that they intended to go back and do some bushranging. Tedbury and Gomil agreed to join with them in some exploits, while Awabakal set out for the coast.

A germ of a thought of returning home was forming again in Awabakal's mind, though he put it aside. Pemulwuy, he thought, would return with some new way of overcoming their present difficulties.

Awabakal became aware of something distinctly different as he walked towards the sea. It took him a full day before he realised what it was. In a full day's walk he had not seen a single Eora.

The next day he went actively looking for people and eventually found one small, pathetic group about six miles from Parramatta. He spent the night with them and learned that the rest of this group had moved closer to the perimeter farms where they could cadge a little food from the British during the bad part of the winter. Awabakal felt a sense of despair among these people, which was typified by the dark, miserable government-issue blankets which were replacing their skin cloaks.

Awabakal arrived on the shores of Tuhbowgule opposite Sydney in mid-May. He found a discarded Borogegal canoe and precariously crossed the harbour. The canoe was old and in bad repair. Awabakal thought that he must steal a better vessel for his return.

After the betrayal, he was very cautious as to whom he approached. He found Bennelong hopelessly drunk. He silently explored further and discovered the young man Bungaree. The boy who had fled Sydney with them many years ago had grown into a young man. Awabakal had not seen him for some time. He learned that Bungaree had travelled a long way by sea with his old friend Captain Flinders. He said that Flinders was looking for another local man to come on a further voyage. Bungaree insisted that Awabakal come with him on board the ship *Investigator* commanded by Flinders. The ship was moored clear of the docks. Awabakal was finally persuaded and the pair took a dinghy out to the ship.

Bungaree went on board first to ensure that Awabakal would receive a reasonable welcome. He returned, and announced that Captain Flinders would be delighted to meet Awabakal. Awabakal climbed on board the magical machine. The lights, the sounds, and the smell of the ship took his mind winging back to his first and only voyage in such a vessel, his voyage to Sydney. Flinders was very hospitable and spent at least an hour talking to the two young men. In fact it was the first and only time that Awabakal had heard himself referred to as an Australian. Awabakal learnt that Australia was the name Flinders used for the whole land. Flinders invited Awabakal to join him and Bungaree on a voyage mapping the coast of the continent. He said it would be very useful to have another Australian on board.

Awabakal had assumed that Flinders would be unaware of what was going on in the land of the Eora. He was not well informed, but he was very interested, and he asked some shrewd questions. Awabakal was rather cautious about saying too much. Flinders, however, pressed him gently and let it be known that he had little time for the Rum Corps.

Little by little he drew the main picture of the situation from Awabakal. Finally Flinders said: 'So you think you have lost a war! My dear fellow, the Rum Corps has never let you fight one. Whatever happens, it is the Corps who has lost. They lost when they made your leader an outlaw.' He looked aside. 'History will treat them very badly.' 'I don't understand,' Awabakal said.

'Well, sir, even if they succeed in killing the man, they are simply executing an outlaw, not winning a war against the leader of a sovereign nation. There is no conquest. Britain can never claim sovereignty here,' Flinders answered. He stopped and thought for a minute. 'But then I suppose it would only be over the Eora country.' He paused. 'It is an unfortunate situation and, mark my words, the future will be held to pay the debt.'

Flinders went on to say that Awabakal should not judge all of the British by the Rum Corps. 'We British also have some history of oppression,' he said. 'Let me show you something.'

Flinders rummaged about and finally produced a worn book. He opened it, eventually finding a reference, and read from it:

'England was occupied for many years by a people called Romans,' he said, 'but listen to this, gentlemen. It comes from a letter written by a Roman called Cicero to a friend, Atticus'.

He read to them in a very strange language he called Latin. Then he translated the passage into English: 'Do not obtain your slaves from Britain. They are stupid and utterly incapable of being taught.'

Both the newly-termed Australians spent the night on the ship. Bungaree pressed Awabakal to accompany them. He said that the ship would not leave until midwinter, or even later, which left him plenty of time for farewells.

Awabakal was absolutely taken with the idea. He reasoned that such a voyage would give him the opportunity to seek more allies in their efforts against the British. Besides, deep in his heart he knew it provided an escape from the hopeless situation he and the others were in. Bungaree and Flinders offered him an escape into a tomorrow.

CHAPTER 47

THE WAITING

Awabakal spent a little more time around Sydney, and then headed for Kamay. Eora people were really difficult to find. After King's edict of 1 May, which made it legitimate for settlers to shoot them, most were prudently keeping out of sight.

Awabakal had dutifully examined as best he could the situation in Sydney. He had seen much, but the most important for Awabakal remained the things that Flinders had said. Somehow he felt that Flinders had told him the ultimate secrets of the British. They were, however, so jumbled that he could not make sense of them. Of all the aliens that Awabakal had known, this man Flinders was the most profound. He seemed beyond the nature of the British, or at least those Awabakal knew. He was truly a strange creature. It seemed that he had left a wife after only four months of marriage. He had done this to wander about the seas. He was, Awabakal thought, like a bird without legs, a creature with no resting place.

Whatever Flinders was, he had created in Awabakal a different way of thought. When the edge was through, it was a dream. Awabakal almost touched it, but then it was gone. He resolved that he must return quickly and talk to Pemulwuy and the others about Flinders.

Awabakal swung back across behind Sydney and crossed the harbour to Kissing Point as Pemulwuy had asked. He then set forth along his westward path to Gittigitti.

When Awabakal arrived at Gittigitti he was disappointed to find that Pemulwuy had not returned. He also learned that Tedbury was very ill and that Boorea had moved camp with Tedbury and Boolayoo to the Hawkesbury.

Awabakal said that he would visit them but decided to spend the night at Gittigitti and talk with Thrush about Flinders.

None of what he told made any sense at all to Thrush. He said that Flinders was a typical well-born naval officer and would understand nothing of the situation of common folk, black or white. The conversation went on a little longer. Awabakal eventually went to his camp with a vague suspicion that the man Cicero might have been correct about the British.

The next morning Awabakal set out for the Hawkesbury. He arrived late in the afternoon and was appalled at Tedbury's condition. His illness looked for all the world like galgalla, but no pox appeared on his body. Boorea had a metal vessel in which she made broth and fed her ailing son.

Boorea told Awabakal that there was nothing that he could do. She said that he should take the child Boolayoo away with him for a while so that he would not catch the disease.

Awabakal left the camp that night, taking Boolayoo with him. The child was now nine years old. He was not as fair as he used to be, and had become quite thin over recent years.

Awabakal called the boy 'Bally', a nickname given him by William Knight. He was a quiet, introspective child and followed Awabakal silently down the river. Awabakal chatted to the boy from time to time, watching him from the corner of his eye. Boolayoo carried a sadness which Awabakal well understood. He seemed to be possessed of an inner calm and had very little of his mother's vivacity or sociability.

What was to become of the child, thought Awabakal, born as he was of two spirits. His father, his mother, his friend, all killed by the British in this terrible conflict. Awabakal wished silently that he had spoken to Matthew Flinders about the boy, as he was after all truly one of Flinders' Australians but a new kind.

They hunted together and Awabakal found the boy to be quite good with a spear. He was, however, never moved to exuberance. Their hunting was productive, but neither of them had any great heart for it. At night in their camp they talked of the realities, the unrealities, and the dreams of their world. Awabakal tried to reach through the mystery of the boy's consciousness to find the essence of his lost companions, but always there was a veil between them through which he could not see.

From time to time they visited Boorea's camp. By the end of June, Tedbury showed signs of recovery, though he remained haggard and worn.

On one of these visits Boolayoo asked Awabakal quietly: 'Why do these sicknesses not touch me?'

Awabakal thought for a minute then replied.

'Your mother and father left you with this great strength. I must spend more time teaching you English. It is another great power to have.'

'Awabakal I can speak English, but my mother said that I should learn to read the marks of English on paper.'

'Yes,' said Awabakal thoughtfully, 'that could also be a very great power'. 'How can I do this?'

Awabakal thought for a while and then said that there were some Eora families who worked with the missionaries in Sydney. They were being taught to read the marks.

Awabakal said that he may be able to arrange for Boolayoo to spend some time there.

They visited Gittigitti in mid-July. The bushranging group had built up again. Horse borne, they carried out two reasonably successful raids. The camp was well fed and in reasonable spirits, but their frame of mind was frayed.

Knight told Awabakal that he wished Pemulwuy would return. Just the sight of him strengthened the resolve of the Eora. He told Awabakal that he planned to make an exchange with some convicts on a perimeter farm. They had been stealing powder and would exchange it for rum. Knight said, however, that he was very worried about Barrington and his patrols and must proceed with great caution.

Awabakal had become very curious about this man Barrington.

'He is like Tench and Carpenter,' said Awabakal.

'No,' said Knight, 'he is a lot more dangerous than them. He is as cunning as a shithouse rat,' he paused, 'I knew him years ago when he was a convict. He was a thief in England'.

'I do not understand why he would now fight for the British, if he was once a convict,' said Awabakal.

'Oh, they bought him off, Awabakal. There are things that you will never know about the British.'

'Are these the things that they learned from the Romans?' asked Awabakal.

'Flinders really got at you with all this stuff about Romans,' said Knight, 'they lived thousands of years ago, they have nothing to do with this' He waved a hand, dismissing this line of discussion, then went on, 'I intend to make this exchange. Thomas is going to make a feint raid some distance away, just in case Barrington has got wind of something'.

Awabakal agreed to join Thrush on the diversionary raid. He further agreed to carry out the exercise from horseback, but said he would not use a musket. Awabakal had little heart for this sort of venture. It was not part of Pemulwuy's war. It was activity, however, and Awabakal needed to sharpen his thinking with action.

Awabakal did some scouting about before the raid and sure enough there were constables about. Nevertheless, the raid was successful, and a messenger assured Thrush that the exchange was proceeding without difficulties. The two separate groups planned to meet some two miles south of the old Goman camp. Awabakal persuaded Thrush and the others to go further west by two miles, while he and the Eora watched the meeting place. Pemulwuy had always instilled in him the importance of listening to the voices inside. They were the whispering realities of old Australia which no alien heard.

Late in the afternoon of the meeting day, Barrington and ten mounted constables arrived. Awabakal sent one of his companions to warn Thrush and tell him to go to Boorea's camp. He and the other Eora left their horses and back-tracked the police. They found the site of an ambush some two miles from the exchange point. Two of Knight's group lay dead and the others were gone.

Awabakal could not make a thorough examination of the tracks, since it was too dark. Curiously, the two small kegs of powder were still present. They hid the powder about half a mile away and then made off, following what trail was visible. When they arrived they found the group had spent time in what looked like a night camp. They had left behind them food and other things, and two dead who had died from spear wounds. But the spears were gone.

Awabakal stood staring at the bodies. There was something he knew he should read here, but his mind was still too full of Flinders, Bungaree and Boolayoo.

Some little distance from the camp they found other tracks. These, thought Awabakal, were made by Thrush and his group.

The whole business was a mess, and Awabakal left for Boorea's camp. They slept for a time during the next day and arrived at the camp late the following midday. Thrush arrived the following night.

There was great confusion. Thrush had returned to the meeting place and found the same situation that Awabakal had reported. Thrush thought Awabakal had attacked the constables. They found out that Knight had been wounded and captured in the ambush. It was concluded that some of Knight's group, who had escaped the original ambush, must have made the attack. Thrush was pleased to hear that at least Awabakal had hidden the powder. George Barrington had been visibly shaken by his midnight experience and considered himself very lucky to have escaped alive. He concluded that the group that had attacked them were highly experienced Eora warriors, probably led by Awabakal or Tedbury. Half his contingent had been wounded. The following day he learnt that the two convicts and an Eora man who had been involved in the plot had been murdered. This was even more unsettling, and did little to enhance Barrington's prestige among the settlers.

He had got nothing from his brief interrogation of the wounded Knight, except a warning. The warning chilled Barrington's resolve to proceed further with his plans. Knight had said that none of them had seen Pemulwuy for months, but he sensed that somewhere out there the crow watched and waited silently to take Barrington's life. Barrington became more and more affected by thoughts of Pemulwuy. He was the first man to write on paper about the mythology surrounding Pemulwuy. Over the next two weeks he also became aware of a crow which seemed to hang about his house. He tried twice unsuccessfully to kill the bird. Barrington had planned to use Knight as bait to trap the rest of the group.

The Chief Constable now told Macarthur that he had decided against the 'bait' plan and advised that Knight should remain in Parramatta. Macarthur would not hear of this and ordered Barrington to go ahead with the plan.

The plan was quite clever. Lieutenant Palmer was to take over the actual field operations. A small detachment would escort Knight to Sydney. Meanwhile, some five or six days before, three separate forces would be strategically located about the route. These groups would be warned of any rescue attempt by Barrington's informants. The whole exercise had seemed foolproof when Barrington had first conceived it. But after two weeks of his fears—and the sightings of the crow—the Chief Constable was no longer quite so confident about who was the fool—he or the humbled but still dangerous Pemulwuy, who was somewhere out there in his silent land.

CHAPTER 48

THE LAST REPRISAL

There was great uncertainty in Gittigitti. Thrush was concerned at facing the prospect of life alone with the Eora. He was sure that Knight would be taken to Sydney and was anxious that an attempt should be made to rescue him. They had received information that he was indeed to be transferred to Sydney on 6 September. Thrush was sure that he would be hanged.

Awabakal thought the idea of a rescue ridiculous. The British, and especially the cunning Barrington, would escort Knight with a substantial force. Worse still, escape from the Parramatta Road area would be very difficult. Awabakal found himself in an odd situation. Thrush was firmly convinced that it was Awabakal who had carried out the midnight attack on Barrington's camp. This, Awabakal naturally knew to be untrue, but he could not find an explanation, no matter how he tried.

The situation became very grave when Thomas Thrush announced that he and four others would make an attempt alone. This infuriated Awabakal, who felt that Thrush was using blackmail to drag him and the other Eora into a suicidal operation. The situation was resolved by the arrival of some very special information, brought by a messenger from Tedbury.

They were told that there was a secret plan. The large escort headed For Sydney was only a decoy. William Knight was in fact being taken to the Hawkesbury settlement by another, smaller guard and would be then transported to Sydney by water. Thrush was overjoyed. Awabakal's information network had worked. Awabakal was inclined to believe that the new opportunity was very good. He insisted, however, that no attack be made until he could be absolutely sure that this was not another product of Barrington's cunning. Among other things, Awabakal wanted to be sure that no secret force waited at Castle Hill.

On 6 September Barrington set forth with a substantial guard reinforced by the Rum Corps. He was clearly escorting four prisoners to Sydney. The prisoners were all masked and the group travelled slowly. Two hours later, a group of six Rum Corps soldiers accompanying a covered buggy left Parramatta for Castle Hill. At Castle Hill a man in shackles was taken from the buggy for a moment. It was Knight.

Within two hours of the news, the rescue force was waiting. Awabakal still insisted on personally acting as watchdog over the operation from a distance. The rescue took place a mile out of Castle Hill. The Rum Corps escort fled at the sight of the relatively large Eora force. The rescuers picked up Knight and were off. At that point, an urgent message came from Awabakal, telling the group to head south and not west. Awabakal had just received information that there was a substantial British force at the Hawkesbury, almost due west of the hold-up site.

The rescue had been completely successful, with hardly a shot fired. Awabakal now feared, however, that the British might come across Boorea's camp. He had reason to be glad that they were using horses in this operation. He galloped to the camp only to find it deserted. The place was covered with the marks of other horses. Awabakal leapt from his mount to examine the camp. He saw a man hanging from a tree by one arm, with an Eora spear through his stomach. The corpse was a European. A little further away he found an Eora man in the same condition.

Awabakal was very cautious. He hid and waited for a while. Finally he approached the bodies and withdrew one of the spears. He knew immediately the answer to the mysteries of the last few months.

'Pemulwuy,' he whispered, and then shouted, 'Pemulwuy!'

During the rescue, Knight had kept warning Thrush's band that it was a trap, with him as the bait, but no trapdoor had fallen. They all arrived at Gittigitti without event and were met by Awabakal, Boorea and Tedbury.

'So that was it,' said Thrush, 'our black guardian angel's still out there'.

Tedbury told them that his father had been watching the British alone, destroying the communication lines and killing the informants. A large contingent of the Rum Corps had been assembled at the Hawkesbury: one detachment moved along the river and the other to the east of the road. The plan was set so that if Thrush and company attacked, the British contingents were to be warned, enabling them to affect an ambush. Pemulwuy had systematically killed off their warning system.

Barrington returned from Sydney a week later after discussing the situation with the Governor. He maintained that Pemulwuy remained the source of the trouble. It was Pemulwuy who had been undermining all their plans by secretly destroying their communications and terrifying Eora and settlers alike. He said he knew of a convict woman who was so afraid of Pemulwuy that she could not bear to sleep without a lamp beside her bed. He said that settlers used the name of Pemulwuy to bring their children in at night. He also reported that Eora people had come to them, swearing that they wanted no more of killing. They had been told by Barrington that the present hostility towards them would continue until Pemulwuy was killed. Barrington had told King that it was quite pointless pursuing Pemulwuy.

He believed that, even though Pemulwuy had destroyed his network of informants, the only way to deal with the savage was to continue to place pressure on the Eora people. King agreed. He said he would write to Lord Hobart in the near future and give a full report on the whole matter.

When Macarthur heard through Barrington of King's intention to report the matter to England, he swore at Barrington and left post haste For Sydney.

Pemulwuy arrived about a week later at Gittigitti. He seemed strange. He was at once talkative and interested, yet withdrawn and secretive.

Awabakal sat with him late at night and told of his conversation with Flinders. Pemulwuy listened intently, asking an occasional question. Finally he said: 'You like ships. Why did you not sail off with them?'

Awabakal looked down at the ground.

'I took Bally to an Eora family living with the missionary. He will learn to read the marks.' He paused, 'I watched Flinders' ship sail away,' he said.

The next morning Pemulwuy said that they must make summer camp far to the south, near the sea in Gweagal country. He said that the women and children, with Tedbury and some of the recently wounded men, should make this journey out west in Tharawal country. They should come into the coast behind Camden. Arrangements had been made for them to pass through Tharawal country.

'And what shall we do?' asked Thrush.

'We will make the settlers think another way about George Barrington,' Pemulwuy said. 'If it pleases you, we shall use horses.'

As they rode side-by-side, Pemulwuy told Awabakal that Barrington depended on his cunning and his successes.

'This English world holds him in no esteem,' he said. 'I have cut off his ears and put out his eyes'. He paused thoughtfully. 'These British will turn on him like a sick worragul. He is no enemy like Tench or Carpenter.' Pemulwuy looked sadly at the sky, and then went on, 'but for every Barrington I kill there are more'.

Awabakal felt elated to be again at Pemulwuy's side. His confused decision about Flinders melted away, and yet he was troubled. Pemulwuy seemed now, for all his strength, frail and disturbed.

During September and early October they began a series of hit-and-run attacks on the settlers. This culminated in a final, brutal attack on Kissing Point at the end of October.

Even in this eleventh hour of their struggle, Pemulwuy seemed again to have completely mastered the situation. Barrington and the Rum Corps were, indeed, blind and deaf, and the terror of the settlers had turned to hate for their protectors. The British had again lost the upper hand in this tragic conflict, but it was different from the past, and even Pemulwuy seemed possessed with a sense of impending doom.

The weather had become quite warm, and the attack on Kissing Point would have been no more than a minor raid with some burning. King had, however, authorised a permanent and heavily armed Rum Corps crop patrol, and this group attacked the raiders.

This was no real problem, and the Eoras expected the situation and were easily confident of evading the patrol. There were no more clever British soldiers left. They planned to break quickly and lead the soldiers into the bush, but it went terribly wrong.

Pemulwuy seemed to take leave of his senses at the sight of the uniforms. He leapt from his horse onto the back of one of the soldiers. The rest of the mixed force of Eora and bushrangers had begun to retreat. They now renewed the attack. Pemulwuy ran ahead, leading them on foot to the houses. He carried a blazing torch in his hand, firing everything as he went by.

Within a few minutes the whole settlement was ablaze. Flames leapt from the thatched roofs, carrying showers of sparks into the night sky with Pemulwuy's fury. The screams of children joined the angry breath of the fire. Enemies and friends were indistinguishable in the chaos that reigned in the settlement.

Awabakal was stunned. This frenzied confusion was beyond his experience. This was different to the war they had been fighting. He turned around, eager to quit the place.

Then Pemulwuy stood before him holding a burning torch in his mouth, his face alight with reflected flames, absorbing the scene, as though he was witnessing the ultimate destruction of an enemy for the first—or the last—time.

He then leapt into the air, waving the fiery brand and calling out strange words. Awabakal retreated quickly. He went to Gomil and asked him to tell Pemulwuy, if he could, that he intended to go to the summer camp by way of Kamay. Gomil nodded but said nothing.

Awabakal left that night. It was a long walk, and he arrived at the north side of Tuhbowgule the following night. His mind remained filled with the image of Pemulwuy with the fire in his mouth. He was deeply distressed by this vision of Pemulwuy's madness.

When he thought back over the years, he decided that there had always been an edge of madness to the man. He sat with his arms about his knees gazing sadly upon the silent waters of the beautiful harbour.

After about an hour, Awabakal began to contemplate some of his more immediate difficulties. He realised that he must cross three large expanses of dangerous water to get to the summer camp this way. He must steal a boat. He walked while he thought about this. The vision of his leader came back to him.

'Pemulwuy has gone completely mad,' he said aloud. He looked up and saw the new moon. She leant heavily on the night about him and gave it a voice of whispers that pursued his thoughts. He listened, looked again at the sky... Yanada touched his cheeks and he caught his breath, and he knew Pemulwuy's secret.

Suddenly Awabakal turned around and began to run back across his tracks of the day.

After the Kissing Point attack, they met up well out in Kamergal country. Several children were said to have been burnt to death in the raid. There was no feeling of elation.

That night at the camp, Pemulwuy and Thrush had an argument, and Thrush came marching past Awabakal.

'The man is mad,' he muttered to himself. 'I am going back to simple bushranging.'

Pemulwuy sat alone and morose in front of a small campfire. Awabakal walked up to him.

'Pemulwuy, we are done for a while,' he said, 'the grass is still too green to burn and we should join the others in summer camp until the sun is on top'.

Pemulwuy looked up at him blankly, then leapt to his feet and grasped a short thick piece of burning wood. He bit the burning embers off it and spat the fire at Awabakal.

'I am strong beyond any of you!' he screamed. 'Go if you must!'

CHAPTER 49

OF CABBAGES AND KINGS

When Awabakal arrived at the Kamergal camp of the last few days it was deserted and cast full of long sad shadows. An emptiness hung gravely about the place. Awabakal sat down to think again but was swept over by sleep until the dawn came upon him. When the sun moved across his face, he awoke and lay for a while in a haze of tiredness.

If he was to be with Pemulwuy, he had to take a different route. He must cross the harbour a little west of Lane Cove and he must eat.

By the dawn of the next day, he had crossed the harbour and lay exhausted on its southern shore. He would lie that day where he was, and by night cross to the Georges River far up from Kamay. He would get to the old Ramedigal camp and wait there.

As he crossed the back of Sydney, he felt Boolayoo's presence, silent and closed. Gurrewe caressed the child that he had never seen in life. Almost beyond vision, just ahead of him, Narewe turned to him...but said nothing.

Yanada walked with him that night, casting what shadows she made. Sun shadows cast upon the ground told Awabakal of the time of day, but these moon shadows told nothing of the night. Except, he thought, they told of some different time in some other secret place.

Awabakal slept again by Kamay. At dawn he made his way along the same path he had travelled twelve summers past. His companions of that past time created for him only a bleak loneliness. He ran along the path; he stopped, he sat down at the place by the river where Gurrewe, with his pale convict skin, waited for them to return from that hunt so long ago. Of those companions, only Tedbury and Bungaree still walked the ordinary Earth. Awabakal stretched out but could not sleep.

Late in the afternoon he ran again until he came upon a sad Eora camp. There was an old woman, a sick young man, and two children. They looked at him in fear and want. The woman held a child in her arms. She whispered: 'O'moon, O'moon, O'moon….'

The plaintive Eora lullaby sounded like the end of a world and it was.

Awabakal was repelled by this vision of Eora society in collapse…he ran on. On the third day he waited. He had reached the intersection where Pemulwuy must pass. He fell into a sleep of exhaustion and faintly hoped that he would not awaken.

Gomil woke him.

'Pemulwuy is gone to Parramatta. He waits by the lightning tree.'

Awabakal sat upright.

'Are you going to the summer camp?'

Gomil nodded soberly.

'All of you?'

Gomil nodded again.

'Then he is alone?'

Gomil looked away in shame. 'Yes, he waits there,' he said reluctantly.

They ate together, these two, who after twelve years of war hardly knew each other.

'Will you come to the summer camp, Awabakal?'

Awabakal nodded, 'but you go on'.

Gomil understood and left.

It took the rest of that day for Awabakal to reach the lightning tree. This was an ancient bluegum, heavily carved and used, but not as a camp site. Pemulwuy was not there.

Awabakal searched the ground carefully and finally parted the grass at Pemulwuy's mark.

He saw the snake, he knew that it was *Yanlarree*; Yanlarree waited for Yanada. Awabakal had no fear of Yanlarree in his snake form. He looked to where the moon would rise, and then turned back to Yanlarree. These two men from different forms of their world stared at each other without speaking.

Yanlarree began to walk away. Awabakal followed him. He knew that he would take him to Pemulwuy.

Awabakal followed Yanlarree quietly, deep into the source of the Eora world.

Yanada rose from the edge of the Earth and embraced her loved one. She cast her light on the path that he and Awabakal trod. In the deepness of that night she lit the place where Pemulwuy awaited them.

'Kiraban, why have you come to me?'

Awabakal fell to the ground and rested on his arm. Pemulwuy sat on a low limb of a tree, all wrapped in his cloak and the light of the new moon. A listening silence stood between them.

'You should have gone to the summer camp, Kiraban.'

Awabakal nodded but still said nothing.

Pemulwuy spoke slowly, 'Kiraban my perfect friend, the long summers between you and I have passed… you should go back home now… it is easy for you to do that now, you can go anywhere in all the land now'.

'And what of you Pemulwuy?'

'I am tired,' Pemulwuy said.

'Yes but not mad,' Awabakal responded.

Pemulwuy looked strangely at Awabakal. 'There are many faces to madness Kiraban. Perhaps it is you who is mad.' They both laughed and thought over the long eventful years behind them.

Awabakal marked the ground with his finger, and then said: 'I have watched Yanada these nights and I know now what our secret truth must be.'

He paused. 'Over all these summers we have learned that there are many ways to win wars.'

Pemulwuy climbed down to the ground. 'To win a war, he said, 'you must make someone lose'.

'It is not even war,' Awabakal said. 'It is just killing people.'

'Ah, but it is war, Kiraban.'

'Then, if it is war, we must lose.'

'Only if we fight, Kiraban', Pemulwuy said strangely.

Pemulwuy smiled and lifted his cloak about him, 'only if we fight,' he repeated.

Awabakal sat up straight. Indeed he knew Pemulwuy's third part of truth.

'And we only fight, Pemulwuy, if you fight,' he said.

Pemulwuy nodded sadly.

Some seven days after this meeting, Kiraban and Pemulwuy were dead, caught by the constabulary and some settlers in an ambush that even Boolayoo could have avoided. Kiraban was killed by a single musket shot in the chest. For Pemulwuy, death was not so easy. He fell to the ground with four musket balls in his body. As he lay there in his own blood, a man moved purposefully from among the British ranks.

'We must be sure!' he said.

With a swift, merciless movement of a sabre, Pemulwuy's head was struck from his body.

EPILOGUE

Bennelong died in Sydney in 1813.

Tedbury succeeded his father. He was captured and imprisoned in 1805, and died in New South Wales. The exact date is unrecorded.

Pemulwuy's amputated head was placed in a jar of spirits and dispatched from Australia aboard the ship *Speedy*. To the best of the author's knowledge the head still lies somewhere in Europe. His body and his spirit have long entered the earth and the Australia for which he gave his life.

Bennelong sat in silence by the moonlit waters of Tuhbowgule, an empty rum jar lay by his side. He was still, as though he were asleep.

A soldier placed a hand on his shoulder and said with surprising gentleness: 'Pemulwuy is dead. They have cut off his head.'

Bennelong bowed his head. 'Then it is over.'

Another solitary figure stood on a small beach near Garrangel looking out upon the darkening sea. He threw an empty rum flask into the ebbing tide and watched it drift away on the dark waters of the South Pacific Ocean.

LANGUAGE AND GLOSSARY

The novel attempts to recreate some of the linguistic atmosphere of the time. This includes certain archaic English terms and seamen's slang. The most important language forms used are English or Australian in origin. These inclusions are mainly from Eora groups with a few words taken from other Australian indigenous languages.

From what can be understood today, Eora people spoke a distinct language of the Australian family known by linguists as Pama Nyungan. These were complex Latin-like languages, which made use of suffixes to form grammatical structures. From records of the time it appears that the Eora subgroups spoke variations of the same language, although some dialects of the tongue showed considerable differences in vocabulary. Some Eora words survive today and are embedded in English used by east coast Aboriginal people; some are used by white Australians.

This novel attempts to make communicative use of the language, and some actual sentences have been constructed so that a more specific Eora meaning can be transmitted. The language is being used for literate human communication, possibly for the first time since it was used by the Eora people in Pemulwuy's time; this is particularly true of Bidjigal.

Notwithstanding all of this, the language of the Eora people is now extinct. The last people to use it for human communication will be the readers of this novel.

The words in this glossary are taken from records of the language held in the Australian Institute of Aboriginal and Torres Strait Islander Studies, or from Aboriginal people who know some words of Eora origin.

Written and oral sources of the language give a variety of spellings in the Latin alphabet. The author has not attempted to create a standard orthography, but has modified the original archaic forms.

Bracketed at the end of each Glossary entry is the name of the language and the actual Eora subgroup if known, otherwise the word Eora is used. Other Australian languages are recognised if known, otherwise Australian is specified. This vocabulary only refers to words and expressions used in the novel. Fuller records of Eora and other Australian languages are held at the Institute of Aboriginal and Torres Strait Studies in Canberra.

Some words from other languages as well as some old English words, are also used in the novel. Some of these are also included in the glossary.

GLOSSARY

WORD	**MEANING** (language)
ABACK	Taken aback, a nautical expression (English)
ALODIM	Meeting or council (Eora)
ALODIM GAERAY	Special meeting (Eora)
ALODIM MURRAY	Large meeting (Eora)
ARABANU	Man's name (Bidjigal
ARAKUI	Australian fruit (Eora)
ARROWANELLI	Place name (Bidjigal
AWABA	Place name Hunter region(Awabakal)
AWABAKAL	Australian people of the Hunter Region
BACOOLONG	Male name (Bidjigal)
BAIDO	Male name (Awabakal)
BAIN MOREE	South wind (Eora)
BALGOWLA	Place name Sydney (Eora)
BENANG	A wound (Eora)
BENNELONG	Male name (Bidjigal)
BEROWA	Place name (Bidjigal)
BERRINGEN	Pretty girl (Bidjigal)
BIAN BENU	Male name (Bidjigal)
BIDJIGAL	People of the Sydney to Blue Mountains region
BINATUNG	Biting insect (Torres Strait Islands)
BINTUNKIN	Male name (Awabakal)
BOOLA	The number two (Eora).
BOOLAYOO	Man's name (Bidgigal)
BOOMERANG	Throwing weapon
BOONGA	Buttocks (Eora)
BOOREA	Woman's name (Bidjigal)
BOOROOI	Number three (Bidjigal)
BOROGEGAL	A distant group, south of Port Hacking
BRITCHES	Trousers (English)
BULLA	The number two (Bidjigal)
BULUMNA	Brother
BUNDICUT	Bandicoot
BUNGAREE	Man's name (Eora).
BUNKILLIKAN	Awabakal man (Awabakal)

BURNIGULA	Setting sun. More correctly COING-BURREGULA (Eora)
BURREWUN	Person's name. Also spelt BURROWUN (Eora)
BURUNGAROO	Woman's name (Awabakal)
CAMYA	Is here (Bidjigal)
CARDIGAN	Man skilled in healing (Bidjigal)
CEUELYEN	Sons of brothers (Eora)
COLELEU	Woman's name (Bidjigal)
CRONULLA	Place name (Eora)
CURRAWONG	Species of magpie, native bird (Australian)
DARUK	An Australian nation adjoining the Eora (Duruk)
DEERABBAN	Original Australian name of the Hawkesbury River—word is Bidjigal, Darak, or Karingai. All seem to use the same word.
DIN YAEGHINE	Pertaining to pregnancy (Bidjigal)
DJURRABA	Musket (Eora)
DJIN	Woman (Bidjigal)
DJORDWUY	Man's name (Australian)
DOOUL	Non-barbed spear (Bidjigal)
DULA IAYANG	Religious ceremony (a fertility rite) (Eora)
DURU	See also WARRANGI. Refers in the novel to a moiety.
GADIA	Penis (Bidjigal)
GALGALLA	Smallpox (Eora)
GANIMANTJ	Large marsupial (see) Kangaroo (Eora)
GARAGALONG	Young men. Also spelt GORAGALLONG (Eora)
GARRANGEL	Entrance to Sydney harbor or TUHBOWGULE
GITTIGITTI	Tickle (Bidjigal)
GITJIS	Kinds of mischievous spirits (Australian)
GOANNA	Large native lizard (unknown)
GOGARUK	Priest, religious man, a sorcerer (Bidjigal)
GOMAN	Campsite near Parrammata
GOMERRY	Female vulva (Bidjigal)
GOMIL	Man's name (Bidjigal)
GONDUWUY	Man's name (Eora)
GONIANA	Woman's name (Eora)
GOORUNGANEGAL	Bribe (Eora)
GROMEDA	Spirit associated with death. Also spelt GROMEDAH (Bidjigal)
GRO MOK	Secret society (Australian)
GUBBA	A modern Aboriginal word that probably came from the word *djurraba* (musket) from these times.

GUNA	Excreta
GURREWE	White cockatoo. Also spelt GARRAWAY (Bidjigal)
GWEAGAL	Eora group possibly south of Port Hacking
KADIGAL	Eora group. Also spelt CADIGAL
KAKUYA	Awabakal man (Awabakal)
KAMAY	Botany Bay
KAMERGAL	Eora group
KANGAROO	Large native marsupial (English, possible Australian)
KARADIGAN	Man skilled in healing (Eora)
KARECAL	Eora group
KAYUMY	Manly cove (Eora)
KIRABAN	Man's name (Awabakal)
KOOBEE	Man's name (Kamergal)
KOOKABURRAS	Kookaburras
KOORI	People or man. Refers today to south-east people (English)
MANGAN ALLY	Husband (Eora)
MAREEMY	Testicles (Karegal)
MATLONG	Good and strong (Eora)
MENORA	First or one (Bidjigal)
MILBAB	Woman's name (Kamergal)
MINYIN	Why (Bidjigal)
MONOE	A game. Also spelt MANNOE (Eora)
MULUBINBA	Place name (Eora)
MUPAONG	Emu (Eora)
MURRA MURRONG	Matter of honour (Eora)
MURRAY	Healing, a traditional healer. Also spelt murri (Bidjigal)
MURRAY	Many or great (Bidjigal)
MURRI-DIOLO	Four (Eora)
MURRI SOOCO	Many (Eora)
MURRORONG	Awabakal man (Eora)
NANBORREE	Man's name (Bidjigal)
NARGEL	Woman's name (Bidjigal)
NAREWE	Woman's name (formal) (Bidjigal)
NUNGEE	Woman's name (Eora)
O'MOON	Hush or be quiet (Eora)
O'SOME	Woman's name (Australian)
PANERA	Blood, also spelt PANNERA (Bidjigal)
PEMUL	Earth (Bidjigal)
PEMULWUY	Man's name (Bidjigal)

PINICOOLONG	Man's name (Kamergal)
PIT MILL	Early form of timber milling (English)
PITJANTJATJARA	Central Australian language
RAE	Birth spirit (Bardi)
RAMEDIGAL	An Eora group
RANMA	'I do not know' (Bidjigal)
SOOCO MURRI WHANI GUNA	'Too much excrement.'
TAMIRA	Hand (Bidjigal)
TANTI	Possum (Australian)
TEBURY	Man's name (Bidjigal), also TEDBURY
TERRA AUSTRALIS	South land (Latin)
TERRA NULLIUS	Land which belongs to no one (Latin)
THARAWAL	Australian group south of Sydney
TUHBOWGULE	Sydney Harbour (Eora)
TUNGO	Tame dog (Bidjigal)
TWIUGA	Falling star (Bidjigal)
TYERABARRBOWARYAOU	'I cannot be like white people.'
UMANA	Spear throwing tool (Bidjigal)
WAHNI	Urine (Bidjigal)
WANUN	Point overlooking Bennelong's cottage
WANEGAL	Eora group (Eora)
WARATAH	Indigenous flower (Bidjigal)
WAROAMA	Place name (Bidjigal)
WARRANGI	Moiety division (Bidjigal)
WARRIGUL	Indigenous Australian wild dog (Australian)
WARRUN	Bay in Sydney Harbour (Karigal)
WAUN	Place name (Bidjigal)
WEA JOWINID	Relating to exchange (Bidjigal)
WEDALYI MINYIN DJALARINJT?	'Is he a man of trust?'
WINDJI	Duck (Australian)
WEDA	Drink (Bidjigal)
WEEAGGI	Bay in Sydney Harbour (Eora)
WEEREE	Bad or evil (Bidjigal)
WE-GUL	Number one (Bidjigal)
WEUONG	Man's name (Bidjigal)
WINGIKARA	Place name south of Sydney (Tharwal)
WORRONARRA	Modern name Woronora River—main tributary of the Georges' rivers system which flows into Kamay (Botany bay)
WORRAGUL	Native wild dog 'dingo' (Australian)

WOYAN	Crow (Bidjigal) (Eora)
YATNADIOU BENANG	To make the first wound (Bidjigal)
YANADA	Moon (Bidjigal)
YANGA	Sexual intercourse (Kamerigal)
YANGA CALLYNE	Sexual intercourse in marriage (Kamerigal)
YANLARREE	Man's Name (Bidjigal)
YANOONG	To watch or witness (Bidjigal)
YATNADIOU BENANG MENORA	'I have made the first wound.'
YELLA MUNDI	Man's name (Bidjigal)
YENNERAWANNIE	Man's name (Bidjigal)
YENOWEE	Man's name (Bidjigal)
YERRINIBEE	Man's name (Bidjigal)
YOO LAY	Religious ceremony (Eora)

ACKNOWLEDGMENTS

I wish to express my gratitude to the staff of the Australian Institute of Aboriginal and Torres Strait Islander Studies for their assistance with the original novel and guidance. I especially wish to thank all those people whose foresight and wisdom created this Institution, which has collected and preserved the secrets and the history of the past on which this novel is built. I also wish to thank those people who read the original draft and offered their advice and encouragement, and to those who did likewise to the second edition. Charmaine Green did all the original and substantial work on the Eora language, and spent many hours arguing with, and advising me, on its use. Finally, to Kevin Weldon for his vision in first publishing this special history and to Alexander Hartman, Peter Scarf and Matilda Books for publishing this new edition.

Eric Willmot

BRIEF HISTORY OF THE BATTLE FOR SYDNEY

The name Pemulwuy means earth: man of the earth. Pemulwuy lived in Australia in the last half of the eighteenth century. He was born around 1756 to a people who believed that their world was brought into being by some sort of an awakening from an earlier dreaming state. A major transcendental entity, instrumental in causing this creative change, took the temporal form of the rainbow. Because of its shape it was and is referred to as the rainbow serpent.

Pemulwuy died in 1802. He took up arms and led the Eora people of the Sydney area against the alien British invaders. He was the rainbow warrior.

This novel was conceived out of his legend and the historical events of the period from 1788 and 1802. This was the first period in which Australians and the British took up arms against each other. After twelve years the Australians lost that war and the British thereafter claimed sovereignty of the continent and its surrounding islands. They did this by means of a deception known as *Terra Nullius*. This was based upon the assertion that the original or Aboriginal-Australians did not own or seriously inhabit the continent of Australia. This assertion has since been shown by historical and scientific examination to be completely false and invalid.

Although Australians in other parts of Australia also opposed the British illegal occupation of Australia, this is a story of the first systematic war of resistance of the Australians to the British, a war that lasted twelve years. The legend of Pemulwuy is part of the belief system and oral history of the Aboriginal people of the east coast of Australia. It is also part of the history of all modem Australians and indeed the people of Britain.

The city of Sydney is built around the harbour of Tuhbowgule upon land owned by Pemulwuy's people. The initial creation of this great modern city occurred during the last fourteen years of Pemulwuy's life. For modern Australians this has always been a period of stories, hidden truths and mysteries. Even the language we use today is embedded with words from that time, such as 'dingo', 'gin', 'womera', and 'bogey'. 'Boong' is a general derogatory term used by some white Australians towards any dark-skinned race and comes from the Eora word meaning buttocks.

Pemulwuy is a fundamental part of that mystery. His story is not different in substance from that of other Aboriginal-Australian patriots like Yagan, Windradyne and Jundamurra. Such men resisted the British invasion and colonial rule in Australia in the eighteenth and nineteenth centuries. However there are two things that set Pemulwuy apart from his later compatriots. The first was that he led the Eora people in the initial major response to the British invasion, and fought the British for twelve long years until his death in 1802. The Aboriginal-Australian resistance is said to have been broken by Governor King in 1805 (Bridges 1920) when Pemulwuy's son, Tedbury, was captured and imprisoned. He became the first official Australian prisoner of war. He died in New South Wales. The second difference was the attitude of Pemulwuy's enemies towards him. The British not only sought to destroy him physically, they, and some of their descendants, attempted to obliterate the very evidence of his existence.

Until the first edition of this book was written and published in 1987, Pemulwuy's name never appeared in any white Australian history, yet he lives on in the unpublished records of his enemies, and in the minds of Aboriginal-Australians. A special kind of mythology has grown up around Pemulwuy. In both legend and history he is described as having unusual powers and a connection with the supernatural. In the television episode, 'Warriors', from the Special Broadcasting Service, Rainbow Serpent series in 1985, Bob Mazza, an Aboriginal actor, describes Pemulwuy as a 'clever man'. In Aboriginal-Australian terms this refers to people involved in activities associated with the supernatural.

In March 1798, Collins, the Judge Advocate at the time, wrote of a myth that had grown up around Pemulwuy as follows: 'A strange idea was found to prevail among the natives respecting the savage Pemulwuy, which was likely to prove fatal to him in the end. Both he and they entertained an opinion, that, from his having been frequently wounded, he could not be killed by our firearms. Through this fancied security, he was said to be at the head of every party that attacked the maize grounds.' (Collins, Volume 11, 1802, p.20). George Barrington, Chief Constable at Parramatta, had reported the same phenomenon the previous year. Pemulwuy and the group he led were clearly at war with the British. His twelve-year campaign and persistent attacks on crops and towns were well beyond the acts of outlaws or thieves. They were acts of war by a people defending their land from an invader. They were determined not to surrender their land or sovereignty to that invader. As the Europeans explored and expanded their domains in the sixteenth, seventeenth and eighteenth centuries, they created many enemies—some weak, some powerful—but none more implacably hostile or uncompromising than the Australian, Pemulwuy.

Governor Phillip Gidley King in consigning Pemulwuy's head to England in a jar of spirits wrote: 'Altho' a terrible pest to the colony, he was a brave and independent character...' (Governor King to Sir Joseph Banks 1802, HR NSW) He was indeed their noblest enemy in Australia. Yet, to the eternal shame of the British soldiers, they dishonoured his body. In 1788 the British landed on the shores of the bay of Kamay, now called Botany Bay. The district surrounding that bay and the great harbour of Tuhbowgule, around which the city of Sydney is now built, was inhabited by a nation of indigenous Australians who called themselves Eora.

The peoples of South East Asia had long traded with these first Australians. When the French, the British and the Russians found their way to the east coast of Australia, the continent was divided into precisely bounded areas of land. Each of these areas was populated by an ethnic group of Aboriginal-Australian people. These people had inhabited the continent of Australia since the beginning of human time here. These Australian groups were all of the same general racial descent, but each spoke a different language and was culturally distinct from one another. The islands linking Australia with Papua New Guinea were inhabited by another racially different group of indigenous Australians. These people are known today as Torres Strait Islanders. Together they formed a community of nations on the continent and its surrounding islands. The area of land that belonged to each of these nations varied in size, depending mainly on the food-producing capacity of the region. The land of some descent groups was larger than several European nations together. Others, located on more productive land were relatively small.

The Eora land area was approximately 1,800 square kilometres in size. It extended along the coast from the Hawkesbury River in the north to Port Hacking in the south. It extended inland to the present towns of Campbelltown and Camden, and a little to the north of the Shoalhaven River (Ellis, 1980). The Eora people were structured into a number of subgroups, who spoke closely-related languages or dialects. These subgroups occupied different parts of the Eora land, and generally had somewhat different economies. The Kamergal, for example, tended to concentrate on fishing, while the Bidjigal were more concerned with hunting animals that inhabited the forests of the region. An approximate location of the different Eora groups is shown in the first map. This map also shows the two major adjoining groups of Tharawal and Daruk.

The first Australians to come into contact with the British were the coastal groups, and they were closely observed by them. The people who lived in the hinterland areas were less well known, and Pemulwuy is known to have been a member of such a group—the Bidjigal. He is described by British sources as a woodsman who roamed over a large area from Castle Hill, Toongabbie and Parramatta, down to the shores of Botany Bay. He is also reported to have travelled as far north as the Hawkesbury River. He is described as being of a tall athletic build with a pronounced caste in one eye. The British, under Governor Arthur Phillip, in 1788 made several unsuccessful attempts to communicate with the Australians.

In desperation they captured a man named Arabanu (Tench 1961). He was reportedly treated well and kept in close association with Phillip, Governor of New South Wales. He became 'quite one of the Governor's family' (Bradley 1969, p.168). Arabanu was kept tied up by the leg until he showed that he would remain at the settlement when he was freed. He was exposed to much of the behaviour of the British, including a flogging which he was compelled to watch. To this event '...he displayed...symptoms of disquiet and terror' (Mulvaney 1985, p.l3). Arabanu experienced much of the new British foods. Some, such as tea, he enjoyed but alcohol he resisted with 'disgust and abhorrence' (Mulvaney 1985, p.13). Arabanu died from smallpox on 18 May 1789, ending the first close contact between these two races of people from opposite ends of the earth. The next contact was quite different and was made with three intelligent young indigenous Australian men of some status in their own society: These three were Bennelong, Pemulwuy and Colbee (called Koobee in the novel).

Bennelong's association with the British is well documented and described by Tench, and Collins et al. Bennelong first appears in records in 1789; whereas Pemulwuy always remains just out of focus. He is first mentioned in 1790 when he is accused by Bennelong of killing a missing convict. In November 1790, Phillip's gamekeeper, John Macintyre, was speared in an alleged unprovoked attack by Pemulwuy. Macintyre declared that 'he had even quitted his arms to induce them to look upon him as a friend, when the savage threw his spear at about the distance of ten yards with a skill that was fatally unerring'. When the spear was extracted it was found to have entered his body under the left arm, to a depth of seven and a half inches. It was armed for five or six inches from the point with sharp, jagged pieces of shells fastened in gum (Collins, Volume I, pp.1–18).

Macintyre died in January 1791 and confessed on his deathbed to his own depredations against the Australians. On 13 December 1790, Phillip ordered an unusually large military force out to apprehend Pemulwuy and his companions. The force consisted of two captains, two other subalterns, three sergeants, two corporals, one drummer and forty privates attended by two surgeons. The force was led jointly by Captain Tench of the Marine Corps and Captain Hill of the New South Wales Corps. Phillip ordered them to bring back the amputated head of any six adult males of Pemulwuy's group. This was a truly remarkable situation. Phillip had previously attempted to befriend the native Australians and, indeed, his direction from the British government was 'by every means possible to open an intercourse with the natives,' and this was to be accomplished in a humanitarian way. Phillip's attitude had certainly hardened by 1790 and it is believed that Pemulwuy was responsible for this. According to Phillip, Pemulwuy's group had by that time been responsible for killing or wounding seventeen English people. White Australian history books record all of these events by saying something to the effect that Phillip was angered when his gamekeeper was speared by a native. This first military expedition against the Australian was, as described in the novel, as unsuccessful, as was a second.

No white Australian historian has described these expeditions as military operations. This is itself extraordinary. The expeditions were commanded by senior military officers, consisted of all military personnel, and against the resources available in the colony at the time, were very substantial. Both expeditions were in fact unsuccessful. At this time Pemulwuy is described as an established leader in Eora society. This means that he must have been at least thirty years of age. He is also described as being shaven, which indicates that, like Bennelong, he must have attempted to relate to the British in other than military terms. Bidjigal men were normally unshaven, as was Pemulwuy in the later period Most of the ensuing events described in the novel, and the time in which they occurred, are based directly on historical records. The actual dates of the attack on Toongabbie and Parramatta have been transposed for dramatic purpose.

These accounts are very sketchy, particularly those relating to actual battles. The casualties involved in these conflicts were probably higher than suggested in the novel. In a four and a half year period at the extreme boundary of the battleground—the Hawkesbury River—John Francis Molloy stated 'that twenty-six white persons were killed and thirteen wounded'. (Dunbabin 1935, p.107). The Australian casualties from armed combat and sickness throughout the period must have been very large, because the entire Eora nation was destroyed.

The anthropological nature and the social structures and organisation of the Eora society of the time are recreated as accurately as is possible today. In most parts of the novel this is explained in the text. In some parts this was not possible. For example, the somewhat puzzling series of events at the Tharawal camp of Wingikari, when Weuong is challenged over the woman O'some, is an example. This scene illustrates the characteristic Aboriginal-Australian brother-sister reaction in such a situation. The somewhat unusual resolution of the situation involves two further mechanisms used in such conflicts. First Awabakal spears O'some as carefully as he can, thus removing the need for mortal combat between the two men. Finally Weuong's adversary uses the ethic of generosity to preserve his own honour in relinquishing his claim to the woman. The reader will also realise that marriage was not celebrated at the time of consummation. The important event was the arrangement.

The reader is given some idea of the depth and richness of old Australian mythology. Little is known today about specific Eora mythology, and some more general traditional Australian mythology is drawn into the novel. The Aboriginal-Australian etiquette of not using the name of the immediate dead is preserved throughout the novel. The form of language, both Australian and English, is interpreted from writings of the times. Some statements in dialogue of the novel are taken directly from these records. These include statements by Pemulwuy, and other Australians as well as the British.

A glossary of language and short dictionary are appended. The Eora language was reconstructed as well as possible from oral and written memory. It is a classical, rather poetic language, similar in some ways to Latin. It is used in this novel for real human communication, expressing at times concepts which are uniquely old Australian and not found in English. The Eora language is, however, now extinct. The readers of the two editions of this work will possibly be the last human beings to use it for communication.

Names used in the novel are historically based, as are the characters. Some names, both British and Australian, have been changed for various reasons. Some Awabakal people were brought to Sydney at the time, but the character Kiraban is a creation of the author. Narewe is likewise an invention, although she is modelled on Pemulwuy's daughter. These two represent all those young Aboriginal men and women who are hurt from a past that cannot be changed, but who would willingly have joined Pemulwuy if they had lived in his time, even at the risk of their lives. Kate Donavan and Sean McDonough are fictional characters and appear in both editions of the novel. Thrush, Wilson, Knight and Barrington are historical characters. Millicent Copley and Penelope Reid are fictional characters and only appear in the second edition.

The term 'Australia' was coined by Matthew Flinders during the period covered by this novel. It was probably derived from the old name of *Terra Australis*. The author occasionally uses the term Australians to refer to Aboriginal Australian groups, which include more than the Eora people. At this point in Australian history it is only the native inhabitants of the country who could be legitimately referred to by this name. Except for the fictional characters, the British characters tell their own story, from their own history. Where accounts in the novel differ from history, names are usually changed. I believe that some of these people may have been sorely judged by their own kind. John Macarthur is one such person. His regard for the native Australians might have been better than portrayed in this novel. On at least one occasion he criticised another officer, Lieutenant Neil MacKellar, who ordered soldiers to kill blacks whenever they met them. Macarthur, then a member of a military jury, asked by what authority he gave these bloodthirsty orders. Mackellar replied that 'they were received verbally from the Governor' (Dunbabin 1935, p.107).

This novel, however, presents Macarthur's character in the way that he has been judged by his own people in modern literature. The novel leaves only one possible suggestion that there may have been more to the man. This is expressed dramatically when Macarthur says, as he stands over the imprisoned Pemulwuy, 'God! Have we actually made an enemy of the earth itself!'

The British characters of Phillip, Ross, Grose, Hunter, King, Marshall, Abbott, Macarthur, Collins, Knight, Wilson and Thrush, do truly represent the people of their notes or as recorded in history. Watkin Tench was the man who led the first unsuccessful military expedition against Pemulwuy. His was an intimate contact, yet his rather dry literary account of his life in New South Wales suspends belief of this most important role of the British soldier who confronted Pemulwuy but never mentions it. Tench had a distinguished military career after leaving New South Wales. Sometime long after leaving he must have recalled that he was the first to be sent out to bring back the head of the worthy enemy, Pemulwuy. Tench was an intelligent, sensitive man and perhaps he deliberately avoided his duty in this matter. Both Tench and Dawes of history were replaced in the novel by Tench and Carpenter, two British Marines who portray a specific and intimate response to Pemulwuy.

The Australian character, Colbee, is replaced in the novel by Koobee for similar reasons. Kiraban is a fictitious character based on an historical Awabakal man.

Records indicate that many more Irish and other escaped convicts joined with, and fought beside Pemulwuy than are described in the novel. What became of them will probably never be known. They witnessed the bleeding and total tragic destruction of the Eora society. Some are remembered in folk songs, such as *The Wild Colonial Boy*.

Pemulwuy believed that the British deliberately infected his people with smallpox. This contention has some support in history, but more importantly in the creation of the Eora word *galgalla* for smallpox whereas no such word was created for other new diseases, such as influenza or measles.

If this is true, then it casts a very dark shadow over this early history of contact. It would mean that the British had become desperate enough during this twelve-year war to use such a biological weapon. A further puzzling aspect of this part of Australian history is that, until now, it has never been told. It has lain for two hundred years in records and legends and yet the spectre of these events haunts the racial memory of all modern Australians. Grassby, in his book, *Tyranny of Prejudice* (1984) provides an understanding, if not a reason, for this situation. He points out that the Irish revolt at Vinegar Hill, two years after Pemulwuy's death, also remained hidden from history until quite recently. Many of those people probably fought with Pemulwuy.

It is interesting to see how the authorities attempted to eradicate all evidence of this battle in a superb Orwellian demonstration of rewriting history. First of all they wiped from the map of Australia any reference to Vinegar Hill. The district was renamed Rouse Hill. Even half a century later when the local people sought to have their post office described as Vinegar Hill this was denied. No reference to the battle appears in any textbook, historical record, or anything that needs an official explanation. So successfully did the authorities expunge all knowledge of the battle, and the reasons for it and its consequences that it took 179 years for the first public commemoration of the battle to take place (Grassby, 1984, p.20).

The battle of Vinegar Hill was in fact first celebrated at the site on 5 March 1983. This was indeed a conspiracy of silence. The same as that applied to Pemulwuy's resistance. It was apparently not in the interests of a crookedly intent or racist establishment to promote such parts of the Australian story. If this is true, then these people have stolen from generations of Aboriginal and non-Aboriginal-Australians a heritage as important, as tragic, and as heroic as that of any other nation on earth.

A series of governmental reports such as *Bringing them Home* and *Children are Sacred* describe a society in a state of collapse, as does the acclaimed modern novel *The Tall Man* by Chloe Hooper. This was about an event and the appalling conditions on Palm Island in far North Queensland. That novel was written this century.

Against all of the above, this novel attempts to provide modern readers with a description and an experience of an original Australian society before it was destroyed socially and economically by an alien invading force from Europe.

The first edition was an Australian best seller and was reprinted many times. This is the first new edition and is both a revised and extended form of the original. This edition is meant to be a teaching tool as much as a novel.

END NOTES & FURTHER READING

Barrington, George 1810, *The History of New South Wales (Parramatta),* Brummell Press, London, 1969.

Barrington, George 1801, *A Sequel to Barrington's Voyage to New South Wales*, Brummell Press, London, 1969.

Bonwick, J. 1882, *The First Twenty Years of Australia,*

Bradley, W. 1969, *A Voyage to New South Wales: The journal of Lieutenant William Bradley* R.N. *of H.M. S. Sirius, 1786–1792,* Ure Smith, Sydney.

Bridges, B.J. 1970, 'Pemulwuy UA Noble Savage', published in the *Royal Australian Historical Society Newsletter,* No. 88, pp. 3–4.

Collins, D. 1798; 1802, *An Account of the English Colony in New South Wales,* vols 1 and 2, BiblioBazaar, London, 2008.

Dunbabin, Thomas 1935, *Slavers of the South Seas*, Angus and Robertson, Sydney.

Ellis, Jane 1980, 'A Troublesome Savage': *The Story of Pemulwuy*, unpublished manuscript, Australian Institute of Aboriginal Studies, Canberra.

Governor King to Sir Joseph Banks 1802, Letter of 5 June 1802, Historical Records of New South Wales IV, pp. 782–786.

Grassby, Al 1984, *The Tyranny of Prejudice*, A.E. Press, Melbourne.

Robertson, G. 1879,. *Australian Dictionary of Dates and Men of the Time,* Historical Records of Australia: Series I, Vols. 1, 2, 3.

Hunter, J. 1968, *Historical Journal of the Transactions at Port Jackson and Norfolk Island. London, 1793,* Libraries Board of South Australia, Adelaide.

King, Phillip Gidley 1893, *The Journal of Lt. Cater (later Governor) King,* Historical Records of New South Wales, Mitchell Library, Sydney..

McQueen, H. 1975, 'Defending Australia', in *Identity,* Vol. 2, No. 4.

Mulvaney, D.J. 1985, *A Good Foundation: Reflections on the Heritage of the First Government House, Sydney,* AGPS, Canberra.

Robinson, F. & York, B. 1977, *The Black Resistance*, Widescape, Melbourne.

Rowley, C.D. 1970, *The Destruction of Aboriginal Society*, ANU Press, Canberra, pp. 308–309.

Stanner, W.E.H. 1977, 'The History of Indifference Thus Begins', *Aboriginal History*, Vol I, pp. 1–2.

Tench, W. 1793, *Sydney's First Four Years: A narrative of the expedition to Botany Bay and complete account of the settlement at Port Jackson,* Australian Historical Society, Library of Australian History, 1979. Reissued Angus and Robertson, Sydney, 1961.

Tindale, R.S. & Lindsay, G. 1963, *Aboriginal Australians*, The Jacaranda Press,

Tindale, N.B. 1974, *Aboriginal Tribes of Australia*, A.N.U. Press, Canberra.

Wiley, I. 1979, *When the Sky Fell Down*, Collins, Sydney..

Closed resources at the Institute of Aboriginal and Torres Strait Islander Studies.

THE AUTHOR

Eric Willmot was Professor of Education and Head of the School of Education at James Cook University of North Queensland when he wrote the original novel. He was then appointed Head of the ACT Schools Authority and later became the ACT Secretary (CEO) of the new Department of Education. In the early 1990s he was appointed Director General of Education in South Australia. He is a prominent member of the Australian Aboriginal community and served as chairman of the management committee for Aboriginal Education programs at both the University of Queensland and at the University of Newcastle in New South Wales.

He was born in 1936 in Queensland and spent his youth as a drover, working in Queensland, New South Wales, Western Australia and the Northern Territory. He is one of those special Australians who has lived close to the earth and experienced the vision of this extraordinary continent, much of it from the back of a horse.

At the age of twenty he was seriously injured in a riding accident and spent a year in hospital. During this period he studied for his matriculation, won a scholarship, and attended the University of Newcastle, where he took his first degree in science.

Eric Willmot then worked in Papua New Guinea. He returned to Australia in the 1970s and followed a career in academia and in the public service. He was a lecturer at the University of Canberra, a Director of research at the Australian National University, Principal of the Australian Institute of Aboriginal Studies and Deputy Secretary in the Department of Aboriginal Affairs. Eric Willmot has taken a renaissance approach to his career. He is one of Australia's leading educationists and was honoured by the Australian government for his contributions in that field with an AM. He was the presenter in a film on Australian prehistory, *Trade Routes,* and is widely published in a number of disciplines, including anthropology and history. He had made many radio broadcasts on a wide range of subjects.

In 1986 he delivered the ABC Boyer Lectures. This is a series of lectures broadcast nationally on subjects relating to Australia in an international context. Each year a prominent Australian is invited to present the series.

The title of Willmot's Boyer Lectures was *Australia: The Last Experiment.* This was a treatise on the nature and future prospects of the new mixed societies like Australia, New Zealand, USA and South Africa. This lecture series was highly acclaimed by the critics and illustrated the extraordinary breadth of Willmot's own research and interests.

In 1980, he found that there were less than one hundred university graduates of indigenous descent in Australia. Eric Willmot is best known in Australian Aboriginal society as the main architect of the national education program began in 1979, which aimed to produce one thousand graduates by 1990. In 1990 that program had produced 1,800 graduates and transformed the society significantly.

He has occupied positions on the boards of numerous statutory authorities and companies.

In May 1987 he was awarded an honorary Doctorate of Laws from Melbourne University. He was awarded a Doctorate of Letters from Newcastle University, New South Wales in 2005.

Eric Willmot has for many years been an accepted authority on the life and times of Pemulwuy. He wrote the original novel and he is also the author of this second edition as well as painting the cover of this edition.

Today Eric Willmot lives in Melbourne, where he is a writer.

www.matildabooks.com

www.ingramcontent.com/pod-product-compliance
Lightning Source LLC
Chambersburg PA
CBHW030818310726
48980CB00006B/542/J

* 9 7 8 0 9 8 7 4 3 8 9 0 4 *